Also by Stephen Swartz

A Dry Patch of Skin

After Ilium

Aiko

The Dream Land

I. Long Distance Voyager

II. Dreams of Future's Past

III. Diaspora

A Beautiful Chill

A Novel

Stephen Swartz

MYRDDIN PUBLISHING GROUP

UNITED STATES · UNITED KINGDOM · AUSTRALIA

ISBN-13: 978-1-939296-30-6

ISBN-10: 1-939296-30-7

www.myrddinpublishing.com

Cover Art by Stephen Swartz

The words of a girl no one should trust,
nor what a woman says;
for on a whirling wheel their hearts were made....

Hávamál 84

(The Sayings of the High One)

Bright One they called her, wherever she came to houses,
the seer with pleasing prophecies, she charmed them with spells;
she made magic wherever she could, she played with minds....

Völuspá 22

(The Seeress's Prophecy)

1

EVERY THURSDAY IS THE SAME. The boys stare all evening and can hardly get any work done, as though her entire purpose in life is to entertain them. Tonight, she glares back at them, just to let the boys know she is onto their game. The first boy, watching her intently, merely licks his lips. The second boy winks, not more than a twitch, as though he has a loose eyelash—or perhaps it is an invitation for a special favor after class. He stays after class sometimes as if waiting for her, follows her out of the building. The third boy simply gawks, unwavering, as though he has never seen a nude woman.

She holds the pose, imagining other times and places, the dabs of reality that have become brushed into memories, and she lands like a cat on snow: fresh, pure, white, brisk, cold and wet against her skin—

December already, and still no snow.

She dreams of snow, wants the icy fingers of arctic winds to grasp her, take her to a place where no one will bother with her, where she can be alone with all her thoughts, free to fight with them. They come upon her like bursting stars yet fall harmlessly into a turbid sea of doomed destiny, scarcely breaking the surface or releasing rings of emotion. She purses her lips. *The Turbid Sea of Doomed Destiny* could be her next painting: purple sky, brown water, red and yellow lightning bolts, a small boat adrift, a man crying for help—

Her eyes wander up to the windows high on the walls. They are painted over white—off-white: eggshell; cream, perhaps. She pretends drifts of snow cover them. A good blanket of snow can hide so much, she thinks. *Já*, like clothing. On the platform nothing is hidden. She holds her breath, counting heartbeats. Secrets, like scars, can be covered yet never erased. And every spring, when the snow melts, the scars remain—like wheel ruts cut into the soil, ruts that dry and harden during summer only to be covered again with the next season's snow.

Time ticks slowly.

A shallow breath—

The Wheel Ruts of Summer—perhaps another painting she will do: two sienna lines cutting through the winter-gray grasses, a black storm on the horizon. She would stare down the storm—she with her pale, thin arms and legs, her body slender and white, without blemish. *Já*, like the pure snow covering the dirty road. There are no scars that are visible—

There was a day in school, back in Iceland where she was born, long before she and her widowed mother moved to Canada. Perhaps she was ten. She drew a picture of a mountain with snow on one slope, a forest on the other, and a fjord across the bottom. Her teacher praised it. At home, she proudly held up the picture for her mother. With only a glance, her mother dismissed it, suggesting she draw Jesus suffering on the Cross if she wanted to waste her time with colored pencils. And she never drew again—not until Toronto, when she would sit in the dressing room, waiting to go on stage and do her dance.

A pang of fear ripples through her, stomach knotting, and she shifts her gaze, hoping to see the clock on the wall but the instructor's head blocks her view. When he turns, their eyes meet. He grins, almost as an afterthought: a snapshot of the instant they both realize she is nude and he is not. He lowers his eyes, and informs the students the session is finished.

"Thank you, Iris," says the professor. "Another productive session."

Some students thank her. A few clap their hands in appreciation. The instructor goes around commenting on their work.

Pulling on a gray, threadbare robe, she takes a stroll behind the easels, catching a look at what the students have done. She admires the shading on the underarm and inner thigh one girl has drawn, compliments her. Another student has concentrated on her head and shoulders, has correctly duplicated the five freckles sprinkled across her nose. Examining another sketch, she wonders if her ribs really do show so clearly. She praises the strong line of back and elegant curve of breasts another woman has drawn, offers suggestions, then takes the charcoal in her fingers to demonstrate the technique.

The three boys on the end give her pause. One of them has focused on her hips, depicting that area in great detail. The other two have no talent: a cartoonish scribble that could be from any porn magazine, the other one even less a work of art.

"This?" she says roughly. "This is the best you can do?"

"He's no artist," says the first boy with a chuckle. "He just likes to look at naked girls."

"You don't belong here," she says.

The professor looks over. "What's going on?"

The boy is scared, then runs out of the studio. The second boy chases after him, an apology trailing.

She frowns. None of them belong in this class. Perhaps she does not belong here, either.

In Iceland, on the first day of school or some such mythic time, a long time ago at any rate, her teacher told her she didn't belong. "No iris grows here, none at all," said the woman at the large desk. "Your parents likely had no intention of you staying. We'll see what good you can do until then. A pretty smile won't get you very far, that's for sure. Much less for that devil's hair you're wearing." She went to her assigned seat and sat quietly, as expected, staring out the frosty windows at the snow gathering against the panes, already feeling the chill—

Students pack up their supplies as she gazes at the windows, sees the darkness outside, and feels tired. For a moment, she feels the weight of falling snow piling up around her, and tosses her orange hair off her shoulders. Something pushes deep inside her gut and she stops to measure the flickering of her heart. The chill is returning.

"You okay, Iris?" asks the professor, approaching.

She nods, then drops to the edge of the platform, sits there, breathing slowly.

"Should I call someone for you?"

"*Nei*, there is no one." She wraps her arms around her bent knees.

"I'm sorry about those boys. I keep telling them to be professional. I'll straighten it out, don't worry." He glances around the studio. "You sure you're okay?"

"Just . . . memories," she says, and lets out a big sigh.

"Art is a recasting of memory," he says, smiling in a fatherly way as he turns to go. "Iris, can you lock up when you leave?"

She nods and waves him out, holding a smile only until he takes a final glance and exits.

There are few memories she would choose to recast as art. Her mentor had encouraged her to try. Inventing new memories seems easier. She can paint abstract metaphors and fantasy landscapes, twisted mythology and self-portraits. *Já*, once in a while, she can be who she wants to be—then quickly decides that is not her, after all.

It is late. Much too late. Perhaps this Art school idea is another dead end. Like the club in Toronto, where she was introduced as the Ice Princess. Or at the university there where Professor Hirsch introduced her to the world of Art. After her widowed and remarried mother kicked her out, she had few choices.

In room 205 of Linden Hall, Eric Schaeffer was sitting with his feet up on the desk, reading the new issue of *Best American Poetry* while his students took their exam. The room had settled into a profound silence, only the faint scratching of pen on paper, when suddenly they were knocked out of their concentration by a horrendous thunderclap. They turned in unison to regard the deluge outside the windows.

"Pay no attention to the storm outside," he intoned, affecting the voice of the Great Wizard of Oz. A few students chuckled. They were in Kansas, after all. He was pleasantly surprised how easily they returned to the exam without much more distraction.

He stayed in his office a while after class, waiting for the rain to subside, and as he sat back, he read a few of the essays the students had written. However, the rain did not let up, so eventually he decided to make a run for it. Of all the days to arrive late and find the faculty lot full! He was forced to park down by the baseball field, a five-minute sprint from Linden.

When he arrived at his car, his sportcoat and shoes were ruined, the rest of his clothing thoroughly soaked. Falling inside, he started up the engine and flicked on the heater. He slapped the steering wheel. One more bad thing in a crazy week overflowing with all kinds of crap. He was going nowhere fast. The storm was a perfect metaphor for his life. He had gotten nothing done over Thanksgiving break, instead driving down to Texas to visit his parents. He could have at least finished grading the stack of papers. Or completed the story for the writers' workshop. Actually, he was supposed to be working on the dissertation: "*La Belle Dame* Grows Up: The Future Poetry of John Keats." He wanted to laugh but feared it might cause more trouble. That was the kind of luck he had.

Just get home, he thought. He had an early class the next morning anyway. Not even a full semester at Fairmont College and he was questioning just what he was thinking taking a position in a place like Wichita. He knew the answers, but dared himself to say them aloud as he backed out of the parking space.

Just get home safely.

"Who in the world could that be?" Eric muttered, squinting between whips of the wipers. He thought of the rainy seasons years before when he'd taught in Japan, all the soggy days he had ridden a bicycle to school. He was lucky to have a car tonight; some students would have to walk and he did not envy them.

One of those poor students was caught in the headlights. She was walking along the drive—trying to walk. Each step was a major effort, holding her dress down with one hand, the other carrying her useless shoes.

A wave of compassion swept over him, wanting to save the drowned puppy. He pulled alongside the curb.

The woman was barefoot, shoes in her hand, her green and black striped dress a second skin, her orange hair a stringy mess.

"Need a ride?" he called, rolling down the window a crack.

She stopped, staring at him as she clawed hair out of her face.

The car door opened and she collapsed inside, wet dress and all, clogs on her lap, hair in tangles, water tumbling off her head and shoulders.

"Quite a storm, isn't it?" said Eric.

Raindrops ricocheted off the car's hood and roof as he gave her a glance.

It was only then that they recognized each other. He held his breath. A flutter of nerves rose and subsided. His belly tightened. She seemed embarrassed but too distraught to care.

"You're Iris, right?" He kept his hands on the steering wheel where she could see them. "We met at the art show, remember? On Halloween night." He looked away, giving her a break. "What did you call it—Samhain? The witch's name for it."

He returned his gaze to her and she nodded.

"My name is Íris. Like the letter E."

"Sorry." He smiled. "Íris, uh . . . Magnus-something. What is it? Magnúsdóttir. Right?"

"Just Íris will do."

He felt the crinkling ice in her voice, and considered whether she wanted him to be driving her anywhere. However, the rain was coming down in sheets. He could barely see. No matter what had happened before, he decided, rescuing her tonight was the right thing to do.

She strummed her hair back as she stared out the window.

"I liked your paintings," he said. "All four of them. There was one I really thought was special. It had a woman sleeping on a bed of roses. Something like that. The thorns cut her cheek. I liked the drops of blood on the leaves."

With that acknowledgement, he felt satisfied that he'd said enough to prove he remembered—whatever it might be worth. Because he did remember. Or perhaps so she would see him as a good guy. Which he was.

Now to get home.

He continued slowly along the campus drive, as though waiting for her to tell him to stop and let her out, that she did not need a ride, did not want to ride with him.

They paused at the stop sign. After checking each direction, he turned the car onto Hillcrest Avenue and went up to the intersection at 21st Street, sat at the stoplight.

"What a night to be out," he said twice, silence inside the car, pummeling rain outside.

When the light turned green, he drove on, struggling to see the lane lines. A truck rushed past them and he hit the brakes as a huge wall of water splashed over the windshield, the wipers already going full-speed.

"That was close!" He caught his breath. "Don't want to have an accident tonight."

"*Já*, I remember," said Íris, as though she had carefully searched her memories and chosen a particular one.

What she remembered was that he promised to buy one of those paintings when he took her home after the art exhibit that night. He was her last customer, her only customer. Her colleagues had sold their works. Not her. She was convinced more than ever that coming to a little city in Kansas from the metropolis of Toronto made no sense at all. Professor Hirsch was wrong. An MFA degree would not make any difference. Her life was like a child lost in a rainstorm, and she just wanted to be warm and dry.

"Yes, I did. And I took you home after that." Eric thought for a moment, grinned. "So, here we are again. Me taking you home. Small world, this town, huh?"

Once upon a time, he had gone to the Ulrich Gallery in the Art building on campus for a Friday night reading by Lance Albright, the writer-in-residence for the year. After the portly, bearded Albright managed to offend everyone with a long rant on the etymology of the word *fuck*, a young feminist poet championed by Dr. Liz Barnes, chair of the English department, got up to recite poetry. Hearing enough, Eric followed his colleague's lead and sneaked out, feigning illness. He felt a little drunk from all the wine at the reading, but he had managed to stumble back through the atrium where he saw an art exhibition was underway.

"*Já*, small world." She looked away.

"I like your accent. You're from Iceland, right? I remember that."

"*Já*—yes," she said flatly, flashing a smile as though they were close friends.

The woman in the atrium had immediately caught his eye: standing barefoot, wearing an elegant black dress, her arms and feet and bosom so white, her hair so orange. He had taken a cup of the red punch and wandered around the room, studying the art, stopping at the four paintings hanging on the north wall that seemed more interesting than the others. She came up behind him as he studied the paintings and, noticing her, he began offering his interpretations. She had acted demure and he became enamored. When he learned she was the artist of those paintings, he offered to give her a ride home. So they could discuss the price.

"I never would expect a rain storm the first week of December," he said. He felt the need for conversation. "It should be snow. I've been looking forward to snow ever since I moved up here from Texas." He glanced at her. "I guess you prefer snow, too. Being from Iceland."

She tilted her head toward him.

"I also lived in Toronto, Ontario for seven years."

"Canada! So you *do* like snow. Not rain. Well, not rain like this." He glanced out the side window at the flooded intersection they were crossing. "It's not even romantic rain. You can't go out singing in this stuff."

She smiled weakly, seeing in the occasional street lamp glow how forlorn he was.

"What a night to be out!" He took a deep breath, exhaled slowly. "So . . . where to?"

"Take me home," she said, laying her head back.

He could appreciate that she was simply glad to be out of the rain. Exhausted, unfocused. She didn't care. Let it be warm and dry. Not like that old house. Her room there was always cold and damp, she had said.

When she invited him up to her room to discuss the painting, all that happened was a cup of tea, questions about the Wiccan altar at the end of the room, and some nudity. She took off the formal black dress, leaving her naked in the shadows of a small lamp. He did not react, then tried to excuse himself. She coaxed him to stay. He sank into the slumping mattress on her squeaky bed, no longer concerned a nude woman sat close by. He soon was mumbling profound thoughts about life and death and how the world had gone crazy, with long pauses to sip the tea. He forgot about the painting.

"Sorry, I don't remember the directions," he said. He looked out at the street sign. "We're already going the wrong direction. Force of habit. I was heading to my place. But that's all right. I'll take you wherever you want to go."

He slowed for the stoplight, rolled to a splashing stop, rain beating against the car.

She spoke softly, eyes closed: "Just take me somewhere warm and dry. Anywhere. Your place."

With the red light blinking its warning, she seemed to be dozing off. Her orange, orange hair curled around her face. The skin-tight dress rode up her thigh, sticking there. Milky white thigh. He watched her chest rise and fall, focused on the V of her neckline.

"Are you sure?" he asked.

A car waiting behind them honked. Eric checked the mirror, then signaled and turned.

"I want to be warm," she said.

Eric was quiet as they drove. He felt awkward, worried about what she might be thinking. After all, his senior colleague, Jack Macintosh, had gotten himself in big trouble by dating one of his students, even though she was his age. Now poor Jack was facing a sexual harassment charge. Eric snuck a peek at the woman beside him. She was at a graduate exhibit, meaning she had to be a graduate student. At least twenty-two. And not his student.

Suddenly, he wanted to kick himself. There was no reason to be having guilty thoughts. He was doing a good deed. Being a Boy Scout. Anyone could see that. Besides, he recalled her saying she usually rode a bicycle. This ride home was perfectly innocent.

Instead of performing some silly old rituals she said were required for her religion, she had made tea. She invited him up for some tea. He never expected anything more. Talk about the painting, perhaps— the one with the woman and the thorns. It was Halloween night, after all: black cats crossing the road, children in costumes. And her witch altar. He fell into a sullen mood, like he was in the wrong place—not her room, but at Fairmont College in Wichita. Nothing like bustling Austin and the huge University of Texas campus where he'd taken his doctoral courses. When a bead of perspiration ran between her breasts, he had panicked. It was too soon to be getting involved with someone new. Before he could consider his options, he was stumbling out of her room, out of the large Victorian house she shared with other students, and back to his apartment with the mismatched furniture of a newly divorced man trying to start over.

"All right then," he said, and turned the car.

They went past shopping, restaurants, large houses rising behind a row of cedar trees and wooden fences, a 24-hour gas station, and a bright, blinking red light that would not change. The rain lessened but remained steady. Going on a few more blocks, they turned into a neighborhood of apartment buildings.

Pulling into a parking space in front of one building, he shut off the engine.

"Here we are," he announced. "You can dry out here. Then . . . ." He waited for her to suggest something. He didn't have any plan, so he made one: "Then I can . . . uh, take you home later."

"Apologies," she mumbled.

They waited for the rain to lighten further, but it did not.

"Maybe we should just go now," said Eric. "We're already wet from head to toe. I have a robe you can change into."

His hand went to the door handle. Then he sprang out and rushed around to open her door. He helped her out and, with his arm wrapped around her shoulders, led her quickly up the sidewalk to the front door. He fumbled with the keys, got the door unlocked, and they fell inside.

Together in the small space at the bottom of the stairs, their shoulders bumped. They stood face to face—close enough to kiss, he measured. Their eyes met, lingered. The sight of their rainy hair in tangles, however, made them smile.

She pecked his cheek. "Thanks."

He went up the stairs first and turned on the light of the bathroom, then she followed. Barely enough light to give the apartment a ghostly tint, but it was a dry hovel away from the storm. Feeling the warmth of the place, she nodded approval.

She peered into the bathroom. That was what she wanted: a hot bath. Her old house only offered cold showers. There had been enough chill for her.

"May I have a hot bath?"

"Sure," he responded. "Let me get you a towel."

First, she needed to get out of the soggy dress. As he stepped away, she was left standing by the wall, across from a cheap-looking bed in the one-room apartment. She took the hem of the dress in her hands. Carefully, she tore it upward a few centimeters at a time, separating it from her skin, rolling it upward until the dress was above her shoulders, caught in her wet, stringy hair. Her pale arms curled up over her head as he returned with some towels and a robe hanging over his arm.

He had taken off his wet sportcoat and shirt, and stood bare-chested before her.

In her crucifixion pose, his eyes took her in a single glance, then zeroed in on the round silver pendant hanging between her breasts, flashing its pentagram and ring of runes on the same horizontal line as

15

her nipples.

She felt his eyes clutching her and could not breathe.

He stepped against her, against the wall.

"Don't say a word," she whispered.

"I won't."

Then his trousers were down past his knees and he was thrusting into her. His hands clasped her hands, holding them over her head. Their lips met and grappled furiously. He pushed in deeper, shifting her hips to find the angle. She pulled her hands free of his and threw off the dress, sending it to the floor. She drew her hands roughly over his shoulders. She stroked his wet hair, rainwater trickling down his back. He pressed her into the wall and her feet did not touch the carpet. She wrapped her legs around his hips, locking her feet behind him, and held on as they slammed against the wall.

When they paused to catch a breath, they found they were soaked again, this time from the ochre of inner fire. They were too hot. They broke into spontaneous grins, surprised what they had done. He softened, dropped out of her. Lowering her feet to the floor, he continued to hold her against the wall—realizing how starved for affection they each had been.

Like a cloud in a dream, she was floating through the small, dim apartment, lighter than air, buoyed in his encircling arms. They arrived at the balcony doors. He slid them open and the coolness of the rain rushed in, settled over them. They watched the rain falling calmly now.

He snatched a blanket off the nearby lounger and wrapped it around them, becoming a cocoon, their skin meshing.

"Are you all right?" he asked after standing together, counting heartbeats. His words were so quiet he wasn't sure he'd said anything.

"Já, I'm okay." Her voice was soft, like a kitten that had died in a blizzard.

He felt energized, noticing the quick thumping of her heart against his chest. He took a deep breath.

"This is what Fate is," she spoke.

His lungs deflated, hearing her words, and his arm tightened around her waist. What about Fate? He thought he knew what she meant, but he could only guess.

"Pardon me?"

Someone was holding her, she realized, someone holding her up, and she forgot where she was, who she was. Closing her eyes, she thought of days when she was a different person. Or wanted to be. She welcomed the days when the snow fell thick and piled high, covering everything. Then it was easy to hide. Then everything was beautiful. Everything was so beautiful.

She shivered in the curl of his arm and a lone tear slid down her cheek.

Not the reaction he wanted, or expected. He wondered if she was planning to go straight to the police and tell what happened. What was he thinking? He was a good guy—a gentleman. That was not him doing that. It certainly was not—

"Did you want to do that?" she asked, staring outside.

His breath stopped cold, awaiting her judgment. Was she saying she *didn't* want to do it? He never paused to check off a long list of signs, or ask her directly if he should or could continue. But she seemed to invite him, he was sure, stripping like that, posed like she was. And what had happened before, back on Halloween, was . . . nothing. Or something. An overture? Halloween—Samhain—she'd also seemed to invite him to join her. Everything that night made this night possible, and yet . . . .

"I was so stupid on Halloween," he muttered. "I—I shouldn't have left like I did."

She inhaled sharply, the life force filling her, awakening her soul—readying her to run away.

"I'm sorry if I hurt you." His voice was weak as he tried to sound sincere. He *was* sincere. He had never wanted to hurt a woman, even when they had hurt him.

The back of his hand pressed against hers. He wanted to clasp it but feared to. Something about that act seemed more intimate than having sex. He cleared his throat.

"I can take you home now, if you want me to."

She remained silent and after a minute he turned to regard her and saw there beside him a wounded waif of a girl. He felt shame boil through him. If he could just get her home, he would be holding his breath until Monday morning.

"I mean, if you want to go now."

She gazed out the open balcony doors at the rainy darkness, like it was another world. *Já*, how far it is from the sunless days of childhood to this strange man's apartment. She didn't know him, not even now, and that made him perfect in one way.

"You don't talk a lot, do you?" he asked.

The coolness of the rain soothed her, the coolness balanced by the heat of his body against hers, skin to skin. A small fire had been lit, a twisted string of flame which needed to be stoked and kindled further, drawn up into a conflagration that would cleanse everything and let her start over again.

She looked up at him. "Do you want me to go?"

2

ERIC WAS PLANNING TO HANG UP AFTER THE FOURTH RING, before the answering machine could come on. That would mean she was no longer there, probably got tired of waiting.

All morning he could not keep thoughts of her from filling his mind, could not block the pastel image of her stretched out on his bed, so lithe and fair, that orange hair in tangles. He knew she was the damsel in distress he was duty-bound to rescue. The words of Keats came to him: *O what can ail thee, knight-at-arms!/ So haggard and so woebegone?* He was the knight in shining armor who rescued women—even if they did not wish to be. He thought of his ex-wife, Marina, the woman he met in Texas. He thought he was saving her from a life of poverty and, in the end, he did. She got everything in the divorce—and still kept the boyfriend.

Someone picked up the receiver on the fifth ring.

"*Halló.*"

He did not recognize the woman's voice, but it had to be her.

"Is this Iris?"

"*Já*, I am Íris."

He replayed her name in his mind, the slippery phonemes and flip of the /r/, a magical incantation.

"It's me. Eric."

He listened to a couple breaths, then: "Who?"

"Eric Schaeffer." He cleared his throat and from his swiveling desk chair tried to swing his office door closed with a tap of his foot. "The guy you slept with last night."

She laughed, something like the bursting of a ripe peach.

"Apologies."

He took a shallow breath, felt his chest tighten. He did not really expect a woman he'd picked up in a rainstorm would still know his name the next morning. Or was it the guy who didn't know the girl's name? Either way, that only happened in movies. Besides, who was he to pick up any woman? Wasn't he always, had been trained to be, a gentleman? He was not some kind of playboy like his colleague Jack Macintosh.

"Are you all right?"

"Já, fine."

"What are you doing?"

He waited for her response, expecting a short list of dull activities she had used to pass the time.

"What are you doing?" she shot back at him.

He grinned into the phone.

"Thinking of you," he said, then wished he hadn't. Too corny for a one-night-stand. If it were a one-nighter. If she stayed another night, he wouldn't feel guilty. It would be a relationship. "This is really the first chance I've gotten to call you. I wanted to see if you were all right."

To see if you are still there.

In and out of class, he pondered why she had agreed to stay. Especially with him. The rain had stopped and he could have easily taken her home. Yet she had taken his arm and escorted him back to the bed. And he followed, already feeling guilty. She was gorgeous, of course; no confusion why he wanted her to stay. She remained quiet, though, a vague sadness settling about her, only speaking enough to direct him as she wished.

He wondered if she was one of those 'loose women' Matt, his younger brother, the church deacon, had always warned him about—especially when he was teaching in Japan. After all, he'd almost married the Art teacher at that school. With a laugh, he decided there must be something about him this orange-haired siren wanted to explore with him, something he could never guess. Just thankful for the rainy rescue? Still trying to sell that painting? He could only guess. Maybe she simply wanted it—needed it—as much as he had.

Need—want—always so close, he considered. It really did not matter which it was.

He jumped up from his chair, as though he had something important to say. But standing in the middle of his office, he heard her soft, steady breathing on the phone line, waiting patiently for him to speak. and he forgot his profound words. In a snap, he decided that might be best.

"You still there?" he asked.

"*Já*—here."

By the tone of her voice, he thought she must be a lost soul, strangely quiet and passive, reacting rather than acting—like so many women in the Romantic poetry he had studied. He was a lost soul, too, he admitted. After all, he had gone to many places seeking something, finding only enough at each place to occupy him a short time, then felt the need to move on. Each time he thought he was ready to settle down, a storm would come along and sweep him out to sea. This time, at least, he'd grabbed hold of a lifebuoy called Fairmont College—just as she apparently had.

"I know there's not much to eat," he spoke up, mentally examining his last look of the kitchen. "I never have much in the apartment, anyway. So I'm going to stop by the store on the way home. I can make dinner for us. Anything in particular you want me to get?"

"I need meat," she said rather quickly. "I want to eat . . . salmon. Can you get salmon?"

"That's what you want for dinner?"

There was a loud exhale. "Oh, it doesn't matter. Food is food, *já*. Can you cook?"

"Can I cook?" he wondered.

Perhaps he had doubts about his ability to prepare a meal for a special guest. He wanted to make a good impression, didn't he? The previous night's introduction was not the right kind of impression. He didn't know anything about the woman. Other than being an art student and modeling for figure classes—and the way she had looked stretched out on his bed: pinkish-white skin, bright orange hair, blue eyes. Deep blue eyes, like a lake surrounded by glaciers. She was from Iceland but had lived in Toronto. And she was a witch of some kind, not that it mattered to him especially. His parents might object, however.

Parents? Way too early for parents.

"Can you?" she was asking when he broke from his trance. She described in detail the kind of salmon she wanted. She seemed to know a lot about fish. Was salmon her favorite food? He furrowed his brow, listening to her lightly accented words.

"Get what you like, Eirík. I will let you cook."

"Great. I'd like to make dinner for you." He took a breath—at last, and his heartbeat returned to normal. What was there to be nervous about? Everything was going well. "So . . . are you staying over tonight?" he asked. *That was subtle.* His tone made it seem as though he didn't want her to stay. "You can stay, if you want to. I mean, please stay with me tonight." *With me? Please?* That sounded desperate. "Okay, Iris?"

Her name sat in his mouth a moment before it felt right.

"Íris," she corrected.

"Sorry. Íris," he repeated.

"I will call work, say I'm sick."

"Oh." He was surprised she had a job. It had never occurred to him that she had any kind of life but teasing him and seeing to his comfort. She became more real. "What is it that you do?"

"Does it matter?" She sounded frustrated.

"Not really. I was curious, that's all."

"I work at a picture frame shop at Towne Square mall. Six dollars an hour. I get frames for my paintings at fifty percent discount. It's okay?"

"Well, that makes sense. I mean, it's good for an artist to work in a frame shop, so you can get the discount."

He went on, comparing a writer working in a bookstore and a few other analogies, then trailed off, realizing how stupid he sounded. What to say next? He heard only the hiss of the phone line and expected she would hang up any second.

"Íris?" He paused to be sure she accepted his pronunciation. "I don't know anything about you. That's why I ask questions."

She laughed, a ripple of sea-breezes. "You know everything that is important. I come from *Ísland*, I'm artist, and I like sex."

"What I mean is, well, I don't even know . . . well, what your favorite color is."

He spied his office neighbor, Jack, peeking into the office. Turning away, Eric kept his attention on the phone as Jack stepped in, loosening his necktie, waiting for a sign from Eric to take a seat.

Eric cupped his hand over the receiver. "I'll be just a second."

". . . color?" she was asking. He expected she would chuckle, but she did not. How could she be offended discussing colors? She's an artist, a painter.

"What about colors?" he asked.

"You need to know colors for sex?"

"Not exactly, but . . . ." Eric turned away, lowered his voice. Jack was distracting. "I—I just want to get to know you better."

"Why?" she asked.

All he could do was stare at the wall. He saw the calendar; he needed to back up all of his computer files for Y2K. *Damn millennium*, he cursed as Jack took a seat.

"Sorry. No more questions."

An apology was the first thing he offered when a woman was displeased. His mother had taught him well. Everything was fine when Íris answered the phone. He recalled his in-the-throes offer to buy the painting—again—as they wrestled on the bed, finding new ways to pass the night. Was last night only to sell a painting? Sure, he'd buy it, but he wanted more. He had to see more, learn more about her, figure out her puzzle.

"I guess we need to talk about it when I get back."

"What's to talk? We did lots of fucking. You must be tired now. *Já*, if we talk about anything else we will be bored to death."

"Well, maybe you're right."

He agreed with her just to end the call. The receiver remained in his hand a few seconds longer as her voice faded.

"You're rather agitated this morning," said Jack.

"Something like that." Eric hung up the phone, felt a grin burst upon his face. "That art student from Iceland stayed with me last night. The one from the exhibit? I found her again."

"Whoa!" Jack scooted to the edge of the chair. "How did that happened? I didn't think you liked redheads."

"What?"

He could not fool Jack, a professional playboy. Eric's neighbor was a younger but upwardly mobile scholar who had a Ph.D. at 29 and, after publishing his book with a big name press, was granted tenure the previous spring. Jack, however, seemed to do everything possible to get himself in trouble now, including that affair everyone was whispering about.

Eric wanted to boast about the night he had, but that was not his way.

"I just picked her up in the rain last night and gave her a lift home. To my home, as it turned out. A place to dry off and warm up, that's all."

"A place to dry off and warm up . . . . Interesting euphemism."

"She's still there." Eric was beaming. "I can't get back until probably five, however. And I need to stop by the grocery. I'm cooking dinner tonight. She might stay the whole weekend."

"Excellent," said Jack, reaching out his hand. "I'm so happy for you."

They shook hands. Congratulations were in order.

"Oh, stop it. I'm a gentleman," said Eric, returning to his chair. "So I shouldn't kiss and tell, as it were." He reached for the can of Dr Pepper on his desk, took a swallow.

"So what are you going to do about the music teacher? What's her name?"

Eric blinked then frowned, wanting to grab his chest.

"Oh. Dominique, the harpist. She—we—heck, all we've ever done is go to dinner and see movies. She's a . . . ."

"A space-saver." Jack kept a straight face, then sat back, satisfied with his jab.

"Jack, you can be so crude." Eric scratched his chin, unshaven for once. "Dominique is nice, but—"

"And you want some naughty."

"No." He thought a second. "I never came here to find someone. Besides, since I'm divorced, how many chances do I get to start over? My hair's gray at the temples already. I'm getting a paunch. I have zero energy—and my back is so sore from last night. I'm forty years old, Jack."

"You should say it like this: 'I'm forty *fucking* years old.'" Jack sat up. "Look at *me*. I'm going bald. At thirty-five! Doesn't stop me. Use what you got; Dear Abby says so. You're cultivating one of those wise old professor looks. Oh, sorry—forget 'old.' Anyway, some co-eds go in for that. It's about confidence, expertise, the danger of the relationship, not your age or looks. They're testing their sexuality on you—"

"No, no, no," said Eric, shaking his head. "That's not what I want. I came here to teach. Didn't you? It's supposed to be my profession. Wait until you're my age. Then you'll understand. You'll see the horizon—where you ride off into the sunset?—you'll see it coming closer and closer, until you can almost touch it, but it'll always be just out of reach, taunting you. Then suddenly it will cover you like night." He rubbed his temple. "And you'll have headaches that grind your precious memories into dust."

"Shit, you really *are* the Romantics professor. Why don't we all kill ourselves and get it over with?" He fumbled with the pack of cigarettes in his shirt pocket, retrieved them. "That's your divorce burning its way through your gut. It'll come out eventually. What's it been, eight months? It's only stress. And frustration."

"Let's stop right there." Eric's face was stone. "We shouldn't be talking about this."

"You want fat divorcées with a couple of kids?"

"*I'm* a fat divorcé." Eric slapped the armrest of his chair. "I'm over the hill, past my prime. Thirty pounds too late. I know it. And I accept it, albeit reluctantly. It's too late for me to start over with the dating scene. Scares the hell out of me. Anyway, I blew it with my ex, Marina. I thought Dominique might be my second chance. Or third. I forgot about my time in Japan. I've lost count."

Eric's mind settled on Sakiko. He had taught her English. When he crossed paths with her at the end of the summer after her graduation, she appeared so mature in blouse, skirt, and heels, so different from that cute school uniform that made her look like a sailor. They began dating. Then the sex started. She taught him a lot—more than he thought she should know. Eventually, she moved to Osaka and got into adult films. He traveled by bullet train to be with her on holidays and vacations—

"You okay, buddy?"

Eric nodded, then let out a long sigh as he held up his soda can. He took a final swallow and slowly crushed the can in his hand, taking interest in the crunching metal noise. Like the earthquake that killed Sakiko in her sleep barely a month after he returned to the States.

"Anyway, I don't know what will happen with the art student." He breathed deeply. "Not until I get home tonight, at least. She might not even be there when I get home. I don't know much about her. She hardly said ten words all night."

"Was that three 'Oh my Gods' and a 'goodbye'?"

Eric shook his head. "You're incorrigible, Jack."

"It's in my job description—"

"But now I need to get to know her—"

"Now that you got the sex out of the way."

Eric thought of that moment, the two of them against the wall, and his heart thumped with guilt. Yes, the sex had come first, he could not deny, but it was not as though it was only a sexual encounter. After their Halloween meeting, on the verge of doing something sexual, well, last night *could* be considered a second date. He smiled to himself.

"She's from Iceland. Did I tell you that? And she's so . . ." He hissed an inhalation. She filled his head, filled his senses, and he could not wait to get back to her and hold her in his arms like a lover. His lover.

Perhaps the future Mrs. Schaeffer, if he dared imagine such a scenario. ". . . pure. Like with snow."

Jack was saying something then. His voice was calm but his words seemed like a warning.

"But I have to get to know her," Eric insisted.

"A girl like that, maybe you don't want to know too much."

Íris sets the phone down on the carpet and rolls back on the futon, studying the mottled ceiling pattern from the coolness of the sheets. She is glad the futon held together as they rocked against it. It did not squeak to let neighbors know how they spent the night. He was not shy this time, not like Samhain night. It was almost perfect, this night with Eirík. Then he calls from his office.

She goes to his lounge chair and sits, tilting all the way back, the footrest rising to meet her bare feet. Relaxing with a blanket coiled around her body, she watches television for an hour, clicking through a dozen channels. No sexy films, only cooking shows. She checks the bathroom since she did not get a hot bath. A bar of half-used soap sits on the rim of the tub. A bottle of shampoo stands in the corner. The ceramic basin looks clean enough. In her old house, she must share the bathroom with four other people. She welcomes the chance to enjoy a bath.

Nearly two hours later, wrapped in a towel with ragged edges, she sits at his computer. The machine hums, the green light blinks, and a bump of the mouse brings the screen to life. The icons are organized. She finds the one for his browser and clicks on it. His home page is personalized with bookmarked websites and saved searches. The weather for seven cities around the world is displayed. She is surprised to see her hometown listed: It is now minus 2° C. in Reykjavík, with snow falling.

She clicks on a link to an online bookstore he has saved. One book he has ordered is a history of Iceland. He has ordered two other books about Iceland. Perhaps this man is checking on her, wants to learn about her life, her homeland.

Another link takes her to a website of Asian women. Artistic nudity, the kind she often posed for in Toronto. And at Fairmont College. The fact that it is on his home page makes him more interesting. She had marked him as a quiet, honest kind of man. Until last night. This man is not *hygginn*, she knows now. All that shows on the screen is simple female nudity—not couples coupling, nothing hardcore, nothing like what they did during the night. When she clicks on some of the advertisements on these pages, however, she is taken to other sites that are more dangerous. A few minutes of staring and she is bored and exits the browser.

Bookshelves line the walls of his apartment and are stocked with the Classics. She read some of them at the University of Toronto; her second subject after Art was English Lit., after all. Her heathen father made sure she read the Sagas, to teach her about their heritage, yet they seemed like silly folk tales and never made her think of religion. She read the *Eddas* and the Saga of the Volsungs, Hrafnkel's Saga, Egil's Saga, and Njal's Saga—all in her native language, *Íslensku*—yet they meant nothing to her. This Eirík is interested in them. Because of meeting her?

This is his life: science-fiction and fantasy novels; Greek plays and Roman histories; books on Celtic mythology; books by Japanese authors in English translation; collections of literary journals; volumes of poetry—old poets like Keats, Wordsworth, and Tennyson, and modern ones, too. There are many reference books: atlases, almanacs, and dictionaries. One book catches her eye: *The White Goddess* by Robert Graves. She pulls it from the shelf and flips through it, reads here and there, suddenly interested in the ancient European cult of the white goddess with the red hair and blue eyes—her ancestor.

On the bottom shelf are books that look as though they were bound at a copy shop. She selects one and discovers the author is *this Eirík*: a volume of poetry entitled *The Dogs of Divorce*. She opens it.

"'She was a dog of divorce,'" she reads aloud, letting the towel drop to the floor, "'howling at the moon/ waiting for her master to come home soon./ As a Schnauzer with docked tail and cropped ears/ she reflected all her master's fears . . . .'"

She continues reading, sitting cross-legged on the carpet.

Other poems are full of words that hurt, words meant as bandages, words as weapons, words intended to hurt *someone*. She understands him now. This man had a dog, had a wife, had a future, a family, everything—then lost them. Today he lives in this simple flat and his only joy is finding a whore on a rainy night. She is sad for him. Here is a man who dreamed of me, *já*, someone like me, for many years, she thinks. There is something familiar she notices. She regards the futon bed, sees a coffin.

Like her, he has been wounded.

Eric unlocked the door, juggling the paper sack of groceries, and entered the dark apartment. He was worried that his guest had left, tired of waiting for him. A faint light shone on the ceiling, however, so he started up the stairs, calling "Sorry I'm late"—and immediately recognized it was the same phrase he'd said before he caught Marina in bed with her lover.

He came to the top of the stairs, shaking off that memory. There was a new woman in his life: the orange-haired woman named Iris—no, Íris. There she was: sitting in his office chair, at his desk, only the pale light of the monitor illuminating the room. She was online, he saw in a glance, a page of text filling the screen.

"So you found some way to kill the time," he called, going to the kitchen.

"I hope you don't mind," said Íris.

"No, it's all right. Please make yourself at home."

He set the sack of groceries down on the counter and took off his coat, went to her.

Nude from head to toe, she had pulled one knee to her chest, her foot on the seat, the other leg dangling. He gazed down over her shoulders and saw the silver pendant resting between her breasts. He leaned down and kissed her cheek.

The way she jerked made him pause. He leaned in again, her lush hair smelling of his shampoo. She continued typing, using three fingers. She was in some kind of chat room, responding to someone's post.

"You are so . . . white," said Eric, more to himself than her.

In the monitor's glow, the faint reflection of her face on the screen made her seem like a ghost, phantom lover, succubus.

"Aren't you cold?" he asked.

He went to the sliding glass door at the balcony and closed it, then checked the thermostat on the wall. It was off so he set it on low. A stream of warm air began to blow. He turned, admiring the litheness of her body, the evenness of her complexion, the curve of her hip. He had slept next to that woman—the two of them naked together under the blanket. It still felt like a dream.

When she finally sent the message off into cyberspace with a triumphant finger strike to the ENTER key, she sat back with a satisfied sigh.

"I did try to get some fish for you. I checked the salmon," he said, expecting she would want to know, preparing her for the bad news, "but what they had did not look very fresh. I didn't think you would want it. Actually, I got to like fish when I lived in Japan. It's always fresh there. They know how to do fish right. In fact, some of my most favorite meals ever were in Japan. Hard to get good fish in Kansas . . . . Nevertheless, I checked. You eat a lot of fish back in Iceland? No wonder you're so healthy."

He waited for her to comment, hoping for some remark of gratitude that he had tried, but she remained silent, staring at the monitor.

"Since it's going to be cold this weekend, they say," said Eric, "I decided to get the ingredients to make chili. You ever have it? It's a kind of spicy stew with beef, and onions, peppers; some people add beans—in a base of tomato sauce and, of course, chili powder. It's Texas food. It's what cowboys eat. It can be spicy. You like spicy?"

She stretched in the chair, yawned audibly.

"*Nei*, I never tasted it, Eirík." She waved him to her side and laid her head back, blinking her lashes at him with what seemed like deliberate comic intention. "Apologies, *já*. I wrote a letter to my friend in Toronto. Beth is her name. This e-mail makes it easy."

"Beth?" He studied her face. "She's your friend?"

"*Nei*, she's more a sister. She saved me when I was living on the streets."

He frowned. "Living on the streets?"

"It's long story to tell. My father died, my mother remarried, so . . . ."

"I'm sorry."

"*Já*, so when I was eighteen, she kicked me out. Beth found me and took me in. She introduced me to her Wiccan circle. She got me a job and she was the one telling me to go to art school. *Já*, she modeled for art classes at the university, and one day I went in her place and met Professor Hirsch. That's how it started."

"Your art career?"

"I showed him my drawings and he liked them. So I got my degree and then he sent me here for MFA. Full scholarship."

"I see. Well, that certainly explains how a girl from Iceland ends up in Wichita, Kansas."

"Long story, *já*." She gazed up at him. "So I told Beth about you— us—last night."

"Really?" He didn't know whether to feel proud or ashamed. "I hope it was good. I mean, what you wrote. That you told her it was good. We were good. I mean, that I didn't hurt you."

"I wrote it was spicy."

He was about to make a joke, then took a breath as she returned to her typing.

Everything felt weird, as though he had stepped not into his tiny apartment after a day of school but into some dream. This beautiful, sexy woman was still in his home, sitting comfortably nude, as though she had no care in the world. And he, back from a mundane grocery shopping stop, was chatting with her like nothing was out of the ordinary.

He gazed at her white shoulders from the dinette corner of the living room. That orange hair was streaming down upon one of her shoulders. He wanted to stroke her shoulder. Then he would slide his hand down her chest and cup a breast—either one. A strong urge welled up inside him: the desire not to grab her and carry her roughly to the bed but simply to ask the only question that mattered: *Why are you here?*

But he dared not ask. He could never ask.

After putting away the groceries, Eric changed to a pair of jeans and a sweatshirt. He offered her a blue and white striped robe—a *yukata*, he told her—that he'd brought back from Japan. She thanked him and pulled it on, tied the cloth belt. He praised how Japanese she looked, except for the orange hair. He glanced down at her bare feet, imagined them in wooden *geta*, then remembered he was no longer in Japan. The door to that room had long been closed.

They both worked to put the chili together. She skillfully wielded the carving knife on the vegetables, cutting them down to size, especially the carrots for the salad. She took one carrot and licked the cut end seductively as he pretended to ignore her. Watching the way she cut carrots made him uneasy. He turned away and mixed the chili base in a large pot, measuring out the chili powder and Worcestershire sauce like a scientist. He threw the big clump of ground sirloin into the skillet and they watched it sizzle. She stood next to him, and eventually his arm slid around her waist, later her arm around his, too. When the meat was cooked enough, Íris snatched a pinch and pushed it into his mouth. It was too hot and he spit it out into his hand as she laughed. He liked her laugh, and thought of snowmen and candy canes. They nibbled from the salad bowl as they continued cooking.

While the chili was simmering, they went to bed to satisfy their hunger for dessert. It was midnight before they had dinner.

"I ran into someone at the grocery store," said Eric as they lay together, their bellies full. He counted heartbeats. "I want to be perfectly honest with you. She and I were dating—something like that—when I first met you. That is, at the art exhibit on Halloween."

"And now, Eirík?" Her voice was soft and emotionless, waiting for some announcement that would ruin everything.

"Now?" He took a breath. "I'm not sure. Not after tonight—last night, I mean. Not now. See, it's just that . . . ." He caressed her bare shoulder, thinking how to put the words together. Her skin was smooth, a pink hue in the shadows. "I guess she and I are just friends. She's not the same kind of woman. What I mean is . . . . She and I—we just go see movies together. Well, she wouldn't understand. I'll tell her next week, and end it officially."

"End what?"

"Our relationship."

Her face changed; perhaps it was the play of light and shadow.

"It matters not to me," she said. "You mustn't change anything for me. I cannot have any relationship with you, so continue going dating with that woman if you want."

Suddenly his promise to Jack hit a wall. *No relationship?* Then why was she here—with him—in bed, *with him*? It did not make sense, not the way he was raised. Unless she was one of those women his brother always joked about: a whore. And yet, she was too pure, too clean, to be a woman who only wanted to play around for a night. He did not have one-night stands; no, it had to be the start of a relationship or he was every bit as—

"That's not why I told you."

"So why?"

He tried to hold her tighter and immediately realized it was a way to control her, but she resisted, pushing her elbow into his ribs. He relaxed his hold but kept his hand on her arm.

"I want to keep seeing *you*," he said. "She doesn't want . . . well, not the same kind of relationship you and I have. She just wants a—a buddy. Someone to talk to. Someone to be there for her."

Someone to lug around her harp, he thought, unable to count the number of times Dominique Vargás had called him to help her. She taught music at Fairmont, played with the Symphony. She also played for church services and weddings. Harps were popular. He was the *boyfriend*, the ever-steady helper—the guy she met at the DMV when he first arrived in Wichita. After being married—briefly—to Marina Ramos in Texas, Eric had no intention of getting involved with another

Hispanic woman. However, there was no one else, and Dominique was pleasant enough.

"*Já*, now you are here."

He was not sure if she was amused or simply pointing out his betrayal of the other woman. The impetuous smile he had seen hiding in the corners of her mouth was gone.

"I don't care if we only see each other on weekends," said Eric. His voice was tight, desperate. "I know our schedules probably conflict— like this morning, when I had to run out so early. Anything is all right with me. As long as I can keep seeing you."

She patted his shoulder like a pet who'd come home dirty.

"So flattering, *já*."

He rolled over, facing her.

"After the art show, and seeing you in your room that way—geez, what an idiot I was!—I thought I'd never see you again. Then, I guess, Fate stepped in. Like you said last night. What are the odds of people meeting in a rainstorm like we did? Not just any two people but *us*— two people who met before and then lost each other. That's what Fate is. And now that I've found you again, I . . . ."

Eric thought of the words that came next, daring himself to speak them, willing to take the risk.

After he'd chickened out on Halloween night, he'd tried to stay away from the south end of the campus, but his curiosity soon compelled him to take a walk on the wild side. He strolled across the campus to Dickerson Hall, the Art building. At first, he simply stood on the knoll and stared at the glass-enclosed canteen that connected it to Everett Hall, the Music building, hoping to see an orange-haired woman.

And he'd thought of her as he drove the twelve hours down to visit his parents in Corpus Christi over the Thanksgiving break. Safe in their air-conditioned condominium, revising his story gave him enough distraction. Then he dared drive past his former condo. At the very moment he turned into the parking lot, there was Marina, fully pregnant, being helped down the stairs by her lover. That was a punch to his gut. Returning to Wichita, he was actually glad he couldn't find this Icelandic witch, realizing how complicated life would become if he had.

But that was last week, not this week.

He smiled, quite sincerely, as for a job interview.

"Íris, I think I'm in love with you."

"Shhhh!" She thrust her finger to his lips. "Don't ruin this moment. If you say it, it will be a lie, and I hear too many lies all my life."

"I'm sorry," he said, always the first words out of his mouth.

She shook her head slowly. "It can never be truth, *já*, not even after many, many wedded years and coming to old age. Even if you feel it, you never say it."

"But what if—"

"Shush now, baby," she said in a different, lighter voice.

She pinched his face between her thumb and forefinger. He grinned, pretended to struggle. Her hands showed him where she wanted him, pulling him into position.

"Again? But I—"

"Don't say a word, baby."

Outside, a faint tintinnabulation filled the silence.

"Listen," Íris whispered in the dark, a streetlamp's glow just touching the bed.

He counted the raindrops for a few minutes, holding her in his arms, cheek to cheek.

"How old are you?" he asked.

"I am legal age," she said with a snicker.

"No, seriously. How old?"

"I am twenty-six."

"Really? I thought maybe twenty-four."

She turned so they were face to face. Her lips brushed against his as she spoke. "And you?"

"Thirty-eight . . . ?" As soon as the words were out, he realized he shouldn't have put the raising inflection at the end; it sounded like a lie. It was a lie. With their noses almost touching, he could not avoid her blue eyes. "No, I'm forty."

"Why did you say thirty-eight?" She seemed disappointed.

"I didn't want to be too old. For you." He studied her eyes for a clue. "Maybe fourteen years isn't too big a difference. It's all psychological, anyway. You're as old as you feel. And you make me feel about ten years younger. Besides, it's not as though I'm . . . well, old enough to be your father."

She was no longer smiling.

"Sorry. I'm forty years old. Are you all right with that?"

"People always telling lies. When people open their mouths, lies come out."

"I'm sorry, Íris. I'll never lie to you again."

"That is the biggest lie of all. Of course, you will. It is human's nature, *já*."

"Human nature," he automatically corrected her, then thought for a moment. "You're right. Everyone wants things to be real. I mean, they want their dreams to actually happen. Or like you: you're a fantasy come true. I mean, you're so—"

Her hand brushed his throat, halting his speaking, and stayed on his cheek. "You didn't shave today."

"Yeah—sorry about that. I had to leave so fast this morning. I barely had enough time to get dressed. I had an early class to teach. And some handouts to print off before it."

Her face froze, then melted, noticing the crystalline patterns in the snowflakes.

He waited for his arrest, listening for the knock on the door.

"Didn't you know that? I'm a professor at Fairmont."

"*Já*, I get it." She smiled quickly, just to be polite. "And I'm a student at Fairmont. We are not supposed to meet this way. Or fuck." She rolled onto her back, breathed deeply. "Don't worry, I won't tell anyone."

That word cut into him, making it all so clear. They did not make love, as he preferred to call it. It was only something bestial. He slowly shook his head. He did not know her, not really, not even now. Yet, if he were going to be charged with anything, she'd had plenty of time during the day to call the police. They could have intercepted him when he returned. But he came home and there she was to welcome him. And they had continued making love—*fucking*, whatever. It had to be love. Backwards, perhaps, but—

"I don't think there's any rule against us being together."

He regarded her eyes. So blue. He was drawn to them but tried not to stare too long.

She blinked, perhaps sending away a tear or two.

What did I say? Eric tried thinking back through his words.

Another tear fell.

"You like what we do, *já*?" She waited and he wondered if she needed an answer. He constructed an answer: *You brought me back to life.* Before he could speak, however, she went on in a weaker voice: "I let you fuck me. I say it's good. I say you're a sexy man. I say you are good at fucking and it makes you feel good. You feel good now, *já*?"

"Good?" His eyes flittered to the wall, the dent in the wall, and back to her, not sure what she was getting at. "It's been a long time. You've already worn me out."

She offered a faint smile. "So you are happy? Feel good?"

"Oh, yes." He laughed. "Oh, my god, yes."

She did not seem pleased with that answer.

"Did I . . . uh, you know . . . satisfy you?" he asked.

He watched her face for a positive sign. Not that he really had been concerned with how she felt. He was loving, he concluded, tried to be passionate, gave some time to her pleasure, but he was no porn star.

"That's all right. You don't have to answer."

"*Já*, you satisfied me."

She blinked. Her smile held steady, so he chose to believe her. He knew he would do more for her, focus on her, if he was given another chance. It was late and they were already sleepy, not making sense any longer. Perhaps there would be no other chance.

"I'm alive again because of you, Íris."

He turned onto his side, kissed her shoulder a few times, a playful act that did nothing to change her expression.

But what about next week, next month? Where do we go from here? It hit him between the eyes. The game had begun, he realized. The relationship game. He now had to be careful. Even to acknowledge it was a game, or mention there were rules, automatically made a player lose. And he had always lost this game.

He tried to hide his grimace of discomfort, wondering what it was about him that kept her there.

"What are you thinking?" she asked softly.

"I'm wondering why me? I mean, why are you here?"

"Where should I go?"

"Just like that? You choose to stay here? With me: a middle-aged guy who happens to like abstract art. Don't get me wrong, I love having you here. I love the way you . . . ." Her eyes had closed. "Iris?"

"*Íris*," she corrected, then opened her blue eyes.

"Are you ready to sleep?" he asked.

She regarded his face, inches away. The slightest of smiles hovered on her lips like a new color of lipstick. She waited and he felt a trick was being played. She seemed to be waiting for him to answer a question she had yet to ask. A question neither could answer. Her eyes remained open, daring him to speak it. He could not so he looked away.

"No matter what happens tomorrow," he said, eyes averted, "I won't ever forget this night—or last night—all this time being with you."

He returned his gaze to her.

"If you wish to," she whispered after a moment of silence.

He broke from his bliss. "Every morning I take a god-awful lot of vitamins, and ginseng, ginkgo, and yohimbe, a lot of other crap. My ex-wife turned me onto those herbal supplements. She was a fitness freak. I don't even know what they're supposed to do, just that they keep a guy my age able to keep up with a sexy woman like you—"

"Don't tell your secrets," she said, putting a finger to his lips.

"I want you to trust me." He took her finger, kissed it. "We can't begin by hiding things."

"You did," she said. "About your age."

Then her stern mouth twisted into something like a sly grin.

Is she joking with me? If she is, that is a good sign. It's the start of a beautiful new relationship. He smiled like a child who got the cookies out of the jar without getting caught.

"Right. That's what I mean. Total honesty from now on."

Her hand settled on his arm, feeling warm and cold at the same time.

"Don't worry, Eirík. It's not you—not who you are. You are a man. *Já*, it's all you give, never hold back. No apologies. You did it, Eirík, and I'm good now. I can go on."

"My ex- didn't think so," he said with a grumble, "so she got someone who could—"

"No secrets, *já*?"

"They're not secrets if I tell you."

"*Mér er skítsama*," she said sharply.

"What?"

"Stay with me, *Eirík*. Stay in this moment. This is what there is: only now. I don't care about your past, *já*. I'm not in your past."

He frowned, thinking of the empty wasteland of tomorrow. In a flash he saw himself twenty years hence, looking back on this moment, when it would be in his past. How would he explain it? He saw grandchildren gathered around him, a beautiful but plump orange-haired woman serving cookies.

"How about my future, then?"

Her face was an icy slate. He could read nothing there. Obviously, she had no plans to be in his future. As she said over the phone: this was only something for now, and it would be done and forgotten. Serendipity. Kismet. Enjoy it while you can. Perhaps Jack was right.

Íris yawned, seemed embarrassed. "I want to sleep now."

"Yes, I suppose we should," said Eric. He faked a yawn. "It's already so late. Tomorrow is almost here."

Instinctively, he leaned over to kiss her but paused. And then, as if by magic, her lips parted slightly. He decided it was an invitation. He accepted and pressed against her mouth, a final kiss, deep and loving, trying to take all he could get of her soul. This was the end, he knew and feared. Tomorrow he would have to take her home. The fantasy would end. His real life would return.

"Thank you," he whispered when their lips separated.

"Thank you," she repeated almost without sound.

Her arms wrapped around his chest and her chin pressed into his shoulder. She left a wet kiss there that lingered as frost.

"You may dream of me if you wish," she whispered.

"I wish."

"And I will dream of snow."

3

ÍRIS RISES WITH THE DAWN, letting Eirík sleep. A glance back over her shoulder at him. She pities him—so confused, so impatient, he is. A miserable man. There is something strange about him, yet familiar, too.

Now is her time, the peace of early morning. She stands on the balcony, feet wet against the wooden planks, her body wrapped in the blue and white striped robe he gave her. The coffee mug is hot in her hands as she breathes in the cold air, noticing how the mighty cedar branches hang limp between the buildings, soft in the mist.

It is mid-morning before he rouses, yet that is not enough sleep for him. He pulls her back to the bed for another hour. He says he sleeps better with her beside him. She throws off the robe and moves next to him, trying the strange activity he calls *cuddling*. As he dozes, one arm securely around her shoulders to keep her close, she studies the cedars outside from her captivity on the bed.

Then they have lunch—bowls of reheated chili, bread on the side—and watch the mist melting away.

Saturday and all is calm. Tomorrow has come. She must go home, they both understand. Her Thursday night dress, the green and black one that got soaked in the rainstorm, is dry but not clean. Otherwise, she has nothing to wear. He dresses her in the smallest sweatpants he can find, ones that no longer fit him, and a bulky t-shirt with the Fairmont College logo on it. She hates wearing pants and is not fond of the logo. With her clogs on her bare feet, she is "fit for public," he says, laughs.

Outside it is cold and dampness seeps into her bones. The city is still asleep as they drive through the tree-lined back streets of her neighborhood. He pulls to the curb in front of the old Victorian house he visited on Halloween night, and comes around to let her out. He leads her up the walk, taking her hand, taking her through the double doors. She points the way up the stairs. On the second floor, she points to the other three doors—her housemates, all guys on that floor—and the bathroom at the end of the hall.

As they enter her room, he suggests they go see a film, anything to keep this dream from ending. Íris hangs up the damp dress and strips off the clothes he lent to her. He says no hurry returning them. When she takes off the t-shirt and sweatpants, he remembers the rainy night. She remembers Samhain night, when he ran out like a frightened schoolboy. Seeing how he looks at her now, she stands up straight, posing just for him. He goes to her, transformed into a big, strong man. He lays his hands on her hips for a moment, remembering, feeling the power he has. They fall back onto the bed as he scrambles to get his pants down. She directs him to fuck her from behind and bends herself over the side of the narrow bed. It is rough. It is the spanking she wants.

Despite seeing him breathing hard, she says she wants to go again, a new position. Now he feels guilty. The full light of day allows him to see it all differently. He thinks he has hurt her, taken advantage of her like some pervert. She shows him what hurt is, pumping him hard with her closed fist—and when he is ready again she makes him release onto her face. The stream is hot against her cheek and runs down to her chin, and for a moment, her mind returns to the club in Toronto, where the men are cheering for her. She was never very good as a waitress, only a little better dancing around a pole, or sitting on men's laps. They found her a job she could do and introduced her to the back room.

She looks up, expecting to see delight in his eyes. He does not cheer. Instead of pleasure, she sees he is horrified.

"I need to tell you something," she says, suddenly solemn. She takes his hands in hers, forcing him to kneel on the floor. "People say I have a problem. The counselors say so. It's a kind of obsession. It is something I cannot control. Sometimes I need to have sex. *Já*, a lot of sex. I feel it come over me, like a shadow or a breeze. After, when I have enough, I am fine again. Yet I hate myself."

"And this is one of those times?" asks Eirík. His words are full of concern.

She nods and her eyes become teary.

His hands tighten around hers, clasped in union and he thinks he can feel her heart through her palm. He does not understand yet he must embrace her, pressing her messy face into his shirt. She does not keep back the tears that gather and fall. She slips off the bed, on her knees with him. Holding each other on the floor, she sniffles and her fingers feel him soften.

There is something in him that touches her, yet she cannot tell him what it is. She is not sure what it is, so she simply cradles his face in her hands, tenderly, and forces herself to gaze into his eyes: brown, beautiful, and open to his soul, a dark place she can only visit for a heartbeat. Otherwise, she will pollute it. Then she is out and swimming back to her own life once more.

He stands and grabs his pants, pulls them on and goes quickly out the door.

"Goodbye, Eirík," she whimpers, not surprised that he leaves.

Most men leave when they are done with her. That's the way it's always been. They walk out satisfied, or angry, or amused—or they die. Her mentor in Toronto, art professor Albrecht Hirsch, died under her as she bounced up and down on his hips. She dared not call the police. Let someone else discover his body. He was old, anyway.

Her room has changed overnight. It is wet—too wet. The window was left open and the heavy wind of Thursday night blew in some rain. Cold air and mist have drifted in. Now the floor is damp. The bed is cold. She does not want to sleep here tonight. She wants to be in the warmth of his aura, in his arms. She can be safe for a while, have a hot bath again. Yet now he is gone, just like Samhain night. She is alone again.

She takes a handful of tissues from the box and wipes her face.

"You *are* here for Iris, aren't you?" asked the skinny boy with the mussed blonde hair and nose ring, fresh from the shower. "She's been gone a couple days so I figured she was, ya know, screwing around again. Never can tell with her." He laughed, grabbing a towel with one hand while extending the other hand. "I'm Cory."

"Thanks for the run-down," said Eric, exiting the bathroom at the end of the hallway.

Cory pushed past him, holding the towel around his hips. "Iris, you in?"

She came to the doorway, half-naked in panties, breasts jiggling as she pulled on a fresh t-shirt.

"*Já . . . .*"

Her eyes widened at the sight of Eric. Perhaps she did not want him to be there. Seeing her acting so free and easy with her nudity in front of this neighbor boy made Eric squirm—and he squirmed more as she confirmed to this boy, in words as plain and dry as a scientific report, that she had indeed spent the past two nights sleeping with *this Eirík.* With this man. Only then did she smile—for an instant.

"So when're you gonna pose for *me*?" asked Cory, the towel slipping a bit. "I almost got the frame done and the clay is on the way."

"I can make time," Íris told him, then gave Eric a brief explanation of the project.

Cory explained further: If Íris were going to pose for his sculpture, they would need to work at school. When it was completed, he would have to fire it there. Moving it from the house to the art building would be difficult.

"I don't mind posing in Dickerson," said Íris. "Your studio or mine?"

Eric calmly observed this side of Íris, a side he somehow never suspected. She had friends—a less intense, more friendly personality, too. He saw a smile, heard a laugh. That surprised him.

"And don't forget the Old Town art show," Cory said as he stepped over to his room, the floor creaking. "Ray's demanding everyone bring at least two works or he's gonna throw a tantrum. Those are Elaine's exact words."

"I could bring what didn't sell at the graduate exhibit," said Íris, adding a sigh.

Eric got the hint. He had not followed through with his promise to buy that painting. He could not quite recall it. Something about roses. A woman resting her head on rose petals? If she still had it, he would pay cash today. He would go straight to the nearest ATM and give her whatever she asked. After last night, how could he not?

He followed her back inside her room. She seemed happy, touching his face. Her fingers lingering against his cheek as she gazed at him, but only for two breaths. Then Íris took a sweater from a stack of folded clothes and pulled it over her head, covering the t-shirt. She gathered her orange hair into a ponytail. He admired the bulky, tan sweater with white and blue lines crisscrossing it, and asked about the design. A traditional Icelandic pattern, made of *lopi*, she said, from Icelandic sheep. He pinched it, rubbed it between his fingers. The green and blue plaid skirt she pulled on swayed around her knees, making him think of school uniforms. Her legs remained pale and bare as she pulled on white ankle socks and slipped her feet into a pair of scuffed brown leather shoes. Catholic schoolgirl. She looked twelve years old.

She motioned him out and closed the door—not bothering to lock it, he noticed. She told him nothing of value was in there. He took her by the hand, an item he said was very valuable, and kissed her cheek, another valuable item, but she did not react—as though she felt nothing. He shrugged it off. It had been a strange enough morning already.

The matinee at the Northridge was less than half-full and although they entered the theater first, they could not choose a pair of seats. He wanted the absolute center of the room. She wanted the extreme back of the room. Eric gave in, still amazed that she was with him at all. Sitting in the back, they shared a small box of chocolates before the trailers began. As the lights dimmed, Eric saw Dominique enter with a large tub of popcorn and move to the center seat.

Eric had mentioned the film to Dominique, and they had planned to go see it. But the rain came. It was an acceptable rationalization, he thought. What did he owe Dominique? They were just movie buddies. Even so, he sank down in his seat. He knew he would have to hurry Íris out as soon as the credits began, before the lights went up; Dominique always stayed through the credits.

He watched Íris watching the film. Except for the occasional bump of elbow or brush of hand on the armrest, she did not touch him or lay her head on his shoulder. He wondered for a moment how they could have had so much sex but not act affectionate when they were in the theater. Different customs. She had no comment, did not laugh when most of the audience did. Of course, he never denied that Dominique was good in public. Íris was at her best in bed.

In the lobby, Íris patted his arm and said, "Thanks for the film, *já.*"

They stopped for hamburgers at a nearby restaurant, sitting across the table from each other, dipping their French fries in tiny paper cups of ketchup and playfully feeding each other. The lovers in the movie had done that. After explaining about each item of '50s memorabilia that filled the restaurant, he watched her carefully remove the lettuce and tomato from the burger before taking a bite, saying she was not a vegetarian.

"So, you're a hardcore carnivore?" he asked, and laughed.

He explained the story he'd shared in the writer's workshop the previous Monday evening. In it, a vegetarian who was head chef at a steakhouse was having an affair with a 'hardcore carnivore' who ran a botanical garden. The workshop members had not liked the story.

Íris grinned, spoke as she chewed: "*Já*, a meat-eater."

When they stepped outside, the gray afternoon had slipped into an evening shrouded with random flurries.

Íris stood on the sidewalk, with Spangles' red and yellow lights throwing stripes across the pavement. She inhaled deeply, breathing in the cold night air and smiling. Her sweater could not have been warm enough, he thought, but she did not complain. He offered her his jacket but she politely refused.

"*Ég fæddist í vetur svo ég eins og kulda,*" she sang to a tune he had never heard. "I was born in winter, *já*, so I like the cold." The north wind caught her voice, amplified it. "It makes me feel alive! And feeling alive is most important."

"What are you talking about? Let's get in the car."

"The cold—the winter coming on," she called. "Hibernation is done, *já. Svefn björninn er vaknaður.* The arctic bear is awake, and hungry." She burst out laughing.

"We just ate, Iris. You want more?"

She went to the passenger side of the car. "It's Íris," she called happily over the roof. "And, *já*, I want more! More!"

He came around to unlock the door. Her hands took his head, turning his face to hers as she pushed him back against the car and planted her mouth roughly on his. She covered his face with kisses. He was fixed to the car until she was done with him.

"The cold always makes me hot," she said.

"Then we should, by all means, make our way home, lest you begin to perspire."

Íris could not follow the film. A blond woman meets a man and tells her brunette girlfriend about him and the brunette girlfriend tries to take the man away from the blond woman by sexual manipulation, yet that only makes all of them closer friends—*fáránlegt, já!* Supposed to be a comedy. It is not so bad going out to a show with him, she thinks, yet she wanted the film to end so they could hurry back to his place. He wants to please her, she knows, so she will give up her body another night. Her heart is a much more difficult thing to give away. She has offered it only a few times yet always it has been returned, unused.

At his apartment, they go straight to the bed, fucking before they finish stripping themselves. He likes the lights on, so he can see her.

She closes her eyes. Tonight she doesn't want to be watched. Something is changing. She realizes she would not want to be with him in public again. She cannot imagine walking with him on campus. People would point. "Look at the Ice Princess—she's frozen another man!" After all, he is fourteen years older than she is.

Já, she thinks, they would be right. She does the math as he grunts and climaxes. *If I were fourteen years old again*, she wonders—

"Are you sweating yet?" he asks, panting over her. She shakes her head and he seems disappointed. "I'll open the window."

She calculates the ages as he goes naked to the balcony, slides open the door. A chill blows in. As he returns, his penis is still fat and red. She feels moisture on her skin now, wants to dry off. She moves to the edge of the bed. As he returns, she takes him in her mouth, makes him grow again. He appreciates her skill—that is obvious—yet he never asks how she developed such a range of techniques.

She adds and subtracts as she enjoys him. When she was fourteen—when this Eirík was fourteen years younger . . . . It makes no sense. She works harder on him and he grabs her head, clenches her hair and holds on to the end. She does not release him until he is spent. He no longer feels shame, she notices and smiles before swallowing. He knows how to use her now.

Standing before her, drained again, he releases her bundle of hair and apologizes if he hurt her. In that instant, she reaches up and pulls him down by his shoulders, falling back on the bed. Her hands direct him and he cannot refuse. He knows what she wants. He knows what to do. His lips, tongue, and fingers work together and she cannot do the math. The ceiling breaks open and she sees stars flickering above, the hot sun on her right with the cool moon on her left, and the earth lies below her, rich and pungent, fragrant and sweet, and she feels the ticking of a clock. He lifts her legs over his shoulders and slides his hands under her bottom, drawing her close. He writes out the Bible, letter by letter with the tip of his tongue as his fingers massage inside her to the beat of some pop song. She can barely breathe. A dull weight settles in her womb, a sensation she has never felt before. It fills her, pressing on her bones, and then, without warning, a stream of clear liquid bursts from

"*Mína píka!*" she shrieks. The echo of her words lasts for minutes.

He grins at her, startled, then sits back on the bed. "Are you all right?"

She is giddy, shaking uncontrollably, unable to speak.

"I learned that in Japan," he says, then wonders if it is appropriate to say.

He wipes his face on the sheet, decides to nibble on her toes as the man in the movie did. Kissing his way up her leg to her belly, he crawls over her, embracing her, sharing his warmth. She cannot speak. She is too weak to wrap her arms around him. He pulls a blanket over them and holds her.

Later, Íris awakens in the dark, next to this man. He is asleep, facing her, one hand draped casually over her belly. She gazes at him, sees a face like the one that hovered over her crib a long time ago. In the ethereal calmness he radiates, she finds herself growing suspicious again. His face is unshaven. The outline of a beard makes her see her father. In this prone position, with his dark hair swept back, she sees a very different man. She wraps her arms around him and holds him tight a moment, and whispers "Thanks." She knows he is only an English teacher, yet there is something disturbing about him. As he sleeps, she holds him—so he cannot get away, so he cannot hurt her. So she knows it is all real. She does the math—again.

This Eiríkur is forty years old, she considers. When she was fourteen, when her father raped her, he was also forty.

4

IT WAS STILL DARK IN THE APARTMENT WHEN ERIC AWOKE. After a few seconds, he realized he was alone in the bed. There was a faint red light coming through the balcony door, silhouetting the roof of the opposite apartment building. A figure was silhouetted by the sunrise. He wasn't sure at first if it was the top of the cedar tree outside, or someone standing on the balcony.

He got up, his back sore, and because of the chill from the balcony, he picked up the sweatpants from the floor and slipped them on, then added the flannel shirt that hung on the bathroom doorknob.

"What's the matter?" he asked, pulling on the shirt.

Íris wore the blue-white *yukata*. Her hair was copper in the dawn light. Her cheeks were white—reflecting a world that was brighter than it should have been.

"It snowed," she said, as quiet as the blanket that lay across the landscape.

She did not move when he joined her at the railing, nor did she seem affected by the cold as she stood barefoot there. Eric looked down at the yard, the drive through the apartments, the buried cars parked along it. The sun was almost showing over the roofs, staining the snow pink. He wanted to put his arm around her, but he felt an invisible force surrounding her.

"It sure has," he said. "Looks about eight inches." He put his hands on the wooden railing beside her, brushed aside the three inches that had collected, and leaned there. "Aren't you cold?"

"Já . . . always cold."

He saw that her eyes were red and her cheek was wet, as if she had been crying.

She looked at the snow. "Don't you want to hold me?"

He curled his arm around her waist and tried not to make it seem he was hesitant. She did not turn against his shoulder.

"Is something wrong?" he asked, certain he had again acted badly.

The snow has settled wet and heavy against the world—each fluffy flake fondling its kin, kissing and cuddling like a happy family reunion, she thought. Já, if only it were so. And with each new snowflake that comes to visit, the snow family grows, and as it grows it transforms into ice, and bears down against the windows, scratching and scoring them in uncomfortable patterns. With time, it crystalizes its history in twisted hoarfrost—

"Nothing is wrong," she said, counting the flakes of snow on the ground. "Nothing that can be mended." All the secrets were covered now, all the dirt hidden. She turned to him. "Thank you, Eirík." She started to reach for him, hesitated. "You are a good man. I like these days and nights with you."

"I like it, too," he said with worry in his voice. He had heard more than a few compliments in his life and most seemed to come with a hidden knife. He tensed.

She blinked twice. "This must be the end."

He stared at her. "If I did anything that hurt you, tell me. Let me apologize."

"You did nothing wrong. You never do—do you?" She raised her head to gaze into his eyes. "It's my fault for getting you into this . . . this trouble." Stepping out of his embrace as though she had now reached the right temperature, she remained beside him at the railing, knowing every babbling brook flows into a deep sea. "I'm full of trouble. I'm one of those damaged people. The kind who needs a counselor. I talk to a counselor here. Fixing my head, *já*. When I was a girl I was bad. I did so much bad. Bad things. Sometimes, I—"

"Íris, I don't care what you did a long time ago." His hand dropped over hers on the railing. She pulled it away. "Whatever you did before we met has nothing to do with us. You aren't my past—like you told me."

"So flattering . . . again. Like a fool."

"I'm serious. Sure, I might be foolish. Nevertheless, I met you at the art show and I fell in love with you. I'm being honest—"

"Stop talking!" She caught herself, about to say more, then took a breath. "Don't say that. There is nothing more for you and me. All we did was fuck. It's not a contract. You don't own me. You don't want me in your life. If I stay, you will be damaged, too."

"But I love you, Íris." He bit his lip. The words had shot out before he could stop them. He stared into her intense blue eyes and she did not look away. "And it's not all about the sex, if that's what you're thinking—which was great!" He didn't know where he was going. "I think we have some things in common, things that we can build on. We like art and going to movies. We aren't vegetarians. We both like to stay in, mostly. We aren't Christians, for one thing. We have to stand together here in Kansas. It's not much, I know, but it's something. Right? I mean, *já*?"

"*Já?* You teasing me?" She stared at him, her face tight. "You are so *heilagur!*"

"What's that?"

"Wholesome, like a married man . . . like a married man should be."

"You're complaining because I'm not some wild and crazy guy?"

"*Nei*, Eirík. Tell me, what is the worst thing you ever did?"

"Me? The worst thing I ever did was marry someone I didn't love."

"Now you act foolish."

The sunrise broke over the rooftops and caught her lips as they pursed.

"How about you?" he asked.

She looked out at the snowfall as the sun mounted the roofs, a clear blue sky spreading over them. She was thinking, he could see; perhaps there was a long list.

"Sorry," he said, offering her an escape. "It doesn't change how I feel about you."

"We don't have much in common, as I see. Unless you want to make yourself over like me. I have a friend who's trying to be me. Her name's Celia, and she changed her hair color to mine, started art classes, tries being a witch like me. All because we went kissing one night. *Já,* she's crazy."

"Oh. I understand," said Eric. He breathed deeply. "So usually you prefer girls."

"No—I'm not a lesbian." She shook her head, thinking. "*Já,* sometimes I like being with girls. Because they are not men. I don't want you to be like me. That is so boring-to-death."

"Okay, I won't. I'll never dye my hair orange. And all I can draw is Snoopy."

"I don't want anything in common. With anyone. I do what I want."

"At least give me a chance to . . . to . . . ."

He gazed into her eyes, looking for the right words.

"Worship me?" She laughed quickly.

He didn't know whether to join her amusement or feel offended by the suggestion. *Who is this girl?* She continued to stay with him. He jokes, he is affectionate, he does his best to make her feel good. He thinks he succeeds. He even angers her—yet she remains. Perhaps, he thought, she really does like me.

"Yes, I'll worship you." Might be fun, he thought.

"Anything you will do for me, *já?*"

"As long as it's not illegal." He watched her thinking. "Or painful."

"Then you must go down there and lay in the snow."

He pointed to the yard below. "Down there?"

"*Já.* Naked, too."

He smiled. "Sure. I'll even make a snow angel for you."

"*Nei,* a snow witch."

She took him by the hand and led him inside. They warmed up with mugs of cocoa and toasted bagels. By eight, they were playing in the snow, and he noticed how she did not seem to feel cold wearing only the sweater and skirt, her bare knees pressed into the snow. Sweeping some snow into the air, he told her how he missed having snow while living in south Texas. Now the snow lay ankle-deep, much higher in drifts, and he scooped enough to make a snowball and tossed it softly at her. Her face surrendered a smile, something of the child within, as they rolled in the snow, spreading out their arms to make the wings of the angels they mocked. They added pointed hats and broomsticks.

They gazed up at the sunny sky, on their backs in the snowy yard.

"I love the snow, I love the cold," Íris sang, breathing hard beside him.

She swung her hand up and dropped some snow on his face. Eric frantically brushed it off as she jumped up and tossed more snow at him before he could climb to his feet. They ran down the yards, across the snow-covered drive and back up the other side, ducking beneath cedar boughs, and back to his front door. She could run quite fast, he saw, especially after pulling off her shoes and going barefoot.

"Are you trying to give me a heart attack?" he asked, panting.

"You would have died last night if you were meant to."

He wasn't sure if it was her accented English or if there was malevolence in her words. Her smile remained firm as they rested against the door, breathing hard, noses and cheeks red, snowflakes spotting her hair. So beautiful. Who was this woman? He kissed her quickly, before she could escape, determined to prove she was real.

"Let's go inside," she said, pushing him, then curling her fingers under his ear. "We must make love. It is good luck for the winter if we make love on the first snowfall."

When Eric chased her down the street and back through the trees, Íris saw a man who looked like her father, Magnús, coming after her. There was a thrill in that, like the fright in a horror film. She recalled times when Magnús chased her out of the house. She ran barefoot through the snow to get away from him. Yet he would catch her and swing her over his shoulder and haul her back to the house. She became used to running in the snow.

Now comes this man who is the same age as Magnús was. She gazes at this Eirík as he kneels and towels off her feet, cold and red from the snow, his hands gentle.

It is not such a rare thing, she has read in the books. The counselors have said so, as well. Sadly, she was not alone. To be sure of it, she searched for a club or chat group online and found several for people like her. Incest survivors. So she joined them. *Sifjaspell*—incest. She dared to say it. That was the easy part.

One group had more than two hundred members. Some of them pushed her to tell about her experiences and after a few weeks she posted her story. Her English was not perfect so there were questions. Because none of them were face to face and they were also victims, she felt comfortable telling the details. She did not want to give out so much detail, yet they encouraged her to tell more and more. Sometimes a group member would post a message, where everyone could read it, saying how exciting her story was.

"*Já*, so flattering. I was not sure of English," she says.

Arms and legs entwined with her lover's beneath the blanket, she feels a lingering spot of wetness on the sheet to remind them of the good luck they will carry through the winter. She waits until he finishes and falls exhausted beside her before she begins her story.

"It frightened me that some of them were child-lovers. They were only there to pop off from reading my experiences."

"There's a lot of sick people out there. But that doesn't matter to me," says this Eirík. He has listened patiently, feeling her angst, tears filling his eyes. "It's not your fault. You were abused. You were the victim."

She glances away, searching for an interesting spot on the wall. She doesn't know why she told him. Perhaps she wants to drive him away. Despite so many years trying to please men, she doesn't know much about getting along with them. Not socially. She could tell him she has a disease, even though she does not. That trick would only make him pity her. Disgust might make him run away, yet pity keeps him close, too close, always ready to catch her when she falls.

"You don't know all of it," she says, sitting up on the bed.

She cannot read his innocent face. After a few heartbeats, she looks away again, afraid he can read her soul in her face.

The sun shines brightly outside yet shadows expand through the alcove, striking the bed. She pulls the corner of the sheet up over herself.

"The thing is . . . . The problem is . . . ."

"Yes . . . ?"

"I—I cannot look at you."

He frowned. Not the answer he expected.

"Why not? Is it something I said?" He sits up and tries to see her face. "Am I too old?"

After a moment's struggle, she gives in and turns to him. His eyes are serious. He is so sincere, she realizes, and he knows nothing about hiding his secrets or his emotions.

"I'm sorry, Íris. I'm sorry for everything that's happened to you. I'm sorry for every man who's hurt you—"

"Stop it!"

Her face goes pale—more pale—and she bites her lip. Slowly shaking her head, she feels the chill returning. If it ever went away. They have been together enough that it should have gone by now. She feels it still with her, and a tear is born in the corner of her eye, falls to its death on the sheet.

"Nothing you said, *já*. You're silly. Not cruel. You are like . . . . *Nei*, I cannot look at you without . . . without seeing my father."

"Your father?"

She sees he is wondering what that could possibly mean, setting up his defenses. He is easy to read.

"When I look at you, I see my father."

She nods twice as she loads her words. She takes hold of his hand, sandwiches it between her hands. Perhaps to keep him from swinging a fist at her? he wonders.

"And my father was the first man to rape me."

The apartment drops thirty degrees before they can take their next breath, the world inside suddenly overtaken by a blizzard. Frost blooms on the walls, icicles hang from the ceiling, and the bed transforms into a sheet of ice. Yet this Eirík has no skates, nothing to keep him from falling. She sees him slipping, crashing against reality, his knees crunching against the ice and the ice cracking, splintering, a bottomless crevasse opening beneath him. She extends a hand to catch him yet he refuses her hand. She hates the terror that bursts upon his face, wishes she could take back her words.

"It's true," she says.

Now he will send her home. He will kick her out like her mother did years ago. Such a dirty girl! He must be afraid, thinks he is corrupted, or given a disease, or made unholy. So now he becomes a target of scandal, ruined for life, the victim of a sorceress. She knows he feels guilty now, too, having done to her what others have done, and he feels shame for it. He is nothing more than the next man to abuse her. The next in line. That is what she sees in his face.

He holds his breath another minute. He fixes his eyes hard on hers, unblinking.

"The first . . . ?"

This Eirík's face is glass yet this time reflects nothing. As she gazes at him, it begins to crack: small lines, then larger ones. She notices a tear sitting on his cheek, refusing to fall. Another one appears before he blinks.

"Já," she says with a rough inhalation—always já on the in-breath, like all Icelanders.

The air is frigid. She feels ice crystals forming inside her heart and that makes her smile. No more hiding beneath the snow. The crystals prick and tickle, reminding her that, against her will, she is still alive, she still exists, somewhere in the world, whether she wants to or not.

"Only my counselor knows."

"A counselor?"

"Now you."

"Me, huh?"

He seems to ponder the implications, rubbing his hands together, clearing them of any evidence.

"And two nights ago?" he asks, suddenly on guard. "I mean, what we did . . . against the wall?" His face is serious. "Was that . . . rape?"

She smiles quickly, like she is paying a bill, and slowly shakes her head.

"*Nei*, that was . . . a handshake."

"I'm sorry," he says. "If I only knew you . . . . I mean, your history, I wouldn't have . . . ."

He looks away, shaking his head as though trying to knock the ice crystals from his mind.

"I am so . . . so . . . sorry," he says. Like an old carnival machine, he repeats his words in hushed voice, afraid to let anyone else hear them. He goes on for several minutes in reverent tone, even after she asks him to stop. She understands he needs to say it. He needs to be sorry for all the men of the world.

"I don't blame you, Eirík."

She can see how he fights with himself, torn between offering a sympathetic hug that protects her from the cruel world or refusing to touch her lest he becomes contaminated. The hug seems to hold in her pain a little longer. Yet the rejection makes the pain drill deeper into her soul where it is more difficult to extract. He wears the same face her counselor wears at their meetings. She can live with that—as she has learned to live with herself—yet it seems others cannot. They cannot decide what to do with her. Perhaps that is the reason she prefers being alone. No one may come too close, nor stay too long.

Until she goes off to take from some unlucky person whatever she needs. And only when she truly needs it. That is the pact she has made with the world so the world will let her go on living. She knows this short period of release is nearly done.

"You need to get help," this unlucky Eirík tells her. She has heard it many times. Help has never helped.

"*Já*, a sad, sad situation," she says, then exhales slowly, as though she believes the bad spirits will depart with the breath. They will not, she knows, because they have a fine, comfortable home in her.

Tired from the emotional ride, she drops on the bed, rolls onto her back.

"It's more than sad," he says, his voice tightly knotted.

"What's been done has been done, and not even the tongue of Thorngren can change anything. These things are what you call fate. You can be sorry for it all you like, yet it is never undone."

He stretches out beside her, arms to his sides. With a thought, he tries to touch her, hand on shoulder, yet she shakes him away. She prefers to gaze at the opposite wall, not wanting to be tested with every glance of his eyes. How long can pity last? When will he take her home? How long must he pretend to want her before he can politely be rid of her? How long must she pretend to be pitiful before she can get on with her life?

"The tongue of Thorngren? What's that, some Viking curse?"

"*Nei*, it's a story I heard when I was a girl in Akureyri," she says in a brighter tone. "It's about a wizard. He wore a purple robe and a pointed hat, waved his hands to make his magic and cast the evil eye on anyone who opposed him. That's what the legend is."

"Sounds like our department chair, Doctor Liz," he interrupts, trying to lighten the mood. He knows it is too heavy for either of them to lift alone. He must try. "She's got this way of looking at a person that—"

"Cast out of his homeland, he found his way to *Ísland*—you say Iceland. He met a girl there, the daughter of the chief."

He runs his fingers through the ends of her hair. "Did she have orange hair?"

"You're listening?"

He sets his hand on her shoulder again and she allows it.

"Yes, tell me a story. A happy story."

"I don't know if it is a happy story." She waits, thinking what to say next, and his hand slides down across her belly. She welcomes his touch; everything will be fine now. He still wants her, for better or worse. She turns to regard him, trying not to see her father there. "The girl, her name was Svana, she fell for this Thorngren yet the villagers feared him. One day, Svana's father caught them making love in the forest. They took Thorngren away. Svana was locked into her house—"

"Sounds like true love to me."

She reverses her position so they face each other.

"Two priests arrived to make the people Christian and they knew Thorngren. They told the chief about him. He went to Baghdad, where he learned black magic from Arab sorcerers. Thorngren went to *Ísland* to escape death in England. Yet he was not evil. He used his powers for good."

"Naturally. The monks didn't like having a magician around."

"*Já*, they turned the village against him. The priest, named Brendan, was an exorcist and offered to remove the evil spell that Thorngren put on Svana. She hadn't spoken since they were caught. The villagers wanted to kill him, so they tied him in the cold waters of the *fjörður* for three days and nights, yet he was fine. They shot arrows at him while he was tied to a stake, yet no arrow struck him. Brendan said Thorngren could not be killed by man or nature. Thorngren must go to some uninhabited land. So they sailed west to find a new land."

"And I'm guessing that's how America was discovered?"

She kisses him quickly on the mouth, just to shut him up. He is surprised.

"Because Thorngren had the evil eye, they dug it out. And he might curse them with words so they cut out his tongue. Because he loved Svana, his genitals were cut off and fed to the chief's dogs. Svana, they tied to a tree high on a cliff above the *fjörður* so she could not see how they tortured him."

He starts to speak, but her fingers push against his lips.

"Brendan sent Harald, his apprentice, off with a crew of the twelve finest sailors. They sailed north to the crystal sea, and followed the ice for days. Everywhere they found land they met bad omens. They came to a quiet bay among green hills, a place Harald took for the end of the earth. He feared dropping off the edge if they sailed on. So there they stopped. They chained Thorngren to a rock on a hillside overlooking the bay. Then they sailed away."

She gazes into his eyes, to emphasize its importance.

"Exiled—yet not forgotten, *já*. Svana watched them sail from the village, up the long *fjörður* out of sight, with Thorngren tied to the mast and his head covered. She heard him speak a spell while they were together. She called from the cliff and Thorngren heard her words." She presses her lips to his ear: "What she called out was the spell of sleep. In nine years time we shall meet, she chants. If not nine, then ninety-nine. If not ninety-nine, then nine hundred ninety-nine. If not then, let the spell be done."

He nods and she moves her fingers away from his lips.

"The story says Thorngren waits for Svana on that far shore."

She notes how focused he is. Something plays in his eyes.

"She could not find him in nine years of sailing about. Not in ninety-nine years, too. She died searching for him. Thorngren remains there until nine hundred ninety-nine years pass. On the night of each winter's solstice, he awakens to scan the horizon for Svana, looking for her until dawn. With first light, Thorngren returns to sleep and takes the form of a standing stone carved with runes."

He stares into her eyes a moment, then kisses her hard.

"Thank you," he says breathlessly. "Thank you for the story."

"Perhaps it is not only a story, *já*."

He wants to know more. He calculates the years, writing numbers against her belly with his finger. She draws a line down his arm with her fingernails, testing him. He does not notice how she hurts him, he is so filled with his story-thinking.

"That would be next year. Wouldn't it?"

"I like that you think it's real," she says as he gets out of bed and goes naked to the computer and begins typing hard. He is passionate—the creative spark has been lit in him. It is clear that he prefers fantasy. She understands. Reality can be so unexpected, so trivial, so disappointing. And it is seldom true.

Sitting up on the bed, she says: "You shouldn't go looking for that standing stone."

She does not tell him that the boat crew, the finest sailors of the village, and Harald, the apprentice priest, never returned home. That is why it is a legend.

5

ERIC CONTEMPLATED THE LINGERING TOUCH OF ÍRIS, her soft hand on his cheek, as he rode up the elevator. He could still feel her warmth against him, taste the scent of her skin, as though it was all a dream. When the doors opened on the fifth floor, Jack was waiting for him. Eric smiled briefly, stepped off. Shuffling the unwieldy stack of student papers in his arms, he dropped two.

"Here you go," said Jack, retrieving them. "Got a minute?"

"What do you want?" said Eric, dryly. This Monday was hell: the cold, slushy weather, a hurried agenda, his students more surly than usual, lots of paperwork, and now Jack.

"Whoa, you sure look like hell," Jack said with laugh. "What happened?"

"Stayed up late writing." Eric opened his office door and dropped the papers on his desk. He rubbed his palms together as if washing his hands. "I have three more piles to collect this week. I'll be grading until next year." He sank into his chair with a groan.

"So that's what's got you bummed out," Jack said, with a glance down the hall. Their colleague, Olivia Jones, was casually approaching. He ducked inside the office, shut the door.

"Things didn't go so well with that Irish chick?" he asked, taking a chair.

Eric glared at him, then stared at the calendar on the wall before his desk: one week of classes, one week of final exams. He could make it.

"Iceland, not Ireland."

"Whatever. I'm sure you did your best. Now it's time to regroup."

"My problem," said Eric with deliberate solemnity, "is that the weekend was much too full. I am thoroughly exhausted—in a very good way." He couldn't keep from grinning. "I had to drop her off at Dickerson before my nine o'clock and rush back here. I was completely unprepared for class." He smiled, remembering how she sprang out of the car with that short, plaid skirt riding up and exposing the back of her milky thigh as other cars on the campus drive waited impatiently behind. No time for a kiss, just her hand on his cheek. He had called after her but she did not hear him and slipped out of sight. "Then again, the way she ran off when I brought her to school, it was like she didn't want anyone to see us."

"Chicks are like that." Jack slapped the corner of the desk. "You buy them food, they treat you rude, and it's thank you, dude. I hate that."

"Yeah . . . ." Eric thought of the green and black striped dress she was wearing when he found her in the rain, how it hugged her body so tightly—how she had stood naked against the wall, dripping wet, her hands clawing his back, her legs wrapped around him, their lips meshed. It had been difficult to concentrate all morning.

"Okay, enough bullshit," said Jack suddenly. "What did you say to Liz? You had no right to say anything to her about my relationship with Megan. What I tell you is confidential. What makes you think you can go telling everybody? And Liz, especially. Are you *trying* to get me in trouble?"

"She asked and I answered," Eric said, his gaze widening. He tried to recall what he might have said back before Thanksgiving break when Dr. Liz pulled him into her office and started flinging questions at him. "I certainly didn't volunteer anything. I only told her what you told me. Just the objective facts, not speculation. Frankly, I told her I didn't believe everything. I thought it would get you off the hook if she recognized that girl's accusation as a co-ed's fantasy."

"Off the hook?" Jack shook his head wildly, then came back with a hard stare. "She's set a hearing date. A committee's going to listen to every sordid detail Megan can think up. I won't get to say a word until everybody else has had their chance to cut me apart."

"She caught me by surprise," said Eric. "I was trying to protect my own job."

"Your job?" Jack jumped to his feet. "*Your job!* What the fuck is that? You've been here not even one semester. One fuckin' semester. What right do you have?"

"I'm sorry, Jack."

"What kind of friend are you?" He shook his head. "I've got fucking tenure. Tenure! That's supposed to mean something."

"So you should be all right."

Jack took a deep breath. "Tenure doesn't mean what it used to. That bitch can say anything and out I go. Tenure! Sure, I can teach any esoteric shit I want to in my classes, rant and rave about my personal political views to my heart's delight, but a few words from a disgruntled slut and I'm history. You'd better be on guard, especially with that Irish chick you took home and *raped*. That's what she could say. She only has to say it. Even if it's not true, you're on your way to flipping burgers. It's her word against yours—"

"She wouldn't do that," said Eric. "We . . . we have a special bond, and some common interests, too."

"Common interests. That's so sweet. She's got her hooks in you already. Anytime she needs something, you'll be snapping to. Money? Sure, here you go, babe. New clothing? Here's my credit card. Anything at all, babe. Just don't say anything to anyone about what we did that night. What you *made* me do. And the first time you cross her, she'll be making up stories of how you seduced her, how you controlled her, forced her into this sexual slavery role playing game. Who are they going to believe? The girl? The victim? Or you, the professor, an older man, divorced—and *obsessed*? Maybe he's got a pocketful of fetishes and perversions he's been hiding. Let's check his house, see if he's got any porn on his computer—"

"All right!" Eric exploded.

Jack leaned against the desk, his index finger raised accusingly.

"You and I have to stick together," he said, calm again. "Megan and this Iris are sisters in the same wacko coven. They're no doubt working together to bring down the whole department, or the whole college. Maybe just us. So we have to work together, too." He stared into Eric's eyes. "Are you with me?"

Eric saw the orange-haired woman in his mind. The beginning was a bit too easy, it seemed in hindsight. She had tried seducing him on Halloween. Then came the rainy night and the sex. His hormones had taken over by then. He had always been the one to expend the effort in relationships. This time was different. Maybe she *was* full of games. She had been evasive with her answers to his questions. What was she hiding? Then she makes up a story about her father.

"I'm with you," said Eric, extending his hand.

Jack shook it, smiling less than usual.

"Okay, buddy. Now we need a plan."

"A plan for what?"

"Before the hearing, we need to do some good ol' fashioned investigation. We need to find dirt on them. Especially Megan. We can point out she's a goddamn witch but we need to dig up more on her."

"Won't saying she's a witch sound a little strange?"

"Right. We need hard facts." Jack frowned. "You see how a simple dalliance can fuck up your whole life? Moreover, you did it with a . . . a foreigner. You exploitive American bastard! You should be ashamed of yourself, taking advantage of a woman—no, a *girl*—like her, a stranger in a strange land."

"I'm sorry," said Eric.

"You oughta be, you sicko."

On the fifth floor, Íris checks the directory. As she scans the list of names, she hears his voice. He comes out of an office with another man, talking. *Eirík* does not see her. She needs him one more time, so she marches up to him, embraces him, and presses her lips to his mouth.

He is completely surprised. He struggles for a second before realizing who it is. Then he breaks free, brushing himself as though Íris was dirt. He is embarrassed, so she laughs.

"Íris," he says, neither happy nor disappointed.

There are four others standing near the elevators.

"I need you," she tells him, ignoring the others. She explains about the art show downtown. She needs him to drive her and her artwork there. Too much to carry on a bus. Other art students have cars but they left already so she missed the chance to catch a ride with them. This Eirík is her last hope. "Can you take me?"

He holds his grin back, glancing at his colleagues.

"I'm free until evening," he says. "Then I have to be back for the workshop."

He takes her hand, casually, trying not to seem secretive, and stands confidently in the circle of his peers. He seems unconcerned that his colleagues saw the kiss. They must wonder who this goddess is. Their stares require an introduction.

"*Halló*," says Íris to the closest man.

"Oh, right. Yes. Sorry," Eirík says. "This is Iris. Uhh, Íris . . . . Umm, Magnúsdóttir."

"Just Íris," she says.

"I'm Jack." The man shakes her hand, a nervous grimace on his face.

"This is Olivia Jones," Eirík says, gesturing at the lanky, blond woman.

"Everett Santiago, hi," says the Latino man.

"Doctor Barnes is our department chair," says Eirík, gesturing toward the stern woman.

"Tina Spencer, nice to meet you," the petite brunette says, shaking hands.

Now Íris has met Eric's colleagues. And they have met her.

"We are lovers," she says, taking his arm so there is no doubt.

He is red-faced and she enjoys that.

Excusing himself, he disappears into his office, returns with his coat on.

The others have departed. Eric and Íris step onto the elevator. As soon as the doors close, instead of throwing themselves into a mad kissing session as she expects, he lectures her about discretion. They have to be careful.

"Careful of what?" she asks. "Is it not normal for lovers to kiss?"

She pushes him against the wall, hooking her leg around his thigh, kissing him—until the bell rings at the ground floor.

They walk hand in hand to his car, passing one of his students, her peers, another one of his colleagues. He points out a few of his students, and they change directions to avoid them. Once inside his car, they resume kissing—until Íris says they need to hurry.

"My work needs a good spot," she explains, "where the lighting is good, with traffic flow. Fantasies are so fragile, já."

He helps her carry four paintings from her studio in Dickerson Hall out to his car, parked in a loading zone along the curb. He almost slips on the slushy sidewalk but catches himself. She rests her hand on his leg as they drive downtown. He knows the way. He helps carry the artwork inside and waits patiently as she sets them up.

Professor Ray Ferguson is there, trying to reserve space for Fairmont College against students from St. Mary's and the community colleges.

"All works are for sale, too," she says, "because we are so starving."

She wonders if he will take the hint, ask her about the painting he promised to buy.

"Do you want me to wait for you?" asks Eric. He checks his watch. "Or, I can come back later." He watches her working. "When will you be finished?"

She is too busy to answer at first. Yet this Eirík is patient, she sees. He is worried that she will forget him if he leaves without saying goodbye. He wants to be a gentleman. How many gentlemen are there in the world? One less will not matter.

"I need to stay a while longer." Her outfit is not good for hanging paintings. When she stretches up, she feels a chill between her legs. She knows he is watching when she gives the hem a tug. "I will catch a ride home with someone."

"I can come back to give you a ride," he says.

Climbing down, she draws a finger along his cheek. "Please don't worry about me."

Yet he does worry. He is not happy, she sees. He takes a notepad from his coat pocket and writes down his number, tears off the page for her.

"Will you call me when you get home?" he asks. "I want to know you're safe."

"You know I don't have a phone."

"You could e-mail me," he says, and quickly writes his e-mail address.

Íris stands before him, eye to eye. He leans forward and she leans back, then again, and again, until she allows the kiss. Apparently satisfied, he smiles warmly, then turns and walks away.

She is wrong about him. He will not go away. She must drive him off, to keep him good. He wants to know I am safe, she laughs, yet he must know I am never safe. She liked teasing him in front of his colleagues. Now he is embarrassing her in front of hers.

Late afternoon on Monday: the weekend has come to its conclusion.

"How about this one?" asks Ray, bringing one of her photographic manipulations. He brought it from his office, where it has been since Íris turned it in for a grade last spring. He gave her an A—"A for arousing," he joked. He said he wanted to hang onto it for a while. "You should include it."

She examines it: a nude woman stands behind the juncture of a wooden cross, embracing it like a favorite phallus. The cross hides her private areas so it is safe for children. The overexposure and negative inversion creates a bright reddish halo around her, as though Satanic forces are at work, so she calls it *Our Daughter Who Art in Hell*. It makes a statement.

"If you think so," she tells Ray. "I just did it for fun."

More than an hour later she has hung up her paintings, including two new works. *The Goddess Inanna* is a golden representation of an angelic entity embracing the rays of the sun. *The Garden of Mefestio* is a portrait of Earth's earliest years, full of spouting volcanoes and flowing lava. Lightning abounds, rocks explode. Goddess is having fun.

"Ready to go?" Ray Ferguson asks Íris, coming up behind her and resting his hands on her shoulders the way Professor Hirsch used to do. After all, Ray was Professor Hirsch's student long ago. When she turns, he is surveying her from head to toe, appreciating how the sweater hugs her torso, how the skirt dances around her legs.

"One minute more," she tells him, tacking up her nameplate on the wall next to *Angel of Death*. She studies it for six heartbeats: *I am her, the Angel of Death*. She thinks of her father, that Eirík, Professor Hirsch, and the other men she has known. She laughs and Ray doesn't know why. He is not even afraid.

In the car, he tells her that his wife and kids are out of town.

6

ERIC RUSHED HOME FROM THE WEEKLY WRITERS' WORKSHOP and booted up his computer before setting down his school bag, expecting to see an e-mail from Íris waiting for him. Instead, his inbox was empty. He stared at the screen. He checked the time, hit Refresh, but still no messages.

If the art show went late, she might not be home yet, he calculated as he prepared himself for sleep. She would be tired. Or her computer was off.

Reclining on the bed, Eric reached out and brushed the sheet where she had been, remembering how good it felt having her next to him. He sniffed her side of the bed, found something of her still there. He breathed it in. Then he grabbed the book under the bed and opened it to the dog-eared page. He realized after six pages that he had been thinking of Íris. He set the book on the floor, rolled onto his back and stared at the ceiling. It felt strange to be alone in the bed.

He regarded the pillow they had shared, head to head. He touched it like a sacred artifact, noticing a single orange hair extending from under it. Gently retrieving the hair, he held it up to the light, then got up to find a place to preserve it. He slipped it between the pages of a book on Iceland on his desk.

After checking his computer once more and finding no new messages, Eric decided to leave it on all night, in case she might stay up late to catch up on e-mails.

The glow from the screen kept him awake, however, so eventually he rose again to set a screensaver playing—a field of stars.

Later in the night, he got up, sat at his computer, and typed more on his new story. He tried to recall their last conversation, not the part about incest, not about rape. No, the one she told about the legend of Thorngren and Svana. After a while, questions made him pause. He clicked on the link to the bookstore and ran searches that revealed dozens of entries. He began checking them. Half-way through the list, he had already clicked seven books into his shopping cart and, realizing the time, he logged out.

He tried to sleep again, convincing himself that it was good to have a night off, a night to recuperate. He reflected happily on the weekend. It was a good backache.

After an hour hovering on the edge of sleep, he got up, splashed cold water on his face. He went to the balcony to reminisce, remembering how they had stood together, regarding the snow.

Soon he read a few more pages of his book, then tried again to fall asleep.

Feeling hungry, he prepared a bowl of leftover chili, and turned on the TV, searched the channels for anything of interest, found nothing but infomercials and sit-com reruns. More than an hour passed before he was ready to give up. With a sigh, he turned off the TV, washed the bowl in the kitchen, and returned to the bed. From the bed, he stared at the dent they had made in the wall until he noticed the graying of the dawn sky and turned off the light.

Between posing in Life Study and her own class, Íris stops in the atrium to check her paintings. All of her colleagues' art has been removed.

Some of it was sold, she heard. Sandra Kinney's paintings of Jesus were grabbed. Her portrait of Mary grieving for her notorious son remains. Nobody wants to look at that tortured face. The fat nudes by Felice are gone. Nudity always sells. Steve's giant alphabet blocks were sold to the day-care center where his wife works. Yet who could possibly have bought Keith's papier-mâché Komodo dragons? What did Roger do with his moaning construction site installation?

Nothing explains her failure. Her four paintings remain on the wall. She realizes she should have taken them to the downtown show. Her painting, *Homeland*, a gently abstract whirl of wintry colors that have no special meaning, is slightly askew but with a touch of her finger, she straightens it. Her landscape, *Glacier*, has begun to melt in the sunlight burning through the south windows. And *Arcadia II*, the painting of underwater ruins and twelve bubbles, is as blue as ever. Then there is the Pre-Raphaelite lady in *Roses* who continues to dream. Íris stares at the four paintings as students pass by between class periods. Nothing about her work draws people's attention. No religious devotion, no childish cuteness, no obese nudity, no nostalgia, no colorful reptiles. All she can offer is fantasy.

When the atrium is clear, she takes down *Roses* and wraps it in the black cloth she brought. Nobody needs to know what happened to it. Let them believe someone bought it. She doesn't want to sell it anyway, she tells herself—too many memories about its origin still haunt her. She will keep it for some day when it rains. Then she will take it out, hang it up, stare at it and wonder *What was I thinking?*

Leaving the atrium, she meets Ray Ferguson on the way down to her studio. He is happy to see her, and tells her his wife saw her at Sophie's Choice, the boutique where Íris works during the holidays. With her scholarship and student visa, she is not allowed to have an off-campus job. Supervising the Open Studio in the evenings is her job. Ray does not care, so she confirms that she is again working there.

She gestures to the slinky blue dress she wears. "I got it fifty-percent discount."

"Looks great on you, Iris," says Ray. "Really goes with your hair."

After a stop in the restroom, Íris heads to her Art History class.

Her final paper is due today, though it is not very good. In 25 pages, she analyzes a painter's body of work. She chose John William Waterhouse, the Pre-Raphaelite painter who specialized in the outcast or marginal women of history. What she noticed while examining his paintings was the number of them that feature women with red hair. There is the famous Lady of Shalott (after the Tennyson poem), and Isolde of Wagner's *Tristan und Isolde*, and Ophelia of Shakespeare's *Hamlet*, and Miranda of *The Tempest*, and the witches Circe and Ariadne, as well as two identified simply as "Sorceress" and "The Mermaid." All are infamous tempters of men, like the trickster lady of *La Belle Dame Sans Merci*.

Other pre-Raphaelites portrayed their women subjects with red hair—Lilith, who tempted Adam; Mary Magdalene, who tempted Jesus; Joan of Arc, who tempted the English; Pandora, the box-opener; Dante's lover, Beatrice; Sybilla the prophetess; the Lady of the Lake in Arthurian legend; both the adulteress Guinevere and her opposite, the incestuous Morgan Le Fey; and many sirens, witches, goddesses, nymphs, fairies, and evil princesses—all red-haired. She sees a pattern. Fuseli paints Lady Macbeth with red hair. Sir Edward Coley Burne-Jones, in *The Rose Bower*, depicts Aurora, the Sleeping Beauty, with red hair. Rossetti painted a red-haired Proserpine and Norman Lindsay painted a red-haired Leda. Maxfield Parrish has a red-haired Cinderella. Jon Collier chooses to give his *Lady Godiva* red hair. Collier's 1887 painting *Lilith* is a mirror image of Íris, except her breasts are larger and she does not wear a snake.

Holding the paper in her hand, turned to the last page, she regards the conclusion. Red-haired Icelanders carry the blood of the slaves brought from Ireland and Scotland. Her mother told her about Oláfur, one of their earliest ancestors, who ran away from the farmstead where he tended sheep and, after several weeks of hiding, came to a church. The priest took him in, told him about the Christian god, and in time, he became a priest. He married a virgin of the congregation; they had four sons and three of them became priests. The fourth was a sailor and was lost somewhere far away. They all had red hair but they were no longer slaves. In school, Íris was teased because of her hair—always the slave girl. Magnús and Heiðr both had red hair, although of different shades. Therefore, Íris is nothing more than the unwanted daughter of a frosty pair of aberrant country folk who descended from slaves.

Feeling depressed, she slides the paper under Professor Norton's door and skips the class.

"I think we parted awkwardly," Eric told Jack as they rode up in the elevator. "Maybe I should send some flowers."

"Are you crazy?" Jack knew what he was talking about. "Why don't you simply shout *loser, loser, loser* from the top of Linden Hall?" He cupped his hands around his mouth to simulate an echo. "Don't forget who the enemy is."

"I have to do something."

"Why?"

They stepped from the elevator.

"You're doing it all backwards," said Jack. "First sex, then dinner, the movie, and now flowers? You're one mixed-up sonovabitch."

Throughout his classes, Eric allowed half his mind to stay on Íris. He gathered the stacks of student papers and during his office hours started grading them. By late afternoon, he was too entrenched in the grading routine to think of anything else.

The evening was a continuation of the grading, punctuated at eight o'clock by the noisy return of his downstairs neighbor and her hip-hop music. An hour later, she shut it off, slammed her door, and left for the clubs. He checked for e-mails at the top of each hour.

Wednesday was the same, except the snow had begun to melt, leaving dirty slush everywhere. It ruined his best pair of shoes.

After his Thursday night class, Eric drove slowly along the campus drive toward the art building. The evening was quiet, and only the glaring street lamps broke the calm. He rolled by the spot where he had picked her up that rainy night. It felt like a month ago. Heart beating quickly, he turned his car off-campus and made his way through the residential streets toward the house where Íris lived. He wasn't sure of the directions, especially in the dark. He circled a few blocks before he happened onto the one he recognized. No lights were on in the windows he thought were hers. He waited for almost an hour, engine and lights off, expecting her to come home—fearing she would arrive, see him, and be angry.

Then he drove home, so reluctantly that a police car came up behind him and followed him for five blocks.

There were no messages in his inbox.

The weekend was equally empty and he could accept that it was over; possibly it was because of something he had said or done. Or fate—like Thorngren and Svana. They simply were not meant to be together. That was fate. She had made that clear enough. Looking at him reminded her of her father, she had said. He stared into the mirror, studying his face.

He drifted through final exams the next week and did what he could to follow Olivia Jones's carefully organized grading protocol. In his office, he added up scores, and then walked across the campus to turn in the grade sheet at the Registrar office. Because he was close, he made himself go to the knoll behind Everett Hall and gaze down upon the Art building for ten minutes, almost expecting to see a flash of orange behind the large windows there. The wind blew hard and cold against him, the clouds darkening, so he returned to Linden Hall.

He packed up a few things to take home for the winter break.

Olivia stuck her head into his office. "Are you finished already?"

Eric looked up with a sigh. "I think so."

After a day of sleeping off the semester, Eric decided to drive over to the house of Íris again. The House of Iris, he thought, good name for a bordello. He felt that he was a special client and thus had the right to barge in. The house was almost deserted, its residents likely gone for the break, though music was playing somewhere. He stood before her door and knocked with restraint. He tested the door, found it locked this time. No sounds came from her room but across the hallway was music. Eric turned to that door and knocked. After a moment, the door opened a crack and a young man looked out.

"Can I help you?" asked the blond-haired young man, wearing only a purple thong.

"I was wondering if you might know where Íris is."

"And you are . . . ?"

"Eric." He watched the young man thinking. "She and I, we—"

"Man, I never know where she's going." He chuckled. "She needs to pose for me or I'll never get the sculpture done." Someone inside his room called and he turned to shout back, "I'll be right there."

"Where would she be at this moment?" Eric asked, checking his watch.

"Oh, she's . . . probably working now. If she's at the mall, she might be home . . . well, not before ten, anyway. You know her, she's always—"

"Thanks," said Eric, and hurried away.

She worked at the mall, he remembered, so he went there next, but after entering and seeing the gaudy storefronts, hearing the canned music and the echoing chatter of teenagers out of school, he paused. Jack was right. Eric would only be demonstrating how obsessed he was by showing up at her place of work.

And yet, she had shown up at *his* place of work. His colleagues probably talked about the incident for days. Or, worse, they wouldn't mention it at all. So he felt justified in . . . what? Stalking her? No, he was not a stalker; he was in love. There was a difference. However, would she see it that way?

He paced the mall, found a directory and noted a picture frame shop. It was at the far end, past the department stores, past the food court, the arcade, the merry-go-round, and the boutiques. He would think of something to say by the time he arrived. His heart beat faster as he moved closer, and he was ready to turn back when he saw a woman with orange hair walking ahead of him—and again when a different redhead crossed his path. Neither of them were Íris.

"So this is where you work, huh?" he muttered, trying out his line as he walked. "Iris, is that you? This is where you work?" No, too obvious. He needed to be more assertive. "Íris, I thought we were going to spend the weekend together again." That wouldn't do, either. *Fuck off*, she would say. "Why haven't you at least e-mailed me?"

There it was: FRAMED!—the picture frame shop. Wooden ones, metal ones. Plastic ones, too. They also sold pictures to put in the frames. From outside, he searched the faces through the windows but found no one who resembled Íris. He let out a sigh of relief instead of being angry. His heartbeat returned to normal.

Because I'm done with you, came the answer, cloaked in Íris' mezzo.

He told himself to give up. That weekend was all there was. Like Jack had said.

As he turned to go, he bumped into a stylishly dressed young woman heading for the boutique next door. He apologized as she sneered at him.

"What happened, Erin?" her friend in the boutique's doorway asked as she entered.

"That creep ran into me," he heard the young woman say.

Was he a creep? That's how he must have appeared, but he knew he wasn't. He could rationalize his actions as research for his writing. He could go home and write about it, let his imagination run free, but that was hardly compensation. He only wanted to see her—not even speak to her, if that was how it had to be. He needed to have another look. One last look. He needed to confirm that she really existed, that she actually had stayed with him that weekend. That she wasn't a dream.

She must be off on her own winter break trip, he thought as he stopped at the mall's bookstore. Perhaps she'd gone back to Toronto. That was her home, wasn't it? She had no chance to tell him her plans because their schedules were so busy at the end of the semester. He laughed at himself for becoming so upset, acting like some pathetic high school kid with a crush. Simple misunderstanding. They had missed each other—in the same way they had met each other—at random, a whim of fate. Now Íris was out of town. It would do them both good to have some time apart; that would make the reunion all the more . . . what? *Passionate*. The word had a nice ring to it.

He laughed, relieved. After winter break, they would pick up where they had left off. Maybe not passionately, but certainly . . . what?

Affectionately? As long as the days remained cold. He had almost three weeks to prepare. To help, he bought the *Dating for Dummies* book. Dinner and a movie was passé.

On the way home, he decided to call Dominique. It was time to make the break official. It was the polite thing to do. He didn't want to hurt her but they had been growing apart even before he met *the witch?* The orange-haired woman was so different. If Jack was right, she would never again be with him. No, he couldn't give up on Dominique just for the slimmest chance to be with the Icelandic witch. Probably for no more than another weekend, if even that. Instead of breaking up with Dominique, he would invite her down to Texas over winter break. They could renew their relationship.

He sat in the lounger and read the first chapter of the dating guide, then put off calling Dominique until after ten. Too late to call.

The next day he felt ready and dialed her number, then became afraid of her picking up the phone. The soft, unsuspecting voice that answered was unnerving.

He fumbled through the small talk.

"Do you want to come to Texas with me for Christmas?" he asked suddenly. He wanted to take it back. He began explaining the virtues of Corpus Christi, feeling excited.

"Oh, I have a Christmas concert to play," she said. "Can you wait a week?"

"I'd like to," he said. "But I need to get out of town right away. It's been a really, really long semester."

"I've been busy, too," she said. "We lost track of each other, didn't we?" She sighed. When the moment of silence became noticeable, she continued: "Eric . . . ? I miss you."

He did not know what to say.

Dominique broke the silence: "Eric . . . ?"

"I'm sorry, Dominique, but I haven't—" and he stopped. Was he breaking up with her after all? He was about to tell her he had found someone else. He paused. It might not be true.

"Haven't what?" she asked.

"I haven't been . . . nice to you lately."

He held his breath, listening, heard only his heart thumping.

"I suppose I'll forgive you," she said at last.

They made plans for January but it was simply a formality.

Once again, he checked his e-mail: only confirmation of his book order.

As the night drew deeper, he thought about Íris and Dominique. Comparing them was like comparing apples and oranges. Dominique was an apple, wholesome and mild, keeps you regular. Íris was the orange, with a tough exterior, randomly scattered seeds, but with a tanginess that was so refreshing. If only he could combine them, make some new kind of hybrid fruit he would call *orple*. The thought made him smile as he sat back, propping his feet on the corner of the desk. He reached for some paper and wrote a poem.

Looking up, he noticed his haggard face in the monitor's screen.

"Am I being ridiculous or what?" he asked his reflection.

In the morning, he stared out the balcony door at the snow flurries, memories firing in the corners of his mind.

When he turned to the kitchen, ready to make breakfast, the perfect angle of sunlight showed him a set of dainty footprints that had been left on the title floor. He dropped to his knees to exam them. The toe dots were prominent, along with the narrow edge of each foot and the faint heels. She had stood there helping to prepare the chili, barefoot, her feet a bit dirty, enough to leave a trace of her there to torment him. He sat back, contemplating whether to scrub it clean, erase her from his memory.

He could not stay alone in the apartment for three weeks, nor did he want to spend Christmas up in Kansas City surrounded by his brother's three children tearing open their presents. Surrounded by his parents' retired neighbors, Eric would be safe. He packed clothes and stuffed his latest writing into his school bag, put them in his car and headed south, where his parents would have plenty of questions for him to ignore.

7

"HAPPY BIRTHDAY, IRIS," SAYS CELIA, tossing her candy red hair over her shoulder. She lays her meaty hands on the bare back and kneads the shoulder blades with her knuckles, then goes for the spine, eliciting moans of stress release and groans of near-pain. "Does it hurt?" she asks.

"Not as much as not doing it at all," says Íris.

Celia's rough efforts are pummeling the toxins out.

Já, it is 30 December once again, happy to be starting a new year. Íris is glad that Celia's parents have gone to the Caribbean for the holidays, leaving Celia alone in the house with a queen-sized bed and a hot tub. Íris cannot stay in her small, damp room, alone in that big house. Everyone there has left for the winter break.

"So how does it feel to be twenty-seven?" asks Celia as she gently turns Íris onto her back and lays a soft, moist washcloth over her face. Celia massages her legs, beginning with her toes and works her way up. Íris relaxes, slips into a quiet numbness.

"I don't feel twenty-seven," says Íris. "I feel like seventeen. Or twelve. *Já*, I want to be nine or ten again."

What matters most, Íris thinks, is starting the new year in the best way possible—with good friends, kindred spirits, and heart-warming rituals.

When Íris did not show up for the Samhain sabbat after her art exhibit, Megan summoned her for punishment. A few cracks of a whip on her back convinced Íris she did not need to be in the circle. It was worse than her initiation ritual. And what they did then wasn't required for Wicca, according to that older woman named Yvonne who was visiting. Íris had endured that abuse. But this time, when Celia defended her, Megan kicked her out, too.

So she and Celia have started their own coven. For *Jól* last week, they went to the nature reserve, to the deepest part of the wood, and in a small clearing dusted by the previous night's snow, they celebrated.

Celia threw her arms around Íris, kissing her face.

"Thank you for letting me join your circle."

Íris smiled at her, ready to light the fire. "Who else could be my first sister?"

It burned low at first, a small bonfire of oak, mistletoe, and holly. The day was overcast, blustery, yet they kept the fire going until the winds died and the fire burned bright. They danced skyclad around it, chanting welcoming words for the new year. As their dancing came to an end, the sky became full of snowflakes, falling over them like glitter. They embraced and wrapped themselves in a blanket, drank their wine and ate their cakes.

Jól is the death of the year, yet also the birth of a new year. They burned some old things they had brought—a letter from Íris's mother, Heiðr, saying she was going to London to take a new research position. All her life she studied fish and thought of ways to make her daughter miserable. Her divorce from Sæmundr, the Canadian man she met and married after Magnús died, was final, but she was leaving the young twins with him. She had shut the door on Íris years before when she turned eighteen and they had not spoken since.

For Celia, a crumpled photo of Megan, who was her one-time lover—before Íris. Celia is such a fickle girl, she thinks.

"That was so good," Íris tells her.

Celia stretches out beside her, drapes one meaty leg on Íris's hip, a thick arm falling across her white belly.

"I love you, Iris," she mutters, half-afraid to say the words.

All Íris can do is smile. After the orgasm, she doesn't care who made it happen. She only wants to lie still for a while.

In this season of good will to women, however, Íris seems to be collecting enemies.

She thought of Erin from the boutique at the mall. "Some people can't stand that witches exist at all, so we are persecuted," said Íris.

"It's not that," said Erin. "It's all that shit about your father. That's too much. I don't know if you are, like, making it up, but it really freaks me out. Now you go on saying you are, like, this big-time voodoo witch person. I don't need that shit in my life."

"I didn't intend to upset you."

"You did." Erin wiped a tear from her eye. "My father—he . . . ."

Seeing her reaction, Íris put her arm around her.

"He abused my little sister," said Erin in a low voice. "I forgot all about that until you bring up that shit again."

"Did he ever hurt you?" Íris asked.

"No. I was older." Erin stared off at the Christian gift shop's neon sign. "Too old for him, I guess."

Erin rejected her shoulder.

"For me, it was punishment. That's what he said. When I was bad, late from school, not doing my tasks, make a poor dinner—he made me do things. If he didn't like what I cooked, he made me . . . ." She shook a little, wanted to hold Erin. "He called it punishment, a lesson."

Erin stared at her.

"Yet I started to like it. It was . . . what's the word? When you feel better after it . . . ? Absolution? *Já*, I liked how I felt after punishment. That is what I wanted, so I did it, just for the punishment. The peace that follows the punishment. When I was sixteen, I was in control. If I wanted something, I promised him sex—"

"Don't talk about that." Erin spun away, her hands over her ears.

Íris feels Celia caressing her breasts, circling her fingertips around her nipples, and she forgets what happened at the mall.

"*Shhh*, you don't have to say a word," says Celia, rising up to kiss her. "Lemme make you feel good. It's your birthday. You deserve to be worshipped like a goddess."

She wants to laugh—or cry.

"Don't say that. I'm not a goddess. I don't deserve to be worshipped."

A goddess would be able to create her world new and fresh each day. For Íris, there is no past, no future, only here and now. Celia foolishly believes in a future. My past is like a heavy blanket of snow, thinks Íris. Like layers and layers of snow, packing down into ice, hard and sterile. That leaves the present—and since it is her birthday, she has received a rough massage, some amateurish oral sex, and a chocolate cake with red roses on white icing.

She thinks of *Roses*, her painting, wondering what its fate will be. And whether she will follow the same fate. That woman will always be asleep, will always cut her cheek on the thorns, will always bleed.

"I am Íris. The *iris*," she mumbles, "the Greek word for rainbow. A bridge of seven colors connecting Heaven and Earth. A link between sacred and profane."

"What're you talking about?" asks Celia.

Magnús and Heiðr have put her here, Íris knows. They taught her to first give herself to others, that she is for others to use. She is supposed to hold back her own desires. She owes Cory posing time. She must sell more paintings to make Ray happy. In the picture frame shop, she gives advice. At the boutique, she praises customers' fashion sense even if they have none. At the club in Toronto she gave and gave—

Íris smiles weakly, fighting the memories. 'You're a good lass, how you make your *pabbi* feel warm,' says Magnús in her head. She feels a chill spreading over her.

"He would pat my head, and I believed I did something good. When he popped off, I knew I was . . . *vá*, proficient—I did something correct. I earned a few minutes of calm. Otherwise, to him I was a stupid girl. Or a whore. He never called me that name unless he was angry. He would call '*Komdu hérna littla hóran þín*' and it was time for my punishment. And I would sit or kneel or lay over the bed, whatever he wanted, and accept what I deserved."

Celia holds her tightly.

"*Æfingin skapar meistarann*, he always said. 'Practice makes you better.' After some time, he learned how I tricked him so he made his requests more difficult."

"That's awful," says Celia, and Íris realizes she has been speaking.

"I didn't plan to tell you," she says, trying to make the confession vanish. "Sometimes I mumble out things."

"Is it true?"

"I never lie," says Íris, knowing it is always a lie. Her eyes are wet. She rises on her elbows, regards Celia. "Except when I say everything is better than it really is. Like for customers." The picture frame shop is what she intends, but it could be Club Venus in Toronto, where she found work after her mother kicked her out. "I tell a man he is good, that I like his cock, that he turns me on, just to get on with it. The rest is acting."

Celia claps her arms around Íris's chest. "You are so strong."

"Don't say that. I am not strong, not like you think."

"Yes, you are." Celia grins at her, but it is not a pleasant expression. "Iris, I want you to know . . . I'm still a virgin. With men. I've never done anything with a man."

Celia is so innocent, thinks Íris. She wants to run away before her touch can poison the girl. Instead, she offers Celia a genuine smile, and pats her shoulder.

"What was your first time like?" Celia asks.

So Íris tells her the story of the day Magnús came home drunk from the pub, desperately looking for money in her room, and caught her with a boy from school. He threw the boy out and, enraged by what he saw, vowed to teach her about sex, if that was what she wanted. When he was done, he walked out.

In the evening, he staggered home again from the pub. At bedtime, he put himself away and ignored her. She bathed, mended herself, and curled up in her bed. She did not sleep. There was no lock on the door, and her mother was away at the research facility on Vestmannaeyjar, an island off the southern coast.

She did not go to school the next day; her father did not notice.

On the second morning, Magnús trudged into the kitchen as she warmed the leftover *hangikjöt* and *rauðkál* for breakfast. She really wanted Prince-Polo, the chocolate waffles her mother always bought, but the smoked lamb and sweet red cabbage was all there was to eat. She thought he must be hungry, so she served it into two bowls and set one on each side of the table.

He stood in the doorway, rubbing his head, unbathed and unshaven, still wearing clothes from two days before. He smelled awful, yet his eyes were alive again. He did not smile but stared across the table.

"I did a foul deed," he muttered after some time had passed.

Íris did not answer. She kept her eyes on the food.

"You know it to be wrong, as do I," he said. "The drink made me crazy. And a crazy man'll do anything. Even foul deeds. Óðinn'll punish me for what I've done, in His good time. Until then, we best keep silent. They'll take you far away if we talk about it. Your mother'd surely be hurt. If we keep silent, everything'll return to good. I'm gonna put aside the drink—no more *brennivín*—as Óðinn is my witness."

For several minutes, she watched his face twist back and forth, until his eyes squeezed out tears. She had never seen him weep before. No matter what had happened, he was her father. She did exactly what she had done years before when Heiðr wanted her to be baptized. She answered the way she was supposed to. She told him she forgave him, yet she did not.

Íris gets up from the bed and feels Celia's teary eyes on her as she walks out.

The Jacuzzi is hot now. The fence is high enough but Íris doesn't care about being nude. Celia is shy. She follows, wrapping herself in a towel that doesn't come together across her bum. Celia enters the hot water, then waits as Íris stretches her arms and legs, as though offering an incantation to the sky.

"You're acting weird again, Iris," she chuckles. "I can't believe you're not freezing your ass off. It's gotta be below freezing out here!"

"I like the chill." Íris gazes around the large yard. The terraces are withered, the gazebo is empty, the flower gardens are fallow, the shrubbery defoliated. "Everything is dead. You see? It's beautiful. This is the moment of rebirth. A perfect existential moment."

"A what?"

"A moment frozen in time," says Íris. She shares a grin with Celia. "At some point in life a dream becomes reality. Or it doesn't. A turning point. Like us, *já*. We go to school for years, prepare for something we want to do. The dream becomes reality. Or the dream ends and reality takes over." She breathes deeply the frigid air. "After that, we live our dreams or give in to reality—and get any job to survive. Then we are trapped. Second chances are rare after twenty-five or -six."

"That's so sad," says Celia. "I don't want to think about it."

"That is all there is to think about."

"Why are you acting so weird, Iris? You getting your period?"

Íris has one foot in the hot, steamy water. The sky is a thin Phthalo blue, the yard Viridian green as the Jacuzzi water goes cold. All she sees is white—everywhere. Snow covers her and she shivers. She returns to a small ice-choked stream trickling behind a hill in northern Iceland. It is not yet springtime, and the snow is spotted with blood.

As Íris looks down at herself, someone calls. She knows *Jól* has passed, that the time of rebirth has come.

Já, rebirth, she thinks and breathes deeply.

Then she announces to no one in particular although Celia is with her, as is Goddess somewhere in the clouds above or the earth below: "It's late again."

Whenever Eric paused to think, he could hear his mother bustling about the condo, preparing New Year's dinner. The intoxicating scents of roast ham and candied yams was too distracting as he pounded the keys of his mother's computer. He had to write while his blood was hot, while the muse favored him, deep into his version of the Thorngren and Svana story.

The keys clicked like hard rain and he dared not stop to take a breath. Eric was the wizard, and Svana was the orange-haired woman named Íris. The rest was pure fiction. His stomach rumbled like the ominous thunder over that fjord, yet on he typed. The girl, Svana, cried out from the hilltop tree where she had been bound. The strongest men of the village lashed the wizard to the mast of their longboat at the command of Brendan, the Christian priest. Brendan cried his directives over the roar of a storm—

Eric stopped, fingers hovering over the keys, electricity sizzling through them. He realized that there had been knocking on the door.

"He's been in there typing for a good part of the day and night," he heard his mother say. "He was up past three last night."

"Let the boy be," his father exhorted, resignation in his voice. "He'll be out when he's finished writing his stories."

Meanwhile, the longboat set sail, was reaching the arctic wastes—the ice sheet, the glaring whiteness—the icy wind—the warriors numb with cold, sick with fear . . . .

Eric had tried to focus on a northern, iceberg-laden seas, despite the sunny, tropical day outside. He lowered the shades, set his fingers once more, willing himself back to the latitude where a single longboat cut the waves, six pairs of oars stroking the sea, bringing them to shores never before seen by man. There they could deposit their sinister cargo and be quickly away.

Eric sat back, pondering his story. When he finally cracked the door, the condo was dark and silent. His parents had gone to bed, the New Year's dinner had been put away, and even the fireworks had subsided. In the refrigerator, he found a ham sandwich with a note from his mother taped to the cellophane: *Happy New Year!* He stared at the note as he ate the sandwich.

He pulled out an armful of ingredients and built another sandwich as the Millennium turned over quietly.

The morning after his return to Wichita, Eric went to the campus with the box of books and papers he had taken on his trip south. Jack's door was open so he looked in. No one was there but the room was a mess, papers in stacks on the desk and books in boxes. He was puzzled. He turned to go—

"Shit, Jack—scared the crap out of me!"

His colleague had a tortured look in his eyes, was dressed in ragged jeans and a dirty sweatshirt. He had let his beard grow out over the break.

"What happened to you?" asked Eric.

"I'm sitting out this semester," said Jack in a tightly controlled voice that set Eric on edge. "Thanks to Megan. I've been suspended. Pending the hearing."

"Wow, Jack. I'm sorry." He didn't know what to say, considering whether or not what he'd already said might have contributed to Dr. Liz's decision. "The whole semester? How can they do that? Don't you have any recourse?"

"I will be allowed to speak at the hearing. After everybody else has spoken." He glared at Eric. "At least I'll have something to use against her. Three days ago someone cut a big star on my car. I don't have any proof it was her, but I sure got gut-instinct out my ass. The police are investigating."

"A star?

"One of those penta-things."

"A pentagram? Or do you mean a pentacle?"

"Just the star. You know what that is, right? A witch symbol."

"Was the point up or down?"

"What the hell do I care? It was cut with a crowbar."

"Down is for Satanists, up is for regular Pagans." Eric felt like an expert after his vacation reading. "Megan is a witch, according to you. It's not the same as Satanism. Pagans want to live at peace with nature. Satanists have a grudge against Christians. And witches work magic to maintain the balance of the elements for the good of everyone—"

"What're you, some kind of apologist?"

"Satanic cults are just teenagers playing pranks. That's what I've read." Eric shook his head at Jack's disapproving scowl. Unperturbed, Eric continued to his office and Jack followed. "I've been reading. That's all." He tried to stare down his disheveled colleague. "When you love someone, you want to learn about her world."

"So now you're in love." Jack grunted. "The Irish chick? Megan's witch sister?"

"It's Iceland. From my reading, your friend doesn't sound like a real witch. She's just—"

"Real, fake, fantasizing, delusional, doesn't matter. She's dangerous."

"Well, what can you do?" Eric asked, tossing his hands into the air. He forced a smile to relieve the tension. "Classes begin the day after tomorrow. I need to throw together a syllabus." He stared at Jack, then became sympathetic. "When's the hearing?"

"A few weeks. They'll let me know. That's about par." Jack gestured for Eric to come to his office. "You can help carry some boxes down to my car. If your politics will let you lend a hand."

"Sure. I'll help you"—Eric grabbed the first two—"anyway I can."

"Yeah? Then you can supervise the Writing Lab this semester."

"That sounds like fun."

"Watch those evening tutors. Last semester, the computers had porn sites marked. Can't have boobs popping up in the Writing Lab."

"Indeed."

They went to the elevator.

"Looks like I'm finally going to be a member of the club," said Eric as they rode down. He continued with a British accent: "Methinks I'll be taking over Shakespeare this semester." He chuckled, but Jack was not amused. "My probation is over."

"How'd you get Shakespeare? I thought you were Romance."

"So did I," said Eric, shifting his boxes. He was better at Romance literature than actual romance, he thought. "I'm the only one left. Blake's on sabbatical. And you're . . . on vacation. Liz had to give it to me. I *have* taken a few courses in Shakespeare once upon a time."

Jack grinned, seemingly against his will.

"Ah, you're stuck to the sticking place, laddy, straight between Lord and Lady Spenser," said Jack as the elevator doors opened, trying to affect a better British accent than Eric. Jack was referring to their married colleagues. "Indeed! There's Chaucer and Milton—and who could forget our dear, beloved Bard? Then comes Blake, Byron *et al.*, and Tennyson—the whole bloody lot!"

Eric almost lost it, amused by Jack's accent. "I can do Shakespeare."

They went to Jack's car, where Eric saw the crooked pentagram scratched into the hood.

"That's too bad," said Eric, setting the boxes down on the trunk.

"I've been following Megan—"

"In high school I was Claudius. You know, *Hamlet*? As an undergrad, I played Friar Laurence in *Romeo and Juliet*. Small parts, granted, but they gave me a chance to—"

"You're in this, too, buddy," said Jack, unlocking the doors. "Tonight or next week, next month, it could be you clearing out your office. What did I do to deserve this? That's what you'll be asking yourself. Then you'll be asking 'Where's Jack?'"

"If I'm going to teach the course, I'd like to do some of the less familiar ones, just for variety. Have you ever read Albright's version of *Cymbeline*? Maybe *Titus*. Well, anything that's not already been made into films."

Jack handed him another box. "Your Irish chick's her friend. Have you seen her lately?"

Eric caught his breath, glanced across the empty parking lot.

"She's been traveling, I guess. And I, of course, went south."

"Good for the both of you," Jack sneered, then started back to Linden Hall.

"One lavish weekend aside," Eric said, catching up, "I think that's the end of it. Like you so vehemently suggested last semester. I've gotten over her now. However, she left me with an interesting story."

"That's so sad." Jack's eyes narrowed. "Now can we get back to my problem?"

"Come on, Jack. Lighten up. You've obviously been obsessing over her all break." Eric rewound what he had just said and played it back. "Let me rephrase that. It's a new year, a new semester. Time to start fresh. So get over her already."

They rode up the elevator.

"One more trip should do it," said Jack, closing the door. Eric stepped into his office.

"Take a look at this." Eric picked up the Manila envelope on his desk and slid out the manuscript. "Here's my novel. Six chapters so far. It's a tragic love story, set in modern times with flashbacks to medieval times." He saw Jack was still working on the plot in his head. "It's a hearty tale of Pagan lust and Christian corruption, Dark Age barbarism and modern commercialism, a true paean to the worst and best in humankind."

"That's great," Jack mumbled. "Must be about you and me."

8

SOMETHING IS WRONG, THINKS ÍRIS. There is snow on the ground and the skies are dark, yet a distant ray of sunlight strikes the earth. She focuses on it as she walks across the campus. Her footsteps seem heavier and she feels off-balance. She stops beside a tree and rests for a moment, until the nausea passes. The first day of classes is a shock after the long break. She finds a bench to sit on.

Later, she runs into her art colleague, Sandra Kinney, who calls it a miracle, a gift from God. Sandra is vice-president of the campus Christian group, Salvation Corps, after all. Íris recognizes she has talent, good at faces and showing emotions. The small paintings she had at the exhibit on Halloween were all bought by local churches: Jesus in his manger, Jesus debating in the temple, Jesus on the mountaintop tempted by the devil, Jesus spread on the cross with Roman soldiers gambling below, and Jesus airborne in golden light.

Íris sees that Sandra is confused whether an unmarried woman is worthy of giving birth, but she believes that higher powers will guide Íris to the right decision. Íris has her Goddess, and the forces of nature. Sandra insists she needs more: "If you'd welcome Jesus Christ into your heart as your Lord and Savior, God would be able to speak to you and advise you." For once, Íris just smiles and nods. It's not that she thinks Sandra is right. She is just tired of fighting.

Sandra has gotten a commission to paint a series of Jesus paintings in the Catholic cathedral. She calls it a miracle, a gift from God. No one has bought Íris's paintings. No one has commissioned her to paint anything. She is not jealous of Sandra. Her work is good. She claims she is blessed. Whatever she believes, it gives her strength and confidence. Talent comes from genes and environment. Yet Íris's mother did not paint, nor did her father. She knew no artists when she was growing up in Iceland.

Já, I guess it was only a knack, she thinks, not talent. Even with Professor Hirsch mentoring her, first as a model for figure studies, then his personal muse, she has come only a little further than where she was in Toronto. He wanted her to become famous. After a year at Fairmont College, she still cannot see her future. She expected more. Now she has more—and she laughs as she rubs her flat belly. She is going to be a mother. She will soon become what she hates.

It may not be real, she considers. The nurse possibly made a mistake. There was only the one test. It could be in error.

Celia told her about a new book at Borders that has a spell for aborting a fetus. "But you hafta do it before the end of the first month," she explained, "and you hafta get a bunch of stuff we don't have in Kansas."

"It's not that I want to be a mother," she tells the counselor, "yet I want this baby. Goddess wants me to have it. It's a punishment for all I have done." The counselor doubts that. "Then it's a gift to the little spirit inside me," she says. "I don't know why, and I don't know how I will manage, yet I want it. I want it to be healthy and happy and a joy to behold. It's perfect. It's . . . clean."

That is what I wanted for myself.

The realization hits her like a rainstorm. There is a psychological name for it—*já*, Cory must know; he's a Psych major—how people want to repeat their childhood and improve it for their own children. That sounds ridiculous, so it must be true. She feels it. What she feels is real.

"Who's the father?" asked Celia the previous evening in her private studio.

"A man," Íris answered, returning to painting. She knows she must paint more. She must create new works, try to sell them. She needs money now. This is her last semester, so there is not much time left for her to become an art sensation and launch her career.

"Is it that old guy you screwed on Samhain?" Celia asked.

"Which old guy? I am not sure which one. There have been so many, *já*." Íris laughed and Celia frowned.

Celia wanted to know if Íris was planning to keep the baby. Her voice was flat. Her expression was different, darker, and for a moment worried Íris.

"Do you love me?" asked Celia and she could not turn away.

Putting down the brush and palette, Íris wiped her hands and carefully embraced Celia. Íris whispered in her ear what she wanted to hear: "I love you, Celia, as my dear sister."

Celia pushed her away. She cursed at Íris, then stomped out, slamming the door. The door didn't catch and it swung open and bounced against the wall, back and forth a few times—

"Like a pendulum," Cory says, hearing the story of her break up with Celia. "Women can be such idiots."

It is night and they sit together in the communal living room, stocking feet on the coffee table, feeling the fireplace warm the room. Their housemate, Jean, joins them, wearing her pajamas and carrying hot chamomile tea in her pink World's Greatest Aunt mug. Her hair is unbraided now, a big mop of hair.

"My classes suck," says Jean, pulling her feet onto the chair, tucking them under her legs.

They moan about the start of classes. They curse their fate.

"I'm taking Graphic Design. Art on the computer," says Íris. "It may be easy, drawing on a computer. Something for fun. Anything but Studio, *já*."

"What could be easier than art?" asks Jean, who can't draw anything.

"Art is very hard," Cory says. "You should try it sometime, girl."

"And I am taking Shakespeare," Íris tells them, then listens to the silence.

"Shakespeare?" they cackle in unison, making faces.

"My second subject at Toronto was English," she says. "Besides, I need an elective for my degree. If I want to graduate in May."

They don't know about her delicate condition. Sandra Kinney knows only because she saw Íris vomiting in the restroom and asked if she was all right. Overcome with nausea, Íris stupidly said, "I will be in eight months." Sandra helped her clean up. Íris asked her to keep it a secret and she agreed. "And don't tell Ray, especially," she added. That made Sandra suspicious.

"Hey, guys, guess what? I heard some girl got knocked up by a professor," Jean suddenly announces. "Pam told Ronda, and she told me. See, Pam works at the student clinic. Even if it's true, I sure wouldn't go around saying it was a *professor*."

"What?" says Tracy, entering, dressed in sweats. "That's so disgusting."

"If you're the girl," Cory says. "How do you know it was a professor?"

"Because Ronda said Pam said she overheard."

"Overheard what?" asked Cory.

"Overheard 'I didn't know he was a professor.' That's what she said."

Tracy waved it away. "It's just gossip."

Cory glared at Jean. "When're you gonna just let people do what they want in the privacy of their own place? Who cares what other people do? I don't give a shit who anybody sleeps with, as long as it's not my mother."

"You should be talking," Jean sneers. "You and your den of iniquity. Or should I say, the revolving door? You're on your fourth 'steady' guy friend in the past year."

"I am serially monogamous, I'll have you know."

"Cory, do you even look at those twinks you bring home? That last one—Toby?—he had a tattoo on his chest that said *Mother*. And he smelled."

Tracy cracks up.

"Iris, what do you think?" Jean asks. "The level of morality on this campus sucks. I know it's not a religious school, but I mean, what kind of girl gets herself pregnant by a professor? That's so Seventies. Even if she loves the dude, there's a little twentieth-century invention we call the 'condom' that prevents embarrassment."

"Sometimes there's no time to grab the magic packet," says Cory.

"Then don't do it," Jean says.

"So girls should carry condoms," asks Tracy, "just in case?"

"It's never the girl's fault," Cory says. "It's *always* the man who's to blame. Like with rape. Doesn't matter what the girl does or wears, it's the man who gets arrested. The girl can hold off saying 'no' right up to the second he ejaculates and she calls it date rape. Men don't have self-control? It's *women* that don't have self-control. I got self-control, Jean. But it takes two to tango. Right, Iris?"

Staring at the crackling fireplace, she doesn't know what to say. No matter what she says, her words will keep her awake. She must choose them well. However, she is an artist, and a picture equals a thousand words. She takes the hem of her nightshirt and rolls it up until her pink panties show, then her white belly.

"So what kind of stupid girl gets herself in trouble like that?" Jean is going on and on. "Did she do it for the grade? What else can there be?"

"How about love?" says Cory.

"Come on. This is the Nineties. Well, okay, the Two-Thousands now, whatever. That kinda shit don't happen no more. Except, well, maybe for those airhead bimbos who can't make it through college any other way."

Cory is watching Íris, listening to Jean. Slowly Íris pats her belly, as though it were the baby's bare bottom. Cory's eyes are on her belly. He understands. Soon Jean shuts up and stares at her.

"Iris, what are you doing?" asks Tracy.

"It's me," says Íris. "I'm the airhead bimbo and I didn't know he was a professor."

After a quick dinner at his apartment, Eric returned to the campus and parked in the student lot near Dickerson Hall, the art building. It was closer to Grundy Hall where his Shakespeare class was than Linden Hall. As he locked his car, Eric glanced up the snow-covered slope and spied a familiar figure already ascending. By the dark hair, he guessed it was Dominique. He shifted his folders of papers under his arm and hurried to catch up with her. Dominique was bundled in knit cap and scarf, long coat and tall boots, carrying a stack of music and a canvas bag of books. He greeted her with a cheerfulness that surprised him.

"How was your break?" she called as their paths converged.

"Started a novel," he called back, their paths not quite coming together.

"Bravo! You'll tell me all about it?" She quickened her pace.

Eric stepped toward her, closing the distance between them. "Of course."

"I'm late now," she said, turning sharply toward the music building. "I'll hear about it another time."

"No problemo." Eric waved as her tracks veered away.

At the top of the hill, he gazed back in the direction he had come and saw how their footprints had transcribed their relationship. They would come together again, he knew.

Eric passed through the main quad. He felt renewed by the cold. With his novel well underway, he had a perspective on the world that was fresh. He felt energized. He came to Grundy Hall, formerly full of chemistry labs. Renovation had been completed over the break and it was serving as general classroom space while another building was being gutted and rebuilt. Grundy Hall still smelled of chemicals, he noticed as he made his way up the stairs.

When he located the room, he ran his fingers through his hair, straightened his necktie, took a deep breath, and entered. Inside, a handful of students were already sitting at their desks. It was a small room but the windows to his left as he stood at the lectern helped it seem larger. The view outside, as the early evening descended, turned ghostly with the moonlit snowy yard. More students arrived.

Eric glanced at the clock on the back wall.

"I guess it's time we start," he spoke up. "Let me welcome you to Shakespeare." His eyes measured the room. At this point, someone would usually get up and leave. "You're all here for Shakespeare?" Nods all around. "Good. For a second I thought *I* was in the wrong room."

Eric introduced himself, spent fifteen minutes talking about his background and how he came to be a professor at Fairmont College. Then he explained the course. "We'll be studying six of the plays, two of which, I should warn you, are not available in any Hollywood edition."

He chuckled intentionally; he wanted them to understand that he knew students usually studied Shakespeare's plays at the local video rental store.

"You'll see from the schedule I'll pass out in a moment that the plays we will look at first will be: *Romeo and Juliet*—I trust you know it fairly well—*The Merchant of Venice*, and *Othello*. Then we'll study *Titus Andronicus*, about the family of a Roman general. Then *Cymbeline*, set long ago in Britain, and last but not least, *Troilus and Cressida*, which takes place during the Trojan War. So, based on the theme that's taking shape, we could call this course 'Shakespeare in Love and War.'"

The boy in front nodded appreciatively as Eric scanned the other faces.

"Perhaps you've seen or read the first three plays?" A few nods. "That's good. The last three will be quite interesting for us to look at, as well. We must keep in mind, especially in this technologically-advanced age in which we live—looks like we all survived Y2K all right—that Shakespeare intended for his plays to be seen, not merely read, so we *will* be watching them on video. I've arranged for us to view the BBC versions, which should be truer to the script, even if they are lacking in car chases and explosions." Some students grinned. "At mid-term, just for some variety, we'll devote some time to the sonnets. That should fill up the semester. We have sixteen weeks to go, so we have to pace ourselves."

He passed out copies of the syllabus. As he counted the papers and handed them to the first student of each row, a new student entered. He handed out the class schedule next.

Eric returned to the lectern and opened his grade book, pulled out the class list the department secretary handed him on his way out of Linden Hall. He began calling out names, making a check next to each name. After a half-dozen names, he called: "Ginger Grundy . . . ?"

"That's me," a woman called out.

"Any relation to this building?" Eric asked, just to liven up the proceedings.

"We're married," she replied. A few students laughed. "But I'm filing for divorce."

Eric smiled. "Good one."

Another late student was sneaking into the room, he noticed. Late ones usually continued being late. This late student was a woman, so he gave her a break and went on checking the roster as she moved to the back corner and took a seat.

"Demetrius Hardeman?"

"Yeah, but I go by Trey. Okay?"

"Sure." Eric's finger moved down the page. "Jason Lawrence?"

"Here."

"Iris Mag—"

Eric's head snapped up. His eyes zoomed in on the blur of orange in the back corner. The student's face was turned down as she organized a notebook. Could that be her? He was hallucinating. He regarded the class list: IRIS MAGNUSDOTTIR. The name was right—the same name that had been pasted beside the paintings in the gallery. The rainy night he picked her up. And the weekend that followed, with the snow, and the sex, all of the mind-blowing sex, then without a word of farewell—

"Nothing," he whispered. The room was spinning.

Eric cleared his throat, again raising his eyes slowly.

The woman had taken off her coat and sat with her arms on the desk, the dark blue sweater's collar snuggling her jawline, the orange hair sweeping down her shoulders. Her eyes did not show any surprise. *Does she recognize me?* Art students don't have to take Shakespeare. *She must be stopping by to talk to me.* That seemed logical; this was where he could be found on Tuesday and Thursday evenings from 7:15 to 9:30. *Then why is her name on the class list?*

He shook himself out of the trance and gazed down at the list.

"It's . . . *Íris*, I believe. Isn't it?" He regarded her. "Íris Magnúsdóttir," he spoke, with an accent close enough to draw a grin from his student.

His student? His *student*. He was a professor, after all.

"You're enrolled in English Three-Eighty? Shakespeare?"

The orange-haired woman from Iceland nodded.

But it's not required for you, he wanted to shout. *What're you doing here? You're a graduate student, for goodness sake, and this is a junior-level course for English majors. You're obviously here to taunt me—*

"Professor?"

Eric gripped the lectern, hearing voices coming at him from all sides. An inquisition led by Dr. Liz? The Viking war council from his novel? He had done nothing wrong. It was all a misunderstanding. *Why is she here?*

"Professor Schaeffer?"

"What?" he said suddenly.

"I'm here, too," the boy on the front row announced.

Eric took a deep breath. "Of course, you are. What's your name again?"

"Vince Logan. I think you skipped over my name."

"Yes, I have you," Eric confirmed, glad to look down at the list.

He finished calling the roll, taking as much time as he could. He grabbed his stack of index cards and passed them out, telling them what to write on the cards: name, major, phone number, and e-mail.

As they wrote, he studied the woman in the corner.

"This class is two hours a session, as you might have noticed from the schedule," he told them as they finished writing. He began collecting the cards. "It's been about fifty minutes so far. How about we take a short break? Then we can get started on Billy Bard."

"Who?" asked Vince Logan.

"William Shakespeare," said Eric. "Billy Bard . . . ? He's also known as 'the Bard.' Well, anyway—it was a joke. Let's take a break."

When he turned away from Vince Logan, the woman named Íris had already stepped out. Eric sat on the corner of the table, leaning against the lectern, quickly shuffling through the index cards until he found hers.

The handwriting was elegant—as he expected, she being an artist;

he knew nothing about analyzing handwriting but the small vowels and large loops on the consonants were lovely. He choked back a phlegm of emotion as he realized it was the first time he'd ever seen her handwriting. His finger traced the script, felt the touch of her pen. Her fingers had touched the card, too.

Now you're being perverse. She's just a regular student. Nothing suspicious. Pure coincidence. Who else is teaching this course?

He regarded the card, memorized her e-mail address.

"Excuse me."

A voice he recognized tickled his ear. He knew it was Íris.

Here it comes: the excuse, the apologies. I've waited seven weeks for this. The way you just left without so much as a word of explanation—

"I didn't know you were the instructor. It was listed as Staff," said Íris, her voice soft and low, just as it had been after they made love in his bed. "Will it be . . . difficult?"

"Difficult? Well, there are several short papers to write. And a longer research paper," said Eric. "However, you should be able to handle it."

She giggled, a sound he had not heard since that first snowfall.

"Will it be difficult *for you*?"

"For me?"

"If it will be too difficult for me to be here." She paused. The other students were returning, slowing to listen to what their instructor was saying, wondering if it might be important. Íris smiled politely. "I can change to another course."

"This is the only Shakespeare course this semester."

"*Já*, I like this Shakespeare. I took some classes at Toronto about literature."

"I see." He didn't see, of course.

In fact, he couldn't regard her eye to eye. He was just tall enough to be able to look down at her. A glance down her sweater and skirt, down her bare legs revealed pumps with low heels on her feet, a couple inches' assistance.

He didn't know what to say, so he said: "You don't have to drop the course, Miss, uh, Magnúsdóttir. I don't think it—that I'll have any problem—difficulty, whatever—with you, uh, being . . . umm . . . in the class."

His chest was tight and his face felt flushed. He was afraid to wipe the sweat from his brow, unwilling to let her see how her presence affected him.

"It's good to hear," she said, and continued on about something.

He stared at her. *She looks absolutely amazing in that sweater.*

Then reality exploded around him. He had forgotten that he *did* want to see her again. After struggling to accept it, resigning himself to the end of the affair, putting it out of his mind over the winter break, he'd been determined to think of other things. His teaching, his novel, his dissertation, his—

Here she is, in the flesh—but clothed. It is winter, after all. That's her season.

"It's nice to see you again, Íris," said the professor to the student.

9

THE FIRST NIGHT PROFESSOR SCHAEFFER TALKED about Shakespeare's life, how he was born in 1564 in the town of Stratford-upon-Avon in central England, married Anne Hathaway in 1582 and had three children with her, then left for London to seek his fortune. Despite rumors to the contrary, he had no mistresses there and he fathered no more children. Shakespeare was a proper gentleman. Or else he was simply too obsessed with the theater to spend his time carousing. None of his children had children of their own who lived to adulthood. He died in 1616 and was buried in Stratford. So sad, thinks Íris, the chances offered, the opportunities missed.

Professor Schaeffer never looks at her, always avoids her corner. He never calls on her, even when she raises her hand. It is better for her to take notes and be quiet. The class is becoming too tense. The way he conducts class, keeping her on the margin, makes her realize he has no more interest in her. She wanted to drop the class because she knew it would be awkward seeing him every Tuesday and Thursday evening.

Já, a weekend fling, that's all. Enough to make her forget everything. That's what she told him. He believed her.

They finished *Romeo and Juliet*, and the cynical slant he put on it was disturbing. They watched two versions on video, one a modern musical version named *West Side Story*, the other a boring British production. Íris didn't get it. She thought the priest must have seduced the girl before she was poisoned—necrophilia, *já*. When Romeo arrived to claim the girl, the priest stabbed him to cover up the crime. That is what she believes happened, yet he gave her a C on the paper, with the comment *Interesting interpretation but stick to the script*.

The snow has melted yet it is still cool. A sunny afternoon has pulled Íris out to paint a landscape of the campus. Dickerson Hall connected to Everett Hall by the canteen, with the three towers of Grundy Hall rising up behind it, a scattering of fluffy clouds, the still-bare branches, students eagerly walking to class. More or less eagerly. Perhaps an art lover in Administration will buy it and hang it on a wall there.

That's where the money is now, says Ray, even as he professes a preference for her fantasy works. Ray paints fantasy in his basement studio, she's learned. Between the wine and the Jacuzzi at his house last December, when she was not thinking about pregnancy, he showed her some of his paintings—a dozen works depicting busty red-haired women in bondage. Not what she expected from her mentor. That is his fantasy: someone who looks like her being whipped and chained by someone like him.

"I have to say, just for the record," Ray told her that night, sitting back in the hot tub after finishing his third goblet of wine, "you are beyond a doubt the best looking, sexiest model I've ever had in Life Study class, Iris. I mean that sincerely. Hirschy was so right when he described you. I'm glad he sent you down here."

Ray watched her intently as she stepped into the swirling, hot water—no swimsuit to wear so she went nude. It shouldn't matter, he said; he sees her in Life Study. He wore shorts and later slipped them off under the water. The cold air did not bother her, so she sat on the edge of the tub with only her legs in the water.

"Last year's girl was a little chubby. She wouldn't do full frontal, either. She was okay. But you, Iris. You have the most *perfect* boobs I have ever seen—in magazines, film, internet, anywhere—absolutely perfect shape, a gorgeous pair of C-cups, pure white with no blemishes, and those ripe, succulent pink nipples. The jiggle-factor is right on the mark, too. Not too bouncy, not too firm like the fake kind."

"*Já*, there are different types of breasts, different tastes in breasts."

"Tastes in breasts." He snickered. "I bet yours have some sweet milk."

He was getting drunk, she knew. He never talked that way to her.

"How about the back of my knees?" she asked as he paused to light a cigarette. "I have good ear lobes, too."

"They're very nice." He took a drag on his cigarette, nodding reflectively. "Yes, indeedy, last year's girl, even though her breasts were too fatty, she did have one forte. She could give one helluva blowjob. I mean thorough—dedicated—like she needed it to live."

"I think my toes are very nice," she said, lifting a foot out of the water.

As water dripped from her toes, Ray became transfixed by the red toenails wiggling on the surface. He reached out and his hands cradled her foot. Then he licked her toes. She had no idea her mentor had a foot fetish—

Íris watches students passing between classes as she sketches.

"What do you mean, should you tell him?" Cory exclaimed the previous evening when they were sitting in the living room. Jean had gone to bed, saying she couldn't stand to hear them talking about 'Iris's delicate condition.'

"What good would it serve?" Íris asked.

Cory shook his head. "He's the sperm donor. You should tell him it worked."

"Knowing that would hurt him," she said. "You don't know him."

"Like *you* know him?" More head shaking. The fireplace crackled, sparks flying. "I'm a guy, and if I screwed some girl, I'd wanna know. Guys wanna know. They don't wanna have to do anything, yeah, but they wanna know their boys are winners."

"You cannot tell someone something like that—not that completely changes everything, if he—especially if he . . . ."

"What? If he wants you to get an abortion?"

"I'm keeping this baby. He doesn't need to know. It would hurt him."

Cory grinned in his silly way. "I got some swampland in Florida."

"He's divorced! His wife was fucking other men. He is afraid of getting tied up again. That's why I cannot tell him." She stops to take a breath. "He's the professor of my Shakespeare class."

That set Cory off. She hadn't put it all together for him. The professor in December and the one teaching her Shakespeare class are the same. Cory ranted how she has to drop the course and hide for the next few months. She let him talk because when Cory's going there is no way to shut him down. What he doesn't understand is that she is all alone.

Já, I have always been alone. I'm used to it and I'm used to getting myself out of trouble. I don't need anyone. I don't want anyone in my life. Except this baby. Not Celia, not Cory or Jean, not Ray Ferguson, not Professor Schaeffer, not anyone. This is something Goddess wants me to do alone. This is my second chance.

"Do you want me to tell him?" Cory offered.

"You?"

"Anonymously, of course. I'll write a note, stick it in his mailbox. What is he, English? It'll read something like: 'That girl you slept with a couple months ago is gonna have your baby.' Is that too blunt?"

"Cory, stop."

"How about a Happy Father's Day card? Not subtle enough?"

"*Já*—stop!" She slapped his knee but he didn't flinch. There was something about him that was different. "You're just teasing me. And it won't help."

Cory was reticent but she could see through him. He was jealous.

She laid her arm along the back of the sofa, let it slide down around his shoulders. He turned and leaned into her neck and she hugged him, brushing his hair with her hand. His hand went to her belly, felt its soft warmth. Then he broke away and rushed upstairs.

After a while, sitting alone in the living room of the large house with the grandfather clock ticking, Íris got up and went to the attic and stood on the balcony late into the night. She breathed in the cold moon and caressed the breeze as it passed her. She thought about everything happening now. Deciding to tell her mother, she drafted a letter in her head: 'Your worst fear has come true—soon you will be a grandmother.'

In her room, she checked the EXCITE website to see what response her previous posting had received. The latest consensus was that she should tell the man identified only as 'ES' that he will be a father. They insist it's the proper thing to do, he has a right to know, and she should accept whatever reaction he has. Unfortunately, the timing is awkward, she typed back to them. Valentine's Day is at the end of the week.

"Someday you'll look back and laugh about it," Jean told her the next morning.

Íris grabbed the last cinnamon roll. "I'm eating for two, *já*."

A few more clouds arrive and the light is different now so she packs up her sketchbook and heads to her private studio in the basement of Dickerson. Inside stands the nearly finished statue that Cory has been working on. The woman who is supposed to be Íris stands hands-on-hips, defiant, one foot slightly ahead of the other, her head tilted coyly to one side, her hair trailing down that shoulder. She is nude, and Cory has made her anatomically correct. Yet she is not me, Íris decides.

"I can't believe you want to change *The Fairmont Review*," said Professor Schaeffer, giving the conference table a slap. "*The Fairmont Review* has been the journal's name for over fifty years. It's the name everyone knows. Who is your audience for *Journatalia*?"

Viki Stafford was the Assistant Editor. She stood up on behalf of her editor, Tiffany somebody, who was thankfully absent, presenting their argument for the name change. With Blake Spenser on sabbatical, Eric not only had the Shakespeare course to teach but he also had been appointed by Dr. Liz to be the faculty advisor for the literary journal. He had little advice for them. They had been waiting for Dr. Spenser's sabbatical to push through the name change.

"Fine," Eric muttered, throwing his hands up in surrender. "Name it whatever you wish. Doctor Spenser will be here in the fall to change it back."

"The Literary Guild's by-laws state that it can only be done during the spring term, at the annual meeting," said Viki. "That's when we change editors. So the name will stay at least until next spring."

The student staff applauded.

"The *Review* is dead," they chanted. "Long live *Journatalia!*"

Eric feigned derision but inside he was actually happy for the change. Anything to shake up the stodgy department.

After the meeting adjourned and Art Director Fiona Graves was given a short deadline to produce new cover art that would reflect the name change, Eric quickly made his way to the elevators from the third-floor conference room.

As he exited the elevator on the fifth floor, Eric noticed that Lance Albright's door was open. He heard the bass voice bellowing in laughter. Probably my novel, Eric thought. He had given his opening chapters to Albright a month ago but the old writer had offered no opinion. Eric's spring semester schedule didn't allow him much time to stop and quiz the visiting writer. Now might be good.

Eric sidled up at the open doorway, saw that Albright was with a student. The woman, red-haired and lightly freckled, looked up at him but did not smile. She was about thirty, he guessed, possibly a graduate student. Her shade of red was closer to burgundy, not the bright orange of the student in his Shakespeare class. She was stockier and, unlike the Icelander who wore skirts or dresses, this woman wore purple jeans and a ragged, gray *Property of Oxford University* sweatshirt. She wore black army boots with the cuffs of her jeans tucked in. Around her neck hung a few strings of Celtic beadwork and a large wooden pentacle on a chain.

Eric extended his hand to the woman, greeted her. She glanced at Albright, who gave a wink that apparently signaled his approval.

"Eric, my boy," Albright chimed, "haven't heard from you since forever. Oh! This is Megan ... uh ... ?"

"Valery," the woman answered, releasing Eric's hand.

Eric blinked, wanting to wash his hand. Here was Jack's witch in the flesh! He stared at her until he sensed she was uncomfortable. Nice looking but clearly too much for Jack to handle. Eric offered the usual pleasantries, inquiring about her status. Graduate, Creative Writing,

110

she revealed. Formerly English Lit as an undergrad, she added under her breath like it was a dirty secret.

"So, you're going into the graduate program?" Eric asked nervously.

"In the fall," she said, smiling with a falseness that made him stay guarded. "Or the summer. Depends on several factors. The job market. I'll need some money if I'm staying in school. But who knows, maybe I'll get an offer I can't refuse."

Eric suggested a half dozen schools; half of them had rejected him.

"Don't listen to him," Albright spoke up gruffly. "You don't need school. Just write, dammit. Publish a couple of books and you can write your own ticket to any university."

"Well," Eric interrupted, "if you're interested in Fairmont College, I'm filling in for Doctor Spenser this semester . . . if you want to talk about the program here." He cleared his throat, then addressed the old writer: "Have you had a chance to take a look at my novel?"

"Novel?" Albright said, scratching his head—like a huge orangutan, thought Eric. "The story about Vikings, right?" He pretended to search his office for the manuscript. "I've got it around here somewhere. Don't worry. You have it on a floppy disk, right? I only got through the first chapter, I should warn you. Viking stories don't sell anyway."

"I gave you four chapters."

"And I'll get to them . . . ." Albright left the words floating in the air.

The woman regarded Eric as if she and Albright had been discussing him. Eric took the hint, smiled awkwardly and stepped out of the office. *Forget them.* He'd had enough of the famous Mister Albright. Fourteen novels of crap which he and everyone else on campus were expected to admire, Eric muttered down the hallway. But the man couldn't even do what he was being paid handsomely to do: teach creative writing to the undergrads.

He stopped. With a deep breath, he turned himself around and stepped back to Albright's open door. *Let's hear how he berates other writers.* Eric leaned closer, careful to stay out of view.

". . . Schaeffer, I think. Or Schneider. Something German, anyway. He's harmless," Albright was saying. "Good example, though. Professors are the ones nobody would dance with in high school. What constitutes dignity for them is how well they get across their sacred message: 'I'm somebody, dance with me.' They chant their mantra of professorship as an excuse: 'I'm thinking important thoughts unsophisticated rubes like you cannot understand. Therefore, I wouldn't *want* to dance, even if one of you unsophisticated rubes were to ask me.'"

"That is so true!" said Megan, her voice full of abject fascination.

Eric weighed the observation: he could see himself in Albright's pointed words. Yes, he might have been like that in high school. And as an undergrad. Yes, he'd used his supposed intellectual superiority as an excuse to avoid participating in whatever social activity his peers might have considered entertaining. He was too good for that low-brow stuff.

"They're scaredy cats," Albright continued. "They hide in academia because the outside world scares 'em to death. Imagine people who actually *like* being in school. They really *don't* want to be in school. They *want* to drive sports cars. They want to fuck the prom queen. They want to score the winning touchdown. But all they can do is rack up the GPAs and claim to 'know stuff.'"

"That is so on target, Mister Albright!"

"That's why I never became a damn professor. Lecturer, yes. A highly compensated writer-in-residence, yes. Academic fodder? Hell no."

"You are so brilliant!"

Eric backed up, getting out of the way of the inflated head he expected to explode.

"I know this girl," Megan said, "and she's really messed up, like, she was a victim of bad stuff as a child. Now she's into sadomasochism and binge sex. I feel real sorry for her, but you know what? I'm glad she's messed up. So I can write about her. Is that sick? I've been using her for a story I'm working on. Maybe you'd like to take a look at it?"

"Why, I'd be happy to, little lady. I'll read it this afternoon."

"That'd be great, Mister Albright."

Eric turned away. *What an asshole!* He would never again pay a visit to Albright's office. *Forget the novel chapters; they're scrap paper.* He didn't want to give him the satisfaction of losing his manuscript.

In his office, the phone was ringing and Eric rushed to answer it.

"*Hola*, Eric." It was Dominique, as usual. "Are you busy now?"

"I just got back from the literary journal staff meeting," he said. "Then I stopped by Albright's office. Big waste of time. The man is an asshole." He took a breath. "Sorry. What's going on with you?"

"Could we change our schedule this weekend?" she asked. "There's a recital on Saturday. Charlotte Becker, the flautist."

He regarded the wall calendar, realizing he had not changed it from January to February. "So you want to go to the movie on Sunday? Is that it?"

"Charlotte needs me to play on one piece."

"We can go on Sunday. No problemo."

"It will have to be the evening," she said. "Is it all right with you?"

"No problemo." The line was silent a second.

"Eric?"

"Yes?"

"Please stop saying 'no problemo.' It's 'problem*a*.'"

He apologized.

After hanging up, he glanced again at the calendar: today was an anniversary. One year ago his divorce was final. He needed to celebrate. Two days later would be Valentine's Day. He did the math: *Dominique + Valentine's Day + impending date = better buy some gift today or else my whole world might come crashing down around me.* The Student Center would have chocolates.

10

THE DAY IS STRANGE—LIKE SPRING, yet there is a chilling breeze; the sun is bright, warm—as Íris pauses in the Plaza of Heroines to gather her strength. The stones forming the plaza's surface and the low encircling wall that students sit on are covered with the names of historic and not-so-historic women with their dates of birth and death, memorials to those who have gone before. As she gazes up at the twisted gray metal that represents Woman rising from the ashes of her oppressed sisters, she knows what is right. She raises her arms upward toward the distant ghost of a moon and the gleaming statue and whispers a prayer to Goddess. A few people watch her, yet she does not care about them.

She sees him. The Plaza of Heroines stands between Linden Hall and the Student Center, so all professors of English returning from lunch will have to pass this way.

"Professor Schaeffer," she calls.

He waves his hand in greeting but continues on.

"Wait, Professor Schaeffer!"

He stops, points to himself, puzzled. She strokes the air, beckoning. He comes toward her, pausing at the entrance to the plaza as two girls exit, seeming unsure whether or not men are allowed.

"I have something for you." As soon as she speaks, she knows the words are ominous.

"You don't have to call me Professor Schaeffer," he says, "not when we're in public." She nods. "Nice day to be outside, isn't it? I like when it's cool but sunny. I remember you like it cold."

"I want to give you . . . ."

She bends over her backpack, digs through her papers. He moves to block the sun, to provide shade so she can see what she is looking for. He always knows what to do. She had forgotten how kind he could be. When her fingers find the paper with his name in the top corner, she pulls it out and hands it to him.

"Here is my paper on *The Merchant of Venice*." She tries to smile. "I know I'm late—*it is* late—but please accept it and do with it what you want." She wants to slap herself. She knows what she is about to say.

He takes the paper and instinctively begins reading the first page.

"You see I follow the script this time," she says and he laughs.

"Yes—good. Taking the party line. I never was trying to introduce any radical new views to the interpretation of Shakespeare's plays, even when they might come up."

"On the subject coming up . . . ." She has to stop, waiting until he gives his full attention. He continues reading. "Please don't read it now. Go back to your office, get a cup of coffee, and relax a while before you evaluate what I have to say."

"All right," he says. "That's a good idea."

"Now, if you don't mind . . . ." She takes a big breath. "I wish to talk to you not as student and professor, but person to person. Only for a minute, *já*. If you have time."

He seems surprised. Yet this professor is waiting patiently. His eyes are so innocent, blinking in the bright sunlight. He is so unprepared for what she is about to say.

"I just want to tell you—now we are talking as people, not as student and professor—when we met last time . . . *já*, last December, on the first snowfall, when we . . . ."

He blushes.

"I'm sorry, Professor Schaeffer."

"Call me Eric, please."

"*Já*—Eirík."

"That's it, with the accent. I love hearing you say it that way."

"*Já*, about that night—one of those nights. I cannot be clever about it, so you must forgive me. The first night, when you picked me up in the rainstorm and took me to your apartment?"

"Uh . . . yes?" His face is red.

"You remember?"

"Oh, god, yes." Probably he has been thinking of that night every night since.

"I really needed to fuck—sorry, *have sex*—I needed it that night." She steps closer, too close for a student and a professor on campus. She does not want any others nearby to hear. "Thank you. I'm sorry to get you involved with me. Yet you were so . . . passionate."

"You're telling me *now* that I was, umm, good in bed?" He laughs.

"*Já*, that. And . . . it was so good I never noticed . . . ."

"Noticed what?"

"It was the right time."

"Time?" He is puzzled.

Suddenly, his face becomes brighter than her hair and he steps back as if he has just been slapped.

"I am going to have a baby," she says.

He is paralyzed, his face grim. She has scared the life force out of him.

"The date is in August," she continues. If she waits even one second longer, either he will run away or she will lose her nerve. "Everyone says I have to tell you. It's the right thing to do. I only tell you so you know. I don't expect you to do anything. I don't want you to do anything. I will have this baby. *Já*, I want this baby. I only tell you because everybody says I—"

"Everybody?" he mumbles. "How many people know?"

"The people on my webpage—"

"Millions of people. You broadcast this news around the globe?"

"I didn't use your name. I never said the name of this college. Don't worry. You are anonymous. No one here knows." She retreats. "I told a couple of my housemates. They can keep secrets."

"So it's true? You've been to a doctor?"

"Yes, the student clinic. In Marlborough Hall. I'm sure they know how to check. And they probably have some record if you want me to prove I went there."

"No, Iris, I believe you. That's not the problem."

He shakes his head, rubbing his forehead with his hand, muttering, *"No problema, no problema."*

He looks up. Their eyes meet for the first time in a very long while. At least, it feels like a long time to her: she feels his eyes penetrating her, pushing against her soul.

"What are you going to do?" he asks in a low voice.

"What do you mean?" She is more cautious than angry. "I will finish school and have the baby. What else is there?"

"I mean, do you need money, or a better place to live?" He waits a heartbeat but she does not answer. "What I mean is, if there's anything I can do to help, I want to help you. I want to take care of you." Perhaps sensing her distrust, he adds: "For the baby's sake."

Then he spins away and begins ranting wildly, talking to himself. She sees how this information has hurt him. He stops and regards her. His eyes are intense. She is suddenly afraid.

"Oh, Iris! I never expected this turn of events, but—but now that it's true, I want to be with you again. I mean, as a couple. As a family. I need you as much as our baby needs us—both of us. This is such wonderful, wonderful news!"

He remembers a small red box wrapped in a purple ribbon that is clenched in his hand and offers it to her. "Here, this is for you."

She takes the box, sizes it up. How could he have known? Was he already planning to give her something?

"It's chocolate, just chocolate, but I want you to have it." This Eirík is giddy. "Please, take it. It's the least I can give you on this momentous occasion." He gazes at her, mumbling, "Sweets for the sweetie . . . ."

"You've given me enough, Eirík."

"I want to give you more. I really have a lot of love to give," he says, as though he doubts what he could only have read from her mind. They are on a wavelength, yet always just miss each other. "But nobody seems to want it. My love, I mean."

"You are unhappy?" she asks.

"Unhappy?" His grin is huge. He places his hands on her shoulders, the first step toward an embrace. "I am ecstatic, Iris! I am blown away! This is great news!" He stops cheering, not convinced she believes him. "I'm going to be a father. A father! Is it true? That means something, doesn't it?"

"*Já*, we matched." Her smile is harder to maintain.

"May I give you a hug?"

She holds out her arms and he steps close. Their arms encircle each other. She enjoys embraces, she recalls from December. If they are genuine. His are genuine. As they part, he plants a kiss on her cheek. When their eyes meet again, there are tears in his.

The conversation has not gone as she planned. She never expected he would have any positive, welcoming response. In many ways, it is worse. She does not want this man in her life. Yet in her baby's life, she thinks, it may be a good thing. She will accept his offer to be the father, yet she will continue to refuse his attentions. After all, she is not in love with this man.

"I know how awkward this may seem to you," he says. "What I mean is I'll help you financially, and with anything else you need for the baby. I'm not asking to return to that sexual relationship we briefly had. It took me a while, but I finally accepted that it ended in December. A weekend fling, sure. That's all. I have no regrets, though I admit I was angry at first. When I couldn't find you, I—oh, I don't want to dwell on that. It's history. The point now is that you're going to have a baby. My baby. *Our* baby. Whatever we can do to make the experience easier on you, I want to try to do."

He reaches out timidly to poke her belly and she does not object.

"The first thing would probably be to have you move into my apartment," he says, rubbing his chin with a thumb. "It's small, as you know, but it's warmer than your place. And don't worry, my neighbor, the one with the loud music, she moved out. I can drive you to the campus instead of you riding a bike. You need to be careful now, and not take chances. I can cook for you. No more chili. Lots of salmon. You'll have a bathroom to yourself instead of sharing it with three or four others. You'll be a lot more comfortable."

"Then where will you stay, Eirík?"

That stops him. His eyes hover in the air before her face, unable to focus. She wants to smile, show him she is only teasing, but she keeps still.

"I have property down in Texas that's being sold," he says, more calm and rational. "I changed realtors because the guy wasn't very diligent, so very soon now I'll have the proceeds. Then I'll be looking for a house not too far from campus. Four bedrooms, one for each of us, an office for me, a studio for you. And two full baths, a family room, garage, and a big backyard for a little person to play in, a garden on the side, a view of the horizon far away . . . ."

He sits down on the low wall and she joins him. He takes her hand.

"Íris," he whispers, careful to say her name properly, "I missed you so much. Seeing you in class has been agony for me. I keep thinking about the time we were together. I know it was short, and I know it was very likely just some random act of kindness, but I—I always hoped we could find something between us, some *thing* that would bring us together. I'm talking about something we could let grow and it would keep us together. I'm talking about compatibility. We talked about it before: we're both creative, we're both anti-social in our own ways, we're existentialists—stuff we can build on. And there must be other things." He laughs and a half-grin materializes on her face. "And now we have a baby. It's such a miracle! This is what I've dreamed of ever since that weekend—I mean, being with you again."

"I'm a witch and a nudist."

"That's what I love about you, Íris."

"People say witches are evil."

"I don't believe in evil."

"And I'm a stranger here, an exiled *víking* princess."

"Then I will protect you—"

"And an artist who is much too demanding."

"I majored in compromise—"

"An eccentric whore. A marked woman. A *vændiskona*."

"Nothing before us matters."

"I'm one of those damaged people."

"I don't care—"

"You will be damaged, too."

"I want you, Íris."

"You may even die!"

"Then that is how I'll go."

His face is a mask of light, eyes shining, cheeks illuminated by the sun. She cannot resist. She leans over and presses her lips to his. It seems strange to be kissing her professor.

"Does this mean I will get an A in your class?"

"Shakespeare?" The question puzzles him. "I hope so." He squeezes her hand. "You're certainly capable of an A. You have a few problems with grammar. I know English is not your native language, but I'll help you—"

"I studied English since I was twelve years old."

"Don't worry. I'll work with you. I'll help you—promise. I'll help you with everything. I can guarantee you an A because your writing will be A writing. If we didn't have this relationship, I wouldn't care what kind of work you turned in. I'd read it and let the grade fall where it might."

"I don't want to study grammar, Eirík." Her smile fades. "Could I just sleep with you?"

"It wouldn't be fair to the other students in the class," he says with all seriousness.

"The others aren't having your baby."

He freezes. He glances down at her belly; nothing yet pushes out her skirt. She lays her hand over it. So quiet. The sky waits and she feels Iceland.

"Fine. You'll get an A," he replies at last with neither anger nor resignation. "Show up for class, turn in papers on time—at least as well-written as they have been already—and the rest will be *gratis*. No matter what I do, though, we have to keep up appearances. I can't be *seen* to favor you, Íris. You understand that, don't you?"

"Yes, of course, Professor Schaeffer," she says.

He smiles painfully.

"And I want to stay in my own place. Where I am now."

He obviously hates negotiating. That is why he is the teacher, she thinks. He knows absolute power pleases absolutely. She reminds him that her lease doesn't end until June.

"Mine, too," he says with delight. "By then, the condo should be sold. Then we can look for a house together. Hmm, together. I like the sound of that. Don't you?"

She does not, yet she refuses to tell him. She does not need this man. The more they talk, the more she cannot understand how it happened. Early on he was charming, kind, and safe—someone who would not bother with her when she left. Because she was so dirty. Now he is a raving maniac who thinks Goddess has blessed him, yet this Íris is no one's gift.

"And you must give in to me whenever I need some 'male attention.' Even if you are tired, or your sports is on the television, *já?*"

"Fine. But you're pregnant."

"I know this."

"We have to be careful while you're pregnant," he says, lowering his voice. "My ex-wife had a miscarriage. In the fourth month. I hate to bring that up, my previous marriage and such, but . . . well, she and I were . . . we were still having sex then. So maybe we should hold off until the baby's born."

"I am very healthy, Eirík. You need not worry."

"My ex- was in good shape, too. It can happen to anyone, at any age."

"*Já,* it matters to you."

It also matters to her. The first time she was pregnant, it was quite unexpected. Being fifteen, it is easy to fix the facts. She did not know what pregnancy was, not until it ended. The purity of the snow made it all clear. Her insides were in tangles and she bled so much—until her body forced something out and it lay there in the snow amidst the blood. She was frightened and thought she was dying. No one was there, so she pushed the bloody thing into the stream with her toe. Magnús did not know until he asked why she was so bloody and she told him what had happened.

"I will be careful," she says, thinking of that icy stream behind the house, when her first baby died. Eirík is speaking yet all she hears is her mother's voice, complaining: "God will punish you if you let the devil inside you!" The world is different now, she thinks, hopes, as she examines his face. Here is a man who will love me, care for me, and protect me and the baby. It might be a good thing to do, to let him play *pabbi*.

"You should leave some clothes in my apartment. It'll be more convenient."

"I don't need clothes in your apartment."

He grins. "That's right. You won't. You're a nudist."

"And I can use your computer to keep up with my webpage?"

"Yes, of course. In fact, maybe I can join your club. I like theological debates."

"*Já*, it is good. We can argue."

"Now how shall we celebrate this wonderful news? Dinner at the best place in town? How about tonight? Before class. Hey, let's just cancel class tonight."

She kisses his lips and he is startled. They hug awkwardly, a little unsettled by the stares of people around them. Parting, she whispers into his ear: "Wait for a rainstorm, Eirík. I'll walk barefoot in front of Dickerson and you drive by, like you are lost, and you pick me up. Then we fuck at your place until next year."

"Or forever?" he whispers back.

"That is negotiable."

11

ERIC WATCHED HER WALK AWAY, saw her steps falling with uncertainty. The sun beat down on him and it was unseasonably warm—or he was sweating from the stress, fighting to keep a positive spin on the situation. The air was cool when it brushed his cheek, and he welcomed it. The forecast was for more snow, but he was already feeling a chill.

He went home earlier than usual, to shower and change for a dinner he had planned in a previous life. In suit and tie, he stopped at a flower shop and bought a bouquet of whatever was left and looked pretty. They had no irises. Then, with flowers in one hand and a fresh run of his other hand through his hair, Eric stepped inside the house where Íris lived.

The house had the scent of fireplace and cleaning wax, dusty carpets and old ladies' perfume. The stairs creaked as he ascended—like the ancient king to meet the goddess in her temple. Doors remained shut on both sides of the silent hallway. He went to her door and saw the tape applied where a peephole would have been: ÍRIS, it announced to the bumbling fools who did not know. He took a deep breath.

"Wait," the voice of an angel called from within when he rapped on the door.

Angels don't get pregnant, he considered, keeping his flower hand poised and his smile intact. In Milton's *Paradise Lost*, angels were androgynous, changing between male and female as conditions required. That was a long time ago. *Forget the details; go with the theme. You've been blessed.* Cursed, blessed, the degree of difference was infinitesimal.

"*Halló*," she said when the door opened.

He fell back under the onslaught of her radiance. The bright red dress sparkled with silvery glitter. The low neckline emphasized her ivory bosom as much as the slit in the side of the knee-length dress revealed her white thigh. Around her pale neck hung a small golden star with a silver crescent moon cradling it. He stared at her feet: pale toes with red nails peeked out from the red two-inch heels.

"Borrowed from Jean," she said to his inquiring eyes. "Except the jewelry."

"You are absolutely gorgeous."

"*Já*, am I not everything you have dreamed?"

"You are." He remembered the flowers and offered them.

"For me?" she said, taking the bouquet. "That's very sweet, Eirík, yet I don't have any vase to put them in. Will you keep them at your home for me?"

"Yes—as you wish."

He cleared his throat, nervous like it was a first date. Nothing was the same, nothing carried over from before. *Time to start fresh. A chance to do things right.* A perfect gentleman was what he would become—as his mother had always insisted.

Eric ushered his date down to the car, which had been meticulously cleaned, a new air freshener added. He held the door open for her. Íris seemed awkward in the high heels, so he supported her elbow as she lowered herself into the seat. The drive was ten minutes to Il Calvino, an Italian restaurant featuring Neapolitan dishes, especially seafood. She liked fish, he recalled, salmon in particular. What else did he remember?

The wine would be white and chilled, Eric decided. Although they were early for the usual dinner crowd, he was pleased to be treated as a gentleman, working through the wine-sampling ritual with ease and assuring her that it was a good vintage.

"I'm pregnant," Íris reminded him, waving the wine away.

The waiter seemed dumbfounded, hearing only that line. Vincenzo was polite and accommodating nevertheless. He sent a violinist over to their table, a college student who proved to be quite proficient. Their oak table stood in the back corner, surrounded by ferns and partially hidden by a plaster column, giving them privacy. This was how he should have started, Eric considered. He should have invited her out right after that art exhibit. He and his beautiful date tonight might be married by now and pregnancy the next logical step. Instead, he had done everything backwards, as Jack pointed out.

That bastard! Jack had gotten Eric all wrapped up in conspiracies, made him fear even looking in the direction of a female student. Meet a woman off campus, then she takes your class and sues you for sexual harassment? Jack was full of shit, but—*You and I have to stick together; Megan and Iris are sisters in the same damn coven, probably working together*—

"Excuse me," Íris called, sensing his distraction as he tore a piece of bread free from the loaf and dipped it in the olive oil before bringing it to his lips.

"Sorry." He smiled at her, gazing into her eyes, wanting to say something about them, something honest. "You're so . . . sexy tonight," he mumbled, then repeated it more clearly. "I want to sweep everything off this table and stretch you out on top of it and ravish you, Íris."

A smile played at the edge of her mouth. "Why don't you?"

His eyes rolled upward as he thought of a reason not to.

"Because we don't want to ruin Jean's dress."

She laughed. "I can take it off, *já.*"

"Well, obviously," he said. He glanced around the restaurant, giving the idea serious thought. More diners were arriving. "We probably should save that for later."

She tore off another strip of bread, dipped it and held it to her mouth seductively.

"I've started work on a novel," he said, watching her nibble on the bread. "I think it's going well. I've written nine chapters now. Should be about twenty in all."

She finished the remaining portion of the bread. "What is it about?"

"It's . . . ." *Actually, it's about you,* he was about to say, then thought better of it. "It's set in a village in Newfoundland where they have a legend about a standing stone that's really an ancient wizard." He gave her the basic plot over the next few minutes and she was attentive. "I was inspired by what you told me. The tale of those Viking lovers."

"You mean that weekend we fucked?"

The waiter arrived at that moment with their dinners and an assistant to help serve them. The plates were hot, the waiter warned. Another plate of bread would be forthcoming. Enjoy the meal. *And the company,* Eric added. The staff departed.

Eric and Íris, boy and girl, the happy couple on their first date, regarded their dinner selections for a few heartbeats.

"So much happened I cannot recall the details," Íris continued.

Eric slid his hand across the table toward hers, his fingers walking like a spider. Seeing the movement, she spread her fingers enough to receive his, like two forks coming together, teeth meshing. She clasped his fingers between hers.

"You are absolutely exquisite tonight, my dear," said Eric, his voice as gentle as he could make it. "We should have come here first."

"It's all very nice," said Íris, and offered a quick smile, one he would have missed if he had blinked. "Thank you, Eirík. For everything."

He watched her intently, lovingly. She pouted, looked away, and pulled her hand free. She retrieved a tissue from her matching red-sequined clutch and dabbed the tissue to her cheek.

"What's wrong?"

"Nothing's wrong," she said. Her obvious distress made it impossible for Eric to believe her. "It's hormones."

"I'm sorry," he said automatically. "I've made such a mess of this relationship. If we can even call this a relationship. So many things I should've done differently. I'm sorry for taking advantage of you. That night in the rain, I should have driven you to *your* house. I should have told you I was a professor at Fairmont. Then everything would be different. Then you wouldn't have been sucked into this mess."

"What mess?" Tears ran down her cheek, more than she could wipe away. "You did nothing wrong. I—I don't—"

He took her hand again across the table.

"I don't deserve any of this," she said, trying not to cry as she pulled her hand off the table. "I don't know what to do. I never did this."

"What? A nice dinner out? You deserve a whole lot more than this. You have always deserved more. I remember what you told me. The bad stuff. I guess that's what I'm apologizing for. Not just for me, but for all the men who ever treated you badly. If you can, please put it away and lock up the past."

"I do like all this." A smile flashed across her face.

"I'm glad." Eric's eyes were twinkling, he felt, like in some Disney animation. They matched her eyes. "Let's consider this night the start of a beautiful new relationship, Íris. Let's start fresh, shall we? Nothing that happened before tonight is important now. Except the baby. Gotta keep the baby." He chuckled, and she followed. "That's beautiful. Your smile. People don't see that enough. Your smile is like everything good." He sighed, tilted his head and recited Shakespeare: "'Shall I compare thee to a summer's day?/ Thou art more temperate:/ Rough winds do shake the darling buds of May,/ And summer's lease hath all too short a date.'"

"I come from winter." Her eyes narrowed and her face, flushed from the tears' touch, cooled. "Summer has never been for me."

"Pale suits you. So does the cold night air. Tonight is perfect."

"It's a beautiful chill."

She smiled, her teeth naturally pearly. He gazed into her eyes, alternately studying the way her tongue crossed those teeth.

"Shouldn't we eat now?" Íris spoke after another minute of his adoration.

He grinned. "I was waiting for it to cool down."

He loved the sound of her laughter, especially when she was trying to repress it.

"Thy eternal winter shall not fade," Eric spoke, giving her hand a final squeeze before releasing it and taking up his knife and fork.

He chewed his veal parmigiana. Íris, enjoying her fillet of sole, was going to be the perfect mother, the perfect wife, if only time was kind to them. His eyes seldom left her as they ate their dinner, and between bites, she smiled at him coyly, sincerely, seriously, warmly, coolly, and with a lingering sensuality that massaged his heart and promised more.

As they exited the restaurant, Eric swept his arm up and around her bare shoulders. They were greeted by snowflakes circling through the air. He glanced at his watch and realized that his Shakespeare students could have been showing up at Grundy Hall only to discover the note tacked up outside the classroom: their professor was ill and class was cancelled. It might be true. Another classmate also happened to be ill. He smiled longingly.

"I suppose we must go to class," said Eric sadly, once they were settled in the car. "The others are waiting. We must not disappoint them."

She leaned in and they kissed. "And tonight's lesson?"

"We begin *Othello*," Eric replied with a sense of excitement, "a lusty story of betrayal and revenge. Everyone betrays someone and is, in turn, betrayed by someone else. It's the way of the world."

He caught her gaze and fixed his eyes on hers and, for a brief eternity, thought he could see into her soul.

When they parked near Grundy Hall, Eric suggested that she should go in first. He would follow after a few minutes.

"No need to get them talking," he said. He gave her a peck on the cheek and she nodded. They stood beside the open car door as Eric removed his suit coat and necktie and pulled a sweater out of the backseat to wear. "Now we won't look like we just went out to dinner to celebrate."

"We did, *já*."

He took her face in his hands, her cold, white cheeks cradled in his warm palms, and pushed his lips against hers. She resisted. He frowned.

"I'm sorry, Íris. I—I love you. I'm in love with you. And I've been looking for someone like you all of my life."

"A whore?"

"No, a beautiful woman who is sexy and artistic and affectionate."

"I'm not affectionate."

"All right. I'm sorry for all the sappy talk, but I want you to know how I feel."

"You want me to know how you feel about me?" She blinked twice. "Put your coat and tie on. Come to class with me. Walk in with me, hand in hand. Then talk to me. Treat me like more than some student you spent the weekend with. *Já*, I am more than that, you say. You called me your 'dear.' Didn't you say that?"

"I did—I think." Eric instinctively shoved his hands into his pants pockets as the wind blew against them. "Do you want me to announce to the class our parenthood?"

She studied the snowflakes. "Not yet." Twenty of them, a hundred, tossed on the breeze, landing on her bare shoulders and hair. She held out her hand, captured several snowflakes, watched them melt. One was the same as any other—until seen up close. The same with men.

"Things are rather tense on campus now. If they think we're having an affair, I could lose my job." His eyes were wide; Jack was barking into his ear. Now he only had this woman's good graces to save him from Jack's fate. Was there some master plan? Was the trap already set? "You know affairs between students and teachers are not allowed. If I lose my job, what would we do? No job, no money. That wouldn't help our baby. Our baby needs—"

"Our baby! You keep saying 'our baby,' but it is *my* baby. My baby!"

She hit his shoulder with the back of her fist, and swung again weakly. Her face was distraught. She swung her arms violently around him.

"You can walk away now and never do anything," she said. "I'm the one who will suffer for nine months, and die in agony when it's born. If I don't die, I will have to work extra hard, *já*, to care for my baby, my child, until he is grown. This child will throw the dirt on my grave!" She sobbed. "It is my baby, Eirík."

"But I *won't* walk away," said Eric. "That's my promise to you. Because I *want* to be a father—*the* father. If I were going to walk away, we wouldn't be having this conversation now. We wouldn't have gone out to dinner. I want to be with you. I want to be the father. It's what I've always wanted." He suddenly grinned. "Not necessarily the diaper changing, cleaning up messes, not the curfews, not the driving lessons, I'll be honest. Seeing my own flesh and blood walking, talking, and doing great things, that's what I want. I need to become a father before I can stop being my father's *boy*. My brother's already got a family. Three kids, and . . . ." He swallowed hard. "I've had a couple of chances before, but something's always gone wrong, and usually it wasn't my fault. I've wanted it since long before I met you, Íris. The fact that I *could* do nothing but I *choose* to care for you—now, and for as long as you need me—that's what it means to love someone. Love is never having to ask for help."

He turned away, shaking his head, leaving Íris stunned, sweating in the cold.

"I'm not one who likes to dabble in romantic crap," he continued, his voice shaking. "I mean, saying all the words men are supposed to say to women to make you love us. There's only one way to say 'I love you.' The bottom line is you're pregnant and I'm the father, and I must take care of you. You have a choice. Go it alone or let me honor my obligations. Not just obligations, but my desire. I *want* you, and the fact that you're carrying my baby—*our* baby—makes you all the more desirable. This is our reality, Íris, and we can't walk away from it. The baby is coming." He had to take a breath. He stared at her: chin dropped, the wind tugging at her hair. "Unless you have an abortion."

She glared at him. Even in the lamplight, he could see a tear roll down her cheek.

"I won't do it," she said, her voice low and firm. "And it has nothing to do with those politics people fight about. I want this baby. Because it is part of me, *já*. I would not cut off my hand because it was dirty. My mother wanted to cut me out of her." She reached up and dug in her hair. "Touch here."

He placed his finger on a ridge that ran across her scalp.

"What is it?"

"My mother's scar. She wanted me out so bad she had me cut out."

"The scalpel did that?"

"*Já*, I was cut out of her. It's a reminder she never wanted me. I interrupted her university studies."

He pulled his finger back. "Well, I want you, Íris."

She turned away, straightening her hair, and flicked snowflakes from her shoulders.

"When I was young," he said, "I used to think, 'Thank goodness if a pregnancy should occur she can simply get an abortion.' In those days I used condoms—anything to prevent it. When I was old enough, secure financially, and damn ready to marry the woman—the abortion option became an out for her. Not me. I wouldn't force any woman to labor nine months if she didn't want to, but when the baby is mine, it matters."

He leaned back against the car, breathing in the cold, raw air. She did not shiver as snowflakes spotted her bare shoulders.

"Once upon a time, when I lived for a few years in Japan, I loved a woman—or I thought I did." It was his turn to look away. "She went and had an abortion before she even told me she was pregnant. That was like having my heart cut out with a pair of scissors and no anesthetic. It still hurts." He met her eyes again. "She killed my child. And told me later. Six years ago! And it hurts as though it was yesterday."

"I don't want to hurt you," she spoke up, folding her arms across her chest. "Can you not see what situation I'm in?"

"You're going to be a mother, physically, emotionally, and socially. Your life has changed. My life has changed. But change can be good."

He tried to smile, then stepped toward her. This time she did not move. He laid his hands on her arms, caressing them.

"I know we may not exactly be compatible, but we should try. Take it as an invitation." He saw a fresh tear roll down her cheek. "I know this has been so backward, but we can start fresh. Can't we?"

He put his hand on her shoulder.

"You know about me, *já*?"

He nodded, trying not to show hesitation.

"And you still want me?"

"I want you." He blinked twice. "Can we start fresh?"

"*Já*, I think so." Standing against him, she took his hands in hers. "I don't love you, Eirík. I am not in love with you. You must understand this. I want to be honest. There is so much wrong with us."

"Okay, so we're not the typical couple."

"*Já*, so much is wrong with me. The best you can do is keep me from going crazy. What I need is a rock to be chained to."

"I'll be a rock." They stood apart. "And a life buoy, if that's what you need. We'll be co-dependents, huh?"

"We have a saying: *Við pössum saman eins níu og sex.* It means 'We fit together like nine and six'—back to back, *já*, fighting against the circle of our enemies. You and me, we stand together against the world."

"Let's not worry about what other people do," he said, staring into the depths of her eyes. "Or what they think of us. Okay, you don't love me—and I suppose, semantically, I cannot love you, at least not at this stage of our relationship—but I'm nevertheless infatuated. Maybe to where love is close. To make that final push, I'm willing to change. I'll be whatever you want me to be."

She grinned, and he thought she believed he was joking.

"*Þú ert skrítinn maður,*" she said, laughing. "You're a silly man."

"Then that's what I'll be for you: silly." He grinned. "So . . . an English professor, an Art student, and a baby go into a bar . . . ."

12

ÍRIS NOTICED HOW HE LOOKED AT HER MOUTH as she ate dinner: the way she chewed, the movement of her tongue, how she wet her lips. He could not take his eyes off her.

Já, he is perverse and old-fashioned romantic at the same time.

Once the meals were served, they ate in silence, interrupted only by the drifting thoughts of desperate conversation. He had to fill the silence with something, no matter how stupid. The topic of family came up. She put off telling him about hers, so he told her about his. Not much better.

When they went to the class, he was so turned on that his lecture was brilliant and very impassioned. *Othello* never had a chance.

"Given his single-minded pursuit of revenge, the character of Iago has often been called Machiavellian by critics," he declared like an actor on stage. "Iago is cynical, choked by his envy and grudges. He's so wedded to his unhallowed principles that he will gladly risk everything to maintain them. In the end, he loses everything because of them, including his very life. Nevertheless, Iago gleefully puts 'the end justifies the means' axiom to work in his bold divide-and-conquer stratagem."

Íris listened intently, scribbling notes on borrowed paper with a borrowed pen. The boy next to her was all too delighted when she asked. He couldn't take his eyes off her bare shoulders, thigh-high slit, and the cleavage showing in the V of her red dress.

"Iago's also been called a 'motiveless malignity' by Coleridge—which begs the question why he does what he does. Every action must have a motive, though it is common to attribute misbehavior to demonic possession—as in Shakespeare's day—or to mental illness—as we tend to do today. Betrayal is the end, in Iago's case, and paranoia is the cause of his will to betray. Why? Because Iago sees himself as a kind of unacknowledged Superman; that is, he thinks he's better than everyone else, and he wishes to take his proper place among the élite. It's almost as if Iago is trying to please Othello, who is a kind of father figure to him, while simultaneously believing he is superior to his surrogate 'father' and hating that situation. Iago wants this father figure to give him the praise he's due—"

He stopped and stared at the back wall as though he'd seen a ghost there. Thoughts of his own father, how they could never communicate with each other, flashed through his head. Shaking it off, he picked up the book and flipped to a page.

"And, as he says, in act two, scene one, Iago wants to, quote, 'Make the Moor thank me, love me and reward me./ For making him egregiously an ass.' And that, ladies and gentlemen, is the theme of our story."

Íris sleeps late, misses her class, because she wants to see if anyone notices. When she arrives before lunch, Cory is waiting outside her studio to tell her that the Student Art Council had a crucial meeting. He nominated her for president.

She laughs. "I will graduate in May."

In the atrium, she meets Sandra Kinney, who tells her she might have a commission lined up for her, a mural in a church—"If you don't mind setting foot inside." She will consider it, yet Sandra insists she must talk with them about what they would like painted.

Then Íris meets Ray, who at first is shy yet asks her if she plans to continue modeling for Life Study. He informs her that he's already spoken to another model.

Já, I have my figure to think about.

She acts as though she never thought of dropping the modeling. Ray is pleased, and lays his hand on her shoulder, just for a second.

"Come see me whenever you're free," says Ray, his eyes meeting hers a moment too long. "We have business to discuss. It's about your fall plans."

"My fall plans?"

She is missed. Yet, she knows she is missed only for what she can do for others. On a day spotted with the return of snowflakes, once again her life is folding in on her. What she can achieve is only what others allow her to achieve. She cannot get pregnant alone. She can paint alone yet no one will see it unless she keeps Ray happy. Friends are what she calls people who will give her the time of day, one out of seven thousand people—not people to whom she can tell her secrets.

Counselors are paid to keep secrets, so she doesn't mind opening the door and inviting them inside. *Já*, here are my foibles and random errors on the shelves to the left, she thinks. Here are my casual faults and indiscretions on the shelves to the right. Straight ahead, overflowing from the shelves there and forming that huge mess in the center of the floor, are all of my serious mistakes, the ones I saw coming and still welcomed, the ones I knew were mistakes yet did them anyway—such as taking my father's side against Heiðr. Such as going to the Back Room at Club Venus the second night. Such as coming to Kansas. Such as getting in Eirík's car that rainy night.

Já, choose any topic. I am an expert.

This Eirík is her teacher and when they are in class, it is easier for her. She only need sit there and listen. Otherwise, he is normal, like her, like any person with desires and fears.

They are so different now from that first night. He is different from the man who took her home that rainy night. Now he is taking charge, arranging for her to have a check-up from a real obstetrician. He also signed her up for pre-natal classes. When the nurse asks Íris about her husband, she doesn't understand at first. When the question is repeated and only then does Íris hear it correctly, the nurse waves her off, saying, "That's okay."

"*Já*, we are a sinful couple," she tells Sandra later. "Sex is sin, they say, so babies are born with sin. They call sex a sin, yet sin creates life. Sin creates jobs. Like counselors. Sex is natural and what's natural must be good, so sex is good. Good sex feels so pleasurable that we think it is about to hurt. When it does hurt, that's sin. Sex is neutral. It is people who make it good or bad."

Sandra Kinney doesn't believe her yet they have called a truce.

This Eirík takes her to a new doctor, a woman in an office near his apartment, to give her a thorough check which is required for the pre-natal classes. As they wait, she holds his arm tightly, afraid of what the doctor might find. When Íris is called back, she doesn't say a word. She speaks better without words, and she doesn't want him to fear anything.

It had been a long time since her last exam and she is uncomfortable having a woman doctor. Is she judging her? Wearing the gown makes her feel more naked than standing nude in Life Study. The nurse draws blood to test for sexual diseases.

"Results in a few days," says the nurse.

As she stands at the checkout station, she sees him watching her. He rises when she comes out. A stream of tears runs down her face. She is embarrassed, wipes them away. Everyone in the waiting room seems to know her sexual history. She hugs him, her face pressed against his shoulder, hiding from the world. After a moment, she gazes up at Eirík, a man she does not know, who does not know her.

"Well, what's the result?" he asks.

She doesn't smile.

He kisses her forehead and she feels the roomful of eyes on them.

He must think by her tears that the result is negative. For a few heartbeats she believes that is the result he wants. Then it will be a problem solved and they can return to normal lives, apart and alone, and forget each other.

Instead, she stretches up to his ear and slowly whispers: "August twenty-eighth."

13

ON MOVING DAY, ERIC ROSE EARLY, had breakfast, finished cleaning the apartment, and sat around waiting for ten o'clock to arrive. Then he drove over to the house, the one set among bare trees that had stood for a century and the snow-crusted yard. Íris was awake when he arrived at the appointed time but she was not ready to move. He gathered the boxes she had filled and carried them down to the car. When he returned, she was napping. He smiled, then searched her clothing rack and selected a few casual outfits to take down to the car.

When he returned to her room next, he sat on the floor beside the bed, patiently studying the face of the mysterious woman who was stepping into his life. Her hair seemed darker, almost copper, in the subdued light. He had strolled down the hair dye aisle at the Wal-Mart, examining the multitude of shades available, considering what her shade might be called. Hers was between Mango Morning and Sahara Sunrise, he decided. He liked how her hair framed her pale face, devoid of blemish—except for five carefully placed freckles across her nose. Her lips, pouty when she exhaled in her slumber, were ripe without lipstick. He had felt her lips dozens of times in previous days and they felt so . . . *welcoming* was the first word that came to mind.

He recalled that perfect kiss they had shared, when their very atoms had merged and they could not clearly define where one person ended and the other began, releasing the supernova of pheromones—

He broke from his trance and licked his lips, then gazed patiently at her placid face until she awoke thirty minutes later.

"Good morning, Beautiful," he whispered.

She seemed confused as she awoke and he almost expected her to ask who he was. She stretched and yawned, glanced at her watch, and extended her arms to call him into her embrace.

"Is it time?" she asked, repressing a yawn.

"Yes," he replied. "Let the family begin."

"I suppose we should get to know each other," she said, standing.

She dressed as usual in skirt and sweater and went with him over to his apartment.

"It looks so different," said Íris, studying the place as he set the last boxes down. "I think you changed something here."

"I moved a few things out of the way," he admitted, "and threw away other things, all to make room for you."

"*Já*, I am so big."

"That's okay. I want you to be big."

He went to her, posing there beside the dent in the wall, and leaned in for a kiss but she stepped away.

She looked into the bathroom where he had scrubbed away every stain, installed a new shower curtain, and set a short vase of silk flowers on the commode. She tugged the blanket on the bed back and saw the flower-print sheets he had put there. The two pillows were new also, fluffier than before. The ugly, old lounge chair had been removed and a cozy new loveseat took its place. On each side were end tables: one with a reading lamp, the other with the TV remote atop a large book. She moved the remote to look at the book: photography of Iceland.

He noticed her apparent disinterest at seeing her homeland.

She's still sleepy. Or maybe she's really Canadian by now.

The stereo system had been set in a black lacquered cabinet beside the television. The oval dining table that had only one chair previously now had two and they matched. A flower basket centerpiece brightened the room and when he pulled the curtains open, they were greeted with the snow-streaked balcony and a view of the snowy yard outside. Nodding her approval, she checked the refrigerator and found a whole salmon fillet waiting to be grilled.

"This will do," said Íris, and promptly pulled her sweater off over her head.

His eyes went to her breasts. "You're so beautiful. As always, Íris."

"*Já*, I am always Íris."

She stared briefly at him, almost an angry look, then went to the computer desk.

"I don't believe in beauty. We are how we are. I hate when people tell me that. What does it mean? What do they want?"

Her hand moved the mouse and the screen came to life. Over her shoulder, he saw the monitor's image: a picture of Gullfoss—'Golden Falls'—a wide, two-tiered watercourse cutting through the barren plateau in southwest Iceland. She regarded it.

"This is Beauty."

"Do you like it?" Eric smiled. "I thought it would make you feel more at home, seeing sites like these. Watch: the picture changes every few minutes. I've set it up with seven pictures. I'd like to add one of you, if I may."

"*Já*, someday." She sighed, sounding exhausted from the busy week.

"You don't have any pictures of yourself?"

"*Nei*. I never take pictures. Other people take the pictures. There may be some on the Internet. If you look hard." She turned to him. "You said I could use your computer? To go to my EXCITE community?"

"Of course. Anytime. Help yourself."

She pulled out the chair, slipped off her skirt, laid it across the back of the chair, and sat nude at the desk.

"Make yourself at home," said Eric, caressing her with his eyes. *My home is already more comfortable just having her here. Maybe I should leave before I ruin it, or say something stupid.* There was a precarious balance in play now.

He excused himself, began preparing dinner now that the afternoon was waning. She was going straight to work at the computer, he understood by the clicks on the keyboard.

"Where are the bookmarks you used to have?" Íris called after several minutes.

"I deleted most of them," he called back from the kitchen alcove. "I don't need them anymore. New life, new lifestyle, right?"

"You deleted the links to the sexy sites?" she persisted.

Clickety clickety click.

"What sexy sites?" he called back. He had to think. Why was she asking? He had stripped everything even remotely questionable from his computer—as Jack suggested.

"The pornography sites."

"I never had any porn sites bookmarked." He hoped that would be a sufficient answer. "I mean, I don't consider what I had to be porn. They were innocent nudity. Just female beauty—like you."

"Are you starting to lie to me, Eirík?"

"So I'm a dirty old man. Most men are after turning forty."

She could see through him from the other side of the apartment.

"I removed incriminating evidence, that's all." Eric bit his lip. Jack had warned him about a search. He never expected the search might come from Íris. "Did you want those bookmarks?"

More clicking.

"You want to see pictures of me, *já*?"

He waited. Enough time to click a few times and find a site, he calculated. What was she looking for? Intimations of immorality?

Concerned, he stepped around from the kitchen to where the computer was.

"Here I am," she said, and casually moved out of the way.

He looked—then looked away.

Sandra Kinney shows up at her studio and they drive over to the Baptist church. At every stoplight, Sandra glances at Íris's belly.

"Plenty of Christian girls get pregnant before marriage," says Íris.

"Too many, yes."

Sandra turns into the parking lot.

"I don't mean to stare, Iris. I was just wondering what it feels like. I've never known anyone who . . . ."

"Sins?"

Sandra blushes. "I wasn't going to say that, Iris. How *does* it feel being pregnant? Isn't it a little bit creepy? Having something alive inside you? My sister—"

"It doesn't feel like anything, *já*." She wonders if Sandra has ever had sex. "And when you introduce me, remember to say *Íris*."

Inside the church, it is quiet, like death, and the building smells cool and moldy. It should be freshly scrubbed with a vile disinfectant. After all, Íris the witch, the unwed *móðir*, the artist and nudist, is setting foot inside.

"My God . . . ," Sandra says, examining the wall.

"Goddess," Íris counters.

Whatever was on the wall before has been torn away, leaving the plaster in shreds and a layer of powdery residue on the floor.

"It will be cleaned up by the time you're ready to paint," a man explains.

He comes over to them and Íris sees he is the minister, white collar adorning his black suit, his thin hair smartly combed, and a smile that doesn't hide anything.

"Reverend Meeks," says Sandra, "this is Íris. She's in the Art department, too. She's from Iceland, but she speaks English very well."

"I lived in Toronto, Canada for seven years," Íris adds.

The minister extends his hand and she shakes it.

Sandra gives the minister her colleague's credentials, including a better-than-expected personal assessment of her ability to paint the mural: "She's very good with fantasy."

"Fantasy?" the minister questions, obviously considering how serious this pagan painter would be about her work. "What do you mean by fantasy?"

"I painted scenes from Norse mythology, and what some people call science-fiction, and from my head." That sounds like a good answer to her. She cannot say they are from her dreams; people would think she was crazy. "I like those because I can paint them my way."

"Can you paint a mural of heaven?"

"I don't know," says Íris. "I have never been there."

Reverend Meeks chuckles, seems guilty about letting go. "Then you'll have to use your imagination."

"You can paint a series of clouds with . . . ," Sandra suggests.

"She'll do fine, I'm sure," the reverend says, "if you've recommended her."

Sandra seems on edge, wondering how many ways Íris will embarrass her.

"Don't worry, Sandra." Íris touches her shoulder. "I know about the Christian heaven. My mother's a Lutheran."

Sandra relaxes.

The Christians drift away and Íris studies the wall, measuring twelve meters wide by four meters high, with double doors at its center leading into the auditorium. Sandra calls it a sanctuary.

"She needs the work," she hears Sandra tell the minister. "She's going to have a baby."

"Oh, that's wonderful," the reverend cheers.

"She's not married."

"Oh . . . ." He sighs, not knowing what to say.

Íris wants to tell the minister that, although she is not married, she is loved.

They say goodbye and instead of returning Íris to the campus, Sandra drops her off at the house. Íris invites her to come up, as a gesture of goodwill. She is afraid.

"Please come up, Sandra," she says. "Let's have some hot tea to warm us. We can talk." Sandra seems nervous. A little more is needed, so Íris says: "Tell me about Jesus."

Eric enjoyed hearing about her week each Friday evening as they dined out. Especially intriguing for him was the way she explained in excruciating detail the mindset, hidden agendas, and twisted world views of everyone she encountered on and off campus—like the characters in *Othello*. He frequently laughed when she described Erin at the mall, or Celia the apprentice witch, or gay Cory, or politically correct Jean, or the evangelist Sandra Kinney. Sometimes she tried to imitate how they spoke and he would laugh. Weekends together was great.

It would be cheaper to live together, however, he kept telling her.

"I'm not here to take your money," Íris said sternly.

He went soft.

"We are in this fix together . . . because we are trying to be a family."

"I know, I know."

He rolled off her, breathing heavily.

"Compatibility is one thing," she said, "yet finance is another."

He knew she was right, but this was not the discussion he wanted.

"When you give me money, I feel like I must do something for you," said Íris. "I don't expect—you don't expect—anything and you don't plan to insist, yet that's the feeling I have. Blame this society, if you are looking for who is at fault. This whole patriarchal monotheistic culture of Western Europe is to blame. A man cannot give a woman the time of day without her feeling as though she must give something back."

She pulled her breast away from his playful attentions.

"It's *my* breast, not yours."

"But I want to play with it—"

"Now you want me to quit my job so I become more dependent on you?"

"That's not what I meant."

Resigned to a discussion, he sat up on the bed and faced her.

"I'm trying to write this novel," he said, "the one you inspired me to write—and all I want is enough free time to finish it. I don't want to teach composition classes, grade papers, go to committee meetings *ad nauseum* and counsel students. I just want to write this thing. Like any artist. What I want most is *time*, time to create. Isn't that what you want as a painter?"

"I am already painting the mural in that church." She cleared her throat. "That is not what I want to paint, *já*, yet they are paying me to paint what they want painted."

"That's the ol' prostitution argument." He sighed. "Artists are forced to create what their patrons want rather than what the artists want to produce. You create for someone else and that buys you time for what you want to create. You need a wealthy patron, Íris. Unfortunately, you hooked up with an English teacher. I'll never be the wealthy patron you deserve, but we can get by." He gently rubbed her belly, expecting her to remove his hand. "I can still offer you time to paint."

She laid her hand over his, lightly but somehow dangerous.

"There are only twenty-four hours in a day." Her voice sounded tired. "I go to classes, teach Ray's classes sometimes, pose for Life Study, and *always* study for Shakespeare, eat a meal or two, and fuck you every night and some mornings. I also have two jobs. When do I have time to paint?"

"I only suggested you quit the job at the mall because I *want* you to have time to be the artist you want to be. The job on campus you have to do—for your scholarship, right? One night a week minding the open studio. It doesn't pay much, but it does waive your tuition. Íris, I'm only thinking of you. That's not being selfish. I want you to paint. I want you to be happy."

"If you give me the same money the shop pays me," she said, "then we return to the original problem: obligation."

"When's your birthday?" he asked, sliding his hand down her until his fingers raked her orange patch. "Let me give you a gift. So you won't have to work at that store. Then you can paint. I want to see you paint. I enjoy seeing you paint, my dear. Isn't that what love is? Never having to say you owe me?"

"*Ástarsaga*," she mumbled dreamily. "You love these love stories!"

The way she said *love* sent a rush through him.

"You should quit your job," said Íris, "so you can finish your novel."

"Now you're being ridiculous."

"I want to support you, Eirík. *Já*, you must be free to write the novel of your dreams and be a success. So I will go out and fuck many men to bring money home."

She turned onto her back, stretching languorously as his fingers made a difference. She breathed deeply. His fingers moved with more conviction.

"Okay, okay," he said.

She placed her hand over his, showing him where she wanted it.

"Two artists can never both be successful financially," he continued. "One person always has to have the steady job. Winner of the bread. Or, at least, they have to alternate. When one becomes a success, the other can—"

"Stop talking, Eirík."

14

ÍRIS NOW KNOWS THERE ARE CERTAIN THINGS she should not tell him. Or show him. He is not ready for all of that.

Look what has happened, she thinks. She has become the object of his desire. He thinks she belongs to him, now that he has tricked her into this partnership. She has seen it before with women friends: men have to mark their territory. Men think they brand women with the tattoo of pregnancy. Now she is branded. She belongs to this Eirík.

It is fate, *já*, yet not his fate.

Íris stands and stretches after sitting in that small desk for an hour.

"Remember, ladies and gentlemen," the professor calls out as they get up for the break, "I'll expect your late *Othello* papers by Monday morning. That way those of you who really do have to work can have the weekend to write."

"Professor Schaeffer," calls Vince from the front row. "What I don't get is, if Othello's so smart he's the general of the whole Venetian army, then how come he gets duped by Iago so easy?"

The professor releases a frustrated sigh, catching a sympathetic grimace from Íris as she slips out the door. Walking down the hallway, she hears: "Because, as a general, Othello's concerned with the big picture. He passes details to his lieutenants. He can't see the forest for the trees . . . ."

Outside, a fresh dusting of snow makes the night luminous. Íris breathes in its radiance, the calm of snow, the sweetness of night. Then yesterday intrudes.

Ray Ferguson's office is a war zone but the original configuration can be detected: mahogany desk set before a wall lined with trophy shelves and bookcases. In the corners, and in every spare nook, are pieces of student art, paintings stacked up, sculptures jammed together, as though the room is more a warehouse of seconds and flawed artifacts.

He spun in his chair to face Íris as she entered, demure and passive in the ragged robe she puts on after posing in Life Study.

"Come in, have a seat, sit down," he said, waving.

He was on the phone as she sat in the chair across the desk from him. He wore his usual rumpled suit and wrinkled necktie, the necktie loosened and his white shirt collar open. His art school days are long behind him so he tries to be an administrator, an art critic, a showman and promoter of others' art. They appreciate his efforts. Without him, many of them would not be artists. They would have been crushed by their first or second or third rejection and changed majors. Except Íris. Art is all she has and Ray knows it.

"Someone wants to buy one of your paintings," he informed her, hanging up the phone. "Anonymous caller. Saw a piece at the student art fair last December but didn't have money. Now he or she wants to know if it's still available."

"Which one?"

"I forget the name. The one with the woman's head on some roses."

"It is called *Roses*," she said, surprised. After Halloween, she took it off the wall of the student gallery so everyone would think she had sold at least one painting. Was it at the citywide art fair in December? She cannot remember exactly. "Who is this art lover?"

"Elaine called me, so I don't know. If you've still got it, bring it in and we'll make the deal. No time to lose."

"How much do you think it's worth?"

"Worth? It's worth what anyone's willing to pay."

"*Já*, art as commodity, not as art."

"Anything that has a frame around it is worth two-hundred dollars, plus the cost of the frame. This is not some starving artist sale, not this time."

"Could I ask five hundred?"

"Ask? Elaine already made the deal. Six hundred twenty."

He stared at her face, to see if she accepted the offer.

How could Elaine make a deal on her behalf? Of course, it is a better price than Íris would have gotten, higher than she would dare ask, so she says nothing.

"Elaine thought that was a fair price," said Ray, "especially since the buyer is willing to let it hang in the gallery here on campus. Isn't that wonderful?"

Wonderful? Her first high-price art sale is engineered by one of the art faculty to some anonymous donor who doesn't want to take it home. So suspicious. She narrows her eyes at Ray. Is he the anonymous buyer? Would he throw six hundred dollars at her because she let him seduce her one evening in a Jacuzzi?

"Yes, it's wonderful."

"As soon as the painting is in the gallery office, they can cut you a check. The price minus the gallery's administrative fee, so you should net about five hundred almost forty. I can't do math anymore."

"It's in my studio downstairs. I can get it right now."

"Tomorrow's soon enough." He grinned, then winked at her. "What I really wanted to talk to you about is your plans for the fall. I know you're about ready to graduate—anxious to graduate, I suppose is the better term, right?"

"*Já*, ready, yet I am only taking three classes this semester."

"Oh . . . ?"

"Studio, the graphic design class, and the Shakespeare class."

"Shakespeare? What the hell for?"

"It is my elective. My second subject at Toronto was English."

"Riiiight. So what does this mean? You won't graduate in May?"

"I would like to stretch it out until summer. I can graduate in

August."

Já, that will be perfect, she thinks. When her graduation moment comes, she will be walking across the stage and go into labor. She will give birth there among the caps and gowns.

She smiled at Ray. "I don't know. Perhaps I am not ready to graduate. I have no plans after graduation, just continue painting. Sandra got me a commission."

"I heard. That's why I asked you to stop by."

Ray sat back, steepling his fingers on the desktop, enjoying the dramatic pause.

"Iris, how would you like to teach here in the fall? And the spring, and summer, and the following year?"

He grinned, as wide as the whole campus.

"There will be an opening in the department for an instructor. It's only an instructor position but it would be full-time, with benefits, and you'd have an office. You'd have your evenings free. No more Open Studio. No more frame shop, hmm? And you'd be able to keep painting."

"I don't know anything about teaching."

"You've substituted in Life Study and my studio classes. You know what to do. Give advice. Tell students what they're doing wrong, how to fix it. Offer a critique. Encourage them. Or *dis*courage them from staying in the program. Had to give the bad news to a kid this morning, You know him. Arty Loomis? The Nazi porn? He took it well. Flipped me off."

"I really don't like working with people, especially if they want my advice. What works for me doesn't work for others." She felt a rumble in her belly and wondered if it was possible for the baby to be kicking so soon. "I have some problems to work on. Teaching would be . . . . I don't want my problems to rub on the students."

"They won't, believe me. I've heard a lot of praise from students. They like your attitude, your straightforward advice. They think you're pretty cool."

She thought he was making up the lie. Students never talk to her. They are afraid of her. Alternatively, they lust for her. She makes boys nervous. Perhaps that is what it takes to be a good teacher. Eirík is funny and relaxed, and students respond to him. Yet she has no humor.

"How can I be the teacher when I am a figure model? They stare at me now as though they can see through my dress."

"I'll give you only freshman classes. Incoming students won't know you. Nobody cares whether you've posed nude or not. Oh—by the way, are you still going to model this term? The advanced class is almost ready for you. I've already lined up someone for the fall. She's been filling in this month."

"Is she this semester's girl?"

She stared at him and he closed his eyes a moment.

"Iris, I apologize. I get a little wine in me and I talk like an idiot. Besides, I'm a man and you're a very attractive woman who happens to have no inhibitions about getting naked in a hot tub. Even with a silly old professor. I hope you didn't think I was pushing you into anything. I was only responding to—to what I thought was your invitation."

She held up her hand to stop him but he kept talking.

"I'm pregnant."

That stopped him. His mouth dropped. "But . . . how . . . ?"

"The usual way, *já.*"

He slumped in his chair, shaking his head.

"I'll have to leave Julie . . . ."

"You're not the father," she whispered, losing her voice.

"Oh." Ray seemed disappointed. "Right. I pulled out."

He began pacing the room.

"I only tell you because I will get fat. Do you want a fat model?"

He seemed to concentrate on the idea, a fantasy come true.

"A pregnant model?" He came out of his trance. "That might be an interesting exercise for the students. We've had all kinds of models, all sizes and shapes, male and female, but never one with the unique dimensions of a pregnant . . . uh . . . ." His eyes were on her belly.

"Woman?"

He grinned, embarrassed.

She watched him thinking, seeing it on his face. Perhaps there were other near-misses for him.

"Who is it then?" he asked. "Wait. Not my business. I apologize."

"Don't worry."

Já, he must think he is the only man I ever—

"Then it's settled. You continue to model for Life Study. Call me when you're showing. Are you showing yet? I didn't really see if you—I mean, when you came in, I couldn't tell."

"It usually takes nine months." She was playing with him. "The end of August."

"August?" He was alarmed. "That'll wipe out the whole fall term."

"I can be ready to teach. I can feed my baby in my new office."

"We need to get the contract ready and signed before July first."

"How long is maternity leave?"

"It's . . . . I don't know. You could take it at the start of your contract, I suppose. I'll have to check. If there's going to be a baby, the medical insurance would be a good thing to have." He looked up, as though he had decided everything for her. "Wow! This is such fantastic news, Iris. I am filled with gladness for you."

He reached out to hug her—she thought it was a hug—but the desk was between them and they barely met. He fell on his chest across the desktop when she stepped back. Scrambling to his feet, he came around the side and tried again. So awkward, she thought, this crazy *bjáni*—

There is laughter coming from the classroom as she returns five minutes late.

". . . decided we are going to pass on *Cymbeline*," the professor says, glancing at her as she sneaks in. "I thought it would be good because we could compare it to a spoof written by our writer-in-residence, Lance Albright. But, in my reading of both, I've determined that—well, quite frankly, they both suck."

The class roars with laughter, hearing the staunch academician speaking slang.

"I mean, come on: we don't really care whether Imogen is faithful to Posthumus or not. That's been done a million times. The real story in *Cymbeline*, as far as I'm concerned—which Shakespeare fails to promote—is the anguish of the king when his etiquette blunder brings on the invasion by Roman legions. He has to think of all the pillaging, the raping, the destruction that will follow. That's left for the audience to contemplate. We know what's going to happen next. But William wrote it as a romantic comedy."

"Go figure," laughs Vince in the front row.

"Indeed," the professor agrees.

15

POOR JACK, THOUGHT ERIC AFTER HEARING what two former students—attractive females, no less—had to say about their professor.

Kari Laughlin claimed that Dr. Macintosh had told her about the policy to keep office doors open when students had conferences, then promptly closed the door. "With this kind of sinister laugh," she added. Annette Collier stated that, while walking across campus, she heard someone whistle at her and when she turned, there was "Dr. Mac" walking behind her, grinning "like some crazed wolf." Bridget Do stood up to confirm that, one time after class, he asked her whether she was dating any *other* Vietnamese, and began complimenting her figure— "He said I was bigger, ya know, up top, than Asian women were, like, supposed to be."—and continued his remarks even after she said his compliments made her feel uncomfortable. Six others had similar statements. Even Belle Phillips, the English department secretary, was asked to repeat what she had once remarked to Olivia Jones: Whenever Jack stopped in the office to pick up his mail, he always paused to run his eyes up her legs to her bosom, "like he was undressing me."

Eric had no idea that Jack's reputation was so politically incorrect.

No one was standing up for him, a man who, though personable and an accomplished academic, was nevertheless . . . an idiot.

The hearing was held in one of the luxurious sanctuaries where the usual campus food service was banned and the flower-printed walls held portraits of past presidents, smiling stoically within their frames like saints on parade. Potted ferns were set in the corners and extra chairs had been brought in to accommodate the many witnesses. It was dark, the curtains protecting the room from the slant of morning sun, and the navy blue carpet and smooth, burnished table further darkened the proceedings.

Eric had been there from the start, but only barely. He rushed in that Saturday morning just as Dr. Liz called the hearing to order, and his harried arrival and subsequent heavy breathing caused her to start over.

"I'd like to call upon Mister Eric Schaeffer," Dr. Liz said from her seat at the head of the conference table.

Mister? Not Professor? Eric flicked a flake of dirt from his sneakers and uncrossed his blue-jeaned legs. He stood, stretching, trying not to meet the eyes of those who had already spoken yet were sticking around to see the hearing through to its end. He stepped forward and sat down in the chair positioned in front of the table, like . . . *like the business end of an Inquisition.*

"Mister Schaeffer," Dr. Liz spoke, "please tell the committee exactly what you told me in my office at the end of the last semester regarding your conversations with Doctor Macintosh."

Eric cleared his throat. The cold soda he had downed as he raced to campus was a much needed supply of caffeine rather than a thirst quencher. It had left a deposit of sugar in his mouth. He coughed, hacked, loosened some of it and swallowed loudly.

"Last semester . . . ," Eric began then paused. The carbonation was working its way through his gut. "Sorry, everyone. Let me apologize for the way I'm dressed and for being late. I completely forgot about this hearing until this morning—and I thought I set the alarm correctly but apparently, I didn't. I grabbed whatever clothes were available and—"

"Noted, Mister Schaeffer," Dr. Liz said, impatiently. "Proceed."

"As I recall, you asked me to come over to your office, where you then began asking me general questions about Doctor Macintosh's, umm, behavior in regard to a certain—"

"Mister Schaeffer, you don't have to speak academic-ese here," said Dr. Liz. "Repeat your answers to my questions in our meeting last semester. I asked you what Doctor Macintosh told you about his relationship with Miss Valery."

"Yes, of course." Eric cleared his throat again, stalling.

What was there to be afraid of? He regarded Dr. Frasier from Anthropology, who was writing on a yellow legal pad. Eric glanced at the History professor, Leonard Jansen, who looked bored with it all. Harriet Glover of Women's Studies, however, was busy sharpening her claws. Eric was helping them hang Jack, a man who had done nothing to him. Other than annoy. But what was worse, he thought, was that he, Eric Schaeffer, was doing exactly the same thing.

He coughed. "Jack told me . . . uh, more than once . . . told me about his, umm, relationship with . . . that woman he was seeing—"

"Did he say her name?" Dr. Liz probed.

"Not at first. Only when she filed the complaint against him. That's when he began to divulge the details—"

"Divulge?" asked Dr. Liz.

"Talk," Eric asserted. *Word choice can kill.* "He never 'divulged.' He always said—*told* me. After the complaint was filed, he told me about that. The complaint, I mean."

"Go on."

"He said—Doctor Macintosh said—that she, I mean the woman complaining, said that—"

"Stop." It was Dr. Frasier, waving his hand in the air. "We are sorry to have to put you through this required function. Just tell us in your own words what Doctor Macintosh told you about his relationship with the woman."

"I'm trying to!" Eric did not intend the outburst; his own situation was weighing on his mind. "Let me start over. One day Jack started telling me about a lady he had been dating—although he phrased it more like 'sleeping' with her. He met her off-campus and, well, she was not a student at Fairmont at that time. I don't know. Maybe she only said she wasn't. My thought, not his. Then, once the relationship turned sour, she—according to Jack—she enrolled in his class. He said he thought she did it just to taunt him."

Eric wanted to share his personal views on the matter but that was out of the question, no matter how the extenuating circumstances were screaming for acquittal. Anything that might benefit Jack's position might also, someday, perhaps benefit his own. The campus was full of mines and any male faculty member was likely to step on one in any given semester. He had yet to be called to account. Suppose they found his story about vegetarian Viki and carnivore Gwen, and their lesbian affair? His erotic poems about Íris? Evidence. At least his computer had been sanitized.

He glared at Dr. Liz.

"Yes . . . ?" Dr. Frasier was prompting him. What was the question?

"Sorry. Was I rambling?" Eric swallowed hard.

"You weren't saying anything," said Dr. Frasier.

"One thing I do remember you emphasizing," said Dr. Liz, leaning forward, "was that you seemed to feel that Doctor Macintosh's rather colorful 'rhetoric,' as you called it, about his various relationships was nothing more than a case of hyperbole. Is that how you recall it?"

"Yes, I thought he was full of *sh*—of himself." Eric straightened up. "I'm new here. I didn't see any point in telling a senior colleague I wasn't interested in hearing his ribald tales of conquest. So I tried to ignore him—as best I could; that is, without telling him flat out to leave me alone. Sorry, Jack, but it's true. Besides, he talked about a lot of things, not only the dating stories. I seldom listened closely to what he was saying. Even then, I figured he was just boasting. Like high school boys. You know, a ten-minute make-out session becomes transformed into an episode of sexual intercourse when the kid tells his buddies later. Boys boast and girls try to live it down . . . or expose the truth." He paused, contemplating his words. "Sure, men have always tried raising their status by inflating their reputations, exaggerating their success, while women maintain their reputation by denying they gave in to seduction. One tries to conquer, the other must defend."

"Interesting point," said Dr. Frasier, and made a note on the pad. "In short, then, you're inclined to believe your colleague's stories of sexual conquest were, as you say, exaggerations?"

"I suppose so, but what I mean is—"

"Thank you, Mister Schaeffer," Dr. Liz cut in. "We'll call you again should we have further questions."

"May I answer Doctor Frasier's question?"

Dr. Liz nodded, shooting daggers at Dr. Frasier.

"I wanted to add . . . ." Eric glanced around the table. "Frankly, ladies and gentlemen, I'm afraid for any faculty member who comes here unmarried. We're set up to be celibates. And yet wisemen—wise women, wise people, whatever. Teachers are still tempted. There's no other way to describe it. Put young, attractive people with bored or lonely, older people perhaps trying to recapture or hang on to their youth, and each of them sharing . . . well, let's call it 'intellectual stimulation'—thinking is such an intimate act, after all—and from focused on-task conversations and debates comes unchecked feelings and emotions. How do we handle that? Each of us, teacher and student—and I'm referring to college students, most of whom are of legal age—is, well . . . ."

He leveled his eyes at Dr. Liz. She looked down at her notes.

"We are just as human as everyone else. The only difference is that to do our jobs we must be objective and censor ourselves. We must deny our feelings, deny our humanity, our very biology, lest we succumb to the same temptations that are normal and permitted for the rest of the population. However, is it wrong to deny ourselves what everybody else is allowed? Are we not also allowed to fall in love? Where else do we meet eligible partners? Are we limited to our academic colleagues, or is that also forbidden fruit? How about our students? I'll concede the obvious conflict of student and teacher being in the same class. But aside from the questioning stares of strangers, aside from the potential age difference, what is the problem? Are we to be denied the right to love, to find happiness, to achieve fulfillment? We're not allowed to have personal lives. It's in our contracts.

"Take me for example—or, rather, a hypothetical person named, umm, *Gatsby*. He's in middle age, mid-career. He goes to his classes for years, works diligently if not always with enthusiasm, and he keeps his nose clean. One day he sees before him in the front row of his class the woman who, he feels, will become the love of his life. She's attractive, yes, but also studious, intelligent. In the end, he awards her an A for the course. She leaves the course, having actually learned something. And this Professor Gatsby, seeing this final opportunity slipping away as the semester ends, gets up the courage to address her—now that they are no longer student and teacher. When they're alone for a moment—yet in a well-lit public place—he nervously tells her that he's fallen in love with her, that they should go out sometime, on a date, or do some interesting activity by which they may get to know each other better, to give compatibility a chance. And he knows—because over the years his heart has become so acute in these matters—that she may very well feel the same way. He won't know unless he dares to ask her. And yet, instead of the joyfully anticipated answer to a simple, honest question uttered in perfect innocence, she coldly informs him that she will now file a sexual harassment charge against him. Because his impassioned proposition has made *her* feel uncomfortable. How *he* feels has no standing in a court."

He scanned the panel of judges.

"So we see how easy it is to completely ruin someone, and for what? For daring to think that he is entitled to a bit of the happiness he sees everyone around him enjoying. What choice does that leave him? Suffer in silence? To be satisfied with celibacy? Loneliness? Death is easy compared to living this way. Therefore, the next best thing he can do is to pretend: to imagine and to maintain such imagination until it becomes real. Or real enough. But it never does. It never does."

16

ROSES IS STILL WRAPPED IN BLACK CLOTH, hiding behind two newer paintings, taking up space. Perhaps she had wanted to forget it, yet why that one and not *Angel of Death* or one of the others? This is one way to get rid of it. For six hundred dollars, she can send it away. She wants to forget it—as she wants to forget so many things about Toronto.

There's a woman, asleep on a clutch of red roses, and the thorns have cut her face. Yet she doesn't feel any pain. *Já*, like the years she danced in the club, stripped, sat on laps, then advanced to the Back Room where she performed on a different kind of stage. Then she went one day to substitute for Beth, her Wicca sister, in an art class at the university, walking nude to the center of the room and waiting on the platform for the class to begin, not knowing what to do—not until Professor Hirsch arrived in a whirlwind of energy. He took pity on her, taught her to model, then to paint, and she quit the club and became a full-time art student. Also his lover. Until he died. She remained numb to the world, knowing she should feel pain yet not feeling anything. Like that woman in the painting. *Stupid woman! Wake up! Feel your pain!*

She must get the painting out of her life. The sooner she gives it to Ray, the sooner the art department gives her a check.

"Hi, Iris!"

She sees Sandra Kinney. Today she is dressed for church and has brought a young man in jacket and tie as an escort. They are both well-scrubbed and bear sinister smiles.

"This is Dylan," says Sandra, and Íris nods. "He's sort of, well, my boyfriend."

Sandra seems embarrassed to admit to a relationship with a mere mortal.

"*Halló*," Íris mutters, impatient.

"They really like what you've done so far on the mural," says Sandra. "I know they'll be quite pleased with it. If you're going to work on it today, we could give you a lift. Isn't this your usual time? You shouldn't be riding a bike, not in your condition."

"*Já*, I am late." She grins at them. "Ray's got a buyer for this painting. I need to get it up to him right now."

"Oh, that's fantastic!" She is more excited than Íris. "The Lord has truly blessed you."

Dylan steps forward, apparently on cue: "Since you've chosen to turn away from witchcraft, the Lord is starting to bless you. It's so obvious your good fortune is the result of God's favor. He loves you and He wants you to be . . . ."

The boy seems to lose his nerve as Íris glares at him.

"It's true, Iris," says Sandra to save him.

"I didn't turn away from witchcraft," says Íris. "I stopped all that because the priestess is a bitch. She likes to whip members who don't follow her rules."

"That's terrible," says Sandra.

"Sandra's told me so much about you, I feel I know you pretty well already," says the boy. "The way the Lord worked through Sandra to arrange the mural job for you, just when you needed a job, is truly a miracle. It's a sign that things have turned around for you."

"She told them I'm a good painter. They believed her, that's all. God's not involved."

"God is involved in everything," says the boy.

"Iris, don't be so quick to deny His blessings," says Sandra. "This is not the time to be looking back over your shoulder. The whole wide world awaits you, once you are born again." Sandra is glowing. "Do you know what that means? Being born again? Now is a good time to dedicate your life to Jesus Christ. He's waiting to welcome you into His loving arms. You *have* been blessed."

"*Já*, that is so nice." Íris wonders if Sandra is referring to her sudden demand as an artist or for the spark of life deep within her gut. "I have to go upstairs."

"We can wait. You won't be long, will you?"

"I must go."

Íris pushes through them, painting firm in her hands.

She arrives on the third floor and returns to Ray's office. He is gone but the door is open so she goes in and sits down in the chair in front of his desk, setting the painting to the side. She stares at the photograph on the desk of Ray standing with Professor Hirsch, both wearing berets.

"Yes, I know the father," she practices answering Ray's question. "*Já*, I'm living with him. Part of the week. He wants to make a family. He wants to marry me. How do I feel about that? I don't know. He is easy to live with, the way we have it arranged, and yet—"

"Yet what?" asks Ray, returning.

"I was just thinking." She holds up the painting, positioning it in her lap so he can view it all at once. "Here it is: *Roses*. Isn't it everything you hate about clichés?"

"No, the myth behind it is very Arthurian. You've managed to capture it wonderfully."

He takes it from her hands and examines it closer.

"It is nice. Very nice. It should make the buyer very happy." He seems much too in love with it to be accepting it for some anonymous art lover. She can tell that he is the one who wants to hang it on a wall— but a wall in the Ulrich Gallery. Can't have that one in his house.

"Yes, very nice," Ray mumbles, gazing slyly over the top of the frame at Íris.

She notices then that her nipples are pushing out her white t-shirt so she crosses her arms over her chest.

He winks, makes weird clicking sounds with his mouth. The same annoying gesture he used when he wanted to fuck. He sets the painting down, staring at her. "Why don't you close the door."

"Thank you for coming so promptly, Mister Schaeffer," said Dr. Liz, sitting down behind her desk. "It seems unfortunate timing," she began —then paused, perhaps choosing her words or simply wanting him to squirm, before continuing—"that I should be speaking to you today about this matter, especially given your highly principled contribution to Doctor Macintosh's defense."

"Matter?" Eric thought he was in her good graces finally.

"Yes, a complaint. From a *student*, a *female* student, in one of *your* classes." Her voice seemed to echo ominously, punctuating each word. "This woman has complained about the plethora of sexual innuendoes that seem to be running rampant in your class. They make her feel very uncomfortable and she—"

"Are you sure you have the right instructor?"

He watched Dr. Liz's eyebrows pinch until they met. He was always careful to cut out the dirty jokes—not conducting a class the way Jack reportedly had done. Was this meeting a joke?

She looked down at the papers, read the instructor's name and the course number.

"That's my Shakespeare class." The mystery darkened. A woman in Shakespeare was complaining about remarks of a sexual nature? The only one who fit that description was Íris, the Icelandic witch. Was this Jack's revenge coming full circle?

"Indeed, it is," Dr. Liz said.

"There's nothing going on in there that's improper. Ask anyone."

"I don't need to. *Anyone* has already told me. Would you like to hear a quote?"

"A quote?" Eric was confused. "At least it proves she's taking notes, huh?"

The department chair did not share his humor.

"Your unit on *Othello* seems to have brought about the worst instances for this young woman. Racist remarks in your lecture on *The Merchant of Venice*, too. This student is Jewish. However, your remarks about chastity and, shall we say, sexual experience were much more offensive—"

"But it's Shakespeare!"

Dr. Liz had a degree in English; she had to have at least read some of the more popular plays. She should simply dismiss this as a frivolous charge of a disgruntled student. *A Jewish student.* Not Íris.

"Shakespeare is known for his sexual innuendoes, double entendres, puns and other phrases that play on sexual references. We just finished studying *Othello*. The 'old black ram' joke? The 'beast with two backs'? Those are some of Shakespeare's most famous lines. All of his plays have these kinds of sexual jokes in them."

"I'm aware of that."

He regarded Dr. Liz, who was clearly content to let him rant on; she knew the verdict.

"I wrote a paper about them in grad school," Eric said, offering evidence. "In *Measure for Measure*, for example: Isabel, the novice, is asked by Angelo, the Lord Deputy, to give up her virginity to him in order to save her imprisoned brother's life—yet she's too faithful to the Church to be willing to save even her brother, Claudio, and so she warns poor Claudio to prepare himself for death. However, she only *pretends* to give in to surrendering her virginity just to trick Angelo into freeing her brother—yet in doing so, she is demonstrating the different degrees of sin: fraud wins out over faithlessness and fornication. It's a morality play in the strictest sense. Nevertheless, this is not a play for children, wouldn't you agree? It's very serious."

Dr. Liz nodded, but did not blink.

"So is *The Merchant of Venice*. It's all about the conflicts between Christians and Jews, but Shakespeare turns it into a farce in the final act, based on an all-too-obvious deception. Forget about *Othello*: there's interracial sex, infidelity, betrayal, deception, murder, political skullduggery—sex, religion, war—it has it all. It's not for children. And I'm not teaching it to children. Are we supposed to rewrite Shakespeare to sanitize it for impressionable students?"

"That's not what—"

"This is a junior-level class, Doctor Barnes. Students should be at least twenty years old when they take it. Heck, they know more about sex than . . . than I do. And I've been married and divorced. What's the problem?"

"Mister Schaeffer . . . ." Dr. Liz took a deep breath, anticipating Eric cutting her off again but he didn't. "This young woman took exception to one of your remarks about chastity. She seems to feel as though you were speaking rudely of those who choose abstinence over a lack of abstinence. That may seem to go counter to popular culture today but it is a valid lifestyle for many of our students. In this day and age, abstinence is something we should be encouraging, even at the college level, don't you think?"

"What?" Eric wasn't listening; he was reloading. "That's ridiculous. They're all adults. I didn't tell anyone to go out and have sex. I'm certainly not suggesting that abstinence—or 'chastity,' as it was called in the Elizabethan vernacular—is not a virtue. Who the heck is this student?"

It was certainly not Íris. She wouldn't be complaining about chastity jokes. And she would never be offended by off-color remarks. Unless this was all some trick of hers.

Dr. Liz held up the paper. "What you supposedly said in open class: You said, quote, 'Chastity was a big thing back then'—by which I presume you mean in Shakespeare's day. Continuing: 'Now a girl is presumed to be unchaste at twelve, if not earlier, and she's expected to be unchaste by fourteen.' Unquote. Does this remark seem out of character for you, Mister Schaeffer?"

"I did say that, but you miss the context." He had to catch his breath. "I was being cynical, not pragmatic—"

"The context is that you should have stopped after 'back then' and left these personal perversions to yourself." Then she mumbled, ". . . unchaste by fourteen!"

"But I—"

"What I have noticed," Dr. Liz spoke up sharply, "and this incident perhaps points it up particularly well, is that you have undergone a drastic change in attitude since . . . since we spoke last semester. It's a change which does not much impress me. I can't begin to imagine the cause of this turn-around. Perhaps you have spent too much time with Doctor Macintosh—"

"I spent as little time with him as possible."

"This is what I'm speaking of: your interruptions, your lackadaisical response to serious situations, such as the hearing. In addition, your inattention to due diligence with regard to your classes. You were not absent once last semester, but you've missed four days in the past month, three of them Mondays. Is it too much trouble to come back after the weekend? Moreover, look at how you present yourself: the sweatshirt and scruffy jeans you wore to the hearing is a prime example. And the dungarees you're wearing today. Has that shirt been washed recently? The whole persona that is Professor Schaeffer has changed and changed dramatically."

She stopped for three breaths, to let her words settle on him.

He was stunned.

"I'm at a loss as to how to interpret this shift in attitude," she said. "Are you still interested in being a part of this institution and of this department? Are you serious about how you present yourself, and our department, and the subjects you teach to our student body? Please explain."

"Doctor Barnes, I am very serious—"

"I should think a weekend would be enough time for you to properly write out your response, not only to this student's complaint, but also how you intend to deal with this problem of attitude reversal in the near future."

Eric stared at her. "You're giving me homework?"

"Monday morning is when it's due."

She was writing something on the papers she had been shuffling across her desk. A reminder to make Eric's life hell? She did not look up.

"On my desk by nine sharp. Good day, Mister Schaeffer."

Eric waited for the hidden camera to be revealed.

"Good day, I said," Dr. Liz repeated.

"You're kidding." He wasn't going to leave until he had confirmed that she did have a subtle sense of humor others had somehow missed. "I can't believe you're serious."

She raised her chin and glared at him. "Oh, but I am. Monday morning."

Eric stood, brushed a lunch crumb from his shirt, and turned to go.

"Also, I'd like in your report," Dr. Liz spoke up as his hand reached for the door, "your thinking behind the name change of *The Fairmont Review* to *Journatalia*."

17

ÍRIS SEES HIM LOOKING BACK OVER HIS SHOULDER at her sitting on the bed in the apartment. He spins his chair away from the desk, letting the screensaver come on, and studies her closely. She sits cross-legged on the bed, in his pajama pants and a ragged tanktop, her laptop on the bedsheet before her. It is a weekend to work. He is writing a report due on Monday and she is writing a paper for his class.

"Íris, let's just get married and go some place where winter never ends."

She types a few more words, then looks at him.

"*Já*, it is too warm in here."

He snaps out of his dreamy trance. "I know."

Getting up from the desk, he checks the temperature gauge on the wall.

"It's seventy-two outside, but it's eighty in here!"

He flicks the switch of the air cooler and for a moment there is a hum, a lurch and the whine of metal on metal. He shuts it off.

"How long has it been? I asked them to fix this thing last October. Then it never got warm after that and they forgot about it over the winter. I swear I'm moving just as soon as the condo is sold."

"Baby, come here," she whispers.

He sits on the edge of the bed, glances at her laptop.

"No peeking before it is finished," she says.

"Right." He holds his eyes tightly shut.

She types on, *clickety clickety click.*

"Should we get married?" he says, holding his eyes closed.

She stops typing. "You are distracting me from my work."

"Sorry," he says and gets up from the bed. He opens his eyes and fixes them on her breasts, pushing out her shirt. She can feel his inhalation. "You're right. We should get back to work. One hour, no talking."

She agrees, and they return to their writing.

Íris wants Eirík to see the improvement in her writing. He has shown her some grammar tricks, some ways to restructure sentences, and he meticulously edited her last rough draft to show how to upgrade her style. He will be amazed at her insights on *Titus Andronicus*, Shakespeare's first tragedy, about a Roman general who defeats the Goths. Yet it is the role of Lavinia, the general's betrothed daughter, who Íris finds interesting. Lavinia is brutally raped, her tongue cut out and her hands cut off. There is much that is similar to working in a certain club in Toronto, yet she will hold back that information. There is a feast in the final scene, where each character murders some other character. Isn't that always the way with Shakespeare? Isn't that the way of the world?

She pauses, thinking.

Yesterday, the weather turned warm, spring sneaking in before its due date, and girls were in dresses and boys dared to wear shorts. Couples lounged on the grass, studying or chatting. Everywhere people cheered the end of winter, the last of the snow melted. She had frowned. Although she wore a skirt and a knit blouse, she was not comfortable under the warm sun and the balmy breeze. After lunch, she found a shade tree to sit under, bending her knees up and leaning back against the trunk.

"Your underwear is showing," someone called to her.

She lowered her book and saw Celia, head-to-toe black Goth. Íris stretched out her legs on the lawn as Celia came over.

"It is good seeing you again," said Íris.

Celia seemed pleasant, so Íris was suspicious why she was looking for her. She got the story of how Celia did not fit in with the Goths, how Megan still hated Íris, how Celia's flunking her classes, how her parents are divorcing, how the "whole freakin' world is going to shit." Celia sat down beside Íris, leaned toward her as though she wanted a hug. Íris hesitated.

"Forget it," Celia muttered, "I know you're living with that man. Hope you're happy."

"*Já*, I think so." She closed the book, held it on her lap.

"Can we be friends again?" Celia smiled, as if she thought it would add sincerity to her request. "I need a friend right now, Iris, and you're the closest I got."

Íris asked what was wrong—aside from the world in general and her college career in particular. Celia explained how her Business Law professor flunked her. It was a course she needed for her major, so she would have to repeat it—with the same professor, since he is the only one to teach it.

"Megan told me about her filing a complaint against a professor," said Celia. "She said he wanted to screw her for an A, so she turned him in. Now the guy's been suspended and she might even get some money out of it."

"You said Megan still hates you."

"Oh, sure, she hates me as a witch, but we still talk. She's in a class next to my Psych class Mondays and Wednesdays. We talk outside, before class. She and I, we're the only ones who know each other."

She stared at Íris for a moment, laid a hand on her shoulder. A favor was about to erupt from her mouth. Winter is coming to an end, thinks Íris. She owes someone a favor by now. It is good luck through the summer.

"Do you think I could do the same thing? You know: what Megan did?"

"You want to file a complaint against your professor?"

"Well, it's not like it's never been done before."

"Not by you, Celia."

"But he treated me very bad—just plain wrong."

"What did he do?"

"He always gave me shitty grades."

"That is not a reason. Did you deserve them?"

"*I-russ!*" Her whiny tone made its first appearance. "He flunked every assignment I turned in. He's got something against me, like me being Goth. He's prejudiced. He needs to be taught a lesson: don't discriminate."

Íris raised an arm and put it around Celia's shoulders.

"I could say he made sexual advances toward me," Celia said. "I could say he suggested after class once—no, twice—if I let him screw me, I get an A for the class."

"Celia, you're a virgin. You told me."

"So . . . ?" Celia shook her head. "They don't check, do they?"

"It is not right."

"But he's wrong. He's wrong for what he said. It doesn't matter if I'm a virgin or not. Not unless I accuse him of rape. That'd sure screw him."

"*Nei*, Celia." It was big sister time. Ever since she learned she was pregnant, Íris felt different. She was not sure what it was, yet she saw everything more clearly. Perhaps it was the hormone surge. "Think about what being a witch really means. We don't get revenge on people who do us wrong."

"We don't? That's no fun." Celia giggled. "Besides, Megan says she's bored with all that shit now. She's changing to Satanism. It's more interesting, she says. Anyway, she says I gotta be initiated. On Beltane. She's going to initiate me as a priestess. Then I'll sure have some power."

"Don't try to get pregnant just to hurt someone, Celia."

"But you got pregnant. By a teacher, too. You get a free ride to graduation."

"I didn't plan it."

"Relax, Iris. I'll just do a spell. I got a new book. It's got spells for everything. Like how to make a man stay with you forever."

"I sure won't need that."

"What do you mean?"

"Eirík is very loyal, too loyal." She likes moving back to her house for half the week. She needs the rest, the solitude to perform her magic: baby magic. At night she speaks the charm of making: *Be good, be strong, be of fine health, little one; be what thee and me wish for thee: be good, be strong, be of fine health; be one with all and all within oneself, blessed be, little one.* "I need a break sometimes."

"I can't believe you ever get tired, Iris."

"I like some peace." It was her turn to laugh. "He wants me every minute. We fuck at night, and in the morning. He is exhausted when he goes to school. Yet he never delays coming home, *já.*"

"But how can you stand it?" Celia was shocked. "With a man. That's gross."

Íris laughed. "Most men are lesbians beneath their skin."

Celia remained serious. Íris leveled her eyes at her: round, pale face framed in stringy black hair. "It is not gross, Celia. It's . . . good. He is the father of my baby." Íris had to stop and think a moment. "He is kind . . . protects me . . . supports me. I like what he thinks and what he says—even when what he says is stupid. He makes me happy. When I am happy, my baby is happy, and that is what I want."

"We could be happy together," said Celia—

An hour has passed and Íris has written six sentences.

Eirík is pounding the keys like a concert pianist, filled with some of the same passion she feels from him at night. He is a new man—less weight, more energy.

She shuts off the laptop and climbs off the bed.

"It is time to stop."

His fingers continue playing the keys, so she begins dressing. Already they are too domestic, waiting for each other, taking turns in the bathroom.

"Done."

He sits back to examine his creation as Íris stands before the bathroom mirror. He reads silently as she measures her curve. When she sat on the bed, she thought she could detect a slight bump. Standing straight now, she sees nothing has changed.

"That's good enough," this Eirík growls. "Liz can kiss my ass!"

He comes up behind Íris, wraps his arms around her belly, leans in to kiss her neck.

"Don't worry, you'll outgrow my pajamas in no time," he says.

Íris reaches back and pats his face—lovingly, some might say. Perhaps she should be an actress. She can be so convincing.

"I am not worried."

Yet she is worried. *Why am I not showing yet? I feel heavier, my clothes have become tight, so I must be growing, já, but my belly is not.*

"Would you excuse me?" she says, and closes the bathroom door.

Inside, she takes a hand mirror and stretches before the mirror over the washbasin, trying to see some sign. She puts a knee on the toilet seat and drapes her other leg across the washbasin to see better. There is no baby inside. There cannot be. It is all an illusion, a dream they have sewn together and wish to be true. What worries her is how much she wants the baby now. She is relying on this baby. It is her life buoy. If there is no baby, what should she tell him?

"You okay?" he calls from outside the door.

She exits the bathroom. "If we are going out I need to paint my nails."

It is just an excuse, of course. He uses excuses, too, like telling her that he must use the restroom before going into the classroom so they do not enter together.

"Can you help?" she asks.

He nods, delighted. She sits on the bed and he pulls over a chair. She extends a leg and he takes her foot in his hand, caressing the arch. He pauses, staring at her toes, and for a second she thinks he will kiss her feet like Ray did. Instead, Eirík begins applying Carnation Red.

18

THE FIRST THOUGHT THAT ENTERED ERIC'S HEAD as he opened the door for Íris was the chance that one of his students might see them. He watched her as she passed through the doors into Towne Square Mall two hours before closing on a Saturday evening. She was the woman he would watch if he were arriving at the mall alone—but she was arriving with him and that felt pleasantly strange.

"Welcome to the shopping mall," said Eric, waving his arms, making a ceremony of it. "Here is the microcosm of America."

"We have these places in Toronto," said Íris.

"Oh. Right." He had to think of something to say. "I don't think of you as Canadian."

"I have dual citizenship."

Eric grinned, nervous. Something else about her he didn't know.

"Even so," he said, "we can see all the social dynamics a person might encounter in the world-at-large represented here, along with the roles of provider, solicitor, and consumer. It's a jungle in here. If we can survive here, we can make it as a couple. As a family." He stopped to suck up his courage. "I hate it already."

"*Já*, I hate it, too." Íris seemed uncertain about continuing. "Let's go home. Let's go back. Let's go back to bed."

He understood what she meant.

"We need this, Íris. We have to conquer this fear we have."

"What are you afraid of?" she asked.

Maybe he did have something to fear. He was getting back into the shark-infested waters. Life vest? Swimming lessons? No, just dive in!

"This is only the second time I've been in here," said Eric, pausing at the directory.

Íris stood next to him, wearing a baby blue cotton top and knee-length skirt, arms crossed over her chest as though she were cold. She always posed that way when she was nervous or afraid, he'd learned. He wanted to put his arm around her, either at the waist or shoulders, and draw her to him. He wanted them to be joined at the hip—like the teenage couples who sauntered past them.

"Are we looking for anything?" asked Eric. "Or are we here to escape the hot confines of the apartment? I sure don't want you to melt." He waited for an answer. "As long as we're here for the cool air, we might as well check out some stores."

"Which store?" she asked solemnly.

"Witch store? There's a store for witches in the mall?" He grinned.

"*Nei.*" She slapped at his arm.

"So what's it going to be? Your old picture frame shop?"

"I don't want to go there," she responded with a huff.

"Shall we go to Waldenbooks? We could see if they have anything new. Something not catering to the lowest common denominator."

He chuckled, always ready to put down the marketing efforts of retailers. It was a bad habit. He watched for a sign, any sign, that she was in the same mall with him.

"How about music?" he asked. "We need to find some music we both like."

"I have a Björk CD, if you want to listen."

"Is that a music group?"

"She is Icelandic singer—"

"Maybe some maternity clothes?"

She glanced at him, catching him locked in a trance of admiration, and she almost blushed. For a moment, her cheeks matched her hair.

"*Já,* we can look for maternity clothes."

Her voice was full of resignation, as though she had no choice but to make her way to what he called the 'pregnant' store. It was inevitable that she should have to wear a sign announcing to the world that she'd become 'infected'?

For a Saturday evening in March, the mall seemed less busy than Eric expected. There remained enough shoppers, teenagers hanging out, and the sordid other denizens to block the walkways and keep the echoing noise high enough that he could not speak to Íris without raising his voice.

Eric led the way through the obstacle course and Íris followed a full step behind. Every few steps he had to let her catch up. He would reach for her hand only to be swept away in the stream of mall rats. Once free of them at the arcade, Eric was able to scan the storefronts as they passed. Íris kept her eyes fixed on some distant point ahead of them.

"This is what normal people do," said Eric with a laugh. "I think we can be counted among the normal people." He gestured at the expanse of commercialism and, from their vantage point on the second level, they could survey the vista of shopping possibilities. "Look at these people. They make a pilgrimage to the mall to lay down their offerings, all the tithes they've saved up since their last pilgrimage. Just so they can remain in debt to the gods of commerce. They go to buy things they don't want and don't need with money they don't have. They're also required to check out other people, sort of keeping up with the Joneses. Someone's probably checking us out right now. Someone wants to keep up with the Schaeffers. The Schaeffers, hmm. I like the sound of that."

He had not realized until then, when serendipity tripped him, but he had brought his lover to the mall to show her how 'normal' couples behave. He needed a refresher, too, he realized at that moment. They needed lessons, models to emulate. A crash course in how to act like a couple when the only thing they had in common was a fetus.

He stopped to lean against the railing, gazing over the food court.

"I'd forgotten what a depressing place this can be."

Íris had not joined him at the railing so he turned, looking over his shoulder, to find her. She was standing in the walkway, staring into a clothing store—for business women. There was longing in her face, something wistful, distant. Someday, he pondered, she would be a customer of this boutique. She could dress in their fashions when she was running a chic gallery, perhaps while he sat home writing his next bestseller. A nanny would mind the children during the day.

He called to her.

She stood amid a stream of young couples, holding hands or with arms wrapped around each other. He saw how easily they touched each other without any concern for how they might appear. Desert island sexuality, he mused. Go with your gut instinct, your basic urges.

"Are you all right?" he asked.

She turned to him and her eyes were moist. "Let's go home."

"Why? We've only been here twenty minutes."

"I don't like being here. It is too—"

"Too many bad memories?" He was joking, but she did not share his humor. "Yes, I'd hate to work here and later return as a customer. Returning to the scene of the crime, as it were. But, hey, we can do this. Besides, we haven't found the store with the maternity clothes."

He reached for her hand, ready to lead her onward. Instead of the breeze where her hand had been in past attempts, he felt her fingers catch and clench his hand. Her grip was too firm to be affectionate. When their eyes met, he thought he understood. In a perfect world she would be the one to watch. Everyone would check her out. He would stare at her, the vixen in the crowd. She had never experienced the view from outside; neither had he.

She grabbed his hand and held it tightly.

Eric's face broke into a warm smile—after being frozen, off-guard, too surprised to respond.

She stepped against him and her head brushed against his cheek. Her soft hair reminded him of other times. Her breath tickled his chin. He wanted to see her face but she turned away. Her hand felt small in his as they strolled.

"Here is Framed—where I was working," said Íris as they went by.

She did not slow as he expected she would. "I don't miss it. I work for you now."

"What's that supposed to mean?" He was more curious than offended.

"Since you persuade me to give up earning my own money, I am working for you. *Já,* I have to keep you happy."

"We went over that a hundred times. What's mine is yours. It's a partnership. We are equals—"

"Iris!" cried a young woman, dressed as a sales associate. She stood outside the next shop, a clothing boutique for the young and hip.

"Erin!"

Íris pulled her hand from Eric's and went to hug the girl, leaving him standing alone.

"They said you quit," said Erin.

"*Já,* I am free almost two weeks now."

"So, like, what're you doing now?"

From his politely removed position, Eric smiled courteously when the girl glanced over at him. She obviously did not recognize him from the awkward bump back in December. Better to keep his distance, he decided.

"Eiрík," his lover called.

Like a good lover, he would dash to her side, eager to be offered as a sacrifice to her endless errors of selection. *What could this goddess possibly see in this old man?* That's what her friend was thinking.

Íris turned and gestured when he did not arrive beside her, so he went.

Íris smiled, saying, "This is Eirík. He's . . . ."

Careful, thought Eric, holding a strained grin but wanting to hide.

"This is the man I sleep with," said Íris.

Eric grimaced, deciding that she had probably misspoken and was not merely with him to tease and torment him. He couldn't determine which way her friend took it. The girl's smile leaned to one side as Íris talked about school. He could tell what the girl was thinking. It showed on her face: *Can he be any good in bed? Does he make a lot of money?*

"God, that's freaky!" Erin exclaimed. "I mean, I—I thought he was, like, your dad."

Suddenly, a cold, steel hook grabbed the back of his neck, yanking him up and away from them, up to the ceiling, leaving him hanging from the rafters of the mall. From that uncomfortable perch, he gazed down upon a man who resembled him only superficially. He dressed properly—conservative, perhaps, but not stodgy. He took care of himself—clean-shaven, often bathed, hair combed, teeth brushed—as his mother had taught him. He had lost ten pounds since December, but still he held in his stomach. He was forty but couldn't change that. What did this girl think? Of course, he had money.

He stepped forward, extended his hand toward Erin.

"Nice to meet you. Íris has told me a lot about you—well, not really much, but some."

"Yeah, I get it." Erin returned her attention to Íris.

When he recovered, he noticed that Íris seemed sad, as though she missed her job, the people she worked with, or maybe it was something else. He felt guilty. He hadn't made her quit; he was giving her what she wanted: more time for art—

". . . going to have a baby in August."

"No way!"

Eric's attention jumped back to his lover.

"*Já*, it's true. Yet I have nothing to show." She tapped her belly.

"You might as well take the baby-daddy in there and show him to Darlene." Erin waved at the picture frame shop. "She'll get a kick seeing your ol' man."

Íris introduced him to Darlene as her fiancé—the only way Darlene would accept her quitting. She needed to prepare for the wedding. Eric liked the idea. However, the forty-ish woman stared hard at him the whole time Íris was talking.

Finally, Íris pulled him out of the store, hand in hand again.

"That wasn't so bad, meeting the folks," Eric said with a quick laugh. "Maybe we can go meet my parents over Spring Break. That would sure be a change of scenery for you, going south to Texas. I want them to meet you. I want to shock them. I want them to see your big belly."

She gazed downward. "I can't see anything."

"Don't be disappointed." He hugged her. "There's plenty of time. That's why it takes nine months. People need time to get to know each other."

When they stop in the Waldenbooks, they part for a few minutes. Íris drifts into Pregnancy, begins browsing. He marches through History, discovers Mythology. He is researching for his book. She is researching for her one-act play that will debut in August. On the way to Pregnancy she pauses in New Age, a place for books the store does not know what to do with. They don't put Wicca books in Religion.

In New Age, she finds a book on spells, one that Celia probably has bought, and she flips through it. Spells to make a man love you, spells to make a man go away, spells to make a man be your slave. Where do they come up with these? Wicca is not about casting spells to make someone do something. She laughs a little and feels better, replaces the book on the shelf and takes twelve steps to Pregnancy.

"Here you go," says Eirík, arriving beside her carrying six books. "These are your kind of books." He shows her books with titles she knows. The sagas of Icelandic literature. She's read them. "They don't have a single Icelandic-English dictionary here. They must think you folks aren't important."

"*Já*, only three-hundred thousand of us in the world," says Íris.

"Three-hundred thousand and *one*," he corrects. "Same population as Wichita."

"Why are you buying those?" she asks, not willing to believe he can be interested in those old stories she studied in school a long time ago. They are tales of the gods and heroes. Lessons to learn, her teachers said. Her father swore by the *Eddas* and quoted from the *Hávamál*—the 'Sayings of the High One'—dictated by Óðinn himself.

"It's common ground," said Eirík. "I want to know about your world. How people think, how they live. Please don't frown at me. It's also for my novel, okay? I need to quote from these. They're part of Norse culture, so a realistic Norse character would quote them. What would

Thorngren say?"

Reluctantly, she nods, thinking of other places. "What would Óðinn say?" She recalls what her father used to say: 'Óðinn, forgive me for what I did: I taught this girl too well: she's much too good at what she does.'

She becomes afraid then and grabs Eirík's shoulder, whispers: "You don't need these books. They will only confuse you, and make you think bad things."

He stares at her, confused.

"We are good people, já. Only a few, like any place, are so cruel. Only a few of *many* are . . . . Such people are rare. We must forget them."

He is caught in her spell—yet it is not a spell.

"I only want to learn about your culture," he says.

"These stories are nonsense. They are like the Bible. Metaphor and symbolism, as you say. To tell about everything, why everything is the way it is. You won't understand them. You won't understand me from them. I am not like people in the *Edda*s. If you insist on studying these books, you should learn my language first, then read in *Íslensku*."

He nods, thoughtfully, pretending he understands.

"*Ert þú búin um?*" she asks, tugging at his sleeve. Speaking *Íslensku* gets his attention, she is learning.

He grins. "There you go again, talking Viking."

She purses her lips, holding back another frown. "I asked: Are you about finished?"

He opens the *Hávamál*, flips the pages, pausing to read.

"You will go mad, Eirík."

"This is good stuff. I need to read this," he says. "Like this one: 'To many a place I came too soon, to others much too late;/ The ale was drunk, or not yet brewed . . . .' I can picture that. How about this one? 'I tell you, Loddfáfnir, heed you this counsel:/ Smile not at the graying storyteller;/ Often is good what the old ones sing;/ Wrinkled lips may speak choice words.'"

"*Já*—I know it. Stop."

"But this is . . . . It's about me. I'm a graying storyteller." He is excited. "So tell me, who is this Loddfáfnir?"

"Loddfáfnir is a dwarf. Óðinn is speaking to him."

"Gods, dwarves, mortal men—this is great, Íris! It's rather Keatsian." He looks at her, wondering if she is educated. "John Keats? The poet? You've read *La Belle Dame sans Merci*, haven't you? *Hyperion* . . . ? *The Eve of Saint Agnes* . . . ? *Endymion* . . . ? Well, never mind."

When Íris does not respond, he turns over a few more pages and reads on, mumbling just loudly enough to prick her nerves:

"'In an enchantress's embrace/ thou mayest not sleep/ so that in her arms she clasp thee./ She will be the cause/ that thou carest not/ for the Assembly or prince's words;/ food thou wilt shun/ and human joys,/ sorrowful wilt thou go to sleep.'"

As he reads, the Icelandic words echo in her head, mocking her.

"'I saw mortally wounded/ a man,'" he continues, giving a glance to his lover, "'a wicked/ woman's words;/ a false tongue caused his death,/ and most unrighteously.' Okay. It's rather vague, but it has a certain wisdom to it. It's a warning, I suppose."

She stands close and whispers the next lines from memory.

"Umm, no kidding," he says. "What does that mean?"

"Nothing. It is all foolish talk. Read it if you want. It means nothing."

"You've got it memorized. Part of your school lessons? You must know the usual interpretations."

"Interpretation?"

She frowns. Her father used to recite it to her when she was a child. He taught it to her like holy scripture, yet she refused to believe it. Gossip of the gods, not words of wisdom.

"Loddfáfnir lived in Valhalla in his youth," she says. She does not want to explain yet she understands there will be no peace until Eirík knows its fanciful truth. "He received advice from Óðinn, advice he ignored. Loddfáfnir is recalling the advice as he sits in the underworld, beside Urd's Well. That is where he fell. He was enchanted by a sorceress and because of that he was not happy."

Eirík's eyes do not leave her. He is fascinated, captured by the words.

She gives in: "In this part, Óðinn is advising Loddfáfnir not to sleep with any sorceress. That's the translation. If Loddfáfnir does not listen to the advice, says Óðinn, he will be filled with such hatred for life he will not care about even the most important matters. He will lose desire for food and good company, and he will go to bed alone. He was told by Óðinn that taking to heart what a sorceress says can cause him . . . an unjust death. He has . . . ."

When she pauses, she finds him gazing at her eyes too long—until her heart starts beating again. This Eirík is a brave man, she thinks. Or he is a fool like the others. It will be his own fault if harm comes to him. Now he has been warned.

He waits while Íris decides on a pregnancy book: *What to Expect When You're Expecting.* He says it's the one his ex-wife read when she was pregnant. That is strange to hear: she is number two in this man's catalogue. Or number three. He mentioned a Japanese woman, too.

They go to the cashier. He puts a credit card on the counter—gold MasterCard. She watches him, wants to laugh. He is part of the consumer machine he hates. And he does not see it.

There is a lot he doesn't see, *já*, about the world, and about the witch from Iceland. She and the world are so different from what he expects. There is no book for him, no *What to Expect When Íris is Expecting* book.

There he is: sliding his card back into his wallet, taking his bag of books, and taking her hand in his, leading her out of the bookstore. They are a couple, she accepts, whether she likes it or not. He wants to show her some of his world. He has done well for himself, he seems to say. *So what am I to him?*

She sees her father bending over her crib, playing with her in the meadow, and contemplates his capacity for affection even when he treated her badly. He could act a part convincingly. Even drunk he could switch back and forth. This Eirík is no actor. Every thought he has flashes across his face. In that way, she knows he is sincere. Too sincere. Her mother was affectionate only during her childhood. Only when she went away to the job in Reykjavík did she turn into a goat whenever she visited home. Even during those visits, Magnús would dare enter her room at night—with Heiðr in the next room. She must have known what was happening, yet she did nothing. It was easier to return to Reykjavík.

In Toronto, the men loved her, could not get enough of her. She owned the Back Room for more than a year. She could be rich by now if she stayed. She could have gone into modeling for magazines, films, or found a wealthy patron. Or she might be hooked on drugs or dead. No one cared about her. They only needed her to be a target for their anger. They paid to abuse her as a representation of all women, to let out the frustration from their emasculation at home or at their jobs. She was playing a game with them. Role-playing games.

This Eirík does not play games, *já*. He sticks to the rules. Yet he criticizes the rules. He demands order yet he dares chaos—like poking a sleeping bear. This Eirík, this clumsy sperm donor, sees something in her that she cannot see in herself. It makes him want her.

It all feels so strange. Taking his hand, she leads him to the food court, where he buys some tacos. As they eat, he talks more about his parents. They are still married, still alive, and he seems to like them— *já*, tolerate them. They live near the beach and his father has a sailboat. She can get plenty of seafood there, he says. They might as well take a trip south for the week.

Finally, they come to the 'pregnant' store.

Íris browses through the racks of smocks and stretchable jeans, and the dresses that hang like tents. She is not showing enough for the clothing to look right on her, yet she tries them on nevertheless, rolls up her skirt and tucks it underneath to see how she will look when she is fat. Not pretty.

Eirík sees her standing before the mirrors and she knows the sight of this orange-haired witch dressed in the uniform of sluthood excites him. He practically glows, anxious for someone he knows to walk by so he can display her like a prize he has won.

"I have nothing to show," she tells him.

"You'll grow into them," he says.

She wants no sympathy. She has come a long way from sleeping on the sofa at Beth's flat in Toronto and dancing in the club because her mother did not want her there to remind her of what happened in Reykjavík. Her mother closing the apartment door, the trash bag of clothing tossed in the corridor, flashes through her mind. Her widowed mother's new husband, that Canadian man, was already leering at the little whore. Time for the whore to go. She's eighteen now. Change the locks and here's some cash to start you off. She wandered the streets, stayed with one friend a day here and there, then with another friend, then no one.

Já, Eirík pities me, wants to care for me, as though I'm a wounded cat he found.

When she returns from the changing room wearing a similar jumper as another woman, it is her turn to be embarrassed. The woman smiles knowingly at her. The jumper hangs low, almost touching the floor, not held up by a protruding belly. The husband surveys her, Eirík notices. That man must feel proud to be there, in this store, with a beautiful woman. When she complains about the fit, the size, or the fabric, he agrees with her. He is putting on a show for them.

When Íris comes out wearing her own clothes again, Eirík calls her attention to a poster tacked on the wall beside the mirrors.

"They're having a fashion show. For maternity wear," he says. "They want to use real mothers-to-be. You're a model. And a mother-to-be. You should sign up."

"I am not even showing."

"You will be in April. Come on, you'll be a fantastic model."

"*Nei*, I do not model."

"I thought you posed in the figure drawing classes." He grins. "It isn't nude modeling. You get to wear clothes. That's the point: to show off the fashions."

She stops posing before the mirrors and glares at him. Already they are squabbling like an old married couple.

"I don't like being on a stage," she says.

"Well, you get to keep the outfit you model, it says. Not interested?"

"*Já*, let's get a free fat suit for the big girl."

She writes her name, age, occupation—*concubine*—and her e-mail address. Then she asks Eirík to write the address and phone number of the apartment. He teases her about not having it memorized. She explains it is only her weekend home.

As they leave the store, he reaches again for her hand but she skips away. He is used to her games.

This time he seems hurt, so she returns to him, grabs his hand and holds it as they walk.

Eirík gestures at the young expectant mother, pushing a baby carriage, approaching them. She is at least the twelfth such woman in the mall tonight, thinks Íris. It must be the season. From cold winter nights come spring pregnancies and summer babies. As the mother passes them with her carriage, Íris glances back over her shoulder.

"I like that dress."

"So do I," says Eirík. "I'll buy it for you. Just tell me when."

"When I can no longer fit into this skirt—"

"Are we going to make it official?" he interrupts.

"What's official?"

"Let's get married, Íris."

She stops, right there in the middle of the mall, with store security fences slamming down around them and custodians unsheathing their brooms.

"It is so difficult." Her voice wavers. "You don't know me, Eirík."

He cannot respond so he simply walks on, expecting her to follow.

That hurt him, she sees. What can she say?

"Sorry I asked," he says.

She sees the couples going hand in hand in that artificial world and knows if she joins hands with Eirík, she can feel she is one of them, a normal person in the thrill of couplehood. She considers the options. She has been on her own for so long. *Já*, so many years of being alone, with only a few, brief partners to break up the time—and they always leave. Or die.

Íris catches up to him, grabs his hand. She pulls on his hand to stop him and when he turns to her she gazes deep into his eyes.

"I think I . . . ."

She cannot say the words. She has never said the words before and meant them.

Holding his face in her hands, he is suddenly afraid. He grimaces as though in pain, perhaps expecting the worst.

"I—I love—you," come the words in her weak voice.

He is more afraid. "What did you say?"

"I love you," she repeats, thinking *Have mercy on me.*

19

"No, Jack, I haven't. Nobody's saying anything." Eric had the phone tucked between his ear and his shoulder. A stack of freshly collected essays sat on his desk and he twirled the red pen through his fingers, wishing they would go away. "I'm sure you'll be among the first to know the verdict. Besides, I don't have a vote."

He let his former colleague rant on.

"You were there, Jack," Eric cut in. "You heard what they were saying. Doesn't look good. I couldn't believe what they said, one after another, the same p.c. crap you should've known about. And I thought you were bullshitting me, but you *are* a . . . what's the term? A dirty old man— except you're young. Gee whiz, what were you thinking?"

Jack told him what he'd been thinking: that he was invincible, on top of the world, eager to take what was his to take, ready to be adored by the female student body. He expected to be smiled at as some harmless eccentric or waved off as a friendly slip of etiquette.

"All right. . . . All *right*, I said." Eric held his breath, about to hang up the phone. "I've got plenty of things to do here, you know. Well, I am glad you found another job." He glanced into the hallway, hoping someone would stop by. "I've got to go, Jack. Really. I have a doctor's appointment. No, it's not my appointment, it's hers. Her: the Icelandic witch. Named Íris. I said 'Íris.' Long E. Spelled like the flower—"

"Here you go!" Viki and Fiona exclaimed, arriving in his doorway like the angels he had prayed for. They held up the latest cover art.

Eric waved them in. Finally, an excuse. Now he was on the defensive, with Jack comparing his troubles with Eric's relationship.

"It's different for us," said Eric. "For one thing, the word 'love' is involved. Also the concept—no, it's not the same." He turned away from his student visitors. "I've got students. Yes, I'll call if I hear anything. Yes. Bye."

He turned in his chair to face his guests.

"Here's the artwork for the journal cover," Viki announced proudly.

It was a pen and ink drawing full of arches and intersecting loops. He was almost afraid to guess what it was. Their first attempt was a set of stylized loops meant to be penises, in keeping with the new name. He had vetoed that cover and they were returning with a different concept.

"It's not penises," said Fiona, smugly.

"Well, that's good." Eric studied the picture, still not sure what it was supposed to be. He was afraid to ask.

Suddenly he glanced at his watch.

"Whoops, sorry ladies, I'm late for an appointment." They seemed suspicious. He grinned sheepishly. "Were we supposed to meet today about this?"

"Yes. You said at noon," Viki replied. "We're even a little early."

He checked the wall clock. "Right."

"So do you like it?" asked Fiona.

"Yes, it's great." He stood and began straightening the papers on his desk. "I'm sorry, but I really do need to rush out of here."

"Is it, like, okay now?" asked Fiona.

"It's fine," said Eric, gathering his jacket and ushering them out the door, closing it after them.

"You heard the man," said Viki to her *Journatalia* partner. "Let's get it to the printer."

Eric hurried across the campus, heading the usual way, along the sidewalk that ran between the Student Center and Grundy Hall.

He spied two women entering his field of vision. On his left was an orange-haired Nordic woman in long skirt and bulky green sweater. To the right was a dark-haired Hispanic woman in a heavy brown coat and calf-high boots. He could see the crash coming but he was powerless to stop it.

"Eric!"

"Eirík!"

"Good morning," he responded in as neutral a voice as he could summon.

His hands were shoved deep into his pants pockets, protecting his manhood. The women stared at each other as they realized they had been calling to the same man. They stared at him. With their intense eyes multiplying the power of their gaze, he stepped back.

"Íris," he said, feigning calmness, "this is Dominique. She's in Music here. Dominique, this is Íris. She's in the Art department."

And I'm in hell, thought Eric.

"*Halló*," said Íris. She extended her hand to Dominique, who refused it and faced Eric with a scowl.

The Hispanic woman regarded the Redhead woman, then the man.

"No wonder you stopped calling me."

The slap didn't hurt as much as he thought it would. Watching Dominique march off was worse. His heart trembled. He hated to hurt anybody but there were no excuses. When Íris entered his life again, he had to drop everything. Now the weight of everything he had dropped was being dropped on him. He couldn't breathe, couldn't move.

"Are you ready to go?" asked Íris, a little perplexed.

He took her hand gingerly, then grasped it more firmly and led her to the car.

"She was your lover before?" she asked once he started the engine.

"Something like that," he muttered, looking back over his shoulder as he pulled out of the parking space. "Doesn't matter now."

Eric waited patiently, thinking what he could have said to Dominique to soften the revelation. During the week of Valentine's Day he was supposed to go out with her. He sighed, drawing Íris' attention. There was nothing wrong with Dominique—and if he had not slipped on the ice princess, he might be here at the clinic with Dominique. No, they would be having lunch in the Student Center, discussing a concert or a colleague's recital. Or his writing. Dinner and a movie. Not a baby—

"Iris and Eric?" the nurse called out.

He grinned unintentionally as they stood, and she took his hand.

Inside the room, she removed her sweater and stood bare-chested before the technician, then slipped off the skirt. She refused the gown and climbed onto the padded table. He stood off to the side, out of the way.

"I'm Alison," said the technician, young and attractive herself in lab coat and glasses. "I'll be doing the sonogram for you today. Is this your first time?"

"Já, the first," said the expectant mother.

He liked the sound of that and his gaze automatically soft-focused around the woman on the table. She was so different now from the woman he had taken home in the rain.

"It's cold!" Íris exclaimed when the technician squeezed the clear gel across her belly. He measured it visually. It seemed to be wider than before and, considering she was on her back, there was a slight rise in the curvature of her abdomen.

Alison tested the machine, then applied the tethered device to Íris's belly. Returning to the monitor, the technician began recording data.

"Everything's looking normal. Do you want to hear the heartbeat?"

Of course they did. With the flick of a switch, the room was filled with a quiet but rapid pulsing from the speakers beside the monitor.

"It's a good, strong heartbeat," said Alison. "Let's see if we can make out any parts of the body." She moved the device across the belly as they stared at the monitor, trying to decipher the black and white streaks that shifted like quicksilver. "I think this is it," said Alison. "You can make out the body here. See it? This is an arm . . . ."

He squinted, trying to make out what the technician was pointing to, her finger pressed against the screen. It was no easier than trying to understand Fiona's abstract artwork. This was moving. Occasionally. And irregularly.

He noticed that Íris was looking away from the monitor.

"You don't want to see?" he asked her.

"I am afraid to look."

"I think I can make it out," he told her, to reassure her. He was still deciding if this blob or that blob was the baby. "Íris, you have to look. It's amazing." And it was: he found it, the baby—fetus, whatever. "I see it. I really see it, Íris!"

Íris slowly turned her head and regarded the monitor, her expression indifferent. He could see her eyes searching the screen for something familiar. In the monitor beat the slippery monochrome lines of a living being. He raised a finger to mark the location.

"I see it, too," she whispered.

He didn't hear her clearly so he leaned down to her.

"What did you say?"

"It is real. It is so . . . real." Tears rolled out of her eyes and she turned away.

"She's all right," Alison said. "That's a very typical reaction to seeing the baby for the first time."

Alison studied the monitor a few minutes longer, switching between different angles, then called his attention to something.

"Do you see this here, this bit of dark matter?"

Eric nodded, concerned. Íris had closed her eyes, her lips pursed as though in pain.

"What is it?" he asked. "Is something wrong? Tell me."

"Nothing's wrong." Her smile confused him. "Unless you wanted a girl."

"What do you mean?"

"I think this is a penis."

"Another ride home?" asks Jean, sitting on the steps as Íris walks up from the curb. It is becoming routine for him to drive her home after the evening class. He waits until she goes inside. "You preggos get all the breaks," Jean laughs, then takes a drag on her cigarette.

"We just fucked in his office," says Íris.

"Well, good for you," Jean sneers.

"And he wants to take me to Texas on Thursday. It's very far south. For the whole week. To meet his parents."

"Oh, you got to meet the parents, girl friend!" Jean chuckles. "That's the rule. They're so gonna love that baby bump. What a way to spend Spring Break, under the magnifying glass of some dude's parents. I don't envy you."

"I don't care what they think of me, *já*." She takes Jean's hand to help her up and Jean swings the door open for her. "It's the hot weather I don't want. I never went that far south."

"Ooo, you're gonna melt, Iris."

The second Íris steps into the house Jean grabs an envelope from the basket by the door and shoves it in her face.

"You got a letter from England!"

There is only one person she knows in England: Heiðr, her mother. Íris sent a letter to her, one elegantly handwritten with proper deference and courtesy—it's necessary, given their lack of contact. Her mother obviously felt the need to respond. It is not every day that a woman learns her first-born will make her a grandmother.

"It's from my mother," says Íris, then steps outside a moment to wave goodnight to Eirík. He won't leave until she waves. He needs to know she is all right.

She waves the letter at them, makes them wait as she tells about her day—backwards. They laugh when she mentions the Korean woman, a custodian, entering Eirík's office and catching them on his desk. Cory jokes about asking the woman to join them, and for a second Íris wonders what it would have been like. Jean teases her, saying that if it had been Celia, she would have invited her to participate. Cory can't believe they did it in the professor's office, on his desk.

"Yeah, but he doesn't count," Cory says. "I thought you were talking about some other professor. Shit, you *are* a horny love-bitch, aren't you?"

"Love-bitch?" Íris smiles slyly.

"By the way, Iris," says Cory, lowering his voice, "Ray called again. Twice."

She glances at Jean, who has perked up at the new topic. Íris looks at Cory.

He asks in a solemn voice, "Are you fucking Ray, too?"

Sometimes she doesn't know which way is up and which is down. The sun rises from the lake and sets in the mountains, and she is a little girl again, running barefoot through the springtime grasses, trampling the wildflowers. It is just a passing scene.

"I went back to Life Study today," she tells Cory, with Jean listening, cross-legged on the rug. "Ray wants students to draw a pregnant figure, even though I'm hardly showing. Can you believe it? He announces to the class I'm pregnant, then pats my stomach like he has a right to. His eyes never left me, not for one second. He had me change pose six times. Then he told me to stop by his office after class, because he had something important to discuss."

"That sounds familiar," says Cory. "From what I heard last year."

"I was not expecting anything important, so I went straight to his office in my robe. *Já,* what's the big deal?"

"The big deal is Ray," Cory says with a grunt. "So . . . what was the news?"

"He told me I got the position for the fall."

"You're going to be teaching in the fall?" Jean asks. "That's fantastic, Iris. I haven't even applied to grad school yet."

"That's rather fast, isn't it?" Cory asks.

"Why? How long is it supposed to take?"

"Longer than a couple of weeks," says Cory. "He's been stringing you along with the hope that you'll get the job, right? Meanwhile, what's he getting?"

She thinks of her visit to Ray's office. When he told her the news, she was surprised. He was excited and wanted to give her a hug. Any excuse to touch her. After the hug, he stepped back and they both noticed her robe had fallen open. He complimented her on her 'pregnant beauty.' Before she realized it, he was saying that some kind of 'special thank you' would certainly be appreciated. For what? For pushing through her application, for making certain it would be approved.

He called her over to his computer as he moved the mouse to bring the screen back to life. The images that appeared there were not shocking to her, yet Ray thought they would be: a nude Asian woman was kneeling as a circle of men masturbated onto her face.

"It's called *bukkake*, a Japanese word," he said. "It's some custom they have there. It used to be punishment for unfaithful wives. Now it's just a porn category."

"Why are you showing me this?"

He grinned. Ray will not ask directly for anything. That is his style. He will hint again and again until she has to play dumb to escape.

"You don't find it . . . intriguing?"

"Is this what's called sexual harassment, Professor Ferguson?"

He was strangely confident this time. Not the nervous, bumbling man everyone sees shuffling around the campus. He calmly stated that because they'd had consensual sex previously that this was not harassment. She told him they never had sex. He reminded her of the Jacuzzi, how he had drunkenly seduced her, how she had let him. He reminded her of how he got the job for her. Then he became angry—or he was acting angry.

"I thought you *might* want to show some appreciation."

He reached over and gently slipped the robe from her shoulders, let it drop to the floor, as he told her about the salary and benefits. When she did not run out, he believed she was agreeing to whatever would happen next.

He went to lock the door and, returning, had his pants open, stroking himself.

She told him it would ruin their working relationship. He laughed and repeated his idea about a 'thank you' gesture.

"It's not too much," he said, "certainly nothing more kinky than you've done before. You were talking about your club days when we were in the hot tub. Seemed you liked it, all the attention, doing things like that, live sex acts on stage."

He set the video playing on the monitor and placed his hands on her shoulders, prompting her down until her knees touched the carpet. He caressed her cheek with his fingers, then with his penis. He patted her head, telling her to open her mouth.

After a moment, she shook her head and spit him out, pushed him away. She shout a curse and got up. Grabbing her robe, she went for the door, threw it open.

Professor Norton was right there, her hand raised as though she were about to knock. Íris brushed past her and pulled on the robe as she hurried down the hallway. Elaine Norton had to have seen the video playing on Ray's computer monitor.

Íris cannot tell her housemates all that.

Cory cuts in: "I can't believe Ray hasn't made the job contingent on you doing some—you know, 'special' chores. I guess he doesn't need *my* help."

"Men are creeps, plain and simple," says Jean.

"So what if he likes to paint porn?" Cory says. "So what if you pose for it? It's not like anybody in the world'll recognize you. But, hey, if he fantasizes about you that way, maybe you should cool it for a while. Stay the hell away from him."

"What a creep," says Jean.

"But it *is* funny," Cory says, "to think mild-mannered Ray Ferguson has a passion for sado-masochism and bondage. Who'd've thought?"

"Not me," says Íris.

She takes the long, narrow envelope from England up to her room. The name and address are typed. A logo is imprinted in the corner: THE UNIVERSITY OF LONDON. Íris purses her lips, feeling disappointed. A secretary likely typed the letter, Heiðr too busy with her research.

Íris carefully tears open the envelope and pulls out the single sheet of thin paper. The cursive letters are strange to her after so many years. Heiðr has written a personal letter. For several minutes, Íris stares at the folded paper, the words showing through, criss-crossed. The paper is so thin. Like their relationship.

When Íris explained she was pregnant and would give birth in August, she did not know what her mother's reaction might be. She might show interest in a new family member. The wild girl settles down. It might bring them together again. There might be some kind of awkward reunion, like they have in the cinema. That she was a graduate student in the U.S.A., producing works of art, might also impress her. Her daughter was no longer earning money in a club in Toronto.

Íris never could read her handwriting, yet she deciphers it. The meaning, in the end, is that this woman she has not seen in many years does not consider the pregnancy to be anything important. Íris is not a member of her family. Furthermore, Íris got what she deserved. "Sin begets sin," Heiðr wrote. The only encouraging remark comes at the end: she wishes her better luck being a mother than she had.

That's something like forgiveness, *já*? I am still out of her life; after tonight she is out of mine. That is what we deserve. 'Ice is sterile; nothing can grow on it,' she heard in a film long ago. Most of all, ice preserves.

Magnús got Heiðr pregnant while she was in university. Her parents said it ruined her life. Yet she returned to the university, got her diploma and became a scientist and, at least in her circle of marine biologists, made something of herself in a life that shattered one November afternoon. A week later, they found her father's boat, frozen in the pack ice. There was no body so they presumed he drowned.

In the morning, as predicted, everything is coated with ice.

Eric sat by his computer, patiently waiting for an e-mail response from Íris. They already had missed a day due to the ice storm making the highways impassable. He studied the weather map: an hour south the roads were ice-free. Looking outside, he saw the road crews had made progress on the main streets. He was ready to drive over to pick up his lover for their Spring Break trip. He would finally be able to go south with someone to show-off to his parents.

This is Íris, he had practiced many times since the city became ice bound. *That's Íris—like the flower, which, by the way, doesn't grow in Iceland. Did I mention she's from Iceland? And, of course, you can see the slight bulge of her belly. That's because we are in love . . . .*

He traced a path in the carpet from the Dr Pepper in the refrigerator to the computer monitor's unchanging weather map. Another day was passing. It was almost eleven. If they could not leave soon they might as well wait until the next morning.

Check your e-mail! She had no phone; her computer was hooked to the wall jack so he could only get a message to her by e-mail. She had to have the computer on to receive it. And she had to open her mailbox. *Stop chatting, Íris!* He sat down, clicked over to her EXCITE community. No activity there. Her last posting was a lengthy account of her clinic visit. She posted a list of "old wives' tales" for determining the sex of a baby. One person had posted a comment: "Over here, we usually just look between the legs: if it's twig and berries, it's a boy; if not, must be a girl." Smart guy. Eric read on. *She's telling them the baby is a boy.* Pride swept through him, then was overwhelmed by feelings of frustration.

Eric shut off his computer, went to the sliding glass door at the balcony, and stared out at the crystalline world. It was pretty. Then a city truck came by spraying salt on the streets.

"If they can make it, so can I," he muttered.

He would just drive over to her house. It would be a start, the first leg of the trip and a chance to test the roads after the thirty-six hour curfew. They could leave anytime; being iced in at separate locations was the worst part.

The car started easily after sitting in the cold the previous two days, and as Eric backed out and headed slowly to the main street he tried to imagine the beach and a tropical breeze, the sun golden, unrelenting. And the oppressive Gulf coast humidity.

Traffic was light for a Friday noon as he passed the campus, silent and empty. He turned down the side streets toward the large, old house he was coming to know well. There were no open spaces along the curb so he went down the street almost a block before finding a place to park. Walking back, he was careful to step across the lawns, avoiding the smooth, transparent layer of ice on the sidewalk.

When he arrived at the house, he proceeded up the walk and nearly lost his balance. Slipping across the ice, he regained his dignity only at the veranda steps. He glanced around, seeing if anyone had noticed.

The door was unlocked, of course, so he stepped inside, shook off a few stray flakes of snow that had floated through the air.

Two people were sitting by the fireplace. On the sofa was a black girl with her hair braided in pigtails and that blonde young man Eric recognized from previous visits. He was there to pick up Íris, he announced. The girl waved him upstairs.

"Think she's still asleep," she called after him.

Eric now liked the creaking of the wood as he ascended and moved down the hall to her room. He rapped lightly on the door, listened, knocked harder. The door opened at last and after a moment to prepare his greeting, he entered.

Íris wore only pink panties and a white camisole, a strip of belly showing.

"Good morning, sweetheart," he said, seeing the messiness of the room. "The main roads are clear so the highway should be open. I checked the weather maps. There's a chance of snow here tonight, so we need to get out of town now or we'll be stranded all week."

She presided over her wardrobe, distributed across the room.

"I got your e-mail," she said, "yet I do not know what to bring." She waved her arm at the bed. "I have no swimming clothes."

Eric chuckled. "I'll buy you a swimsuit when we get there."

He winked, but she was regarding her laundry, neatly folded on one corner of the bed. The way she stood, with one hand behind her hip, supporting her back, made her belly project a little more.

"Íris . . . I do believe it's gotten bigger," said Eric, his voice full of fake surprise.

She looked up. "What?"

"Your belly." He pointed. "I meant it as a compliment. It's a good sign."

"So I'll be too heavy to run away?"

"Don't worry," said Eric. "There are probably a hundred shops selling swimwear. We sure won't be alone—unfortunately. It happens to be one of the big Spring Break havens for Midwestern students. I booked us a nice condo, though—on the island, near my parents' condo—so we should avoid most of them. They don't cater to spring breakers."

"*Já*, I don't like crowds."

"Because you come from a sparsely populated country?"

"Because I don't like people."

"Oh. I see." He watched her trying to organize her wardrobe. "Need help?"

"I just need some time."

He took the hint and excused himself. He studied her Wiccan altar at the end of the room. It seemed to have not been used for a while. The candles had worn down to the holders and the tiny bowls of powdered this and that were almost empty. The dull-bladed athame lay on the tabletop beside the silver chalice. Signs of a lapsed Wiccan.

He turned and watched her packing.

"I'm ready," said Íris, covered at last in a thin dress with pink and yellow flowers that hung from her bare shoulders by spaghetti straps and dropped to mid-thigh. She pointed to a sagging duffel bag on the bed. "This will be enough, *já*. We are only away this week, and you will buy swimming clothes for me."

Eric examined her. "That's a lovely dress, but it's not summer yet. Not here in Kansas. It's cold outside. Shouldn't you wear something warmer for today?"

She smiled and went to him, kissed his cheek. "I am trying to think positive, *já*. I am thinking of the beach."

He persuaded her to pull a cardigan over her shoulders, but her long, pale legs remained uncovered. As they exited the house, her housemates wished her a good time. They cheered enthusiastically, joking that now they would have some peace.

"I can't believe this," Eric growled on the veranda, "a damn ice storm just as Spring Break comes. Look at this . . . this winter wonderland!"

"*Já*, it is beautiful."

He started across the icy lawn, but she continued to admire the scene.

"Watch out on the walk there," Eric said, coming back for her. "I almost bought it on that patch of ice."

She stepped down slowly, paused, and stepped out of her rubber-soled sandals. She carried them by their straps as she continued barefoot across the yard.

"Be careful," Eric exclaimed. "Don't want you to slip. Or fall. Think of the baby."

He stopped to notice how she walked barefoot across the ice, not slipping at all, not feeling a thing, oblivious to the cold.

20

GRAY SKIES MERGE WITH THE SEPIA LANDSCAPE as they drive along the highway that crosses Oklahoma. Twice Eirík points to where trees had been cut down by past tornadoes. The trees are broken, splintered, forlorn. A dirt trail across the landscape shows the storm's path. Then, because Íris asks him what he did during the ice storm, he begins to tell her about his novel, *A Winter's Tale*.

She takes her foot out of the sandal and brings it up to the seat, her knee in the air. The toenail polish has worn off and she wonders if she can paint as they drive. Her short dress pulls up and when he glances at her, his eyes catch the narrow strip of pink cloth between her thighs.

"I wish you wouldn't do that," he says.

"Do what?"

"It's distracting," he explains, nodding at her exposed panty. Then he apologizes, explains that he *wants* to be distracted, but not when there is no place to pull over and relieve his guilt.

Íris laughs and puts her foot down.

He continues telling the story of children who discover a magic rock that is actually a wizard who has been transformed into a standing stone. Then, on one snowy night—

Several cars pass at high speed. They are full of young men and a couple of girls—spring breakers. The last one honks as Eirík moves to the slow lane.

"Damn spring breakers!" he curses, then mutters under his breath how the road is still slick and how they might not make it to their destination the way they are driving.

"Then let them be," she suggests and he gives her a strange look.

"You don't care if they have a wreck?"

"*Nei*, it's their choice."

"Is it the choice of the other car they crash into? Is it their passengers' choice to die?"

That shuts her up. She has never ridden so long in a car. In a bus, yes, coming from Toronto. She had packed a suitcase and a large portfolio for the three-day ride to Kansas. The bus stopped in Detroit, Chicago, and St. Louis and she changed buses in each city. No chance to bathe and not much opportunity to eat a good meal, only what she could buy in shops along the highway. A fat woman with a squirming toddler sat beside her the first leg of the trip, then a young man on leave from the Navy for the next part of the trip. A man just out of prison sat next to her from Chicago to St. Louis and flirted with her. When he started grabbing her, the bus driver stopped and made him get off, right there in the middle of the night.

"We might as well stop for the night near the border," says Eirík after some time. When he picked her up, she asked for lunch before they left town. Then they had to get some snacks and drinks for the trip.

"*Já*, we can stop and stay in a hotel."

She pats his thigh and the car suddenly swerves.

"I'm driving."

"What did I do?"

"Sorry—you caught me off-guard," he says, with a glint of humility.

Five minutes of silence passes.

"So, what happens next?" she asks.

Outside the village, there is an old woman who senses something is going to happen on this snowy night, so she puts on her boots and leaves her cottage. She doesn't know what it is, but her mother is concerned and follows her. The young man in the tavern, the local tour guide, senses something, too, and despite the innkeeper's insistence it is not a good night to go out, the young man follows his intuition.

Eirík has caught up with one of the cars that passed them, the one that honked.

"Well, here we are again," he grumbles.

"Do you want me to show them my finger?"

He acts surprised. He still believes she is an innocent child. She decides she will show all of them, Eirík and those crazy college kids in the red sports car. She climbs up onto the seat and twists her rear to the window, drops her panties and lifts her skirt just as they shoot past.

"What the hell are you doing?" Eirík yells. "You think that's going to make them slow down? No, they're going to try to keep up with us from now on, hoping to catch another look at your butt!"

"A harmless joke," she laughs, sitting down. "It is Spring Break, *já.*"

"Okay, Spring Break is the time for getting wild and crazy," he says, "but not at the risk of . . . . It's a long way to the next service station. Or hospital, if there should be a wreck. It can happen. People are killed every Spring Break horsing around like that. When I was in college, my roommate was killed on the highway at Spring Break. He was going to graduate that May."

What is there to do during this time of fun?

He is the teacher and yet he promised to take time off from his work. She put aside her mural painting for this week, even though she could have finished it in three more days and gotten paid. She could work at the picture frame shop, yet he got her to quit. It is all because she is pregnant. She is not her own woman in his mind. That is what she thinks, yet not what she wants.

She reaches up and unties the strings on her shoulders and the top flap of the dress falls to her belly, exposing her swollen breasts at the precise moment the carload of spring breakers passes by. One of the young men is displaying his rear. Eirík shakes his head, trying to be patient, trying to maintain control of the vehicle.

He is not getting into the spirit of the season, so she leaves the dress top down and stretches her arm across the back of the seat behind him.

"I want to warn you," she says, "I'm going to lean over and kiss your cheek. Please do not be alarmed. It does not mean I want to distract you so we crash. I only want to kiss you. Are you ready?"

He nods his head, lets a small grin show.

She leans over and kisses him. She kisses his cheek, and stretches up to kiss his forehead, then the top of his head. The car slows suddenly. A nipple is in his eye. He says nothing.

"Forgive me," she says, sitting back in her seat. "We should definitely stop at a hotel."

He agrees.

Eirík resumes his story: how the old man turns into the standing stone at sunrise and how the children age faster than their parents, and how only that one young man who left the village as a youth was not affected.

He pauses to inform Íris of the police car approaching from behind and suggests she put up the top of the dress and tie the strings. She does and the police car passes them. He hopes it will catch up to the spring breaker cars. She crosses her legs, rubs her thighs.

"I want you so much," he says, voice firm, eyes on the road. He explains how his parents will question him, how they will regard her. "No matter how old I get, I always worry what they think. It's weird. Neurotic, maybe. When I live away from them—like when I went to Japan, and now in Kansas—I can get out from under their scrutiny. Matt—my little brother—he doesn't have that problem. I'm the elder son so all the crap fell on me. I had to be the good one, the steady son, while Matt was the one who took risks. I cleaned up after him. Now he has the garage door company and the money, the wife and kids, and I have . . . you."

"And you want me, *já*."

"Damn straight," he mutters. "You make it a tie game."

Her arm is still behind him, resting on the seat, so she caresses the back of his neck.

"You are too nice, Eirík. You cannot let them push you." She has no idea what she is saying; she heard it on a TV show. Her parents ignored her, gave her no responsibilities. She cannot understand his family. "You need to shock them. You need to let them know you are free. Do something outrageous."

He reaches out and pats her belly. "I think this will do."

She thinks of big bellies and remembers Celia. After a few minutes, she must speak.

"I have a friend, and she asked me for a favor. It is a personal thing, yet I will ask you. Would you be interested in getting together with her? What I mean is, to have sex, the three of us. That would surprise your parents, *já*."

Instead of being offended, he laughs. "How would my parents know about it in order to be shocked? Should we videotape it?"

"Can we?" she laughs and he frowns. "I don't know why I asked. A long trip, *já*. It's Celia. She wants to lose her virginity. Yet she doesn't want some fraternity boy pawing over her, or going around boasting about 'doing' her."

"Why doesn't she just meet Mister Right?"

"Not likely. She's kind of a lesbian. And she's getting fat." She watches him keeping his eyes on the road, maintaining a steady speed, obeying the rules. "She wants to accuse this guy of assaulting her, just to mess with him."

"What?"

"She needs to tie the game."

"But why?"

"She got a bad grade. She wants to accuse him of raping her, but that's too—"

"Criminal!" He snorts. The car suddenly goes faster. "What the hell's she thinking? We got enough trouble on campus. She's . . . . Another bitch comes forward! Men get accused of enough shit without crazy chicks setting them up. It's like blackmail. That's the all-purpose revenge, isn't it? The accusation of sexual misconduct. What a f—"

"I already told her it was crazy idea."

"I'm not interested."

"I don't care what her reason is, I just thought . . . ." She looks away. "That's why she asked me, yet I was thinking only of something fun to do. Especially since I am getting big and you do not want to have sex with a big me."

"I want to have sex with you. We just need to be careful."

"*Já*, careful." She grins at him. "You need to 'lighten up,' as Cory says. I thought you were the same as me."

A few miles pass.

"I am not . . . the same," he mumbles, obviously deep in thought.

More miles fly by.

"Sandra Kinney got a tattoo. It says 'Jesus is Lord.'"

He laughs. Of course, she has told him about Sandra before.

"There's a girl who logs on at my website, too. You know her: she's China Doll. She's quite flirty. She lives in Kansas City. We exchanged some pictures, too. She's quite beautiful. She is like me, yet Chinese. She wants to get together for some fun, *já*. You know what that means. I e-mailed her that I live with my baby's father yet it does not matter to her. It's okay with her if you join us."

The car swerves as he takes his eyes off the road then fixes his gaze back.

"You have some weird friends," he says softly.

"And you do not?"

"Not like yours." He sighs. "Not since Japan. Not since—"

"Japan! You love these Asians! So you will like this China Doll, *já*."

He laughs. "Where the hell do you come from, Íris Magnúsdóttir?"

"From Hell," she mutters, frowning.

He seems serious and she is afraid the trip is finished. Then he chuckles, slow at first then rising to a great eruption of laughter.

"Your whole world is turning upside-down," he says. "The Christian girls are getting tattoos and the lesbians want to have sex with men. Strange women want me for threesomes. Next thing you know, your witch sisters will be waving gold crosses and singing hallelujah!"

She starts to respond, then she has to think about what he said.

Miles go by.

"I'd like to get the myth of the White Goddess into the story," he says. "The goddess has to anoint the sacred king, like what Mary Magdalene did for Jesus. She has to anoint him so he can restore life to the land. It's like the Grail legend. Otherwise, he has no power. It's her sacred duty. That's like the Great Rite for you witches, I read. It's sympathetic magic. The power of suggestion . . . ."

He continues on this theme until they pull off the highway.

The town is Ardmore, just north of the Texas border. They park in front of the room and he carries the bags in. It is dark already, past the dinner hour; yet after hamburgers, she is hungry for something more.

He showers and they go to bed.

"Shit, I can't get to sleep," he complains after tossing and turning for an hour.

So she gives him the best fellatio he has ever had and he gets rid of his frustration.

In the morning, they shower together. After, he kisses her and pats her belly, which presses against the front of the dress she puts back on. She does not sweat, he notices, so the dress is still fresh. He helps her into the car and soon they are on their way again, skipping breakfast for the promise of a better brunch down the road.

"Can you see the border?" he remarks after twenty minutes. "It's over the next hill, across the river. That's Texas. Where anything goes—as long as you're a Texan. The rest of us have to be careful. The rules are different there."

Eric concentrated on the highway as more vehicles bound for Spring Break venues joined them. It was Saturday now and classes were done. He kept to the right, letting the youth have the fast lane.

Íris gathered her hair up, tied it in a ponytail, then laid her head back, feeling nauseous. He knew a great place to get brunch that was a little further down the road.

"I need something to eat," she said. "If this trip is going to be so long, I better buy a magazine to read. I also need to pee."

"We'll be there soon. Can you wait?"

"There's a book store," she said, pointing at a billboard. "Next exit."

"It's an adult bookstore."

"*Já*, I am adult."

She's just tired and hungry, he decided.

"I need to pee," she said. "You can get something to drink there, too."

He exited reluctantly and circled back to the frontage road where Fuzzy's XXX Books & Video stood in need of fresh paint. Three cars and a pickup were parked in front at the mid-morning hour.

As their car rolled across the gravel and into a space between the red sports car and the small black truck, Eric decided he also needed to use the restroom.

He opened the door for Íris and the two men inside stopped their conversation in mid-syllable as the orange-haired goddess in the short, flowery dress stepped inside on long, pale legs, licking her pink lips as she surveyed the store.

"*Gaaaw*dang," the one decked out in blue denim from chin to boots muttered, leaning against the counter. He gave her a thorough look, from her red toenails to her orange hair and all of the curves between.

"Do you have a lavatory?" she asked. Eric smiled at her accent.

"In back," said the burly man behind the counter, pushing his cowboy hat back on his head and giving her a wide grin. "All the way ta th' back, past th' video booths."

"Thank you." She turned to her boyfriend. "You can look at the magazines."

He saw how the eyes of the men followed her, lingering even after she disappeared through the arched doorway. He glanced at the sign over the arch—TO BOOTHS—then scanned the rest of the store.

It was like any bookstore: metal shelving forming shoulder-high aisles, magazines on one side, videos on the other side, a section of sex toys near the cashier. He had never seen so much pornography.

Eric was tempted to flip through a magazine or two, *just out of curiosity*. They were just rags featuring . . . *well, every niche of sexual perversion*. He strolled up the aisle, scanning the selections: blondes, busty, Scandinavian, or flat-chested, and brunettes, short hair, long hair, Asian, Latin, Black. And Middle Eastern—*Harem Girls*, he noticed. There were the usual boy/girl magazines, the slightly more interesting girl/girl, and the more daring threesomes and foursomes.

Roman Orgy caught his eye. Next to it was Group Sex, Bondage, Sado-Masochism, Foot Fetishes, Latex Fetishes, "unusual insertions," special fellatio issues, the cunnilingus and analingus do-it-yourself pictorials, and every possible combination of acts to bring arousal.

Eric repressed a laugh.

He thumbed through a magazine featuring threesomes and paused at a pictorial showing two women and one man in contorted positions. Íris had suggested such an arrangement with her Chinese friend and with her chubby gal pal so he wondered how it might look. Research. That's all. Threesomes couldn't be that common, he decided. He would not be willing to share Íris with anyone.

He put the magazine back.

Stepping casually down the aisle, glancing at one magazine cover after another, he helped himself to a classy-looking magazine devoted to the art of fellatio, remembering the previous evening. As he flipped the pages, concerned about leaving fingerprints, he felt eyes on the back of his head. He returned the magazine to the rack as nonchalantly as possible, reached for another. Before opening it, he pretended to check his watch—as though he was not there for the magazines but just to kill time.

Eric felt a tap on his shoulder and slapped the magazine shut, crumpling half the pages between his hands. It was not his mother and he was not thirteen. It was Íris, his lover, mother of his child.

Her hair had come untied and she was perspiring. She took the magazine from his hands: *Busty Redheads*.

"Sorry," said Eric, "I'm . . . I guess I'm hooked on women who look like you."

"*Já*, don't worry. If you want it, I will buy it for you."

"You're not angry for looking at naked women?"

"What else would you look at here?"

He was nervous, used to being a model of propriety in public. He'd been taught too well, no matter how he fought against it. In Fuzzy's, he could not peruse the pages without worrying who might be standing behind him. He was not going to let himself become aroused. Not in public.

215

"If you're ready to go, I'd better stop by the restroom," said Eric, returning the magazine to the shelf.

"I will get a magazine," she said, turning away.

He stopped short. "You're not going to buy any of these, are you?"

"That's why we stopped, *já,* to buy a magazine for me to read."

He seemed offended. "Not much to read in these."

"Of course not, Eirík. You are so . . . conservative!"

Surprised by his reaction, she selected a magazine at random from the rack and thrust it angrily into his hands.

"What do you think of this?" she asked. The magazine offered women in very compromising situations, submissive, humiliated.

"It's gross. Why would any girl let men do that?"

Íris snatched the magazine from him and set it on the rack.

"You like that kind of thing?" he asked.

"*Nei.* I am saying—"

"I'm conservative?"

"You need to let yourself go wild before you get too old."

He grinned. "Actually, I thought I'd done all that back when I was in Japan. When I was young. When I didn't care much about anything."

"Japan again! Why don't you take Asian girls to meet your parents?"

"I don't know any," he said. He took a breath. "Because I'm interested in red-haired Icelandic witches now."

She blushed. "So you know how to have a good time."

"Well, I thought I did." He glanced at the front, saw the men there were talking, ignoring them. He turned to Íris. "I thought I'd gotten over all that, umm, playfulness—that frivolity, horniness, whatever." He pursed his lips, frustrated. Where was a thesaurus when he needed one? "Then you came into my life."

She was about to make a comment, but he waved her off to go to the restroom, unable to wait one minute more.

Three young men in t-shirts and shorts were bulling their way out as Eric tried to enter.

"Damn was *she* hot," one said to the others, who readily agreed.

Eric entered, muttering how spring breakers were always getting in his way. He hated them—fit, energetic young bulls. They had no conscience or brain function. Just booze and women. Forget studying. Burn off some gray matter, instead. Good luck finding a decent job after graduation. Good luck graduating. He sidled up to the urinal. None of that was true, he knew. They all graduated, and they would easily out-earn him. It was exactly as Albright said to that woman in his office: he was a perennial wallflower.

Perennial . . . wallflower, he laughed.

When Eric returned from the restroom, Íris was at the cashier. A pink-covered *Cosmo* was tucked under her arm, a box of mints in her hand. She was unscrewing the cap of a Mountain Dew bottle. She took a sip as he arrived.

"Want some?"

Eric reached for the bottle. He raised it to his lips and chugged down half.

"All set?" he asked, satisfied.

"*Já*, ready to go."

"Have a real good trip, ma'am," said the cowboy behind the counter.

She glanced at Eric: he was taking one last look at the store.

"Are you coming?" she asked, opening the door.

"In a store like this, how could anyone not?" Eric mumbled, and the cowboy chuckled. It was a deep, Santa Claus laugh Eric heard, and reminded him of Albright.

"Y'all come back now," said the cowboy.

She nodded without a smile, stepped out.

The warm Texas breeze caught the hem of her dress and her hands were slow to smooth it down. Her hand pinched the hem to keep it in place as she went to the car.

"Have a good one," a fellow sitting on the hood of the red sports car said. His two buddies, leaning against the car, were smoking but paused to smile at the sexy lady.

Eric recognized them: the three he bumped into at the restroom.

"*Já*, enjoy your holidays."

Eric quietly unlocked her door and helped her in, then went around to his side, got in and started the engine, flicked on the A/C.

"What was that all about?" he asked, watching the young men as he backed the car.

"Nothing," said Íris. "They asked where I was going. I said I didn't know the name. They are going to Padre Island."

She waved at them as Eric pulled the car out of the parking lot.

"What is the matter?" she asked, as they roared onto the Interstate.

"Nothing."

"Are you angry at me?"

He expelled a sigh that shook the car.

A mile down the road, he said: "I'm sorry. I guess I was jealous."

"Jealous? I do not know them."

She stared out the window for a few minutes.

"I think you are starting to be possessive. I don't like that."

"Let me say I'm sorry again."

"*Já*, that's good. Say it again." She turned to him. "I am with you because of what we have in common. I am with you because I want to be. *Skilurðu?*"

He had learned a few phrases; now she was testing him.

"Yes." He coughed, cleared his throat. "*Ég skil*. I understand."

Íris pulled her feet up onto the seat with the seatbelt loosened. Suddenly she unbuckled the belt and stretched over to kiss his cheek.

"Satisfied?" she asked.

He smiled, nodded.

As she repositioned herself, he caught a flash of orange. Normally, he would enjoy the sight, maybe pull over to examine it more closely, maybe even pull off the road—

"You're not wearing panties anymore?"

She hesitated, then: "*Nei*."

"Too hot?"

"I had an accident, so I threw it away. I have others."

"Do you want to stop and get another from your bag?"

"It is not required."

She watched the road, straightening her dress.

They stopped in Waco for a late brunch that was by then officially lunch. In only three months, Eric saw, the restaurant had changed from barbecue to Chinese. No longer was there a famous Buddy's Roadhouse to introduce Íris to. He sighed. The only thing about Texas he truly enjoyed was the barbecue. Now it was gone.

He pulled in a parking spot and sat, thinking.

"Do you like Chinese?" he asked, cautiously.

"I am hungry for anything now."

He was a gentlemen, opening doors, ushering her to a table, helping her decide what to order, taking the lead in ordering, making requests on her behalf—everything he was taught to do. He remained polite, even though she had turned sullen. He tried to make jokes. She stared out the window at the overcast skies.

"So what does your fortune cookie say?" he asked at the end of the lunch. He cracked open the cookie, pulled out the paper. "Mine says: 'It is easier to ask for forgiveness than to ask for permission.' Hmm, interesting. A tasty bit of existentialism."

She fumbled with her cookie, so he took it from her hand and broke it open, returned it to her.

"It says: 'All misfortune happens for a good reason.'"

Eric took it, examined the paper. "Look at this. The fortune's written in Spanish on one side, English on the other. Only in Texas—where the rules are different."

21

ÍRIS IS GLAD IT IS DARK WHEN THEY FINALLY ARRIVE, so she has a chance to hide.

Eirík pauses at the top step, glances back at her to make sure she is ready to present, and rings the bell. A kindly-looking old woman opens the wooden door, then unlatches the glass door and holds it open for them. The old woman eyes her thoroughly as she passes by. Inside, the sitting room is decorated in an old style—hardwood furniture with heavy fabric upholstery—remnants of life in a cold climate. Not wicker and mahogany like in the front office, with tropical plants, and seashells adorning every surface. Out from the lounger comes a grizzled old man, his hair cut short, his clothing tropical. The two of them stand side by side, blocking their way, forcing the visitors to notice them. She feels her hand being taken by Eric's.

"She sure does have orange hair," says the old man.

"Mom, Dad, this is Íris," says this Eirík. He drops her hand and places his in the small of her back, giving her a gentle nudge forward. She extends her hand and his parents shake it in turn. "You can call her Iris, if you like. She won't mind. Her name's spelled like Iris but it's pronounced Íris. That's because she's from Iceland."

"Another foreigner," the father says. "You still working for the goll darn Immigration Bureau?"

"Actually, I'm from Canada," says Íris. They must begin by being honest, já. His parents are still married, and they welcome him into their home. That is unfamiliar to her, so she feels awkward among them. "My name is very easy to say. It is Eeris, like the letter E, já?"

"Já means 'yes.' She says it a lot," Eirík explains. "She was born in Iceland."

"I moved to Canada when I was sixteen—"

"She has dual citizenship, though, and she still speaks Icelandic, so I think of her as being an Icelander."

"Your mother's got dual citizenship," his father says with a laugh. "She's a Preston and she's a Schaeffer."

The mother smiles, excuses herself for the small kitchen, with a window open to the sitting room. She has been cooking and the smell of roasted meat tickles their noses. It is long past dinnertime yet she will warm up the food.

"Dad, be nice," Eirík cautions, then continues his list of lies about her.

She could never tell her father how to act, especially not in front of guests. If she were ever rude, she would be punished. This is Texas, she remembers him saying. The rules are different here. Either way, she does not know what they are.

The mother returns with a tray containing a plate of cookies and fruit juice.

"Do you like it? It's mango," the mother announces, setting the tray down on the kitchen counter. "Have you ever eaten a mango?"

Íris smiles politely, as she has been trained.

"It's so good of you to come visit us, all the way from Kansas," the mother says, laying her hand lightly on Íris's forearm.

Naturally, Íris is suspicious, waiting for claws to unsheathe. For now, she likes the mother, who seems harmless, a plump German matron who tries not to smile.

"Eric hasn't told us very much about you." She turns to her son:

"Matt called. He said you had a new lady friend. We never imagined how pretty she is."

Já, they think he is too old to attract a pretty girl.

"Well, here she is," Eirík exclaims, happily. This is a new man she sees. "And I should tell you, she is special. Very special. We're going to be getting married soon."

Íris glares at him. "What?"

"But we're kind of living together right now. To save money."

"*Já*, I sleep with him on weekends."

He grimaces. "Until the lease is up on her place. In fact, as soon as the condo is sold and I get the proceeds, we're going to buy a house. Something with a spare bedroom, so you can visit us whenever you wish—"

"I must graduate first," she jumps in to shut him up. "In August."

"Íris is an art student," he starts again. "She's working on a Master of Fine Arts. Oh, and she has a commission to paint a mural in a church. What is it? Lutheran?"

"Baptist," she says.

"Close enough for your mother," the father says. "Aren't we all gonna sit down?"

"You two must be starving," the mother says, anxiously. "The food is almost ready. It's too bad you were delayed. We missed having dinner with you. Ten minutes more. Waiting on the rolls. You like roast beef, don't you, hon? So many girls today are vegetarians, I hear."

Íris gazes at Eirík, then wets her lips. "*Nei*, I like meat." Eirík nudges her, so she says: "Thank you for your hospitality, Missus Schaeffer, yet I am not so hungry."

"She's gotta keep that figure," the father snorts. "Eric likes a svelte gal."

"Dad! Be nice." Eirík pouts a moment, then grins. "What I like most about Íris is that we both have the same views on a lot of issues, like politics, religion, art . . . . And we both are creative. The only problem is we need privacy to do our creating."

"Someday you'll work on a project together," the mother says.

"Actually, we already have," says Eirík, and gives Íris a wink.

"*Já*, Eirík is writing a book," says Íris, "and I inspire him."

"It's a novel set in Viking days," he joins in. He always loves to talk about his work. "Also in modern times, up in Newfoundland. I was working on it last Christmas—"

"Newfoundland? Canada?" the father growls. "God bless America! You can't ever do anything with your own country, can you? Goddamn years wasted in Japan. Jesus Christ! Can't even write about your homeland."

Eirík reminds his father about the novel he wrote that was set in Missouri, about the Scouts on an Ozark campout who uncover a spy plot.

"You never sold that book," the father summarizes.

"Dad never reads them," he tells her, "he only knows what I tell him. He doesn't like fiction. He says there's no point reading anything that's not true. Isn't that right, Dad? And she"—meaning his mother—"can't bear to read all the 'realistic' dialog. In other words, profanity."

"Are we ready to eat?" the mother asks.

They sit around the dining table with place settings and a flower centerpiece. Dishes are placed on the table and everyone serves themselves and passes the bowl or plate to the next person. Her portions are small because she really is not so hungry, yet the mother insists she eat more. She orders Eirík to give her more potatoes and meat. The father sneaks an extra dinner roll onto her plate. During dinner, she drops out of the conversation as they catch up on local news and family gossip.

"So, have you set a date yet?" the father inquires as they sit back at the table to allow the mother to clear off the dishes. Earlier, Eirík told Íris not to offer to help. It would only embarrass his mother, because Íris is a guest. She sits back, too, and feels her belly rumble a little. She yawns softly.

"We haven't set a date yet—for the wedding, I mean. But we do have one more or less firm date to plan."

"We have to wait until August," says Íris with a smile. "That's when the baby's due."

A couple of plates crash on the floor behind them.

"Baby?" the mother exclaims, rushing to the table.

Eirík blushes, brighter than Íris's hair.

"Yes, that's right." He glares at Íris. It is out now, so he jokes about it. "Don't you see the slight bulge in her belly?"

"You're pregnant?" the father asks her directly, his eyebrows pinched.

"*Nei*, I had a big lunch. Chinese. With fortunate cookies."

Eirík laughs, nervously. He takes a huge breath. "Yes, I know it's backwards. But, well, we happened to meet last year and we've been dating ever since—"

"I took him home with me on Halloween and we made love all night. *Já*, I'm a witch and I needed him for the Great Rite."

Íris is the only one in the room with a straight face.

"She's kidding," says Eirík quietly. He turns to Íris. "No, we didn't. I was a perfect gentleman that night." He faced his parents. "She had an art show that evening."

"We tried to forget each other after that," Íris continues for him, "yet he picked me up a month later, on a cold, rainy night." She knows Eirík is waiting nervously, afraid of what she will say. "We were drenched, so we just ripped off our wet clothes. Then we went at it so hard we made a dent in the wall. It's true. The rest is like history." She cannot keep from laughing. "*Já*, I told him about the baby on the Valentine holiday, and this Eirík, he was so thrilled to hear the news! He gave me a box of chocolates. *Já*, we are so much in love we cannot be separated."

Father looks at Mother, who looks at Eirík, who looks back at Mother, then at Father, and then they all look at Íris. For a full minute.

"That's wonderful news, Eric," his mother says to break the silence.

"I guess at your age, you can't wait for a wedding," says the father with half a chuckle. "The girl might run off before you take her down the aisle. Besides, it's a modern world. People have babies before they know what to do with them. The world still turns. It's all a learning process. Young people today just have to learn what to do."

"Did you know what to do with me?" Eirík asks his mother.

"Sure, she did," the father cuts in. "She'd hand you to me and I'd have to take you over my knee and whip you with my belt whenever you raised hell."

"You abused Eirík?" Íris asks, alarmed.

"Abuse? Hell, no. Taught him a lesson. Only way a boy'll learn anything."

The father seems offended at her suggestion.

She can imagine this man pulling a boy down and slapping his bum with a stick. He seems like someone who could abuse a child. She studies them as they talk about Eirík's childhood. They tell her a few anecdotes, intended to embarrass him—yet she is not listening. She knows what she needs to know.

"So you're from Iceland. Isn't that where all those volcanoes are?" the father asks. "And everything is covered in ice, or bare rock. It's a barren place, from what I hear."

"It is only named such because the first visitors arrived to the southeast coast and they saw the ice cap there: Vatnajökull. Most of my country is green, *já*. Very green. And blue. And white. My grandparents had a dairy farm. My father was a fisherman."

"Oh, really. A fisherman? Did he have his own boat?"

Now the father is interested in her.

Eirík moans. "Here we go."

"I'll have to take you out and show you my sailboat," the father says, grinning. "His mother won't go out in it, scared to death of the sea. And this boy won't try it either."

He calls his son 'boy'—even though he is forty years old and has a baby on the way. She is understanding this Eirík more.

"It's not the sea, Dad, it's taking orders from you." Eirík does not seem completely angry, yet there is something burning under the surface, she can sense. "You're starting too late in life to be captain of a boat."

"What's too late? I'll be sailing around the world next year. All I need is someone to go with me. Someone who knows a couple of things about sails and rigging and basic navigation." The man turns to Íris, a glint in his eye. "Your pop teach you sailing?"

She answers honestly yet in generalities. She cannot tell the truth. The expression Eirík wears reminds her that she is a guest.

The man talks on and on about fishing, and because he has always been interested in history, he gradually moves to the topic of fishing in protected waters and the sovereignty of nations dependent on fishing for their economy. The 'cod wars' between Britain and Iceland in the 1970s pique his interest and they discuss it rather passionately for almost an hour.

"Dad, she doesn't want to talk about boats or fishing," Eirík says eventually, trying to rescue her. "Or her father."

"Your father?" He shoots a glance at Íris. "What's wrong with him? He was a damn fisherman, wasn't he?"

"Her father's dead," says this Eirík, who then explains about her mother's remarriage and divorce, moving to England, being estranged—

Íris glares at him. He did not have to tell them that!

Já, it makes no difference, yet now they will ask what happened. *How* it happened. He drowned. He got on his boat and sailed away. It was November and he ignored the gale warning. It was to be expected. Nobody cares what he was thinking after he ran out.

"I never saw him again."

"So the only family you really have is . . . Eric," the mother says so plainly.

The three of them regard each other, then all face her. She is the outsider, the one to be examined. *Is she worthy?* That is what they are wondering.

A bell rings on the countertop. The mother announces that dessert is ready.

Dessert is a ring of chocolate cake she calls 'devil's food'—covered with a caramel-coconut frosting that is too sweet for Íris. The mother offers coffee and Eirík refuses for her.

"Shall we adjourn to the living room?" the father suggests.

They all sit down, Eirík and Íris side by side on the sofa, the father in the lounger, the mother in a straight-backed dining chair that her son pulls over. The silence is too loud—

"Oh my," the father suddenly blurts out.

"What is it?" the mother questions.

"Uh . . . nothing, nothing to worry about," says the father with a snicker and a wink.

Íris realizes that sitting on the sofa has made the short hem of her dress ride up and given the father a good look between her legs. She is wearing nothing.

"Excuse me," she says, standing. "Could I change clothes? I have worn this dress for two days and I would like to—"

"Yes, of course, dear," the mother says, jumping up and playing the hostess again. "I'll show you to your room. Eric, bring her bags up."

"Mom, we got our own place at the Surfsider."

"You're not staying with us?" The mother is shocked. "You're just throwing money out the window, aren't you? You don't make that much being a teacher."

"Let the boy be," the father says. "He 'n' his lady friend need some privacy."

He tells Eirík to get a change of clothes for her and the 'boy' goes down to the car and returns with her bag. Eirík takes it into the bedroom, following his mother, and Íris follows them. When Eric leaves, Íris unzips the bag and selects a skirt and top while the mother gets a towel and a fresh bar of soap. The mother insists she use the shower—"if you care to" with a tone suggesting she needs it.

The mother is shocked again when Íris pulls the dress up and over her head.

"Oh dear."

The mother glances at the famous belly, then acts as though she was not looking. Íris does not know if she is more shocked to see a nude woman standing before her, or that she now understands Íris was not wearing any underwear when she sat on the sofa. These garments are required for all respectable women, and especially for pregnant wives. Everything must be held in place.

"Missus Schaeffer, thank you for welcoming me to your home," says Íris. "You need not worry about me. I often go nude when we are together. It's so natural to go without clothing, *já*. Very healthy."

She is dumbfounded, staring at Íris.

"What is that?" she asks, pointing with her chin.

Íris looks between her breasts and sees the pendant dangling there.

"A pentacle," she says. "A symbol of the four elements of nature and the spirit of humanity. Everything in the universe."

The mother continues to stare.

"It is not evil." Íris raises the pentacle and kisses it ceremoniously.

"Here's your soap and towel," the mother says, now afraid to touch the witch.

The shower is cold, no matter how she spins the dial, yet it is refreshing that way. She feels much better—alive, ready to challenge convention.

When she exits, wrapped in the towel, the mother is not there. Íris can only imagine what she told the men. She laughs to herself as she slips into fresh clothing, including panties. Her knit top is white and her skirt is red/white plaid with Velcro on the side to make it easy to rip off herself. On stage, she performed as a Catholic schoolgirl.

Íris rejoins them to the praises of the men. They like this transformation. They pick up their conversation, about Eirík's ex-wife and her baby—a girl named Alicia. They changed realtors and the condominium has gotten a few offers but not close to what they have been asking. Eirík is willing to wait rather than lower the price. He knows the condo's appraised value and he needs that amount to buy a house in Wichita. Íris nods through the discussion, like a good little wife.

"So what do you like to do?" the mother asks too innocently.

Eirík looks at Íris, daring her to answer.

"We like sex." She smiles at Eirík. "That, mostly." She lays her hand alongside their boy's face, turns his head and gives him a noisy, wet kiss on the mouth. "I want a good grade in his class, *já*."

22

THE CRIES OF SEAGULLS AWAKENED ERIC and his first instinct was to reach for his lover. He sat up. Yawning, stretching, barefoot and shirtless, with the baggy lounging pants sagging on his hips, Eric wandered out to the balcony and gazed at the gray sky stretching across the brown Gulf waters. He spied her down on the beach, sitting on a towel, dressed in a green wrap-around skirt and white knit pullover. She sat with her knees bent and a sketchbook balanced on them. By the time he had pulled on a pair of shorts and a t-shirt and joined her, the sketch of the seascape was almost finished.

"It is so peaceful here," she said, gazing seaward. "I can't remember anything that happened before I awoke this morning."

Except for a few early-risers who walked along the shore in the distance, they were alone. Birds squawked overhead and called to each other as tall grasses waved along the crest of the dunes. Despite gray skies, the air was warm, humid. It was difficult to remember the ice storm a couple of days before. Even so, as he watched her he knew she was out of place. Her skin was so pale in the morning light, her hair the brightest point on the beach as far as he could see in either direction.

After breakfast, they went into town to find her a swimsuit. The town had once been a fishing village; before that, a Civil War lookout post, an Indian village, and a place for pirates to bury their treasure. Now it was full of souvenir shops, restaurants, hotels, and vacation condos. The main street had a dozen swimsuit shops.

They crowded into one small boutique and dug through the racks. Íris selected a mauve one-piece suit with tropical fish swimming across the waistline. Eric held up his latest find: a metallic-purple thong. He joked that the total amount of fabric used was less than the sleeve of his t-shirt. Íris frowned. She took it and her selection, as well as three others, into the dressing room.

Eric waited a while, grew impatient, called into the dressing room that he was stepping out for a moment.

Outside, he leaned against the wooden railing. The storefront was decorated as a wharf, fishing nets strung along the posts, a few plaster seagulls bolted to the railing. Girls in swimsuits or shorts and tank-tops strolled past on the sidewalk, some with boys in t-shirts or no shirts accompanying them. Everyone was heading to the beach or returning from the beach.

He was admiring some of the passing girls when someone tapped his shoulder. Spinning around, he saw Íris standing there in the purple bikini he had chosen. Her orange hair tied up, her shoulders were left exposed. He noticed how the skimpy purple fabric accented her pale skin, made her seem even whiter.

"You like this?" Her smile was sunshine. "You picked it."

She turned around in place on the shop's wooden deck as several young men stopped to check her out. Standing sideways, the skinny straps were nearly invisible and made her appear completely nude. Nothing covered her backside but a narrow strap.

"Well, I didn't think you'd wear it out of the store."

"I bought it already." She showed him the receipt. Her clothes were folded and stuffed into the shop's bag. "I still have some money."

He saw the slip of paper but was actually calculating the effect this purple strip of cloth against her pale skin was having on him.

"This is closest to nude as possible," she said.

"Absolutely." He could not take his eyes off her. "We need to get some sunblock, too. Strong sunblock, to keep you from burning."

A group of boys had gathered in front of the store. One called to her, asking her name and where she was staying. Eric put his arm around her as she waved at them.

"Maybe you'd better put the skirt on as long as we're in town," he said. "And a shirt."

After she changed, they walked four blocks down to the grocery, the only one on the island. Inside, the checkout lines were six customers deep, but Eric waved her on, saying the lines would be shorter by the time they were ready to go. He wanted food to cook in their condo.

They were in no hurry as they walked around the store and gathered items in the basket.

"Hey, what're *you* doing here?" a male voice called.

Eric was not concerned until he looked back and did not see Íris.

"This is where I'm going," he heard her say, around the corner.

"No shit," said a different male voice.

"We're staying down the road."

"It sure is a freakin' small world!"

Eric stepped around the end of the shelves and saw three bare-chested young men with cases of beer in their arms.

"Hi, I'm Brad," said the tallest one with short, bleached hair and a small lizard tattoo above his left nipple. "Guess we never were, ya know, properly introduced." He extended his hand and Íris shook it without any smile. "This is Lee and that's Frank."

She looked at her escort, gave him a nod. "This is Eirík."

"How's it going?" the boy offered.

Eric did not care how it was going, but he did not want to make a scene in front of his lover. There was enough tension left from meeting his parents. When Brad extended his hand, Eric shook it. Then Lee and Frank shook hands with him and with Íris.

"So you're, like, married or something?" asked Frank.

"We are more like, how you say, co-dependents," Íris responded. "He likes to have sex and I like to be protected."

Eric *tsk*ed, shaking his head. "She's kidding, of course."

"Yeah. And your name was . . . ?"

"Íris," she said quickly, lowering her voice as though it was a secret.

"That's unusual," the one named Lee said.

"It's Icelandic," said Eric, suddenly proud. "My girlfr—my *fiancée* is from Iceland."

"You're sure a long way from home," said Brad.

"But we're glad you're visiting," said Frank.

"Yeah, have a good time," said Brad.

"A *real* good time," Lee added with a sly grin.

"Well, dear, I guess we should be going now," Eric said, deliberately.

"*Já*, time to go."

"See ya round," said Brad. "Maybe on the beach, yeah?"

"*Já, já.*"

The three men turned and walked down the aisle with their beer.

Eric regarded Íris. "Who are they?"

"You do not recognize them?" She acted as though everything was normal, that he was the one out of touch. "They were in the bookstore where we stopped."

"Those guys?" He watched them joking around at the opposite end of the aisle. "And they followed us here?"

"*Nei*, they just came here, too. This is the destination. Everyone is coming here for Spring Break holiday."

"The only grocery on the island . . . ."

Eric led her to the cashiers.

"I thought they meant *South* Padre Island—two hours' drive further south, far away from us."

He cooked dinner: shrimp and vegetable stir-fry with rice. After eating, they lounged on the balcony and watched the stars, listening to the steady rhythm of waves rolling to shore.

In the morning, Íris was on the beach again under cloudy skies, only the purple bikini and a skirt covering her, sketching another seascape. The breeze danced with her skirt, tossing it around her legs. The fabric was thin enough Eric could see through it from the balcony.

They spent the day on the beach and when she stretched out on the large beach towel, he gladly rubbed sunblock on her. He started with her thighs, working his way up her back and then across her shoulders. The overcast was dissipating as she rubbed her arms and chest.

She decided she was bored, so Eric locked up the condo and they strolled down the beach to see what the crowds were doing.

"Hello again," a man called to Íris. Eric saw that it was the one named Brad. The boy jogged up to them. Eric saw the boy's eyes widen at the sight of Íris in the skimpy purple bikini. "Wow, great swimsuit! What part of the beach you hang out on?"

"We're just walking down from our *condo*," said Eric. He intended his tone to indicate he had money for a nice beachfront condominium while they, being poor college boys, were splitting the cost of a cheap motel room.

"Too quiet up that way," said Íris.

Brad called to his friends and the guys, with girls in bikinis, joined them. Brad introduced everyone to Íris. The guys examined her quite brazenly, and the girls noticed the guys' attention and pulled them away. Eric wished then that she'd gotten the one-piece suit. The purple bikini was for him.

"We're planning a party Friday night," said Frank. "It's kinda . . . call it a farewell to Spring Break bash."

"You're invited," said Brad.

"Bring your ol' man, if you like," Lee added, gesturing at Eric.

"Sounds like fun," said Íris, and turned to see Eric's slight tilt of his head. "I will see if I can join it. You know . . . busy schedule."

Brad glared at Eric. He was clearly an "ol' man" if ever there was one.

Eric saw it differently. He was here with his *fiancée*. He was a professor. These were kids, students—someone's students—and they should not mix. Jack's voice was shouting in his head. Eric answered: *No, the situation with Íris is not at all the same as yours!* He meant *other* students, students he would give grades to, not this one he'd met before she was his student, before she was pregnant with his baby. *With my baby!*

"We need to take it easy, sweetheart," said Eric softly. "Remember what the doctor said about *the baby*. We want to get some rest. That's why we came here, isn't it?" He stressed the word 'baby' for the benefit of the testosterone-drunk audience. Brad, Lee, and Frank took a moment before congratulating her, saying she looked "hot" even while pregnant.

Eric did not like the look Íris gave him but she told her new friends that she needed to consider the baby. She patted her belly for effect. The two girls stared at her belly. Oh, yes—they could see it, now that she mentioned it.

Eventually, Eric was able to separate Íris from the crowd, escorting her past two police cars, blaring stereos, kids dancing and drinking, Frisbees and footballs being tossed, dogs running around unleashed, surfboards being swung haphazardly—back to their stretch of beach.

She released his hand when they arrived at the condo.

"There was nothing wrong with talking to them," she said. "We were just talking. You had to jump in and show them how much a control person you are."

He apologized. "I was only looking out for you. These Spring Break gatherings can erupt in violence at any time. The kids are crazy, and some of them are on drugs, and most of them drink. Why do you think the police are patrolling the beach?"

She sat on the bottom step as he remained standing, poised above her, seeing how the purple top barely held her breasts. He also noticed how she had cowered as he lectured her on the evils of springtime fun. He stopped. What was she thinking?

A tear rolled down her cheek.

He went down the steps and knelt in the sand before her, tried to take her hand. She pulled back.

"You make me feel like some little girl who knows nothing," she said. "I do not want you to protect me. I do not need it. I am twenty-seven years of age, and I have taken care of myself for more than twelve years. I do what I need to do. I am making new success with my art. Where are you going to be? You going to follow me to galleries and exhibits? You going with me to New York, Paris, or Milan? Do you expect me to keep in the studio in the house? You going to chain me there? A golden cage is still—*vá!* Is that what I am to you, a pretty little witch to fuck? You don't know anything about me, yet you act like you have the right to control me. When you think you are fucking me good, what you don't know is that I am giving nothing to you, Mister Schaeffer! I am *taking* from you what *I* want. *I* am fucking *you!*"

"I'm sorry, Íris."

"Please be quiet."

"I need to tell you—"

"Shut up!" She looked away. "I need time alone."

"I understand."

He paused, hoping she would look up. He wanted to see her face, those blue eyes that made her special.

"I'll be inside."

23

THE WATER IS TRANSLUCENT TODAY. Regarding the endless waves, Íris knows somewhere out there is a land where she has buried her heart. It is decaying, returning to the soil.

When the volcano erupted and her father ran out of the house, Íris climbed off the bed, so confident in her sixteen-year-old nudity as she stared at Heiðr. *Here is your daughter.* Magnús had shoved Heiðr aside in his escape and she glared at the girl from her crumpled position on the floor. She said nothing as Íris stepped to the waste can and spit, wiped the back of her hand across her chin. Heiðr got up and slapped her face several times and she took it, every one of the strikes, until Heiðr was too tired to swing her hand and the girl's lips and nose were bloody.

Throwing on a dress, Íris ran outside, trying to catch up to him. She soon realized he was too far ahead. She went to the harbor, thinking he would go to his boat but his boat was gone when she arrived. She sat on the wharf, arms wrapped around her knees, staring at the November sea, the dark skies and darkening waters, as the night deepened. A storm was approaching yet she did not feel the chill. A harbor pilot found her asleep there and took her home to a house that was empty. Heiðr was out, looking for her, she thought. She waited until morning yet Heiðr had not returned.

She went to school. The headmaster called her into his office. Two women teachers were there and they seemed to know everything. One of them insisted she must be sent for counseling, that she must be insane. The other suggested she needed more time with her mother. The headmaster thought she should be punished, and had a plan for her to work around the school in her free time, to teach her discipline and let her reflect on her sins. At home, she should be treated similarly.

When she went to the classroom, the students stopped their work. They snickered and the teacher had to silence them. They knew Íris was a girl who was kind to boys. She sat down at her desk, got out the history book, turned to the assigned page, and was called upon to read the passage there.

The passage concerned the punishment put on pregnant girls who were not married. It was after the conversion to Christianity in 1000 A.D. The girls were drowned, or they were burned to death as a priest held up a cross in an attempt to save their souls. At the same time, the fathers of these unborn babies were rich men, landowners, so they were untouched. Many of the girls were slaves in those households—red-haired handmaidens, descendants of slaves brought from Scotland and Ireland. They were required to do more than cook and clean. Instead of aborting the unborn babies in those days, the woman was killed to keep the honor of her master's family. It was the woman who was the temptress, according to their Christian thinking. Women were devils in disguise, who provoked God-fearing, married men into sin. Yet always it was the girls who died for the sins committed as a couple, or for acts forced upon the girls by the master or the master's sons.

The teacher selected this passage for her benefit, everyone could guess. Some of the boys laughed. They understood. Some of them knew her well.

She closed the book and ran out of the classroom, out of the school.

Heiðr was still not home. Íris cried for hours—until nightfall—and ate nothing. Fearing she was now completely alone in the world, that

Heiðr had left her, too, she went to the one place where she was always welcome: the *erótísk bókabúð* in Midbaer, the bookshop for adults. As long as she fulfilled the expectations of the men who stopped by, she was appreciated. Some gave her money, others merely their thanks. No one asked her name, nor her age when they pushed into the booth. When the night grew late, she crept home no happier and did not find Heiðr there.

The next morning Íris awoke to see Heiðr standing over her. Beside Heiðr were the headmaster and two stout women in white coats. They grabbed Íris, bound her hands and feet as she screamed and struggled. They wrestled her into the car outside, then drove her to Kleppur, the mental hospital on the north shore, facing snowcapped Mount Esja across Faxaflói Bay.

She stayed in Klepp and endured their tests and counseling sessions, wearing a gown they gave her or, just as often, tearing it off and running naked through the corridors. She learned to survive there, to give them what they wanted while keeping herself alive inside. And every night she watched the moon rise over Esja. She was examined by a doctor and passed the sexual diseases test—she had none. She passed the pregnancy test—she was not. Everyone was informed that she was, as expected, no longer a virgin. In that Lutheran land, she might as well be dead.

Her mother never visited and Íris thought she might never return to collect her from the institution. She watched Esja all night long, the stars and the moon lighting her, the snow covering her, the beautiful chill freezing around her heart. One night she bit her fingers and, using the blood, tried to draw the mountain on the plaster wall.

After three months, she was behaving as they wanted—yet it was only acting. Three months more and she was released and delivered home—to a new home in a new block, twelve buildings looking the same, blue and white, yellow on the balconies. In this new home, a flat on the fifth level, was a new Heiðr, who tried to be kind and not let her anger out. She told about her father, how they found his boat locked in ice yet no body. He was listed as drowned.

Then Heiðr told her she had met a Canadian businessman after that and they were going to marry. They would be moving to Toronto in a few months.

Íris just smiled at Heiðr, as she had practiced in Klepp.

The sun is high now, and the horizon no longer bleeds into the sea. Clouds drift by and the air is hot, moist, even as the sun stays hidden. The dunes rising behind where Íris spreads the towel hide her from the condo's deck. She stretches out on the towel, reaching for the future. Her eyes search the shoreline. The beach is not deserted. There are a few people far off in each direction, heading away from her. She sets down her sketchbook—how many seascapes can she draw?

After a while, she gets up and steps across the sand, over strings of seaweed, down to the surf, to the water's edge, and lets the waves roll over her feet. Her toes dig into the wet, brown sand. A tiny crab, no bigger than her thumb tip, crawls over one foot, then the other foot and continues on its way.

She feels weak. To fight it, she runs into the surf, submerges herself in the water up to her chin and splashes around like a child. When she has had enough fun she wades up to the beach, rising from the waters like the Venus of Botticelli.

With water running off her body, she sees that a few admirers have gathered. It is Brad and his two buddies. She sees in their faces that something is amiss. She notices that her top has come untied, hanging loosely around her neck.

"How's the water?" Brad asks.

"A little cold," she says.

"I can tell," says Lee, staring at her nipples.

"I didn't know this was a topless beach," says Brad, trying for humor.

She regards them, their chests muscular, becoming tanned, their swimming shorts, baggy boxers in bright colors. They stare too hard.

"You never saw nude woman before?" she asks sharply.

At the same time, Lee says "Sure, all the time," and Frank says "Just in magazines."

"Excuse me," she says coldly, and returns to the towel.

Standing on the towel, she suddenly feels like she is on stage, so with practiced grace she ties the strings of the bikini top. She turns to give them a show, shoveling her breasts inside the tiny purple triangles. As she performs, she offers them a slight grin, enough to acknowledge that she knows their interest has risen.

"Hey, as long as we're passing by," says Brad, "have you thought about the party?"

"Now is the middle of your holiday and you already plan the end?"

"We really want you to come," says Frank, with a leer.

"You can wear clothes. Or not—whatever you like," Brad says. "It's not really clothing-optional. Well, some girls take their tops off, if they get wasted, but it's—nothing is, uh, you know, required. You can just meet people and do whatever."

"We'll have good music, food, tacos and nachos, and lots of beer—"

"A *lotta* beer!" Lee cuts in.

She realizes these three are standing within arm's length of her, closer than the boys in Life Study who always leer. It seems strange that their presence does not bother her, does not make her nervous.

Já, they are so innocent.

"The party's at ten o'clock," says Brad, "but it'll go til morning, so you can stop in anytime. Should be about thirty people. Just guys from our fraternity—any brothers who're down here from any college. Plus any girlfriends they want to bring. We're gonna have lots of food."

"Where is it?" she asks, crossing her arms over her chest.

"It's down the beach. About half a mile," says Brad. "At the new motel."

"I will need a ride," she says, and she wonders what she is saying. "If I decide to go."

"That's cool," says Brad. "I can pick you up, or . . . . Is your, umm, co-dependent going to join us? It's okay, I mean."

She shakes her head, then stares at the surf.

"He—he has his own way of seeing things. Sometimes I need to have my own fun, *já*." They think they understand and applaud her decision. "Everything is different now. He is . . . . It is difficult sometimes."

"Yeah, he *is* a lot older than you," says Brad. "We thought he was, you know, one of those gentleman friends."

"Your sugar daddy," Frank says.

"*Nei*, he is my professor."

They nod, giggling. Now they understand.

"It's a class about Shakespeare. I sit in the back. Sometimes we fuck in his office."

"You'll get an A for sure," says Lee.

"Hey, that's cool," says Brad. "If you really dig each other, why not?"

Brad tells about an affair he had with his Anthropology teacher, a Miss Fletcher, a graduate teaching assistant actually, but his buddies hoot that he is delusional.

"We met on campus, but he was not my teacher then," she says. "We fucked one night, and I never expected to see him again."

"Like you never expected to see us again, huh?" says Frank.

She nods.

"You got a baby, too. That's kinda weird." Brad grins, awkwardly. "So, are you gonna get married sometime or just stay co-dependents?"

"I do not know. He asked me a few times yet I keep putting him off. I'm not ready to belong to someone." She gazes at Brad, who seems to understand. "This trip is to meet his parents. He wants us to like each other. He worries too much—"

"Must be serious," says Brad.

"*Já*, serious . . . . Everything is so serious."

Íris gazes out at the sea, remembering a man in Reykjavík who taught her things she had no reason to learn—yet, having learned, found them useful. He taught her how to bend to keep from breaking. He told her it was better to be a living whore than a dead virgin.

"What I want," she tells them, "is—is do something outrageous. *Já*, I want him to watch me. Yet it is impossible. He would freak out. Is that the right word?"

"That's it, awright," says Lee.

"If I go to your party, I will be alone."

"Hey, that's great," says Brad. "We'll be looking forward to whatever."

Frank scratches his crotch. "We sure would welcome you, even if you just, like, show up to just dance. You don't have to do anything else. Whatever you want. Total freedom."

Brad takes over: "We do have a private room where we could all, uh, hang out and . . . ."

She turns to them, glances up at the condo, all but the roof lost behind the dunes, then stares downward. Her red toenails are partially covered by the sand. She sees her pale legs, the knobby knees she hates, and the narrow purple cloth. They cannot see the beach for the sand.

Brad's eyes gleam, and the testosterone lingers on the breeze. She feels something burning inside her, screaming at her to maintain control. This is not Iceland. It is not Toronto.

"*Nei*, it is impossible," she says finally.

She has discovered that because the world has changed and the rules are different now, she must change with them. She touches each boy's shoulder, to let them know she does not want to hurt them.

"There are things I want to do yet I cannot. It is not me. It's not the woman I am trying to be. I am not the whore I used to be. You know? So let's not meet again. We—my boyfriend and me—we are having a baby. We are trying to be a couple and a family. It is hard yet we try."

She glances up again at the condo: the bedroom window is visible.

"It's not like you're engaged," says Brad. "Like you said, you're just co-dependents. Right?"

His friends add cheerful rationalizations. They desire her, and she desires being desired.

"Whatever you want to do is okay," Brad says.

They stare at each other a moment too long.

24

ERIC SHOUTED FROM THE LIVING ROOM TO THE BEDROOM: "Hurry, the reservation is for seven. That's the latest my folks would wait for dinner. You know how old people are: early to bed, early to dinner."

Íris appeared. "Early to bed, early to rise, he never has fun, so early he dies."

"Very funny," said Eric, looking over his date.

Nothing was too fancy on the island, and an elegant romantic dinner in higher priced restaurants required nothing more than a tropical shirt and khaki slacks, sandals optional. For the women, any dress that was colorful, and required no heels was appropriate. Íris wore a too-elegant dress of gold with emerald highlights shimmering through the fabric like glitter. She said that her housemate, Jean, had insisted she bring it, "for the big date, when he pops the question." Her legs were bare and she had put up her hair, leaving her neck exposed, so he went to her and kissed the nape.

"Am I satisfactory?" she asked, playfully.

"You might be overdressed for the island." He looked at his own outfit: khaki slacks and a mauve shirt with white palm fronds. "Maybe I need a jacket."

"You look fine, my dear," she cooed. "I won't kick you out of bed."

They met his parents at The Blue Pelican, one of the few upscale restaurants on the island. His parents greeted Íris, and his father, grinning slyly before sweeping his arm to gesture at her seat, praised her "spiffy outfit" and called her a "princess." That was what Eric had called her: his Viking princess. Íris smiled demurely. Eric's mother wore her usual dowdy flower-print dress. His father wore the red Aloha shirt Eric had bought for him. His mother complained about him spending so much money on them when they could as easily eaten at Joe's Rib Shack or The Luau Buffet.

His father sat back, surveying the decor. "Well, looky there," said his father a dozen times before the server came to take their orders. His father pointed to the stuffed marlin and swordfish hanging on the far wall, talked fishing with the 'boy.'

They dined on grilled snapper, tuna steaks, shrimp, pasta, Caesar salad, stuffed mushrooms, zucchini, and Mediterranean coos-coos. As Eric chewed the snapper, he recalled the evening five years before, an evening such as this one, when it was Marina he had been introducing to his parents. She had been so flamboyant, self-assured, knowing everything. The snapper was a little tough, he decided, and reached for his iced tea. It was bitter. His mother saw his face and handed him the sugar packet tray but only the sugar substitutes were left. Íris was quiet—reserved in manner if not in dress. Two packets made the tea suitable but the coos-coos was overcooked.

"I got a call from the realtor," Eric mentioned half-way through dinner. "He had a couple look at it yesterday. They made an offer. It's close to our asking price."

He remembered the day he came home to the condo, went straight to the bedroom and found Marina, his wife of almost a year, naked and sweaty on the bed, flat on her back with a tan, muscle-bound lummox between her legs.

"Oh, you're home," she had said, matter-of-factly.

The big lummox looked up at him: "Hey, man, you must be Eric!"

His automatic reaction was to close the door. Yes, he thought, block the scene, pretend he had not come home at all. He waited in the hallway. In movies, the appearance of the husband would put a quick halt to the illicit sex. The big lummox would come rushing out, a bundle of clothes in his arms. The woman would remain on the bed, tearfully begging forgiveness.

However, Eric had waited. He listened at the door: their passionate moans were increasing. They were not stopping! He barged in, shouting: "Are you about finished?" They were breathing too hard to respond, so he slammed the door as loudly as he could and left the condo. He went to the beach, watched the sun set, then rise.

Too many days were the same routine: the afternoon delight, the stoic response to his criticism, the feigned apologies. It almost became a joke. Soon it seemed as though her lover was a part of the family: the houseboy who collected the mail, did the dishes, ran errands, yet was always ready when Marina needed him. Eric lived there, too, on the sofa and in his home office, until he found his own apartment.

"Would it be safe to assume that you and I will no longer be having sex?" he asked her in the cynical whine he saved for special occasions.

"It would be safe," Marina responded.

"Now that that's clear," Eric said, "would you tell me exactly *why*?"

She had not hesitated one heartbeat. "Just look at him!"

What she meant was that the big lummox—the name Marco was applied after a few more intrusions—was the man she wanted. Plain and simple. The marriage contract was an illusion. A piece of paper that made two sets of parents happy but actually counted for nothing.

Nevertheless, it *was* a contract, he pondered: to love, honor, and obey? He loved her, honored her, obeyed as much as he could, though she never commanded him to do much of anything. Except when he barged in and she would yell at him to get out while they finished lovemaking—"and don't let the door hit you in the *be*-hind on your way out!" She knew he was a gentleman, that he would not become violent, that he'd just take it.

"Hey, I'm real sorry your ol' lady's such a slut," Marco told him.

"Then why don't you stop seeing her?" Eric had asked.

"Cuz she's so damn hot!"

"Maybe in a couple of years," Eric sneered, "you'll get to experience this from the other side."

"Huh?" said the lummox.

She must be breaking some kind of law, Eric had considered. So he sought legal advice from Rex King, attorney-at-law.

"Adultery is certainly immoral," said King in his easy drawl, "and it is on the books as a crime in many places, but fact is, Mister Schaeffer, you kin sue her fer divorce but you caint have her arrested. Wives're no longer property. They kin do whatever th' hell pleases'em."

"You mean, even bringing some lummox into our home and refusing to send him away when I show up?"

"Mister Schaeffer, she kin use yer hard-earned money to hire a gigolo, pick him up in yer luxury car, drive him home an' feed him yer food an' let him drink all yer beer, an' screw th' hell outta him. She kin do that and it's all kosher precisely 'cause she *is* married. It's the same as when a husband hires a call girl t'come over t' the house. It's all tacitly done with the spouse's knowledge an' approval. That's what matrimony means: it's a goddamn partnership. What's yours is hers and what's hers is yours. You could put on her dresses an' make-up if you want an' you'd be perfectly legal."

He had met with King on a Monday. Tuesday the next week, the papers were served, and on Wednesday, she gladly signed them. They arrived in King's office on Friday. It was a done deal: no-fault divorce, a mutually agreed settlement, property divided, and no children to fight over. Eric was so eager to be divorced from her that he had agreed to everything. *Money is no object, just get me out.* Rex King saw to the details, collected a fair but modest fee, and a few weeks later the papers arrived in the mail. Valentine's Day. He was free. He laughed, realizing he was free in exactly the way a sailor is free who jumps into the ocean from a perfectly good boat, leaving all the supplies on board.

"What are you thinking?" asked Íris, nudging him out of his trance.

"Sailing," he muttered. Finding himself back in reality, he smiled at her. "I was thinking how beautiful you are this evening."

"*Já*, it has to be said." She slid her hand atop his. Eric saw his parents' eyes focus on the affectionate gesture, knowing their impression of her

250

was improving. "Now tell me, what were you truly thinking?"

"Seriously? I was thinking of Marina—that's my ex-wife—how she was such a bitch." He saw his parents flinch. If he's using profanity he must be grown up, Eric sensed them thinking. "And how I am so happy to be getting closer to dumping that condo." He gazed into her eyes. "We're one step closer to buying our dream house, Íris."

Eric and his father fought over the check then divided it evenly as the women visited the restroom. They all went to the parking lot together, chatted a few minutes more, and each couple got into a car and drove away.

Parking at the Surfsider, Íris leaned over in the car and kissed him, stroked his chest, moved her hand to his lap. He laid his hand over hers and moved it off. He climbed out of the car, went around, and opened her door.

"Eric, are you angry?" she asked. He stepped back from the car.

"I'm angry . . . but not at you."

"Your parents?"

"No, the condo. And everything in it, then and now. The memories."

She went to him and he let her hands caress his face. They walked up the stairs arm in arm. Inside, they went to the sofa and began kissing in the dark.

The sound of firecrackers going off down on the beach broke the mood.

"Idiots," said Eric.

"They are just having fun," said Íris, quick to defend the anonymous rebels. "That is what this holiday is for, *já*. Fun and frivolity."

"Fun and frivolity? Hah!"

He regarded her, ran his fingers slowly through the hair she had let down.

"Eirík . . . ?" Her hand rested on his thigh.

"Yes, my dear?"

"It is a strange place here. I like the peace, yet I think I have reached the limit of peace. I am bored."

"We'll be leaving soon," Eric assured her. "Just thirty-six hours."

"You talk like it is some punishment we must endure."

He laughed. "In some ways, it is."

"I do not want to sit here waiting to leave." She glanced away, in the direction of the beach, even though the balcony door was closed and the curtains were drawn. "I want to do something fun. And frivolous."

"I think we've done about all that's possible here. We went to the beach. The souvenir shops. The restaurants. The beach. Met my parents. Toured Dad's sailboat. Mom's baking lessons. You got your fish and seafood. And a sexy swimsuit. Oh!—did I mention the beach?"

"*Já*, that is what I mean." She kissed his cheek. "We could go to that party tomorrow night. That might be fun."

"What party?"

"You remember. The students we met. They invited us to the party."

"You want to go to a frat party?" He made a face, like he had swallowed something bad. "It's just a bunch of idiots seeing how lewd and crude they can be. It's a keg-emptying contest, and the winner pukes out his guts while the others laugh hysterically. That's your kind of fun and frivolity?"

"It's not that," Íris said. "They came up the beach yesterday. I talked with them. They invited us again. They are having tacos, he said. You like tacos, *já*?"

"We can fix our own tacos, right here, Íris."

"That is not the point, Eirík!"

He saw she was upset. All it was, he told himself, was a stupid frat party. Of course, she was a member of that generation. She needed a moment of escape, but he did not get it. When he was in college, he never found anything entertaining about those kinds of parties. He didn't see the point of getting drunk and acting stupid.

"I don't want to go," he said calmly. "And I don't think you should go, either. I mean, you're pregnant and shouldn't drink alcohol. And they'll probably have too-loud music—it'll disturb the baby, make him grow big ears or something." He brushed her hair. "Come on, we'll have fun here, just the two of us. Doing what we do best. Making love is fun and frivolous, isn't it?"

"We did that," she said, crossing her arms. "I want to go to the party. It is something different. It is going on all night yet I can go for only an hour or two. That is all I need."

"Need? Nobody *needs* a party like that. Forget fun and frivolity. It's dangerous."

He knew what he was talking about. His roommate in college was a good example: fatal car crash coming back from spring break. Another drunken friend took a dare and jumped off the dormitory, and now drove a motorized wheelchair. Eric, despite being a legacy, dropped out of the fraternity before completing the pledging. Running naked across the campus at midnight covered in whipped cream did not seem to have too much to do with earning a degree.

He laid his head back on the sofa cushion and sighed.

"Íris, I really don't think you should go to that kind of party. It's just not, well, *proper* for a pregnant woman, and it's certainly not right for any woman who is . . . ." He was going to say 'pledged' but decided not. "Don't you want to be here with me? I want to be with you. I want to make love to you—before you're too big for us to do it safely."

His arm curled around her shoulders. His hand gave her arm a gentle squeeze, then he leaned in to kiss her cheek.

"I'm sorry to have to be strict, dear."

"*Já*, it is for my own good. I heard that coming."

She laid her head back, resigned to her fate. They stared at the drawn curtain, imagining the beach outside, and listened to the surf grating against the shore.

25

THE MOON SHINES THROUGH THE CURTAINS, waking Íris. She checks Eirík, naked on the bed sheet, sleeping peacefully. She is attracted to the light and goes to the sitting room, pulls back the curtain. The moon lights the beach. There are two men staring up at the condo. She recognizes them: Brad and Lee. It is two in the morning by the kitchen clock. She picks at the lock yet when she looks again, they are gone.

She waits a while longer, watching the beach, then returns to bed. As she reclines beside Eirík, she feels something in her belly. On her back, she feels it again. It is too early for the baby to kick, *já*. It does not happen again. She rises on one elbow and studies Eirík. He smiles in his sleep, as though he is dreaming of their last sex.

After breakfast, Eirík goes into Corpus Christi to see the realtor. He says he's going to visit his attorney, too, about how to divide the profit from the sale. She will be bored, he says, so he leaves her in the condo, in this small tourist village on the coast. Television is not enough, nor is the swimming pool. No point going to the beach again.

She puts on a short skirt and a t-shirt that Eirík bought for her that has 'Surfer Girl' in large red letters. She can surf the Internet, *já*.

She walks out to the main street, turns the corner, and continues into town, about a kilometer. Asking directions, she finds the library, a white brick building. Inside are three computers set up and, because it has been a week since her last confession, she logs on and goes to her EXCITE community to see if anyone has noticed she's been gone.

There are only three new postings in five days. She types out a few rebuttals, nothing earth-spinning, enough to let them know she visited.

She clicks to her e-mail and finds nothing but spam. Because she has the entire afternoon ahead of her, she clicks on one link that seems innocent and is taken to an adult website: *Dirty Harry's Teen Babes*. She clicks BACK but a new window opens with more erotica. She keeps clicking BACK yet new windows open. Finally, she gives up as more windows open like a deck of cards until the computer freezes. There is *Babe-A-Licious* with 24 thumbnail pictures of hardcore acts—

"Excuse me," says a woman. "What do you think you're doing?"

Íris looks up at the librarian, a middle-aged virgin. She has a cross dangling around her neck, yet it is hers to bear, thinks Íris.

"They popped up on their own," she says.

"That's against library policy," the librarian declares, her voice a bit louder. "You'll have to leave. Right now."

The librarian takes hold of her arm. Íris shakes her off and stands.

"I did nothing wrong. I got attacked by the pornos. You should put a filter on computers so people do not break your rules." There is scorn in her voice. "Oh, *já*, that would mean censorship, and we cannot have any of that! What about the children?"

"Yes, what about the children?" the librarian roars, waving her hand toward the children's section.

A toddler there is watching the noisy confrontation. The screen is still visible, so Íris gives the computer the three-fingered salute and sends it to reboot hell. The librarian acts as though she has destroyed evidence.

"You need to go—now."

"I am going!"

She storms out, leaving a storm inside the library. She laughs as she goes down the sidewalk. These dirty spring breakers, the librarian must be cursing.

People pass her as she walks through the souvenir district, young people in swimsuits or other beachwear. Young men with their muscled chests and tight abdomens. The girls who accompany them are busty, skinny, flirty. Their goal in life is to look hot. There are all kinds, yet all have one thing in common: they do not notice her. Being aroused by a pregnant woman is a fetish on the Internet. She moves through the crowd like a ghost, untouched. She realizes she wants to be touched.

Back in the condo, she strips as she enters and relaxes on the sofa with the curtains open so she can see the ocean. Bikini girls walk by on the beach and bare-chested young men follow.

She touches herself, waits for it to feel good. This is her time. There is nothing else in this moment. Not until the sky explodes and she rolls off the sofa, limp on the floor. When she catches her breath, she laughs.

Later, Eirík returns with a sheaf of papers to fill out. He asks Íris, dressed again, what she has been doing and she tells him she has been packing for the trip home.

"Home?" he asks. "To Kansas?"

She laughs and he is puzzled.

"Is that not our home?"

She goes to the bedroom and gathers her clothes. The dress she wore on the trip down is on a hanger, fresh from his mother's washer and dryer. She will wear it for the trip back. Other clothes she will take back in a laundry bag.

Dinner is a delivered pizza and they feed it to each other, sharing the same slice, sitting on the sofa, laughing at a comedy on the pay channel. A cop drama follows so they turn it off and go to bed. Morning will come early and the twelve hour drive will be exhausting, he says.

"I guess we are not going to the party," she says out of the blue.

"I thought we settled that."

He is not angry, perhaps upset that she questions his wisdom.

"*Já, já,* the baby will not like the music."

His mother calls as they get into bed and he talks to her, then his father, about the condo sale—the buyer's paperwork has to be sent in, and the loan approved by the lending institution. Thirty-five minutes later he hangs up. He apologizes to her.

They kiss. She slides her hands down his body. He reminds her of the early start in the morning. It is a long drive. He says he needs to get a good sleep.

She stretches out, staring at the ceiling, moonlight on her belly.

Eirík is quickly asleep.

There is a party going on down the beach. She can almost hear the music—or is it in her head? There is a lot that is in her head tonight. Tomorrow, she returns north, to the coolness of early spring, knowing summer will come soon.

The sheet is moist under her back, so she rises quietly, not wanting to awaken this man. The palms outside sway, dancing seductively, and she wants to join them.

She takes tomorrow's dress from the hanger and pulls it over herself. It is two inches shorter, thanks to his mother's hot drying machine. She steps barefoot onto the deck, slides the door closed. Leaning against the wooden railing, she slips flip-flops on her feet. She gazes up and down the beach—all is quiet, calm. She sits on the top step, wraps her arms around her knees, enjoying the breeze, listening to the moon, thinking about being sixteen. Warm air blows through her hair, tossing it against her face. When she brushes it back with her hand, he is standing on the beach below the stairs.

"I was wondering if you'd come out," says Brad, wearing shorts and an unbuttoned tropical shirt.

"It is too warm inside," she explains when she gets to the bottom.

"The party's still going strong," he says, "but I had to take a break. Too damn loud, like you thought."

"I do not like loud."

She looks up at his face, a blank mask that shows her nothing.

"What do you want?" she asks, knowing the answer. "I cannot go to any party with you tonight. You know I'm pregnant, and my boyfriend is in the condo. He is a very light sleeper."

Brad grins in the moonlight, sure of himself.

"I was thinking you might be out," says Brad. "That's one thing I've learned about you. You like to sit outside and stare at everything, like the sea and the beach. You know, Iris, sometimes you look absolutely homesick. But you're not from here, so it's cool."

He takes her hand, pretends to kiss it. When she does not object he really kisses it.

"Would you like to take a walk? Down the beach?" he asks, releasing her hand. "You can check out the party, then come back if you don't want to stay. You should have a good time and not be so bored here. Your boyfriend doesn't know how to have any fun."

"Or frivolity," she adds without a thought.

The earth shook and Eric awoke with a start. In the first few heartbeats, he thought he was back in his apartment in Kansas and snow was falling. The sound of palm fronds brushing the siding of the condo was like the dull roar of snowflakes. He sat up, thinking of the dissertation he had started before being hired by Fairmont College. He reached for the small notebook on the nightstand, began writing his idea before he could forget it. Knowing the writing would be unintelligible, Eric fought to keep other thoughts out of his head as he got up and went to the living room where he could turn on the light, not wishing to disturb his sleeping beauty.

Before he could turn on the light, he saw the sliding door ajar, and the curtains open. There was some movement outside so he went to the door and stared. A man was standing at the bottom of the staircase.

He scribbled a dozen lines of text in the faint glow of the kitchen nightlight, then returned to the bed and noticed the sheet was twisted and tossed back to his side. No one was there. He glanced at the dark bathroom, then went back to the kitchen.

No Íris.

Maybe she went for a walk, he considered, opening the front door despite having no clothes on. All was quiet in the parking lot, the palms waving in the breeze.

He rushed back to the living room where the balcony door framed the moment perfectly: a woman sat on the lower steps as the shirtless man, shorts lowered to his ankles, stood before her. It was clear what was happening. Eric pressed against the glass, studying the scene. The man held himself in place, one hand on each wooden railing and, as Eric watched, the man's head rolled back as he was overtaken with ecstasy. He lost his grip on the railings and fell back.

Eric heard the woman giggle as she sat back on the steps.

It was Íris.

He went to the bathroom and splashed water on his face, trying to stay calm. He sat on the rim of the bathtub, rubbing his forehead. What should he do? What would a gentleman do? What had this so civilized man done before and regretted ever since? He should have shot the big lummox, then Marina. Forget the damn law, forget the arrest and the imprisonment—

"It's over," he muttered.

All of her teasing, flirting with other men—defending them when he called them fools and idiots, when it was he who was the fool! He was the idiot. So often she put him casually in his place. Now it had come to this. He breathed hard, his throat tight, his chest aching. His hand went to his neck, felt the artery pumping away. A heart attack might come any minute, he thought, wishing it would save him from torment.

It had been too good to be true. How could a woman like her ever fall for some poor divorced loser like him? With her background, there was no telling what kind of screwed up head she might have. She'd told him about her father, sure, and about being a dancer in Toronto—and some parties, and boyfriends and girlfriends. How could he possibly know her? Who was this witch from Iceland? For all he knew she could be a native Kansas girl putting on an act for his benefit. Why go to the trouble of learning an obscure language like Icelandic? Because no one would check. While she claimed to know the literature and history of the place, she refused to discuss it with him. Maybe she didn't know it. Maybe her whole story of childhood abuse was a clever fabrication. Maybe the baby was not his.

He heard a noise and recognized it as the balcony door, so he rushed to the bed and lay on his side, facing the wall, pretending to be asleep.

The moonlight filtering in through the blinds provided enough light for him to see the woman enter, wearing a dress.

He held his eyelids closed to slits, watching her. She looked in his direction but did not smile. Going to the foot of the bed, she pulled the dress off over her head and stood naked in the moonlight stripes. She seemed dirty, sweaty, and her hair was mussed. Dropping the dress on the corner of the bed, she went to the bathroom, leaving the lights off, and stumbled over to the toilet. The lid went up with a *clink* and Eric next heard vomiting. Then a flush.

She ran the water in the sink for a couple of minutes.

"Are you all right?" he asked her with no hint of emotion.

"*Já,*" she said. "I'm okay."

She left the bedroom and he listened to her footsteps across the hardwood floor to the tile of the kitchen, the swing of the refrigerator door, pouring a beverage.

When she returned to the bedroom, he was on his back with his arm bent under his head, a corner of the sheet covering his hips. He watched her climb onto the bed, on her hands and knees. She rolled onto her side, facing away from him.

"Íris . . . ?" he called softly. "Would you give me a blow job, too?"

She turned to him. "You want that?"

"Please."

Crawling over his legs, she pulled back the sheet and began. It was difficult to maintain his concentration, as thoughts of what he had just witnessed stayed in his mind. At last he was nearing climax and her efforts slowed. Suddenly she stopped, released him.

She sat back on her heels, running her fingers through her hair but looking away. In the moonlight, he saw a tear roll down her cheek, cling to her chin, and drop.

"Too?" she whispered.

26

ÍRIS EATS THE TWO REMAINING SLICES OF PIZZA for breakfast as he grabs his bag and takes it down to the car. When he returns, she is ready. The flower-patterned dress is stained. Anyone can see it. She tosses it in a plastic sack and digs out a new outfit: a tan skirt and red cardigan that are too warm for this place. She does not know why she brought them; it seems fate knew.

He takes her bag down, then comes up to lock the door.

"Let's go" is all he says.

They both understand completely. She can feel his anger, though he does not slam doors and kick the furniture. He wears no scowl on his face. Yet she knows what he is thinking.

They are not engaged, have no marriage plans, she insists. He called her his fiancée once or twice in front of his parents. Yet there is not one instance where she agreed to be his slave or servant and submit to his will. She is her own person, and she is free to do what she wants with whoever she wants. That is the fact he does not understand. She is with him because . . . .

She has to think, and she has many hours to think on this silent drive north.

Vá, I never said I would marry you, she thinks, preparing her speech as they go up the highway to San Antonio. I never said I would be your spouse. That day in the Plaza of Heroines, I decided to tell you a fact you had a right to know. My words meant nothing else. You misunderstood, Eirík Schaeffer, not me. So we got to know each other, a ritual required of parents. I thought we might make a good family, and you did, too. There is too much left unsaid between us now—and she sighs, unable to continue.

She watches the grasses along the highway bend in their wake. Somewhere ahead is the border he showed her. There is a sign, yet the border is invisible. There is no list of acts and their consequences. There is no warning. Cross at will, at your own risk. Be suspicious of everyone. Anyone could be Loki, the prankster god. Your closest friend could be Satan in disguise, Sandra Kinney would say. *Nei*, she would not say that. She would tell me *I* am the devil, and I would not be able to prove her wrong.

Brad told her she did nothing wrong. If everyone consents, there is nothing wrong, he said. They knew there would be no future meeting.

"It's Spring Break," he said.

There was a party and she was an independent woman. He escorted her down the beach. He introduced her to everyone, kept his arm around her. She did not resist. They sat around the bonfire as his friends danced to music coming from a boombox. Brad showed her the refreshments, handed her a paper plate of tacos and a plastic cup of beer. She only sipped it. New people arrived so he introduced her to them, all college students.

"Where's Lee and Frank?" asked Brad. His friends said they were with some other frat brothers in a motel room "watching porn videos."

She had laughed at that.

"If you want to check out the videos," Brad said, "I'll take you up there."

"I have seen enough," she said.

He swung his arm around her like they had been lovers for a year, and herded her toward the dunes. They could get some privacy there.

"It is too early," she said. "Let's see the videos."

On the way, she leaned against him and he wrapped both arms around her. She whispered that she was feeling hot. He slid his hand under her dress and, finding no panty there, let his fingers explore. She said she wanted to do something outrageous, that she cared nothing about the party.

"Are you sure?" he asked.

She nodded and he knocked. Lee opened the door—like Big Joe escorting her into the Back Room of Club Venus. Her heart was beating fast. Lee called to Frank, on the far side of the room. Inside were about a dozen young men—frat boys. On the video were two busty blondes playfully working over a skinny man who had a silly moustache and a big penis.

"Everybody, this is Iris," Brad called out, then quickly kissed her.

Just north of Austin, she realizes she has been refusing to admit the truth. The hours have been silent. Eirík does not play music, does not listen to the radio talk. He does not know she is in the seat beside him. He wishes she were not there. As Íris leans against the window, they race up the highway. She can whimper at her fate yet nothing can change it. She does not know why she did it. Why does anyone do anything? For a while she was back in the club: she was the most important person in the room. Everyone's attention was on her, everyone wanted her.

"I am going crazy these last few weeks," she told Brad as he walked her back to the condo. "I don't know what it is, yet since I got over morning sickness I get aroused so easy—the shower, breezes, clothing rubbing against me."

"That explains why you enjoyed flashing your twat in the bookstore john," said Brad, with a laugh. "We all thought you wanted us to do something. But you never told us what."

"That was an accident," she told him. "I was trying to not let my bum touch the toilet seat—it was so dirty. My panties got peed on, so I took them off. I wasn't flashing you." He seemed disappointed. "I did not see you until I finished."

She had grinned at them, washed her hands, and exited. Thinking about it on the beach that night, she could imagine them laying her down on that dirty floor or bending her over the filthy washbasin. She told Brad and he laughed.

"You sound like you're drunk."

"*Nei.*" She looked at the stars. "When I get hot, I do anything to keep it going. It was diagnosed as sex addiction. I am a sex addict."

"No kidding?" He gave her hand a squeeze. "Does that mean you need to have a lot of sex to stay, uh, in control?"

"*Já,* that's it."

She counted the stars. He counted the strands of her hair as she gave him a quickie version of her life in Toronto: immigration, her mother's second marriage, kicked out on the streets, found by witches, the job in the strip club, sex acts in the back room, then art school, nude modeling and Professor Hirsch.

"Looking at you now, I can't believe it," said Brad. "Watching you in that motel, shit, I can't believe anything else."

The beach seemed like a Surrealist painting, and because she knew she was leaving in a few hours to return to reality, it was a place for confession.

"It's not something to be proud of," she said. "Pride is not the right word. It is like . . . ."

"Like a batter having the strike-out record," said Brad, "even if he also knocks fifty homers in a season. Why boast about being bad?"

They had stopped at the staircase leading up to the condo.

"Some people get a thrill from being bad." She tried to kiss him but he stepped back. "Most do not want to take the risk, *já.*"

He gazed into her eyes for a minute before dropping his shorts.

The miles flew by, the cities and towns vanished, the farms spread out toward tomorrow, and the other vehicles on the road were mere glimpses dashing away over the horizon. Eric's hands gripped the wheel, and his mind sharpened on the woman sitting beside him. Who was she? The more he thought he knew, the more he realized how much was an illusion.

The car roared down the highway, weaving in and out of traffic, ignoring patrols. He was anxious to get home as soon as possible, eager to dispose of this cold, cold woman. The chill had turned into frostbite. The once delicious ice cream had melted, then soured—

Eric glanced at her leaning against the window. *Let her feel bad. Maybe she wants me to forgive her, tell her everything's all right, that I know she'll never do it again. That's not the point. Trust is the point.* He'd never had any reason to think about trust. That's what trust is.

North of Ft. Worth, she asked him if he wanted to talk about it.

"There's nothing to say," he would say, keeping his eyes on the road, keeping his voice carefully under control. "You understand, and I understand, what has transpired. No negotiation, no counseling. Nothing can change it. It's finished, dammit." That's what he wanted to say.

Instead, he shook his head and muttered: "No."

He was glad to focus on the road. He could not meet her eyes. They were optical illusions that twisted the truth into some kind of rationalization. When he had met her eyes—for two seconds while they had sat in line back in the highway congestion outside of Waco—they were red, puffy from crying, ugly to behold. He'd turned away. She was a different person.

As they approached the Red River, four hours remained between their awkward couplehood and the freedom to begin again. Over the next hill, he knew, would be the adult bookstore where they had stopped on the way south. She had seen the video jackets, the hardcore magazines. She had showed him one and asked what he thought of it. What had *she* thought of it? Was that when it began?

They came to the tornado tracks across the Oklahoma countryside, and Eric slowed to consider them. He had never been good at reading signs or at divining the future. The trees were broken, the grass torn up, blown away, the fields barren. Like his life.

He stepped on the gas.

The sun was setting to their left, throwing tangerine rays upon the lavender clouds. He wanted to look but he knew she was gazing at it. She worked with colors. She was sensitive that way, creative, but utterly uncontrollable. He felt sad to discover that. Whatever she had done and whatever reason she had for doing it, the fact that she now was going away made his guts knot. It was as though she had murdered herself just to deprive him of the goddess he worshipped. Goddess is dead, he sighed; mankind killed her.

A few lights were on in the house as he pulled up to the curb. The skies were dark but the last of the sunset silhouetted the bare branches and the house. A Halloween scene, he decided, remembering the first time he had driven her to this house. He had returned to where it had begun, full circle, a witches' circle, a coven, lucky thirteen and black cats, and curses, back to the scene of the—

He shut off the engine and immediately climbed out and opened the trunk. The cool air revived him, and he tossed her unzipped bag onto the curb as she got out and stood on the grass. Clothing fell out of the bag as it landed. He grabbed a few articles of clothing left in the trunk and tossed them down beside the bag.

"We have to talk about it," she said. "We need to understand—"

He snatched the plastic sack containing her dress and slapped it to the grass.

"There's nothing to talk about."

"I know what I did was wrong, but—"

"Take your fucking books, too!"

Volumes of the Sagas and the *Edda*s, sources for his novel, splashed against the curb in front of her. He was reading them to understand her culture. That was not what he needed. It was all bullshit. Her real culture came from seedy downtown Toronto, not Iceland. There was no more Viking in her than her name. The essence of Íris Magnúsdóttir was her art, and he was not referring to her paintings. Not even to *Roses*, the painting he had bought. Six hundred twenty dollars was supposed to buy his mistress a bit of encouragement. However, *Roses* was a fantasy: an illusion of the tragic fallen woman, cut by thorns, yet her sleeping face bears a smile—as though she enjoys her suffering, as though she welcomes her fate, knows what she deserves—

"Please let me apologize. Please listen to me."

She stepped toward him and he held his ground.

"*Já*, I did go to the party, the one you told me not to go to. I did not go because you told me not to. It was my choice. I am not a little girl. I am not your . . . ."

"Girlfriend?" he answered for her.

"It's okay if you believe nothing." Her eyes were wide, welcoming. "I am crazy, *já*. I am sick in the head. Yet I want you." Her hopeful face melted at his staid expression. "I gave in to temptation, yet who hasn't? It was the wrong thing. Yet I could not turn away. I have addiction."

The night darkened as a cold wind blew between them.

"Don't you want to hit me?" she said, bracing herself.

He stared at her, his hand quivering. He raised it, extended a finger and pointed it at her. "I will never do that."

"You cannot even hit me. You are a weak man."

"Weak? It takes strength for me not to punch you in the face."

"Then do it. At least my father beat me! And fucked me whenever I was bad."

He glared at her. "You are a sick, sick girl. You know that? And a real bitch! Why didn't I see that before?"

"And you are a—a snowman! You stand so frozen you cannot feel anything!"

"I feel plenty. Now it's pity, most of all, pity for you." He swallowed hard. "You just go on with your whimpering victimhood and you keep making yourself a victim every time. That's not a life."

"Then you are the abuser. Because you always let me be the victim so you can enjoy rescuing me! *Ja*, I don't want to be rescued! I don't need saving! I am my own woman."

"I'm not going to rescue you this time."

"Good," she said. Her mouth twisted suddenly and a fresh tear fell down her cheek. "You should hit me. Then you be a man."

He stepped back, his hand a fist. Somewhere her voice had changed to the voice of his father.

"No—I won't do that." He turned to the trunk. "I just need space. I need to figure out how I feel."

That was the most generous remark he could make, Eric considered, and he almost congratulated himself for not giving in to sheer rage. It was tightly bottled, dangerous.

"I just need time."

She took a step closer. "Time for what?"

"I don't know. To decide what to do with you."

"To do with me?" She laughed, or maybe it was the wind. "You still want me?"

He stared at the pile of clothing and books at her feet.

"I don't know."

"When will you decide?"

"I don't know!"

He slammed the trunk lid with all his anger. It hit and bounced open.

"Maybe a week, maybe forever."

"Will you call me?" she asked.

"No."

"No?"

Eric slammed the trunk again and it caught.

He jumped into the car without looking at her, started the engine, and sped away, wishing he could go farther than his apartment, farther from the orange-haired witch—the sorceress who had entranced him. How could he have been so stupid?

He would not make that mistake again.

What mistake? he asked himself.

Believing.

27

PEARL-GRAY SKY ON A SUNDAY MORNING, and Íris has been up all night. After the long ride returning to reality, her back aches. She sits on the floor, legs crossed, waiting for tomorrow and the next day to come and go. Only then will she know if she lives or dies. Such drama! She listens too much to Cory talking about his soap operas, and thinks too much about the Shakespeare plays she studies.

By now, the whole house knows what has happened, because she told Jean and Cory, and they passed it on to everyone else. Like a disease.

When Íris stepped inside, with all of her clothes dangling from her arms, only Cory was there, sitting on the sofa. He welcomed her home.

"It's Iris. She's back," he called out.

Then he saw she was crying. Jean entered from the kitchen, followed by Tracie, microwave dinners in their hands.

Íris could not see them through her tears, strange droplets of pain she had long avoided. Jean came up and hugged her, helped her carry her things up to her room. They talked there and later she went across the hall to talk to Cory.

On this quiet morning, the music from downstairs bleeds into her room, some ballad, a woman singing about reality being relative. It is, she thinks. The mirror in her room shows her reality. She is nude, in profile, wondering how she will return to Life Study. How can she look Ray in the eyes, or take off her robe in the class? How can she pose for students? She sees her belly's small curvature. There is a baby inside, and she cannot deny it. It is growing quicker now.

She searches through her wardrobe and there are few skirts she can adjust to fit her new waist. She opens the door and steps into the hall.

"Jean, can you take me to the mall this afternoon?"

"She's already gone," a man's voice answers. It is Richie, who spends most of his time in chemistry labs. "Long time no see, huh? How ya doing?"

"I'm fucked up," she says, because it is true in several different ways.

"You must be," he laughs, gesturing at her nudity. "I can take you to the mall."

"Thanks, yet . . . ." She steps behind the door. "I can wait for Jean. I need her opinion. I am shopping for clothes—maternity clothes, já."

"Yeah, I heard. Congratulations."

Congratulations? How can he say that? She retreats to her room.

Monday comes before Sunday ends, and still she waits for reality to be relative.

She turns to her laptop and logs on to her Excite.com website. She struggles with the wording, then deletes it and starts again. There is nothing worse than a confession. Nothing worse than a confession where so many details must be held back so they don't offend anyone. She has made a habit of offending people. She knows the facts; she can see the episode "in a new light," as Jean says. She needs to justify what she did, and get sympathy, or perhaps encouragement—

Nei, I do not want any of that, she decides. They must tell me I am right! I have nothing to feel bad about, nothing to apologize for.

"I am a woman," she speaks to the laptop. "It is my body."

She wanted to enjoy the moment, so she took it. People do what they want to do. They move toward enjoyment. That is normal and natural—

Nei, that is not it. That it is difficult to write must mean it goes against her values. "If it harm none, do as thou wilt," the Wiccan Rede says. Who has she harmed? A good many more were pleased than were hurt. Only Eirík was hurt—yet it is in his head. He thinks he is hurt. She did not intend to hurt him, so he cannot say *she* hurt him.

She takes a couple of hours to write it straight out, everything that occurred that night, and, despite too many adjectives, it makes a good erotic story. Yet it is not a confession. According to Sandra Kinney, confession implies some sense of regret at slipping, a realization of wrongdoing.

Já, people do not confess what they do not feel guilt for.

Eirík is an academic person, a man who anyone would expect to overreact. He knows who she is. He said he needs time, time to get over it. Even if all of her housemates think she is the ultimate slut and has broken some unwritten laws, he should be ready to forgive her. Eirík is no Christian, yet he must know the rules of forgiveness. She apologizes and he forgives. Simple. He must understand there are only two choices: to forgive or to forget. Because he cannot forget what happened, he must choose to forgive. When he realizes this, he will return to her. If he cannot see the moment and climb over it, then the world will end for her. The world will end for him, too.

Já, that's what it means to be co-dependents.

Today the campus is so bizarre. Everyone is walking around in a daze, worse than after the Thanksgiving holiday.

When she goes for a late lunch in the Student Center, she meets Sandra. She sees Íris at a table, joins her, wants to know how her break was, so she tells her. Íris holds back nothing as Sandra consumes the meatloaf, potatoes, and peas-and-carrots with the utmost etiquette. It is a perverse kind of entertainment, seeing her expression change as Íris reveals the details.

"How can you *do* that, Iris?"

"Sex is normal," says Íris. "For normal people. Not Christians."

Sandra frowns so Íris waves at her, taking it back. Bad joke. She does not feel like hurting Sandra, or anyone, today. She sees Sandra is trying not to judge her. Her housemates have already pushed her away.

"Sex is an urge," says Íris, "like hunger or thirst, or that fight-or-flight instinct. It can be suppressed, but not for long. I can distract myself for several days, keeping busy doing another activity, yet when I have a moment to catch my breath, there it is, waiting for me, like a shadow. It's like feeling a chill. Like an itch that needs to be scratched. So I scratch it. Sometimes, I scratch very hard trying to get rid of it and it becomes too sore to touch. Then I need time to heal. It's more complicated than that, *já*. What's your priest say?"

"I don't have a priest," says Sandra. "I have a minister, and he has a lovely wife and three boys and a baby girl." Sandra smiles, embarrassed. "Of course, I learned all about sex in school like everyone else, but it's not appropriate to talk about it in public, like you're doing now. It's a private subject."

"How does anyone learn anything if it is kept private?"

"There are good books out there on the subject," says Sandra with a wink. "And there is the Good Book, of course."

"There's a lot of good sex in the Good Book," Íris laughs.

"You've read it?"

"*Já*, my mother made me."

She tells Sandra she has not bothered to memorize chapters and verses. Sandra provides a few, however, and Íris grimaces.

"That is wonderful," says Íris, mockingly. "What is it supposed to mean?"

"Sex is love—or it should be," Sandra explains. "And love is sacred, holy, and it should not be like what you do: for recreation. What you call 'good sex' should be only between a man and a woman who love each other deeply and commit themselves to their church-sanctioned relationship through a stronger bond with God."

"Bondage? You make it sound so romantic!"

She continues preaching and Íris notices how she resembles Renée, the shy girl from Québec who was her lover for a semester in Toronto. They have the same brown hair, the same brown eyes, cute nose, high cheeks. Sandra takes care of herself.

"I will tell you what good sex is." Íris takes a sip of hot tea. "Good sex should be so pleasurable that you know it is about to hurt. It should feel so good that you are on the edge of pain that never comes—"

"Stop it!" Sandra quickly looks around to see if anyone noticed she lost her composure. She seems genuinely angry for once. Íris likes seeing the ceiling of her Sistine Chapel crack. Yet there is something else she sees behind her eyes: sincerity.

Íris apologizes to her.

"Thank you." Sandra takes another bite of her lunch, chews, and Íris studies her. She soon swallows, then: "So what are you going to do?"

"I do not know. Collect my check for the mural?"

"No, I meant about your, um, lover." Sandra smiles. "Since you mentioned . . . . I know you don't like to go to church, Iris, but they will be dedicating the mural next Sunday. You should be there. You don't have to do any Christian rituals, as you call them. But you may."

"I always go to my dedications," Íris laughs, able to count on one finger the number of dedications she has had. "*Já*, it might be fun. To see how the other half lives. Can I wear my pentacle?"

"Everyone is welcome," she says, her eyes sparkling.

Íris takes a swipe at the air over Sandra's head. "No halo?"

"It's invisible."

They gather their dishes and take them to the conveyer. Sandra reminds her to first toss the paper trash in the wastebasket. It is easy to dispose of some things, she thinks.

"He's going to some conference the end of the week," Íris tells her as they begin the walk to Dickerson Hall.

The afternoon is teasingly sunny, temptingly warm, and a team of groundskeepers are digging up flowerbeds for a new season.

"So he will get his 'time to think,' as he wants." Íris breathes in the moist air, fresh from an early morning shower. "When he gets back, he will be ready to forgive me. Then we will be a family again. We have to think of names for the baby."

"What's his name?" Sandra asks, leaning close.

"Eirík," she replies. "That's how we say it in *Íslensku*."

"It's funny, but you never told me his name."

"*Já*, that is because it is not important. Eirík is a professor."

Sandra stops. "You got pregnant with a professor?"

"You did not know?" Íris smiles. "I thought the whole campus knew. Was it not in the school paper? Now you need to say longer prayers for me."

"Iris, you really need to set yourself on the right path. God has been blessing you for a while, but now? You have no idea what you've done, do you?" Sandra shakes her head. "Think about Eric, your so-called boyfriend. He must be torn up inside. What were you thinking? You knew it would hurt him, and if you didn't think it would hurt him then you were being just plain dumb. You go on a trip with the father of your baby, then you skip off down the beach to have be with a bunch of jerks because you want to exercise your free will? I'm talking about you being unfaithful to your partner. He *is* your partner—"

"We didn't agree to anything!"

Sandra has made her angry. She never likes hearing someone else's truth.

"*Vá*, that is the point! I never agreed to a relationship. I did not want a relationship with him. He keeps asking me but—"

"Then you're stringing him along, using him." Sandra's hands are on her hips, her face stern. "But I have no idea what you're expecting from him—other than some sort of financial support. Is that what you're after? If all you want is money, why are you going through with the pregnancy? I would've thought you'd get an abortion, just to be rid of the baby and the father both!"

"You are such a hypocrite!" Íris shouts at her.

"You're the hypocrite!" Sandra snaps. "I'm real sorry I got you that commission. You don't deserve it."

"I never wanted it!"

"I'll tell you what you deserve." Sandra is in her face, pointing a finger at her nose. "You deserve whatever happens to you now."

"My mother told me that, so you are not saying anything original!"

"God bless you, Iris. You're going to need it."

28

PROFESSOR ERIC SCHAEFFER LEANED against the lectern in his Tuesday evening class and stared at the back corner of the room, not too surprised his lover was absent. How could she face him again after her infidelities? And yet, he wished she would appear. He wanted to see her.

She also might benefit from discussion of the next Shakespeare play, *Troilus and Cressida.*

"Ladies and gentlemen, this is a case study of various degrees of betrayal, both political, military, and, shall we say, amorous." His voice sounded weary, reluctant to go on. However, he had to, for his own sake and for the students. "That is the theme of this play. I'm telling you what it is, in advance, because I want all of you to be looking for instances of betrayal . . . as you, umm, watch the video. Try to figure out why character A chooses to betray character B. What is the motivation? And what are the consequences?"

He gave them a short talk on the style of the language, realizing it took a certain degree of attention to follow the original text. To enjoy the play took even more effort. He himself had less attention to devote to it tonight than he would have wished. The parliamentary filibuster on what to do about Íris occupied him. He pushed on, trying to make the lesson worthwhile for students still hung-over from Spring Break.

"Of course, the story of the Trojan War is well known to us, especially from Homer's epic poems. What do we know of the history behind it?" The students sat dumbfounded. "All right, I'll tell you, since I've done a fair amount of research on it." The students were glassy-eyed as he talked for twenty minutes on the history, modern excavations, and how it influenced the play.

Eric dimmed the lights and started the video, a four-hour BBC production that his students would finish watching on Thursday evening while he was away at a conference. He moved to the side and sat among the students.

Having already watched the video before Spring Break, he was free to think of the weekend. The Saturday night was too short. He had intended to stay up and brood, slam his fist into the walls, but the drive was too exhausting and he instead slept late into Sunday. The bed felt particularly empty when he awoke without Íris beside him and for the first minute he had not remembered what had happened to ruin his life. He sat up, examining the dent in the wall where they had made love—where the woman had been tacked up, Christ-like, in her suffering. In her *rape*.

That was what she could say. But would she? She might—especially if it suited a vindictive mindset. A few words, enough proof still existing, and he would be put away forever. He laughed unintentionally, realizing the situation. Like Jack, who was about to be convicted by a college infractions committee, Eric would be convicted. He and Jack could be roommates. Perverts and reprobates!

Jack had called Monday morning, concerned about the delay of his fate. Dr. Liz had given Jack a deadline to produce a written response to the ten key accusations against him.

"I'm not writing a report for that witch," Jack said.

Eric cautioned him about using "witch" in that derogatory tone, then decided that his own witch, Íris, did not deserve any special treatment.

"What is with Doctor Liz?" Eric asked. "She made me write a report on how I was going to improve myself the second half of the semester. She thought I was getting cocky, too comfortable, taking life for granted. I needed to get back on track."

"What a bitch," Jack growled. Everything he said was a growl now. Eric noticed his own voice losing its fluidity, settling into a hard-edged gruffness. "I don't need this bullshit from her."

"You didn't do anything horrible," said Eric, thinking of his own situation. "You should get off with a slap on the wrist. What was it, a few cat calls, a slip of the tongue, and sex with your girlfriend before you broke up? They have no case. Besides, it's not Liz's decision alone. The whole committee has to vote."

"I'm tired of playing their games," Jack growled. "I've got a position lined up at the community college. Okay, it's not my specialty, but it'll pay the bills for a year while I send out my C.V. to bigger schools."

"I'm sorry you had to sink to that level."

"Community college?" Jack laughed. "They've got lots of co-eds. And they're not as smart. Clever, I mean. Don't know how to backstab."

"You haven't learned anything, have you?"

"Yes, I have. I've learned how to spell 'take your tenure and shove it up your Ph.D.' Write that five hundred times on the chalkboard, Liz! I've got a sealed envelope in my hand this very second just waiting for a stamp. Inside is my letter of resignation. I'd rather get the hell out of Dodge than wait around for the posse to hang me. I get out on my terms, with my balls intact."

"Well, that's an appropriate metaphor, I suppose." Perhaps that was what he should do, too, before Íris made a claim. He thought of insurance: she was attacked, made pregnant, now she filed a claim and collected damages. Like a car crash. It was all too neat.

"Now tell me what's gotten you so screwed in the head," Jack insisted.

Eric hesitated. Then, feeling there was no one else who could ever understand his delicate situation, he divulged everything. Jack had sympathy for him, the kind he wanted but could not afford. He needed cold, clear objectivity to prepare a defense, not a mindless cheering section. Jack laughed, and that had set him on edge.

"I did nothing wrong," Eric insisted, preaching to the choir.

"Of course, you didn't."

"I met her outside of class—she wasn't even my student then. At that art show. Then in December, I picked her up in a thunderstorm. I took her in. We fell in love. I provide for her, chauffeured her to the doctor's office, her job, anything."

"I hear you, buddy."

"And then she goes off to some frat party because she's *bored*?"

"You have a case, my friend."

"Does she still want to be a couple now? A family? Or will she just want money?"

"You nailed it."

"And to make matters worse, I'm teaching *Troilus and Cressida* this week," Eric told him. "It's nothing but women having sex with men who aren't their husbands. Did you know the word 'cuckold' is used more in that one play than in anything else in English literature? This infidelity shit . . . must've been the biggest problem of Shakespeare's day. And today. Everybody getting laid by a non-spouse. The more the merrier."

"*The More the Merrier*. Wasn't that Shakespeare's original title?" said Jack, adding a hearty guffaw. "*Hamlet* was about scandal in a small village. And *Measure for Measure* was about penis enlargement."

At least his old colleague had been able to joke about it, Eric recalled, now that Jack was leaving on his own terms. Eric, however, needed to play it cool—according to Jack, becoming a perverse kind of mentor. Eric was in his first year of teaching at the college; he still had his dissertation to finish; instead, Íris had inspired him to start a novel. He had to patch things up quickly, be nice, be forgiving, display generosity and understanding. Until she graduated in May—no, it was going to be in August, same as the birth. Then dump the stock. Jack was full of metaphors on Monday. Worse than Eric's. Too much time living in one's pajamas and perusing the Want Ads all day.

Not satisfied with Jack's advice, Eric had called his brother, Matt—just to touch base, as Matt liked to say. Jane had a bun in the oven, their fourth. Business was good, finally opening that new store, his third.

Yes, Eric's visit to their parents down in Texas was a big success. More or less. Mother liked the new girl, Father tolerated her. They had talked about boats and fishing. Then came the details he tried to gloss over. Matt had no empathy, suggested he shouldn't have trusted Íris.

"She's a foreigner, right? She's only after a green card."

"She's already got a work permit," said Eric.

What was Matt saying? That he suspected her *because* she was attracted to him? What kind of brotherly support was that? Eric wasn't that far over the hill. Forty, yes, but he had a full head of hair. And Íris, the Icelandic witch, had inspired him to perform great feats of sexual strength and endurance. His ex-wife would've been impressed.

"We had a genuine love affair going," said Eric. "It just fell apart. Before Spring Break everything was great. But somewhere she decided to abandon me."

"Eric, she decided she had you wrapped around her finger tight enough."

"Not the other way?" Eric was sick of his brother's attitude.

Then Matt, in his impeccably unsubtle way, cleared away the gloomy clouds that had accumulated around Eric's sensibility: "Have you gotten a paternity test?"

Eric held the phone away from his ear, repeating the words in his head. She came to him to tell of her pregnancy. Ten weeks after their weekend together. If he were not the father, why would she come to him? How could she be certain who the father was? Other than her assertion that he was the only man she had sex with that week. Correction: the only man she had *unprotected* sex with. Unless it was, as Matt suggested, just a conspiracy, a set-up, or an elaborate prank.

"No," he answered.

"If she slept with you," said Matt, "chances are she'll sleep with anybody. And she did, didn't she? Weren't you at all suspicious when she wanted to go home with you? And then be so easy? Those witches are always after something."

"That's got nothing to do with it." He had been fighting his urge to curse witches. "Nothing to do with Wicca. She has a psychological problem. It's called sex addiction."

"Oh, come on! That's one of those New Age alibis these loose women use to get out of society's moral code. You fell for it. There's no such thing. And if there was such a thing, it'd be the same as for any other addiction. Simply stop. Get counseling, fight the cravings, get some backbone, and just don't do it."

"Oh, yeah?" Eric had frowned—as he was now, watching *Troilus and Cressida*.

"You need to pray for her," Matt had said. "Pray for her *more* if you want her back."

Troilus and Cressida drifted in, filled his awareness, and Eric sat up, stiffly. The boy next to him smiled, catching his professor asleep in class. Eric grinned sheepishly, noticing that someone else had chosen to join the class. In the usual corner desk sat Íris, her hair tied back, wearing what appeared through the flickering light of the video projection to be a maternity jumper over a white, long-sleeved blouse. She had sneaked into class under cover of darkness. Was the late arrival intentional, to avoid eye contact with him? Or was she innocently late to class? Innocently? He bit his lip. Did she have a rendezvous before class? If so, who did she come to campus with and how would she leave campus?

She was becoming too big to ride a bicycle comfortably. Should he offer her assistance? a ride home, no strings attached? That was how it all started: giving her a ride home. With her belly showing, he couldn't imagine how she pedaled, but a hand clenched his heart and another slapped him across the face: What if she fell, or a car hit her? If that were his baby inside her, how would he reconcile his refusal to see her home safely? How would he live down the shame? *His* shame?

Eric grunted. Like poor Troilus, who believes in his heart that his unfaithful mistress, Cressida, is innocent to the end—even when he sees his young betrothed in the Greeks' camp flirting with the soldiers, taking delight in their lusty attention. Even when Cressida beds Diomedes, the Greek captain, and gives to him the virginity that she had always promised to Troilus, she remains redeemable. Eric would still want her, he realized. She was who she was, after all, and that essence of her was what had attracted him. Still, how could any man choose to be with a woman whose list of lovers was so long? That took either a fool or a pervert: the former to pay no attention to the heavily trodden path to her door, the latter to welcome the open door as extra incentive to be impressive.

"At least get the paternity test," Matt's voice returned to Eric—as Ulysses in the video counsels young Troilus not to fret over his lady. "That's the most important thing. If the baby is yours, then you'll know what course of action to take. If it's not yours, then, well, I guess you're free and clear. Meanwhile, start going to church. Meet some decent women."

Eric sighed, wanting to look over at her. He glanced at the door, wishing he could exit before the video ended. In the morning, after his classes, he would hit the highway, driving three hours to Kansas City for the annual conference of Writers & Publishers.

Yvonne, the only real witch Íris had met at her initiation into Megan's circle the previous spring, responds to her e-mail. She wants Íris to call her to discuss what to do about getting herself out of the mess she is in. Yvonne always sees straight through to the truth. Yet Íris has no telephone. She also needs privacy from her housemates. So she sends an e-mail to Yvonne suggesting she try calling in the evening when Íris supervises Open Studio.

Thirty minutes into Open Studio there is only one girl. The phone on the desk rings.

"What a great e-mail," Yvonne says, sounding like she has a cold. She goes on about how much detail Íris put into it, how it showed her true passion, the depth of her trouble, and the sincerity to seek a solution. That impressed Yvonne enough to call.

"I am sorry to need your help," Íris tells her in a low voice. "You are the only one who will give me straight advice."

"Unfortunately," says Yvonne, "what you had to experience is all too common among women in this day and age. It *is* painful. You can't undo it. How you choose to carry your pain will determine both your future and your child's future."

"*Já*, everyone tells me that."

"Iris, there are so many things I picked up on in your e-mail, mostly because you share info in rivers. I don't know if you're aware of it, darling, but there's a lot of anger that comes out of you in various ways, along with high risk, self-destructive behavior. My hunch is that by engaging in that kind of provocative behavior, you attempt to gain control. Now, I don't pretend to know all you went through growing up. I only know what you've told me. Yes, you were abused and you had a rough time as a young woman on her own in the big city. The damage never goes away. That's why I stopped going to the sex addicts meetings. I concluded that I am who I am, and trying to change that fundamentally is a dubious endeavor at best."

"You're a sex addict, too?" asks Íris.

"Oh, yes, but that's something I've had under control for the last ten years."

"How do you balance that with Wicca?"

"Iris, darling, you should know better. We're not sex addicts. We witches have the same demographics as the greater population, the same percentages of normal and crazy people."

"*Já*, I know, but—"

"You and I are damaged goods, darling. And damaged people are dangerous because they know how to survive. You've been getting by and you'll find a way to get through this, too. That's part of who you are, Iris: you're a survivor. You will always survive. You learned early how to live with pain and how the world really works. Not like these soft-hearted assholes who think they've got everything figured out. Put them on a street corner with empty pockets and they'll be dead in a week. You, on the other hand, are tough. But you've got this strange side I can't quite understand."

"I told you everything about me."

"Probably not everything, Iris. Remember the business card I gave you after your initiation? I'm head of Human Resources at a national corporation, so I've learned to be a good judge of character. But you I haven't managed to figure out and that's driving me mad."

"Apologies."

"It's always a dilemma when I encounter someone who is in extreme pain," says Yvonne, shifting to a softer, motherly tone. "The natural inclination is to want to rush in, hug the person, tell the person that everything will be okay, try to make the pain go away. I'm going to resist the temptation to paint a smiley face on your life. You've overcome quite a lot, darling, and you should be damn proud of what you've achieved. You should use that to build a foundation for the future. At the same time, you're aware of your tendencies, and, frankly, I'm not sure you could change them now even if you focused every atom of your being on the effort. Real change is impossible, dear."

"Then what do I do? I already promised to change, yet I don't know how."

"Take it easy, Iris, darling." There is a pause on the line. "I've got another call coming in, so I have to leave you. I'll call you right back."

The line is dead and so is Íris. The student looks up, returns to painting. Two others come and go as she waits. Thirty minutes more. The phone rings.

"Yvonne!"

"Okay, Iris, this is one thought that went through my mind while I listened to my boss bitching about the monthly reports. As I was reading your e-mails again, I saw where you mentioned your list of secrets. Remember? Last fall, you wrote in your EXCITE group that you have a list of three hundred things people don't know about you. Do you see the irony of sharing some of the most intimate, personal, even embarrassing moments of your life in an open forum like that online, but at the same time you amass a list of so-called secrets? And they involve some of the same events? It's this sort of 'going in opposite directions at the same time' that caught my eye. On the one hand, you present this kind of in-your-face, totally liberated, bi-sexual, care-free, fearless, independent, in-control person. Then, on the other hand, here is a very reserved, even shy individual with a list of secrets."

"When I told the first secret, I was being clever. It's not what you think. I thought they would laugh. They would wonder what it might be. It was fun, that's all. I don't really have a list of secrets."

"I think you do, Iris."

"Unconscious list somewhere, *já*. Not on paper. The website is where I'm free to express myself. That includes telling some about my past—anonymously. Who really knows anyone on the Internet? No harm done. For example, when I stated what I like for sex, that was true. As for my sexual statistics, that is also true."

"I guessed so. Iris, this is a significant part of your problem: the two lives you lead inside your head. You are a madonna and you are a whore—at the same time. The former is what you were expected to be as a child growing up, and the latter is the reality that you've since become. It's one of those eternal conflicts. So who do you want to be?"

"I get aroused thinking about it sometimes, thinking of the past or fantasizing in the present." She looks up, checks on the student behind the easel, then lowers her voice further. "Sometimes it makes me sick. I can relax only by playing it out online. Else, I do it for real. When I feel that chill—*já*, that's how my problem began. That's how I met this Eirík. He wanted a whore and at that moment I wanted to be a whore."

"Now that, darling, is the truth of the year. But it will only split you further apart. What we're trying to do is patch you together so you know who the real Iris really is."

Yvonne waits for her response yet Íris is too stunned to speak.

"I'm not pointing it out to find fault or criticize you," says Yvonne, hearing sniffles on the line. "I'm trying to focus on what I see as your pain. There's no right or wrong here. I'm keying on the fact that there appears to remain a lot of very tender areas in you despite the tough, outer shell. Sort of like an M&M: the tough candy coating makes them melt in your mouth, not in your hand. A lot of women are sluts inside but wear the hard candy coating. The reverse is also true: slut on the outside just to get attention, but inside scared to death of really being a slut."

"You think I'm a slut?"

Two students who are painting look up and Íris turns away.

"That's a good question," says Yvonne. "Are you?"

"If 'slut' means a woman who likes sex or can't get enough sex . . . *já*, it's still different from how men use it—"

"Okay, Iris, this is from the gut," says Yvonne. "What I was feeling as I read your words, what you wrote about how many times you've been gangbanged, is this: It's one thing to see someone I don't know and don't care about get all her holes plugged, but it's quite another to hear someone I respect glorifying that kind of sex. I guess it has to do with how men react to the women they screw. They don't respect them—they see only pieces of meat. In your case, Iris, I feel you are mostly the victim of your asshole father, and you've been compounding that fear and loathing, playing the same role with every man you meet. I don't know if what you did at that club really hurt you—or if you allow it to keep hurting you now—but it hurts me to read about it in your e-mails. I don't want to judge, so I try to deflect that pain with humor. The truth is, darling, it hurts when I imagine you putting yourself in that kind of degrading position when there's so much more to you than that. And until you realize it, and let yourself catch a break for once, you will continue to solve your problems by escaping into superfluous sex."

"I'm sorry," Íris whimpers.

"It's not a matter of being sorry," says Yvonne, like the mother Íris wishes she'd had. "Listen, I need to get off the line now, but just remember: you can't stop hurting people you fall in love with until you stop hurting yourself. And you can't stop hurting yourself until you point the finger at the people who hurt you first."

29

THE SOLITARY THREE-HOUR DRIVE up the Kansas turnpike reminded Eric of the return trip from Texas just a week before, and he instinctively glanced to his right. There she was again: the lovely Íris, his mistress, a ghost, leaning against the window, sobbing, not offering an apology. She was sorry she was caught, he sneered, not that she had acted . . . how? What word would suffice? Improperly? Too nice. Like a whore? Perhaps too harsh. He thought a while. Outrageous. That was the word. That was what she had instructed him to do: be outrageous, break the rules, have a good time.

"Have a good time," he muttered disdainfully, flipping the radio on.

The Writers & Publishers conference was held in one of the elegant old hotels that had suffered through years and years of renovation and modernization until all of its original charm had been scrubbed away. Now the hotel stood before the Allis Plaza in downtown Kansas City like some carnival funhouse facade tacked onto the sturdy frame of a historical building. He parked his car in the underground garage and took the elevator up to the main lobby. A line of people were checking in: the famous and not-so-famous, writers and editors, publishers and publicists. And the famous wannabes who stood by, watching curiously.

As Eric rode the escalator to the second floor where the meeting rooms and main hall were located, he passed his colleague Olivia Jones coming down. He recalled hearing that she wrote children's books. He waved politely and she called back that they should have a drink.

A refreshments table was set up outside the Grand Ballroom. He helped himself to coffee and went to the registration table. A perky blonde girl, probably working her way through the conference, pinned the name tag on his lapel and handed him a packet of papers.

Inside the main hall, Eric found the perfect seat, the exact center of the room, almost directly under a huge chandelier. He briefly pondered what the effect would be if it were to come crashing down on him during the keynote address, to put him out of his misery.

Sitting, he shuffled through the papers, found the program book, and began looking at the list of featured speakers as others gradually came in and took their seats.

The keynote address concerned the state of publishing in America: the how and why and why not of being an author or poet in these difficult times. The mergers of small- and medium-sized presses with large, international conglomerates, reduction of mid-list publishing, increase of celebrity products, and the generally low morale for anyone involved with the industry, left the audience depressed and anxious to hit the bars.

Eric repressed a sigh, though a sound did escape. He saw a petite woman in gray business suit sitting nearby, her mousy brown hair tied in a bun. She glanced at him, pursing her lips as though holding back a grin.

Browsing through the stalls of publishers, taking any preview copies they offered, Eric happened upon the stall of his one-time publisher, then balked at introducing himself. They had accepted his manuscript, a novel about a man who goes hunting in India as an ancient ritual to restore sanity, and sent him a small check. He told everyone of his success. He made plans, cleared his schedule for the inevitable book tour. Then they dropped the project and he was left with no options but to take the teaching job in Japan.

"Are you *the* Eric Schaeffer?" asked the clean-cut young man behind the table. His white shirt and black tie made Eric wary that a religious group had taken over the company. The smile was painfully sincere.

Eric playfully looked at his own name tag. "Yes, I think so." *Therefore I am*, he thought with a grin.

"I remember your name," the young man said, pointing to Eric's nametag.

The man's tag read DARRELL ROSS. Apparently, Darrell had worked for a literary journal previously and only recently moved to the book field. This was his first conference with the publisher.

"You must have me confused with someone famous," said Eric.

"No, I definitely remember the name." He tilted his head, scratched his ear. "Japanese story, right? The girl drowns herself because her American lover isn't coming for her. But it was the grandmother who kept his letters from her so she wouldn't leave."

"Sounds like one I wrote," said Eric. During his first months back from Japan, he'd crafted such a story.

Darrell told him how, as a screener, he had passed the story up the ladder, all the way to the senior editor. She was the one who rejected it. She had roomed with a Japanese girl at NYU and didn't believe a real Japanese girl would act so traditional in modern times. *I met such a girl*, Eric thought. Darrell had tried to argue that the author had styled the story in such a way so the girl would have plausible reasons to act traditionally. Feminism, they moaned simultaneously.

"Writing is subjective," said Darrell.

"So is life," Eric added. "Even so, I appreciate knowing someone actually read it, enjoyed it, and considered it."

They shook hands.

"It's great to meet you," said Darrell. "Keep writing. And send me something."

He handed Eric a business card.

"Thanks." Eric nodded, wanting to launch into a description of his latest work, the Viking novel, but he suddenly felt sick. He decided then and there to put it away and not work on it until he was over that orange-haired woman. Or forever. That would be Albright's advice.

Then something caught his eye: there was the old writer himself, decked out in red turtleneck shirt and a Navajo-patterned vest, browsing the stalls three aisles over. The fluorescent lighting reflected off his bald pate and his fluffy white beard was down to mid-chest.

Eric made a line for the exit.

After a couple of breakout sessions, more panel discussion than an escape from the confines of conference etiquette, Eric was ready for the opening night feast. He milled around the long tables where hotel staff were setting up the banquet's dazzling Sterling silver serving plates and bowls. As his stomach growled, he wanted to sneak an hors-d'oeuvre. All he had to do was lift the plastic wrap and slip one out. Or two. Who would care?

He should wait, he decided.

Screw the rules. He was hungry. He had been following rules for too long, and what did he have to show for his propriety?

He noticed the same woman from the keynote address standing alone by the tall windows that looked down on the tree-lined Allis Plaza, staring out those windows. Eric studied her. Solemnity engulfed her like a balloon. She held her hands clasped, drawn up under her chin like a nun praying. Normally, he would be unconcerned, but the way her face was set so sternly made him curious what might be wrong.

He pulled out several hors-d'oeuvres, wheat crackers with cheese and olives, and grabbed a paper plate left from earlier refreshments.

"Excuse me," said Eric. "Is everything all right?" He held out the plate to the woman. "You look like you might like a bite."

She shook her head, mouthed "no thanks" and returned to her pensive pose.

Fair enough, he thought.

"My stomach's empty," he said, with a chuckle, "so I thought you might be hungry, too. I'm not trying to invite you to join me in gluttony. It's just that I know listening to all of these speeches can make a person hungry."

She feigned a polite smile, crossed her arms over her chest.

"Sorry to bother you." His voice remained cheerful. He was not after anything. With a polite smile, he turned to go.

"No, it's all right," she said, giving him a longer look.

She took one of the hors-d'oeuvres, and he took another.

"They're not too bad," said Eric. "I hope you like it because I might have to go to jail for stealing these before the banquet officially opens. Rules are rules. But I'm willing to take the risk. Supposedly I'm learning how to be outrageous."

She was about to thank him, but lost control and began crying.

"I know it was a bad joke, but I didn't think it was that bad."

He glanced around the hall: no one was paying attention to them. It was left to him to deal with whatever the problem was.

"I'm Eric," he said despite her consternation. He did not know what to do, so he reached out and patted her shoulder.

Suddenly, she stepped awkwardly into his space, almost against him. After another minute, she regained her composure, stepped back and wiped the streak of tears from her cheek, apologizing.

"Are you okay?" asked Eric.

She nodded unconvincingly before the dike burst once more and her words flooded his ears and swept him into her story as the hotel staff uncovered the serving dishes and the feast began.

Laura was her name, and Eric introduced himself again, cautiously. He was an English professor at Fairmont College. Never heard of the place? Doesn't matter.

He directed her casually into the line and they gathered their food, returning to the corner where they had met. Their conversation turned lighter, leaving Eric to wonder what had caused her to cry before. Nevertheless, he was glad to be away from the stresses of fidelity. He was among his own kind: writers and publishers. Real people living real lives, not denizens of fantasy worlds populated by witches and trolls. He told her about his poetry, about the novel he was working on, and the teaching position he held.

She also wrote poetry. In fact, much to Eric's chagrin, she had two volumes published, with her latest, *Days of Their Lives*, coming out in

May. Eric told her about meeting Darrell Ross, his number one fan. Laura laughed. Then, between the last morsel of main course and the first sample from a dessert tray, she asked Eric if he wouldn't mind reading some recent work she had in a notebook. It was in her room.

About six lifetimes ago, it seemed to Eric, he'd met a woman at an art show in a similar moment. He had chickened out that night, but he was ready this time. Laura, a professional poet, seemed all too sincere for the kind of games to which he was becoming accustomed. And his status? He was a free man.

As the conversational din expanded through the hall, Eric grabbed a few mints from a bowl on the dessert table: silver foil-wrapped squares with dainty green string bows.

Laura led him to the elevators and, going up to her twenty-second floor room, no words were spoken. Eric knew he would compose a poem about the experience. Lines were already coming to him as she tried to slide her key card into the door slot without success. He took hold of the key card and tried shoving it in as she remarked that it must be too large for the slot. Finally, he found the right angle and pushed it all the way in. She sighed in delight and her warm, dark room opened to him.

Entering with equal parts excitement and caution, Eric saw her clothing laying about, hosiery and bra hung up in the bathroom. Laura apologized, explaining that she'd arrived late the previous night and had overslept, missing the maid service. She invited him to sit, gestured *there*—as she removed her jacket and slipped off her pumps.

Eric sat hesitantly upon her un-maid bed, his hands touching the sheets that had been tousled in her restless sleep. He breathed in her fragrance—it had settled upon the pillows—and thought ahead. Only the wall lamps at the head of the bed were on.

She retrieved her notebook: a pink pastel thing, its unlined pages filled to the edges with love sonnets and lonesome laments. She had filled half of it since her fiancé died, she told Eric. There was mistaken identity, a rough patch, jealousy and late night calls to check on her. Eric wanted to glance over at her breasts but kept his eyes on the notebook in her lap.

She paused to catch her breath as they sat shoulder to shoulder on the bed, reading intimate poems composed in her elegant handwriting with hardly a scratch out to break the mood. She brushed his thigh as she turned the page.

There she saw the poem, *that* poem, and recalled the pain. She had written a poem about a male friend who was not her fiancé.

He read it aloud: "To rid himself of a twisted mind; that's what he said . . . " and finished it silently. He took a deep breath. He felt warm, too warm, and removed his sport coat. The lamps were too bright so she dialed down their intensity. Eric blinked.

Reading her poem, he was thrown rudely back to his own distraught moment when he'd considered ending it all. To make Marina sorry she was so callus with him. At the last instant, he decided not to give her the satisfaction and veered back onto the highway, leaving the concrete buttress for someone else.

"I can understand why he . . . ."

She felt his tension and cupped her hand on his knee, part comfort, part warning.

A glance at Laura's breasts, bunched together in the hot V of her crisp, white blouse, prodded him. He focused on the notebook. Tears had spotted the page. Hers. He felt a strange passion there in those heartfelt words. When she at last divulged what had happened to her fiancé, she could not hold back the tears.

Laura fell heavily into Eric's arms.

"We were supposed to . . . to come together to this . . . convention." She tried to speak but sputtered. Her arm curled around his back, pulled him close. Her hair brushed his cheek. "We were having some problems. But I—I never thought he would—that he would put a bullet through his brain after reading a poem I wrote."

Her sobbing softened him. He wanted her face to dive against his chest, into his shirt; he wanted to feel her wetness—and with one hand, he grasped his necktie and pulled it loose. He carefully wrapped his arm around her shoulders and she melted, kissing his cheek, then his mouth, and with a pause to allow him to refuse her, proceeded to kiss him frantically until she was satisfied. By then, he was massaging her neck, her shoulder, her back. After she had taken off the blouse and lain back in her camisole, he stretched out beside her and held her willowy figure until sleep overcame them.

He awoke later, opening his eyes to the darkness, looking out the window. He still held her. Moonlight streamed through the curtains, silhouetting the gentle curve of her breasts as they rose and fell with each calm breath. His hand rested against one breast, then slid down to her thigh and stopped. He watched her sleeping for a while, until the thought flashed through his head that he could just take her, right then and there in this bed, that she might appreciate his attention, that a brief encounter might be just the prescription for the hurt that had caused her heart to decay.

Then he noticed her eyes darting beneath the lids; she was dancing with someone he did not know.

With a long exhalation, he climbed off the bed they had shared and pulled on his sport coat. He gently kissed her forehead and placed a foil-wrapped mint from his coat pocket between her sleeping breasts.

Eric stumbled out of Laura's room, his eyes blinded by the corridor lighting, and found his way to the elevators.

"You did the right thing, you ridiculous fool," he muttered to himself, stepping onto the elevator, trying to smile. "What have you learned tonight—this morning, whatever?"

That it was much too easy to be tempted, and it was much too easy to desire. It was easy to give in, too. And yet, he hadn't, and he didn't understand why. He had wanted her, this Laura, the poet. If he had, the world would know. His room would be discovered unused, his bed unrumpled. What would the cleaning staff make of that? That it was difficult to resist the sure thing.

Eric could not find her for two days as he wandered from workshop to workshop, from poetry reading to book signing, through the elegant corridors of the luxury hotel.

On the final evening of the conference, he spied her in the lobby.

She wore a long, formal black dress that was slit up one leg—the same kind of dress Íris had worn at the árt show. Laura sat across a coffee table from another man, dressed for the farewell party and closer to her age. They made a good couple.

Eric was surprised that he felt no jealousy.

Pulling out his pen and pocket pad, he watched her new life unfolding, and started a poem. He saw a frozen lake with skaters, an oily roadway with drivers, a dusty floor with ballerinas. People were crossing, at random, always expecting to maintain a certain decorum. Then tragedy would strike. Some people kept better balance than others in slippery situations, he considered. Some look like fools as they flail about, trying to keep their balance. Others simply fall. Most get up again. Some stay down.

30

ÍRIS KNOWS HE IS GONE. Although he says he will return next week, it feels as though he has fallen off the planet. The campus is empty without him. Linden Hall leans a bit to the side, the sky is a darker gray, and the wind blows harsher. A cold front has arrived and a chill settles over Íris as Sandra drives them to the church. It is Palm Sunday, dedication day, and Íris is dressed for religion, for the sacrifice. Her belly marks her sin.

Sandra shows Íris the engagement ring on her finger.

"We wrote out a courtship agreement," says Sandra. "It specifies what we shouldn't do in order to stay pure for each other. For example, one is 'Make no provision for the flesh.' That comes from the book of Romans. We also shouldn't 'put a stumbling block' before each other, as it says in Romans, chapter fourteen, verse thirteen. We're only allowed to hold hands, shake hands, have only friendship hugs, and no mouth kisses, no making out or other touching, no hand to body contact—"

"When do you get to know each other?" asks Íris.

"We are getting to know each other during courtship," she says.

"*Já*, if you're compatible sexually."

Sandra's explanation of sexuality not being so important makes Íris laugh.

The dedication goes well, and Reverend Meeks offers flattering remarks about the mural. It is as heaven is described in Jesus's own words, he says. Íris did not know that. She painted it how she thought it should look. There is no Valhalla set on an icy mountain peak, only fluffy clouds with cherubs. Sandra praises the rays of light that shine down from the ceiling—the actual light comes from recessed lamps. The effect is that a higher power, not just Kansas Gas & Electric, is projecting light upon the clouds.

They will not give Íris the check during the ceremony. Money is dirty. She must sit through the hymns and the sermon, the invitation to change her life, and the spectacle of a family of four marching up the aisle to kneel before the minister and beg for acceptance into the church. It is all about belonging to the group. No one is allowed to stand alone.

"Hello, Iris," says a voice she is afraid to recognize.

She turns and sees Ray in a blue suit and red tie, standing with his wife. He introduces her: Julie, the one with the trick jaw, who refuses to do oral sex. Ray has spoken of her.

"What are you doing here?" asks Íris, surprised. "You came to see the mural?"

"Naturally I would come to see it, Iris," he says, as his wife beams possessively, "but we come here almost every Sunday."

"We're members of the church," says the wife, proudly. She praises Íris's painting skills, not knowing her other talents. Probably Ray has avoided telling his wife about those.

Íris thanks Ray's wife for the compliments, staring at Ray. He lowers his eyes. She could say anything at that moment and although no one would believe her it would at least cause Ray some trouble. He would have to explain why she might say such a thing.

"You are both Christian?" asks Íris. Ray fidgets.

"Oh my, yes!" says the wife. She has her arm looped around Ray's arm. They make a handsome couple.

"I thought so. It shows."

"It does?" says the wife. "That's so kind of you to say."

"Professor Ferguson is such a great role model," says Íris, her voice dry. "He always goes out of his way to help students. He got me the job in Life Study. That's where I pose nude for figure work, twenty-five dollars an hour."

The wife's face goes pale even though she must know the kind of classes artists take. The way Íris shoves herself into their comfortable life seems to shock her. Especially now that she has a belly to show. She gives it a pat.

"He thinks it's good practice for them to draw a pregnant figure."

"Indeed."

"The paintings he did of me are especially provocative, considering the bondage and sado-masochism themes. Have you not seen his work? In his basement studio? You should take a look."

Íris parts rather abruptly, leaving the Fergusons with an interesting discussion for their afternoon tea.

Sandra takes Íris to her aunt's house for the noon meal and introduces her to all Sandra's cousins and their spouses and their children and a few grandchildren. What a joyful clan! How do they make so many children if they all follow Sandra's plan?

Her courtship? That is what they want to know about as they eat the baked ham. Sandra explains that Íris did not have a courtship, that she is—how should she put it?—a fallen angel. She means someone who is essentially good but who has been dealt the Devil card from a deck of Tarot.

"I still love him," says Íris, rather quietly, not wanting to let the moment go, "yet he does not love me any longer. I hurt him, so it is my fault. That is the reason I have this belly growing without a man to share it." That satisfies their sense of decorum. "I'll be all right. I have my faith."

They smile warmly, assuming her faith is the same as theirs.

Faith? The night Eirík brought her back to reality, she gathered the books from the curb, the books he bought to learn about her history and culture. She took them up to her room. She was more curious the next night, after the Shakespeare class. Rather than read a play about a love affair during the Trojan War, she chose the *Edda* of Snorri Sturluson and read it for the first time in English. She was amazed to see things in it she had not been able to see before in *Íslensku* words. She saw the truth of the Æsir.

"They were not mythological characters," said Íris, preaching to Cory after dinner one night. "They were real, flesh-and-blood mortals. They were some of the refugees from Troy!"

"Whatever," Cory muttered, then yawned. "Does it blow your mind?"

"*Já*, it blows my mind!"

"Well, good for you."

She told him how, reading in her native language, the names are *Íslensku*; they all sound like myths. "Like fantasy places."

Cory could not understand her excitement.

"In English, the places are clear. The chief god of the Ásatrú, Óðinn, was a prince of Troy. He was married to a daughter of King Priam—the same Priam being the father of Troilus that Shakespeare wrote about."

"You had a mystical experience."

"I'm not certain," she said, thinking—remembering it as she relaxes in Sandra's aunt's sitting room, children playing noisily around her.

Íris picks up a Bible from a table there and flips through it, as if looking for a page or a verse. Sandra notices. The Bible gives Íris more ideas to match with Snorri's *Edda*. It is easy to understand what ancient people were actually experiencing.

Cory was curious that evening and finished his dinner as she explained it all to him.

"Today we know what an aircraft is," Professor Íris had lectured, "and what a rocketship is, what computers are, what genetics is, and a long list of other scientific discoveries—things that no one thought of even a hundred years ago, much less five thousand years ago."

Cory agreed with her. When she mentioned Jules Verne, he knew what she meant. In the 1840s, the French writer described Iceland in his novel *Journey to the Center of the Earth* and wrote about electricity as a power source for an underwater city in *10,000 Leagues under the Sea*. Cory smiled, getting it.

"What would Jules Verne think of a microchip?" asked Íris. "Or a map of the 100,000-plus genes in every chromosome? What will we discover in the next ten years no one knows about today?"

"I have no idea."

"Someday everyone will carry a tiny telephone in a purse or pocket and everyone will talk through the air with no wires," she preached, "and everyone will join one big community on the Internet, like my website yet bigger, and share their opinions about everything."

"You're right, Iris," said Cory. He took her hand and shook it firmly. "Congratulations. You should go to Rocket Scientist school."

"Stop mocking me!"

He apologized. "Okay, I can read the story of Ezekiel. I get how he saw some airborne vehicle land and take off. I can accept that he didn't know what the heck he was seeing and he did his best to describe what he saw in the terms that he knew. Yeah, that I understand."

"So how would he describe a computer with speakers?"

"How?"

"As an 'ark of the covenant.' He hears the voice of God coming from it. The music of the spheres was radio static."

Cory was quiet for several minutes, contemplating.

"Mom never taught me that," he said. "Guess she was already set in her ways."

"I know many people who refuse to change," she told him.

Já, they are people who insist that what was true millennia ago must still be true today—and everything must still be true no matter what new information people learn since. Nothing changes, they insist. They accept, they believe, they hope for the best. That is what *they* call faith.

She pressed Cory: "Who is who in the Norse pantheon is clear in the English translation: Óðinn, the king of the gods, and his followers, the Æsir. As in 'Asia,' as in Asia Minor, what is now Turkey. The Vanir come from the area of Lake Van in the east. One of this Óðinn's sons is the mighty Þórr—"

"Yeah, but if Jesus is a myth, then those Norse fuckers are, too."

"It is all connected, Cory. We also have a place like the Christian heaven. It is *Ásgarðr*. It's where the gods live in a continuous drunken orgy. I made a painting of it, remember?"

"You told me that before, but that's no Christian concept. A drunken orgy? Come on."

"In the center of *Ásgarðr* is a palace reserved for the slain heroes, those who died in battle or otherwise distinguished themselves in heroic deeds that required strength and courage. It is called Valhalla."

"Heard of it. Never been there, and don't plan to."

"Most children in the West grow up with these tales pushed into their heads as myths. For the children of Iceland, they are not myths, they are history, the real history that Christians tried to hide. They do not want us to believe that Óðinn really existed, that *Ásgarðr* is real."

"But it can't be proven. That's why they suppress it. It's only myth."

"*Vá*, it is the Christian myths that need to be suppressed, Cory!"

"Calm down, girl. I'm only playing with you."

"These are the facts! They are fundamental to our way of life, our thinking about everything. The Norse people! And me. This translation explains more than what I ever read in *Íslensku*. Now the names are put side by side with other names that make the world turn upside down and spin backwards."

"You're the one spinning around."

"No, I am coming to a stop—finally. I have been spinning all these years—around a broomstick! All those silly rituals count for nothing. So many rules, and if I miss a meeting I get whipped by that bitch Megan. No more. Now the curtains that have hidden the truth from me, they draw back. Now I see this play. Read it yourself."

"I've got psych chapters for tomorrow."

She watched Cory for a while, letting him crack the cover of his psychology textbook, pretending to read.

"If the Norse gods can be the survivors of Troy, who were thought to be gods by the people they met in northern Europe, then how likely is it that what we call gods today, from anywhere in the world, all have similar origins? Just think! If Homer composed that *Iliad* poem about three-thousand years ago and the Trojan War was more than three-thousand years ago, consider that a thousand years is long enough to turn mortals into gods. The cult of Óðinn was wide-spread by the first Viking visit to Britain in A.D. 572!"

"Geez, did you memorize the whole book?"

"No, yet I read it twice."

With a dismissive wave, Cory returned to his reading, leaving Íris to ponder her new wisdom. It was that American professor of English who showed her the heritage she had forgotten. Not her father who secretly prayed to Óðinn, not her mother who cursed Óðinn, nor all the silly teachers in her schools. It was this sad, angry Eirík who opened the door, who showed her the homeland she had abandoned. And she hurt him for no reason.

On the way to her house, Íris asks Sandra if she would deliver a message.

"I must be sure Eirík understands me. He must know how ashamed I am for what I did, and I'm willing to do anything to bring back our relationship. I am willing to let him do anything he wishes in order to restore the balance. If he wants to do as I did, to play for a night with a woman of his choice, I will look away."

Já, when we are both wounded, we will again have something in common. From our injuries we can build a life together again.

"But only if you do me a favor in exchange," says Sandra. "Next week there's a rally, and the Salvation Corps"—she's vice-president of the campus student group—"will be spearheading it. Because you're a new mother-to-be, I'd really like you to join us. Iris, you don't have to be Christian to participate. We have some Jewish people. A few agnostics, too. Anyone who believes that Life is sacred. That's why I thought you'd be perfect."

"Me, perfect?" Íris is suspicious. "What do I have to do?"

"I'm hoping you'll give your testimony," she says, voice full of joy, "about choosing to carry your baby to term rather than turning to abortion as a solution to your unexpected pregnancy."

"My testimony?"

"We'd like to hear your thoughts about Life. About five minutes. Just tell us what it's like to be a witch and still be pro-life."

"What are you talking about? Witches aren't against life. I want this baby because he's mine. Not because of politics."

"It doesn't matter, Iris." She is so sincere she believes what she says. "I'll help you get back together with the father of your baby *because* you stood up for Life. We need people to speak out against abortion, even those who don't happen to be Christian. That makes you the perfect witness. We need your testimony. Will you help me help you?"

Íris regards her a moment. "Do I have a choice?"

There is a lot of free advice on her website, Íris discovers. She reads through the evening and the consensus is that she is a slut, though none of them use that word. Their suggestions range from giving sincere apologies to seeking professional counseling. Most of them question the authenticity of her love. She must prove her love to him. Even so, no matter what she does, a smart man would never trust her again.

"Where is Cory when I need to talk to him?" she mutters, opening the door and glancing up and down the hall.

"He's out on a date," someone answers. She sees Richie. "Can I help?"

He convinces her that he can be a good listener and will not judge her before hearing the whole story. He turns down the music he's playing, all drums and chanting, Buddhist stuff. She talks, he listens. She sits on the bed, he on the floor.

"All I can say, Iris, is if he feels he can't trust you, you've already lost him. I know that to change any behavior, you have to replace it with something else. Do you really love him? If yes, then do whatever it takes to prove he can trust you in the future. But do you want to change for him, or do you want to change for you?" He notices her skeptical frown. "I only say that because it seems like you've hurt yourself, and you knew it would hurt you, even if he never found out. Think about it: would you want a lover who thought your actions were okay? Even someone who objects to your liberal attitudes about sex? Why'd you even ask his permission to go to the party? Did you want him to tell you *not* to go?"

"I do not know," is all she can say.

"Do you really want to change? Only you know the answer."

Já, I want to change. What would I change?

The next day Íris catches Cory with his sleepover partner and she teases him about his 'liberal attitudes about sex.' To make her take it back, he consents to hear her report and offer his advice. His mother is a psychiatrist, after all, and that makes his advice a bit more relevant than others. For this act of charity, he sends his date home.

"My mom once said that the reason women want commitment from men is to create an emotionally and financially stable environment for raising their children," says Cory, sitting on the bed in his white briefs. "Stability is very important to a child. I should know. I never had any. But one decision you have to make is what priority your child has in your life. Iris, how much are you willing to change for the child? What'll you give up? My mom gave up custody of me to pursue her career. Now she makes six figures but we never talk. You need to be honest with yourself, too, because a lifetime is a very long time. What kind of mom are you gonna be?"

She needs another opinion, so she seeks out Tracie on the ground floor, who's heard it all from Jean. In exchange for her advice, she gives Tracie a massage. She talks about commitment, a word Íris hates.

"Ya didn't commit to each other because of compatibility and love. It was because of necessity," she explains. "Well, that ain't a bad thing, and it certainly don't mean y'all ain't compatible and don't or won't or can't ever love each other again, but ya need to really take a look at why ya made that commitment—and just how much commitment ya really made."

Íris finishes the massage as she goes on about what 'committed relationship' means to her—*já,* opposite of Magnús and Heiðr. Tracie sits up and pulls on a shirt.

"It ain't necessary to raise a child with two equally-committed parents but it sure makes things a whole helluva lot easier. And what kinda rules're ya gonna have in a committed relationship?"

"What does that mean?" asks Íris, wringing her tired hands.

Tracie gives her a hard look. "Are ya willing to let him do what you did? I mean, play around? Are ya? Shit, Iris, from what ya said, it seems like *you* are the playboy on the prowl and he's the lonely housewife fretting at home. That's ass-backwards."

Not true! Íris sits back and rubs her belly, feeling the weird warmth there, and realizes that she has been blind for so long. She knows nothing about what real people do for each other. She never had a relationship longer than a few weeks. Her lovers leave when they get enough.

"All your sex talk is just some asinine distraction from what the real issue is," says Jean later. "Iris, you need to ask yourself why you snuck out in the first place. These kinds of questions don't just stand up and shout to you. Sneaking out was what put you into the mud, girl friend, and the rest was a slide down the hill. It's time to be brutally honest with yourself—and I'll help you do it. Put aside the guilt—you know what that is, right? You hurt him. You're confused and feel guilty—or you should be—but you need to find answers to these questions before you can be sure you won't ever hurt him again. That assumes you don't *want* to hurt him."

"*Nei*, I don't want to hurt him," says Íris. "I never wanted to hurt him."

"That's cute," Jean sneers. Íris can see this is unpleasant for her. "So do you really want some kind of a sexually exclusive relationship with him? I wouldn't, but that's me. I need a more . . . a more *black* man. That's a matter of taste. If the dude gets you going, go after him. Confusion and doubt is normal at the beginning of relationships, but do you honestly feel you'll be able to live the kind of lifestyle this relationship will demand? Can you see yourself being Missus Professor, with a baby boy named Lyle or Dylan or Regis?"

"Never Lyle or—"

"The biggest issue you created in your night on the beach was trust. Trust with a motherlovin' monster T. How can the dude ever trust you again? Are you gonna sneak out again? One out of three times? Every time? Never again?"

"Never again," says Íris, lowering her head.

"So why *did* you sneak out? He said it wasn't *proper* for a preggo to party, but you thought he was just being a hard-ass. He is a professor, right? Didn't you read between the lines? He was really saying he was freaked out at the chemistry you and those boys had. He was afraid you'd leave him for one of them. And you did, didn't you? Damn, girl, can you ever give up the slut life? Will your art suffer if you do? I know you put a lot of sexual shit in your art. But why's it there? Does it come from the addiction you think you have? Personally, I don't buy the whole sex addiction thing. You like sex. That's normal. The real question is why you weren't getting it from him."

Long after midnight, Íris stands on the third floor balcony and watches the clouds drift across the sepia moon, seeing how the branches have begun filling with leaves. Tears fall from her eyes and she is surprised. It is like her conscience is leaking out.

Já, my place in the world has been swept clean. I have been chained to a rock. A falcon comes to peck out my eyes, yet they grow back each night. And my baby boy, born and grown to manhood, is forced to watch from the rock where he is also chained.

That is the dream that disturbs her sleep. God has commanded too many people to rise up and twist her life around, spin it into dust. They are part of a conspiracy to make her insane. She is powerless to stop it.

Now I understand the value of Eirík. He doubles my strength against the world.

She clicks COMPOSE and types out a message. She needs to see him, to explain that she has changed and wants to beg for forgiveness. She had a revelation. He needs to see for himself. Only then will the world stop shaking, trying to throw her off. Only with what Sandra calls a 'reconnect' will the balance in her universe be restored. A life squirms within and knocks on her door. He asks where his father is.

31

THE DRIVE BACK FROM KANSAS CITY WAS A BLUR, thinking of Laura and thinking more of Íris. They were opposites, and yet there was similarity in their situations. He could have had sex with Laura, Eric calculated. However, he chose not to. He put away his libido and left the scene of the crime—without the crime. No one in the hotel or driving along the highway could know of his noble choice. And that was how it should be. Somehow, the day was brighter.

He thought of his phone conversation with Matt, a quick call before leaving town.

"After much soul searching and a lot of internal anguish," Eric told his brother, "I have decided that I will forgive Íris. Then we will proceed with our relationship. If we still can. That's contingent, of course, upon such acts never again occurring, and, as you have advised, upon the positive results of a paternity test."

"There's the professor we all know," said Matt. "But are you sure?"

"I can accept that there is such a thing as sex addiction, but as with any addiction, a person has to learn to control it. I agree with you on that. She needs to seek treatment. In your parlance, I shall hate the sin but love the sinner. I have to help her, Matt. At least give her the chance to help herself."

"Be careful," was Matt's last advice.

Eric slowed, glimpsing a state trooper parked in the shadow of a tree.

"It's not her," he told himself, "it's that there is no one else."

When Eric returned to his apartment, he unpacked his bag, setting the conference packet and a stack of review books on his desk. He routinely switched on the television, clicking through channels until he landed on the old movies channel. There, in all its Romantic glory, was the musical *Camelot*, just as melancholy Franco Nero was singing to tearful Vanessa Redgrave how he could never leave her in springtime. Or winter, or fall—or summer, for that matter, she being the infamous Queen Guinevere and he the notorious Lancelot. Eric realized that he had always identified with the sadly noble King Arthur, played by Richard Harris, who ignores their affair and suffers in silence for the good of the kingdom. Every woman Eric ever fell for was this kind of Guinevere, it seemed, and every rival was a deceitful Lancelot. It was life imitating art.

"Art exists where words end," he whispered. Íris had said that after an evening comparing his writing to her painting. "The artist doesn't depict symbols," she told him. "Viewers see symbols from their own minds and their experiences, and they lay those personal symbols over the art."

He continued watching *Camelot*, comparing the infidelity in the film with his own situation. How perverse! How Romantic! The land suffers when the king is wounded, went the myth. Eric's sanity suffered when his ego was wounded.

He sighed, then let out a stirring rendition of "If ever Iris would leave you, it wouldn't be in springtime . . . ."

Viki and Fiona stopped in to show Eric the latest batch of submissions for the literary journal: 19 stories, 32 poems, and 5 essays. He'd sent a memo around to the faculty, asking them to remind their students of the deadline. Now the selection process could begin: students sorting the good, bad, and ugly, then he, as adviser, selecting a certain percentage from the top and passing them on to the final judge, visiting writer-in-residence Lance Albright. Those that Albright picked would be published.

He sighed, seeing the folders of ragged pages, some handwritten, some with strange fonts, formats all over the spectrum.

"Do you want to read them first?" Viki asked.

"Oh, you guys should go through them before me," said Eric, not ready to dive into the mess this week.

"How about we each take half, then switch next week?" said Viki.

Eric agreed.

The first story he saw when he opened the folder was "My Bitch" by Megan Valery. He stopped and examined the cover page: professionally done, neat, correct, inviting. The name of the author, however, sent shudders down his spine. He'd never suspected Jack's troublemaker was a creative person. Still, for a journal recently renamed *Journatalia*, this woman had the right story. Without stopping, he read through the lesbian bondage tale. It had a plot, was amusing in places, erotic in others, actually rather good. He had a problem with the submissive character named Irina, of course.

Judgment time. Ms. Valery had crossed the line. Eric liked the story, but it had no place in a student publication. Freedom of speech? That only applied to speeches. In the English department, democracy was often discussed but did not really exist. There was a god—or, in this case, goddess: Dr. Liz—who ruled over all, and if the demigods did not behave, they could be struck down and transformed into mere mortals.

There was no way "My Bitch" was going into *Journatalia*—

"Eric, my boy," a familiar but unwanted voice bellowed outside his open door.

It was Lance Albright, in all of his beer-belly stoutness, Santa Claus beard, and Il Duce pomposity, pushing his way into the office without hesitation. Eric nearly tumbled out of his chair, caught by the surprise of the invasion. Albright had never visited his office.

"I've finally read those chapters you gave me. Lost them for a while on the desk. But I gave them a good read. Here you go."

Eric accepted the manuscript, puzzled by the meeting. None had been scheduled. And what was Albright doing calling him 'my boy'?

"I made a few marks," said Albright, hovering over the desk. "Hope you don't mind." He plopped himself down in the chair beside the desk where Jack always sat and let out an explosive exhalation, as though he had just walked up the stairs to the fifth floor. "My assessment—which is, I believe, what you expected when you gave me the manuscript—is that it needs a lot of work yet. You probably knew that when you gave it to me, but it's a rough draft, so I gave you the benefit. Get me?"

"Thanks, I guess. So what are the main problems?"

"Well, I'll tell you," said Albright and stopped to catch his breath. Then he launched into an uncharacteristically friendly talk about the novel's contrasting story lines, how they kept crashing into each other. He liked the shifts between the modern and medieval settings of the Viking tale, but encouraged Eric to write on through to the end before attempting to revise the early chapters. "By now, you've hit your stride and you're on a roll, right?"

"Sure." He decided not to divulge that he had put the novel away for the foreseeable lifetime. Without his source of inspiration, there was no motivation to work on it.

"There you are!" The infamous Megan Valery was suddenly poking her head into his office.

"Here I am," said Albright.

"Just want to ask if you finished the story I gave you, the new one?"

"The lesbians?" He grinned at Eric, who carefully closed the folder of stories. "Almost done."

"No hurry," said Megan, leaning against the doorframe. "I want you to know I turned it in for the magazine."

"Magazine? What magazine?" asked Albright.

"The literary journal," Eric explained. "It used to be the *Fairmont Review*."

"Oh, that one."

"They changed the name," Megan told him excitedly. "Now it's called

Journatalia."

"Journa-what?" asked Albright, and his student—female friend, whatever—gave him a brief history of the campus-shaking decision. She threw in a couple of nasty epithets for Blake Spenser, wishing death upon the ultra-conservative faculty advisor.

"Anyway, good luck with your reading," said Megan, bowing out. She took a step, spun around and returned to the office. "Lance—you *are* coming to the party afterwards, aren't you?"

"What party?" asked Albright.

"Don't be silly," Megan teased him with a playful slap on the wrist.

"I remember." Albright was smiling. "That bacchanalia thing, huh?"

"I'm counting on you to be our guest of honor."

Megan patted the old writer's shoulder, gave him an air kiss, and departed in a whirlwind.

"What's that all about?" asked Eric after a moment, seeing the old writer still grinning.

Albright reluctantly returned to reality. "Oh, she's planning some party for after the reading. Calls it a Beltane celebration. I'm invited, like I'm some kind of celebrity. The woman's a little wacko, but she's a looker. So what the hell? Might be fun. Good way to wrap up my year here, and a better way to finish off a reading than last time. Get me?"

He winked at Eric, who chuckled. They shared a joke, he realized. Despite feeling awkward, Eric decided he enjoyed it. Editing his manuscript, this friendly visit, socializing with students? Albright must be going senile. In that case, thought Eric, he should be extra nice and give the old writer something in exchange. Like a warning.

"You'd better be careful. Some of the women here are working to bring us down."

"Us? Who's that?" asked Albright.

"Men. Especially faculty. They're dropping like flies around here."

Albright moved to the front edge of the chair, leaned on his knees.

"Eric, my boy, if there's one thing I've learned in my forty years of adult life, it's how to keep my balance in changing times. These co-eds, they're still after the same thing they were thirty years ago. They want to be respected, sure, but they also want to be cuddled and coddled."

Albright sat back and scratched under his beard. "How can they expect to have it both ways? Well, I'll tell you: so do men. We like to kick butt at work, right? But we also like to be—how can I put it delicately?—to be *pleasured* when we get home." He caught his breath, and, just as Eric was about to speak, continued: "So I'm gonna go, just to humor the woman. I'll have a few drinks—wife says she doesn't care. So I'll shake some hands, sign some autographs, say some words of encouragement to the ladies—those who aspire to be writers, like yourself—then I'll go home." He gave Eric a wink. "And I don't care which one I go home with!"

"Your wife lets you go to these student parties?"

"Hell, yes. Gives her a break." Albright chuckled.

Eric shrugged and picked up the manuscript, flipped through it to see how much marking Albright had done. The pages were covered in red pen notes, arrows, and cross-outs. Had Albright ever worked as hard on a student manuscript?

He cleared his throat. "I've written twenty chapters now, but I've hit a mental block."

Albright snickered. "Just take a walk around the campus, clear your mind, and focus."

Eric shook his head slowly. That was how his troubles had begun. "The woman who, shall we say, inspired the story has, uh, turned out to be . . . . She's not . . . ." Albright waited patiently for him to finish. "We broke up. Now, whenever I try to write on the novel, I think of her. That makes me sick. And I can't write."

"Used to happen to me all the time," said Albright, with a slap to the desk. "That's why I got married: so I always have inspiration. Some area of normalcy is required in a writer's life. It's the fooling around that gives him something to write about. Get me?"

"I got you." More than he wanted to, and more than he'd expected to. Eric smiled to himself. He glanced at the wall calendar: no, it was not Friday the thirteenth, not yet.

Albright lifted himself out of the chair, reached for the doorframe, then looked back.

"Gotta be going, but here's the all-purpose remedy: start another story. Put that whore-inspired crap away for six months. If you cross paths with her, start the six months over. Meantime, start something fresh. Complete opposite."

"That would be the apple," Eric mumbled.

"Pardon me?"

"Nothing." Eric looked up. "I said, the opposite would be a story of a Hispanic lady in a tropical setting. You know: jungle love, that sort of thing."

I have to get out of Dickerson.

Íris needs to run away from the eyes of sophomore boys who now know how a pregnant woman looks when she is put on a pedestal.

Ray leers at her while she poses. His eyes are always on her. When he stands behind the students, he runs his tongue across his lips. Yet she cannot accuse him of anything.

So Ray has other ideas. He brings in a male model. A new challenge, he says to the students, and positions the man behind her, his arms around her hips as though they are the happy parents-to-be. Fifteen minutes into the pose, she feels the model's penis pushing against her. She mumbles to him to think of sweaty old men but he continues pushing. She breaks the pose.

"What are you doing?" she asks loudly.

"Nothing! What's your problem?" says the model.

She wants to slap his face; instead, she glances down and is briefly impressed. When she steps away, his secret is exposed. Ray is caught, too, not knowing what to do.

She sees that the boys on the front row are excited and turns angrily to them, hands on hips: "Is this what you like? Looking at naked women? *Já*, you should try it! Off with your clothes! Take them off! Now! See how it feels, *bjáni*! Strip down!"

The boys are so surprised they start unbuttoning their shirts. One pulls off his t-shirt before Ray stops them. When he turns to check on her, she has left the studio.

She does not go straight to her studio, not this time. Pulling on her robe, she passes barefoot through the atrium to see Cory's sculpture.

In greenish-gray fired and stained clay stands the life-size Íris, nude as nature, everything about her rendered in perfect anatomical detail. She is amazed. There is an opening in the hand between the curled fingers and someone, perhaps Cory, has placed a single purple iris there. A real flower. The plate on the base gives the title: *Iris*. Without the accent mark.

Is it me, she wonders, or is it the flower she is holding? She enjoys the joke. Everyone who passes through Dickerson will see her now. The students and faculty know who this Iris is. Those who have not had the pleasure of seeing her in Life Study can now see her anytime they wish in the atrium. That is all she is to anyone: a cheap fantasy.

Catching Íris in the hallway, Elaine tells her that *Roses* has finally been put up in the Ulrich Gallery. Evidently, there was some dispute whether it was to stay in the gallery or go home with its new owner. In the end, the curator convinced the owner to leave it in the gallery for everyone to see. Yet what will they see in her painting? An abused woman satisfied with her punishment?

After putting on her maternity dress, she goes to see it.

She stands before the pallid face, full of regret, resting calmly upon those damn thorns. She is surprised. It seems like a different painting now, as though someone else painted it and she was only the model. The hair seems brighter, redder, changing with the seasons.

Já, the seasons of a lifetime, she thinks, regarding the painting and touching her belly. She is no longer maid, in Wiccan terms, but mother. When her child is grown she will become the crone. Such is the cycle of life, a woman's grand cycle. The wheel is turning. She smiles yet feels a tear in the corner of her eye. This time next year, she will be bouncing a child on her knee.

Íris has learned that mirrors can lie. The woman she sees is not her, can never be her.

"Get over it," says Jean, who has driven Íris to the mall to help her choose the maternity clothing she will wear in the fashion show. Stork Fashions left a message at the house: they want Íris to be in the show. There is no money, but she may keep two of the outfits.

"You're one hot mamma, Iris. Don't let anyone tell you you're not. I've seen some pregnant women that look plain ugly, like the baby was sucking out all their looks."

She puts on the next dress and turns to the side. She poses first with her back to the mirrors, then faces it. This is how she will look when she models. She sighs, visually measuring her belly.

"Let's try on the pants," says Jean, lifting the garment from the hanger. "They look baggy enough for you."

"I cannot wear pants. They rub too much."

"Okay, no pants."

She finds two more dresses and a jumper.

"Did I tell you my sister had her baby?" says Jean as Íris tries on the clothes.

"Boy or girl?"

"Girl." Jean laughs. "She's gonna have so much trouble raising girls. She's a tomboy herself—six brothers, four uncles. At least she knows what to expect from the boys when it comes time to start dating."

Íris frowns before the mirror. "This one makes me look fat."

"You're supposed to look fat in maternity dresses."

She shakes her head, and pulls off the dress.

"I will teach my boy to respect women. None of this playing games. No testing a girl's love by demanding sex. I know what that is about."

"You go, girl friend."

"I think I was testing Eirík," says Íris. Jean helps her pull on another dress. "Cory said I wanted to see if he would stay with me, no matter how bad I was. Or I was trying to drive him away because I'm afraid of a relationship."

"I vote for the second one."

"This dress is not good, either," says Íris, studying herself in the mirror.

"You wanted to get caught," says Jean.

"*Nei*, I wanted it—and more."

Suddenly she feels sad, and she sits down on the bench in this big, clumsy dress. She stares at her red toenails, wiggles her feet, making sure they are hers before she loses sight of them.

"I know what you are wondering, what everyone's been wondering. *Já*, she cannot really love him if she goes out to party with other men."

"Nobody thinks that," says Jean. "Honestly, nobody cares what the hell you do."

"I liked being with him."

Jean sits beside her with a loud sigh.

"Even though he is too old for me," says Íris. "He made me a better person. *Já*, I always felt smarter. My creative spirit was bright. Now it's all gone. I have no creative energy."

"You're slipping into soap opera land, Iris."

"He was so excited when I told him about the baby. The first thing he said was he wanted to be a family. He never asked what I wanted. He took charge. I never asked about marriage, if he wanted to marry me, or if I wanted to marry him. We were here in the mall—outside this shop—when I dared to tell him I love him."

"Ohmagod, you said that?"

"*Já*, and I never said that to any man before."

"That's a big tamale."

"What?"

Jean laughed. "Come on, you need to change. Let's try the jumper."

Íris stands and slips off the dress.

"I have to be more responsible." She turns to Jean: "Can I be afraid of commitment?"

"Sure, why not?" She hands her the jumper.

"I have been on my own since eighteen, *já*, really since fourteen."

The jumper is emerald green with a pattern of royal blue butterflies running through it, white clovers around the waistline. Iceland's colors. Not its flag, its landscape.

"That's the one I like," says Jean. "It's the real you."

32

FEELING LIGHTHEADED AFTER TWO HOURS OF GRADING, Eric knew it must be time for lunch. He was still on island time even after being back for three weeks. When his stomach was empty, he could not concentrate. There were still seven papers on the sonnets for him to read and grade. Eight, if the student named Íris was going to turn one in.

"Excuse me," a woman's voice called softly. "Eric Schaeffer?"

His office was becoming the center of the universe, everyone coming and going, revolving around him like planets about to collide but always just missing.

Eric looked up, saw the young woman standing in his doorway wearing a modest shirt and slacks, her light-brown hair in a ponytail. A large gold cross hung around her neck, settled between her breasts like some VERBOTEN sign.

"What can I do for you?" he asked, instantly suspicious.

"My name's Sandra Kinney." She stepped into the office, clasping her hands demurely in front of herself. "It seems that we have a mutual acquaintance. Iris?"

"Iris . . . ?" He got up out of his chair. "What happened?"

"Nothing's happened, Professor Schaeffer. She's spoken of you so I wanted to meet you."

He let out a sigh. "Call me Eric," he said, gesturing to the side chair.

"I'm a graduate student in the art department, a friend of Iris. Well, as much as I can be. Sometimes it's hard to be her friend. I'm sure you know what I mean."

Eric nodded. Today was understatement day.

"I'm here as a favor to her," said Sandra, "acting as a sort of middle man. She's really very upset—this is from me, not her. She wanted me to talk to you, and to find out what she must do to get you back. I agreed to help her because I believe it's the right thing to do. For the baby, that is. I want to help the both of you."

Eric grinned against his will. "This is going to take a while, I'll bet. Actually, I was about to step out for lunch. If you'd like to join me, we can talk there."

She thanked him and they left together, awkwardly. He considered that this woman was the confidant, so he wondered what sordid details she must know already, and what kind of slant Íris had put on those details. Was he already the bad guy in Sandra's eyes?

"I see her hanging around Linden," he told her on the way, "like she's waiting to catch me coming or going. She comes by my office, too, just to see if I'm in."

"I didn't know that. No wonder she asked me to speak for her."

"Is she all right? I mean, medically?"

"The baby is doing well, she said. But she's afraid of you, I think."

"Afraid . . . ?"

"Yes, that you'll reject her. Like you've been doing."

They went to Golden King, a small Chinese restaurant across from the campus. Eric was indulging his renewed craving for kung pao. Sandra chose vegetarian, ordered for herself. Eric told her he'd pick up the tab, his gesture of appreciation for her charitable act.

"I do love Iris. I mean as a fellow artist, and as a human being," said Sandra, "but she thinks I'm trying to convert her. Which I am, but passively. I want her to want to change. I know she wants to change. She said so."

The hot tea was served. Next came the communal bowl of rice and the dishes they had ordered. Sandra bowed her head and mouthed a prayer as Eric waited. Small talk was followed by Sandra's observations of their mutual friend. Íris was agonizing over what she did to hurt him. She knew she sinned—Sandra's lexicon—but she was willing to do whatever it took—Sandra's words again—to make it up to him, and anything else he required in order to return their relationship to the way it was before Spring Break. With a baby on the way, Íris wanted to get back together with her lover, this man named 'Eirík.'

He chuckled at the way Sandra imitated how Íris pronounced his name.

"She told me something about her teen years," said Eric, breaking his crab Rangoon open, "but I never wanted to hear any details that might turn me against her. Whatever she did before I met her does not concern me. If she has any kind of sex addiction, it needs to be treated like any other disorder. That's what concerns me: that she get help. If we get back together, that'll have to be a priority: getting her help. That has to be one of the conditions for a reunion. You didn't know all of that about her, did you?"

"I had no idea." Sandra was pale, hearing of her colleague's past life. "It makes me feel more sorry for her. I can't imagine how she managed to go through all of that. Alone, especially. It's amazing that she's come here to be an artist after that kind of life." She took a bite, chewed. "But I can't believe she would do those kinds of things while she's pregnant."

"It doesn't seem rational for a pregnant woman to do what she did." He ate some kung pao, then reached quickly for the water glass. He drank, cleared his throat. "That's got some 'pow' to it, all right!" He recovered, coughed. "So her rational mind simply ceased to function. That sounds about right. I've done stupid things, bad things, and I've demonstrated poor judgment a thousand times. My brother thinks I did when I first met Íris. Still, that kind of irrational behavior sounds like addiction to me. That's what it was. We didn't have a fight. She didn't storm out, as you might think. She didn't do it to spite me."

"Yes, that's what she said. She doesn't know why she did it, but she wants you to forgive her. It wasn't a matter of not loving you, or not wanting to be with you. In fact, Iris says that, afterwards, she felt like it was somebody else who was . . . uh, doing those things."

The waitress checked on them and Eric waved her off.

"Well, I guess you know the graphic details," he said, and sighed. "She wanted to go to the frat party and I said I didn't think it would be good for a pregnant woman to be there. You know, the drinking, loud music, potential for violence. Wasn't that realistic? To be concerned about those problems?"

"You acted appropriately, in my opinion."

"I suppose what I was really trying to say was that a pregnant woman who was mine—not to be possessive or chauvinistic—but she shouldn't be at some party with other guys. Maybe she took exception to my 'controlling' statement. I don't know. I can understand that I'm getting old, not as fit as I used to be, not uh . . . ." He took a sip of tea. "Well, commitment is commitment, isn't it?"

"That is the most important thing in any relationship," said Sandra, then explained some of her courtship agreement as Eric patiently listened. "So without some agreement that you are with her and she is with you, there is nothing. Nobody can base a decent relationship on an 'anything goes' philosophy. Like her witch-ism beliefs. It's all about flaunting convention."

Eric cleared his throat. "Convention?" He considered whether to spend the effort correcting her misperceptions about Wicca.

"She said it was pure coincidence that they came by," Eric said, "and she happened to be sitting outside. Two hours later, she returned and I clearly saw two people engaged in an act of oral sex. Considering that single episode, I can only speculate how much more must have taken place at the party."

"Actually," Sandra spoke up, "and I shouldn't be repeating this, but one time I heard her say to a friend of hers that she was doing *quote* everything she could *unquote* to keep you satisfied—everything sexual, that is. I guess so you'd stay with her."

"I have been wondering if our 'good times' were just that: enough to keep me on a short leash. But why wouldn't I stay with her?"

"What do you mean?"

"Look at her: she is so beautiful, sexy, talented, intelligent, fun."

"Eric, the devil is a beautiful mistress, too."

He nodded. "In other such relational discord," he said, shifting into professorial formality, "I've often asked myself this: Given the present situation and what I know, would I ultimately be better off with the woman or without her? And that assumes that I'd subsequently find another of equal or better quality. That's the bottom line here. Is what I had better than the great unknown?"

"Put your faith in Jesus Christ," she said. "He'll show you the way."

"That's not necessary. I've already decided."

She perked up. "You have?"

"It has taken time and a lot of prods from extraneous sources," said Eric, choosing his words carefully, knowing Sandra would repeat them to Íris. "I've decided that, if the baby is mine, I will forgive everything. And I'll stay with her. Presuming she still wants me. If not, then . . . we'll stay apart."

"You want to know that the baby is yours?"

"Shouldn't that be the first step?" He could guess what Sandra was thinking: Where does that leave the baby? "I considered a paternity test the first thing. If infidelity occurs once, it's likely it has occurred before. Right?"

"I really have no idea what goes on in immoral relationships. My boyfriend, Dylan, he's a hundred and ten percent faithful to me."

"If that's possible." He sipped tea. "I've already checked on it. The cost is a whopping six-hundred dollars. Insurance doesn't cover it. But it's fundamental to how we live the rest of our lives. If Íris agrees to pay, let's say, two hundred of it, which is probably all she can afford, I'll pay the rest. She needs to pay some of it. Symbolism, if nothing else. She'll want to know, too, I'm sure. Who else is there on campus who could be the father if not me?"

"She hasn't mentioned anyone else." Her eyelids batted and she was staring out the window for the first time during their lunch. Eric wondered whose side she was on.

The waitress brought the check and two fortune cookies on a small tray.

"Pending the results," he continued, "if it's positive, I will forgive her. Completely, and without obligation. And if that *is* the case, I would sincerely hope that our experience of mistrust does not make our relationship forever strained. I mean, I wouldn't want to live with the idea that she always 'owed' me for my forgiveness. I don't want that."

"I'll tell her."

"And if the test is negative, then—well, I suppose my life will simply have to start over again without her. In that case, she can . . . . She can do whatever the hell she wants."

"That seems fair," said Sandra, breaking her fortune cookie open.

"I think so." Eric picked up his cookie. "That's the best I can do. I want things to work out. I'm in hell just as much as her—umm, don't tell her that. The only way past this is to have the test and go from there. Then we can get some professional help for her."

"I'll report everything to her tonight." She paused to read her fortune, then crumpled it up and left it on the plate. "You said there were conditions?"

"Yes." He sat back, thinking. "First is to have the paternity test. If it's in my favor, then the second condition is to get counseling for the addiction. She has to promise never to give in to it again, or if there is temptation, allow me to help her through it."

"Is that all?" She had taken out a pen and was making notes on the paper napkin.

"No." He waited until she finished writing. "In order to confront this problem of hers, she needs to write a letter, a letter explaining all of her history and how she came to have this problem, how she will prevent it from occurring again. It should force her to examine why she has this addiction, how it started, recognize the patterns that will appear as she writes, patterns of when and where and how she has given in to the addiction. I want her to recognize those moments of weakness. Full disclosure. Doing so will help her to avoid them. I think that's straight out of the Psychology 101 textbook."

Eric watched Sandra writing and thought of what reaction Íris would have to his three conditions. He was not being harsh, he decided. He wanted her back, but he needed to be sure that the problem would never again ruin their relationship. The only way to do that was for her to get to the source of the problem and fight her way out of it. He would dedicate his life to the change.

He broke open his fortune cookie, a little fearful of the prediction.

"I think what you're doing is wonderful," said Sandra. "It's clearly the thoughts of a rational man in an irrational situation. Iris has to appreciate that. I know she will."

He examined the slip of paper from the cookie and laughed.

"What is it?" she asked, perplexed.

He showed her the fortune: *Two Wrongs Don't Make a Right*.

"I think I've had that one a few times before," he said, getting up. "It must be popular."

33

ÍRIS SITS ON A BENCH OUTSIDE DICKERSON HALL, gazing into the woods that border the campus, trying to sketch the way the sun highlights the branches spotted with new leaves. The breeze is warm yet she shivers. Summer is coming. This is not a good day for drawing. She cannot easily translate reality into two-dimensional fiction.

She thinks of the previous evening as she sketches, hating how much she struggled over what to post as her response to online friends who wanted to know how she will solve her problem. By midnight, she had written and posted a short statement:

> he told me to think hard about how & why i have this addiction & what i plan to do about it so it doesnt happen again. he said i must write a letter explaining everything- all the way back to iceland. it is hard to write about those events yet that is what he wants so i am writing it. i said i was willing to do anything. when he reads the letter he will know everything- so then no secrets between us. then no reason for him to reject me. im going to be completely honest & i will swear to get help & swear to be faithful to him. i will finish it this weekend & give it to him monday. wish me luck.

The letter will be the document that reconnects them—a contract between them. And a pledge to him. Sandra suggested she make it like a confession, like a plea for forgiveness. Íris is not such a good writer, however. English is not her native language. She only started learning it at age twelve, and she was hardly a studious girl. She was not prepared when she arrived in Canada—

Já, the wheel is turning. She counts the years, sets down her pencils, leans back on the bench, and inhales the springtime around her.

A shadow falls over her. She turns and is shocked to see Megan.

"Here you are," says her former coven leader, dressed in scruffy jeans and torn sweatshirt. "Your art friend—Cory?—he said he saw you come this way."

"He did?" Íris wonders why she has followed her to this secluded corner of the campus.

"I wanted to see you again, Iris."

"You forgot, it's *Í*ris. With an *E*."

"Yes." Megan comes around to sit beside her on the bench. "I've missed you. There isn't any better way to say it. I acted like a real bitch after Samhain, and I want to apologize for that. I hope you can forgive me." She offers a big smile. "This has been a fascinating semester for me, and I'm going to be able to graduate in December."

"I graduate in August." Íris is suspicious. "I had to cut back this semester because of . . . this baby," and she gives her belly a pat.

"Yes, Celia told me you got pregnant."

"Celia can't keep secrets."

"It's no secret now. Look at you: you've got a beautiful bump going there. I know that baby is gonna be a cutie! Celia said it's a boy. May I?"

Before Íris can react, Megan presses the palm of her hand to Íris's abdomen, shifting it three times, like a doctor.

"Do you know who the father is?"

"*Já*, of course."

"But you're not getting married. Are you going to just live together?"

"We have an arrangement." What it is she isn't sure.

"That's cool." Megan chuckles and tosses her hair back. "I thought you might've gotten pregnant on purpose, to get something out of him.

Some women'll go to that extreme. For me, it was real simple. A few minutes of fornication and I've got a semester of homework, lectures, and bullshit papers out of the way. Sixty percent of my A grades have been achieved in an hour or less. Only that asshole Macintosh is giving me grief, but he's going down. I hear he resigned, the fool. Hah! My psychology courses are paying off."

Íris stares hard at her, into her gray eyes. "Why are you here?"

Megan laughs. Íris knows her. Megan doesn't do anything without a reason.

"I just wanted to see how you were doing." Megan's smile is a mix of strained sincerity and genuine mirth. "No matter what happened last year, not a single day has passed without me thinking of you. I guess that's what it was that disappointed me about you: you are so like me. I am so like you. Have you ever looked into a mirror and thought, 'Who is that woman and why can't I be more like her?' That's what I felt ever since we met. Goddess, you were so *hot*! I wanted you to be someone else, someone I had in my head who would be the perfect partner."

"You whipped me because you loved me?"

"No, that anger was because I hated myself."

Íris tries thinking like Yvonne would, with her way of cutting to the core of things, so she says: "That's a bunch of bullshit."

"Listen, Iris, darling," says Megan.

"Íris."

"I know you've been going through hell the past two, three weeks. You're confused and worried. Celia told me. And I know from my Tarot readings. Your sisters feel your pain, too. They had visions, and you're in them, suffering, with monsters and demons surrounding you."

Íris is beginning to feel comfortable with her. There must have been some traumatic event that changed Megan's mind about everything. She has a new, different attitude that is puzzling.

"We want you to come back and rejoin our circle," says Megan. "I'll restore your full privileges. We'll all offer you some sort of retribution. We know we treated you badly and we're sorry. Whatever you wish for us . . . . You can whip me if that will restore the balance between us."

"The rule of three applies?" asks Íris. If she can whip Megan three times for every lash Megan laid on her, she thinks, it may be worth rejoining the circle.

"If you wish." Megan lays her hand over Íris's on the bench seat. "You know, with Beltane approaching, it would be perfect timing for you to return. The great holiday of fertility would allow you to consecrate your own fertility. Your baby will be blessed under the protection of the Goddess. He will grow up big and strong, and blessed."

Íris's eyes are wet suddenly, and she wipes a hand across her face.

"Iris, darling, what's wrong?" asks Megan.

"I don't know anymore. Everything is wrong at once." She sniffles back tears. "I learned today that my Eirík wants me to get a paternity test. He does not believe the baby is his, yet I was only with *him* during that time. If the test proves he is the father, he will forgive me and stay with me. I am so afraid of the test. What if the test somehow shows the wrong answer?"

"He will understand the truth, Iris. I promise you that."

"The test costs about six hundred dollars. He is willing to pay most of it. I agreed to pay a hundred-fifty—but I really need that for rent. He made me quit the job at the mall. Now I have little money."

"So you need money for the test?"

"He demands the test and it costs money that I do not have."

"Hmmm. I know a few men who would pay you for an evening. Even pregnant. Couple hundred, at least."

"I can't do that. Then he'd never take me back."

"Listen, Iris." Megan squares herself to Íris and lays her hands softly upon her shoulders. "You're looking at this from the wrong perspective. You don't belong to that man and you don't have to wait for him to take you back. You should be the one taking charge of the situation. You say to him: 'This is the way I am, take me or leave me. If you don't want to stay, then good luck finding someone else as good as me who's willing to fuck you.' Let him know you're the boss."

"I have to prove I can be faithful. Sandra said so."

"Your Christian friend? What can she know?"

A tear runs down Íris's face and Megan catches it on her fingertip, rubs it across her own lips as though it were a balm.

"I will have to prove my faithfulness to him every day the rest of my life, yet I know, after some time, I will regain his trust and everything in the future will become wonderful."

"You don't have to prove anything," Megan says with quiet intensity.

"Yes, I do."

"Why?"

"I need to restore balance."

"In the universe? Or just for you?" Megan leans toward her, slides an arm around her. "Listen, darling: I feel your pain, and I want to help you. We can do things to ease your stress."

"I know he's concerned about me. I heard he's agonizing over this, too. He wants me back. Yet he worries I cannot control my behavior. So I have to prove—"

"You sound like you're back in junior high! She said that he said that you have to do this or do that or he or she won't love me any more. Give me a break, Iris!" Megan kisses her cheek. "For Goddess' sake, take responsibility for your actions. Forget that jerk. He's a man. He's a loser. He doesn't deserve you."

"I have no one else."

"You don't need anyone else, Iris, darling. You've always been strong on your own. If you need to belong somewhere, come back to our circle."

She hugs Íris, then sits back. They are eye to eye but Íris's are teary and what she sees of Megan is distorted. She is not Megan—she is someone Íris does not know.

"He won't be able to trust you, but so what? You can't promise him you won't do it in the future. It's something you probably don't have any control over. That's the nature of addiction. But instead of using your insight to face your addiction, you chose to run away. Whoa! You weren't even content to just do that! No, you had to glorify it—like you were the injured party, like you were some martyr."

Íris looks up. How could Megan know so much? There were only a few postings on the website. The only possible explanation is that she joined the EXCITE community anonymously. So Megan has been spying on her private thoughts—meant only for the members of her EXCITE community!

"You always like to hide in victimhood," Megan continues. "That's the essence of the real Iris: everything always comes back to you. It's all about you. Maybe you were so damaged by what happened before, back in your youth, that you have no other recourse. It's enough to be able to get up each day and not kill yourself."

Megan holds Íris close and brushes her hair. The harsher her words are, the more Íris hears the truth. She should not have left the circle or abandoned her sisters. If she had stayed she would not be in the situation she is in now.

"Your life is a living hell, Iris," Megan whispers in her ear. "You've probably done as much damage as a woman can do to herself and still be alive. And you're about to inflict that pattern on your son. You always have excuses for everything, but now you've come to this place—this motherhood thing—where you won't just affect yourself by what you do, but also an innocent child. Your innocence is in the toilet, but it seems that you'd've at least seen this pregnancy as a reason to take stock, stop running, and try a new beginning."

"*Já, já*, I know, I know."

Megan releases her. "Or, maybe you're just a whore, after all."

"*Nei*, no longer."

"Iris, darling," she says, her voice soothing despite its edge, "your thinking is distorted to such a degree I've never encountered before. It's not immediately apparent because you do still have some tremendous gifts that aids you in survival. But rather than working for you, your gifts always work against you. Maybe they help you survive."

"Survive?"

"Yes, rather than *thrive*."

34

THREE TIMES SHE STOPPED BY HIS OFFICE, always after lunchtime—during his office hours, like she was a student waiting for a conference. She *was* his student, Eric reminded himself, though it was difficult to consider her that way if he counted her absences in Shakespeare. He was supposed to drop her from the class, according to the rules. Since the first class after Spring Break, she had missed four in a row.

Now he was going off to find her, the ice princess, somewhere in the world of art.

Dickerson Hall was filled with the scents of paints, sprays, fixers, and other products that tickled his nose. He sneezed—twice. Students were preparing for the end of semester exhibition, it seemed. That brought back memories. This exhibition, held Friday night as the flyer on the wall announced, was for undergrads.

"Excuse me," he called to one young woman in paint-spotted overalls. "Where might I find Íris Magnúsdóttir? She's a graduate student."

"Oh, Iris?" The girl seemed to know her, scratched her nose with the back of her hand. "She's probably . . . ." She thought a moment.

A boy came by and she quizzed him.

"Now? She's in Life Study," said the boy with a wink.

Eric got directions to the studio and thanked them. Down the stairs to the basement, along a bare concrete corridor to the double doors with windows. Paper had been taped on the inside of the windows. He listened at the door, heard nothing. Was there a class going on or not? He reached for the handle, intent on opening the door only a crack, enough to check.

Suddenly, he thought that he might see Íris posing nude in there. He would be called a peeping pervert, so he released the handle. Still, he did not have a lot of time. He had to get back for yet another meeting, this time a mandatory department meeting. Dr. Liz promised to update them on policy changes needed since the Jack Macintosh scandal.

He checked his watch, made himself wait another three minutes. By then, a stirring inside caused him to stand back. The doors opened and students began streaming out. He peered over their heads and saw an orange-haired woman in a gray robe stepping down from the platform.

"Okay, let's talk," he said as Íris exited the studio.

"Not here," she said with a grunt. She stepped quickly away.

He followed at a distance, up the stairs to the main floor and across the atrium, then down again to where the private studios were located.

"Wait," she commanded, then locked herself inside the small room.

After a few minutes, she emerged, dressed in blouse and jumper, the maternity uniform. She gathered her hair up into an elastic band and grabbed her book bag.

"I'm sorry for everything," she said, voice low. "For missing classes, for not turning in the papers I owe you. Yet is that enough reason to stake out Life Study? You wanted to catch a peek of me, *já*?"

Eric grimaced. "I didn't know you had that class. I just followed the directions a student gave me. And here you are." He glanced around. "So this is your private studio . . . . Mind if I take a look inside?"

"It only has painting supplies and old artwork."

She gestured at the closed door, then noticed how he watched her. He was focused on her face, studying it, searching for a clue, curious about something. She unlocked the door and switched on the light.

"There. Look."

Eric stuck his head in, saw that it really was an art studio, and he nodded. He was not sure what he expected to find there. Two or three men hiding?

"You do all of your work here?"

"Sometimes I use the attic at my house."

He withdrew, simpering.

"How many times do I have to apologize?" she asked with a sigh.

"Once. If it's sincere."

"Every apology is sincere." She looked away. "*Já*, it is not a good time. Everyone is against me, so I am apologizing a lot. It is tiring. I have no energy."

Regarding her, he reached into his shirt pocket, retrieved a slip of paper.

"Have you spoken with Sandra?"

"*Já*." She turned to lock the door. "She said I have to do three things. Make a promise. Write a letter. Take a test. Is that all?"

"I think so."

"You already made up your mind, have you?" She crossed her arms over her chest. "This is something like homework. It is not necessary. It is to punish me. You give me assignments that take time away from the exhibition, or writing a paper for your class."

"No, it's for you to understand why you do what you do, and how you can stop. You're supposed to reflect on your sins, as Sandra calls it. It's not that I've converted, but her way of thinking does have merit."

"She is concerned."

"I'm concerned, too." He handed the paper to her. "Here's the time of the appointment. It's the same clinic. They already know to expect you. I mean, what you're there for. I gave them a blood sample this morning, so now it's your turn."

She looked at the paper. "Are you going to drive me there?"

"I have a meeting in twenty minutes." He looked at his watch. "Besides, maybe I shouldn't be there, not this time."

Her face shifted. "In case I turn out to be a whore?"

337

A tear popped out of her eye, ran down her cheek. She reached out for his shoulders with both hands, something to cry on. Without thinking, his response was to step back—and he immediately wished he hadn't.

"Can I hold you?" she asked.

"What good would that do?"

"It would give me hope."

Her weeping became a noisy sobbing for a minute and two students walked by, staring, and hurried away. He wondered if it was an act.

"Everything's been arranged," said Eric. "Sandra will pick you up and wait with you. She volunteered. They'll know the results in four to six weeks."

"And what do I do until then?"

"You could write a letter."

They wanted it in certified bank draft, Sandra reported the next day. She drove Íris to the credit union branch on campus where she had her account.

Eric nodded his approval.

"Then we went to the clinic," said Sandra, sitting across the table in the Student Center cafeteria where they agreed to meet. "She said she'd been there before so I let her out and waited in the car. It only took about forty-five minutes."

"You didn't go in with her?" he asked.

"Let her have some privacy, Eric. It's embarrassing enough without having the chaperone accompany you. Besides, the exam is private."

Eric nodded. "Everything went all right? No problems?"

"Íris said the baby is fine, growing well. Her blood pressure was up, but considering the stress she's been under, it's no surprise. Also, her blood type is A negative. Mine, too. Except, I'm positive."

"Of course, you are. But that's good to know, in case there's any violence." Eric was distracted, lost in thought.

"Oh, don't worry," Sandra laughed. "You know, I read in a magazine that about half of new fathers admit they had thoughts about not being the baby's father. The article said if you ask these men whether they suspected their wife had an affair, they're insulted by the suggestion. Well, it makes sense. On a logical level, it's a 'disconnect,' but on an emotional level there is something else going on. I think men dwell too much on their inadequacies."

"You're right."

"It's nothing to worry about," said Sandra, tapping his arm across the table. "Really it's about God, if you think about it. The father says, 'This is too big of an event, a miracle, so how could I be responsible for it?' They feel small. They know something greater than themselves must have created it."

"I suppose. I do know that, sexually, I have a reasonable chance at being the father, even if there were others. What I'm saying is, I did the job, and I now have proof to my satisfaction. What I can't prove is exactly what day and hour her ovulation began. No one really knows but her—if she even knows. And maybe her doctor. He won't tell me because—guess what?—we're not married. No spousal privilege."

"I'm sorry, Eric. It's kind of . . . a touchy subject with me."

He caught sight of Dominique by the cashier, carrying a tray of food. She wore her hair up, had her overcoat on, and was not as tanned. The winter could do that to tropical people, he thought, refusing to duck down.

"That woman over there, for example—she used to be my girlfriend. Way back in September, I thought we were progressing nicely, getting romantic, the whole nine yards. We even tried to make love once—unsuccessfully. She sent me out to get condoms and when I returned she'd lost the mood."

"Eric, that's a private matter, so I shouldn't be hearing about it."

"I'm not trying to offend you, but people do have sex and people talk about what they do. The point I'm making is that I was dating her, with no sex occurring and no official relationship, when I met Íris. So, in a weird way, I cheated on that woman with Íris. Of course, it was only—"

"Stop!" Sandra exclaimed, loud enough to call attention to them, including Dominique. "I said I don't want to hear about any of that."

"I'm trying to make a point—"

"I got the point! You and everyone you associate with is unfaithful. They're all cheaters, and they all have the morals of baboons. Point taken."

She got up and stalked away with her tray of dishes. The diners' eyes remained on Eric, and Dominique sauntered past his table, pausing to sneer at him. No doubt she thought he was working on yet another student. His reputation was so downhill.

On the way back to his office, Eric swung by Albright's office to check if the old writer had made his selection of winning entries for *Journatalia*. The door was open but no one was inside. Eric went to the English department office and asked Belle Philips where "Lance" was; the ladies were allowed to call him by his first name.

Eric checked his mailbox: a couple of advertisements, a late paper, two late entries for the journal, a story and a poem. Nothing from Íris.

"That's it for me," said Eric, turning to exit. "Let the weekend begin."

In reality the weekend lay somewhere between 7 p.m. Saturday and noon on Sunday. Before and after that, he was thinking about classes, committees, students, or wayward colleagues. He relaxed through the evening, fell asleep watching TV and awoke before dawn. He stared out the balcony door at white petals drifting on the breeze, imagining them as snowflakes. He shook off the chilly memory.

After a small brunch of Friday's leftovers, he realized that a stack of composition papers was calling him. He had to return for them, or he would never have a moment's peace—even if he did not actually read any of them during his days off.

Eric drove back to the campus, parked in Dr. Liz's reserved space, and hurried into his office, gathered the papers, and was ready to leave. He read the first sentence of the top paper, then read the paragraph. He sat down, read the first page, then sat back and finished reading it, wrote some notes on the last page and assigned it the grade of A. He reached for the next paper, then stopped.

You must be going mad, Mister Schaeffer.

He had a life outside of school. He just didn't believe it any longer. Kicking himself out of his office on a Saturday was a start.

Outside, the afternoon sun was turning warm, melting away the overcast, as Eric drove over to the Towne Square Mall. Íris had been accepted as a maternity wear model, said Sandra. So he went and stood at the rear of the crowd, not wanting to be seen, not wanting to distract her. With his hands stuffed into his front pockets, Eric watched the show. Pride welled up inside him.

Look at her: so beautiful, even in maternity clothes. And she could be mine, if I would only give her a break.

A lapse of judgment. That's all it was. Who has not made a mistake? He could think of several he had made in the past year, most of them related to Íris. And Dominique. And Marina, Matt, his parents, his colleagues in the English department. By the middle of April the list of bad deeds done and the favors owed was extensive. He owed himself a lot, too.

Everyone's screwing with me. When is it my turn?

All he wanted was a good night's sleep. That, first of all. Then a hearty dinner in a fine restaurant, preferably good company with a witty conversationalist, a pleasant face to gaze upon, a winsome disposition to soothe his soul, and, if time and circumstances allowed, some passionate and sustained lovemaking with a reasonably talented and enthusiastic partner. Was that too much to ask? Even once in a lifetime?

But I had that. One weekend in December.

His attention shifted back to the stage as his once-upon-a-time lover walked to the end, paused, turned, smiled at the crowd, turned again, made the jumper swirl around her knees, and walked up the runway for the last time. He thought back to the early days of his obsession, when the orange-haired ice princess, the Pagan artist and witch, had taken a surprising interest in him, and made him break the rules, taught him to be outrageous.

35

SUFFERING IS THE BEGINNING OF CONSCIOUSNESS, wrote someone named *F. Dostoevsky*. Professor Hirsch had told her that saying one evening after she modeled for him, snapping black-and-whites of her nude figure, just the two of them in the studio. He had been worried about retirement, about losing his creative energy, losing his muse. "All part of the art," he told her. "To suffer is to be pulled out of the ordinary and forced to act." That is what makes us human, thinks Íris, hearing his voice in her head. Or is it Eirík's voice now? We must act, either for good or ill, or simply to maintain our stubborn neutrality. Balance must be maintained at all cost.

Earlier, while she waited for Jean to take her to the mall, Íris sat before her laptop, trying to start the letter. Nothing came to her.

Já, I was born, I was a child, I reached adolescence, my first blood came 25 *Febrúar* in my eleventh year. I knew who I was on that day and how my life would flow. As a girl, I was intended by God to be a dutiful wife and nurturing mother. So my mama told me. Now I am trying to remember how everything went *brjálaður*—crazy, foolish, wild, there are many possible translations, none quite right.

At noon, Jean took her to the mall, saying she would return in two hours.

"I got a life," said Jean. "Don't need to see preggos walking a runway."

A woman named Georgia was in charge of the show and directed Íris to the rack where the outfits she chose were hung. Íris would model seven outfits. Three girls from Stork Fashions helped the models dress behind a curtain. Íris measured the other bellies and saw that hers was the smallest.

Íris went first, luck of the draw, and stepped out from behind the curtain as Georgia introduced her: "This is Iris, our lovely redhead, at five beautiful months," and began telling everyone about the jumper she wore. She walked to the end of the runway, raised about a meter off the floor, turned and paused, walked up the runway. She was used to holding a pose, not walking in a pose, so she felt stiff and awkward. Quickly, she changed behind the curtain.

On her second walk, as she paused at the end, she caught a glimpse of a woman who looked somewhat like Megan. Íris smiled at the crowd: the housewives with children, young couples, middle-aged career women, cliques of adolescent girls, single men interested in any woman who was modeling, and a few older men ready to relive their youth. Megan was up front in black leather vest and red jeans. Íris smiled to herself, eager to see her ex-priestess with a big belly to carry around someday.

Íris tried to look at the crowd on her third walk, a dozen more people there. She spotted a man who looked like Eirík but, after she turned, was not. Megan was still there and applauded.

Já, he persuaded me to sign up for this stunt. Now I am here without him.

She searched for him in the crowd on her final two trips down the runway yet no face was his. He must have been in the crowd, she wanted to believe. *He would not miss it. He wants me.* Yet she was blinded by camera flashes. She was deafened by the applause and the amplified voice of the hostess.

Smiling at the crowd, she wanted to cry. She tugged at the dress, wanting to tear it off. Her smile crumpled and when she returned to the curtain she was in tears. It must have been more than hormones. It was a taste of how life would be without him. She had already forgotten how she had survived alone for so many years. What was that Eirík anyway? A stupid, lucky man, *já*, that's all.

After Georgia thanked the crowd, the seven models bowed as best they could, their bellies lined up smallest to largest.

When Íris had changed back into her own clothes, Georgia presented her with the jumper she chose, the green one with blue butterflies. Íris asked about the second outfit and Georgia explained that the models could keep only one. She wanted to protest but Georgia complimented her performance and said she should model for them again, after the baby is born. Georgia asked when Íris was due. August, she said, and Georgia gave her a business card for another store, Li'l Darlings, a baby goods store she also owned.

"Tell them you modeled today," said Georgia. "You'll get fifty percent off everything."

She insisted on exchanging hugs and air kisses—

Now the big show is done. This is the time Íris has set aside for writing, not just any writing but the story of her life, or as much of it as she can tell.

Já, the letter is all-important. It is an application for redemption.

The more she writes, the further she sinks. The night grows darker, until it is deathly silent. Her heart does not beat. Soon there is nothing surrounding her but her wasted life. She cannot stop typing. With every ENTER, she insists she is only the author, not the poor heroine. The heroines of the Sagas and the *Eddas* were women of strength, who took a harsh life and bent it to their will. They made the land obey them, organized the men around them, and remained wise through it all. The books Eirík left with her have given her strength. She is not like them, she feels, not like Guðrún in the Laxdæla saga, or her sisters under the *Óðinn* sky. There is much she has seen and felt, and it all has come to this: composing a saga of her own, full of the senseless acts of a wild child, the brutal cruelty of a teenage girl who realized her own powers too soon.

There she was: a beautiful young girl who played innocently in the meadows. She became a girl who tried to take her own life, late in the afternoon on the third of November in her seventeenth year—after her mother had the twins, Dagrún and Birgir, with her new husband, Sæmundr Arnórsson, in Toronto and Íris became extra. She had felt dizzy staring down from the cliff at the icy waters of Lake Ontario and had stumbled backwards, tripped and hit her head on a rock. It was dark when she awoke, and on the walk back through the park, three men came out of the woods. At the time, with Death refusing her, she had not cared what would happen and made it easy for them. A few months later her mother would kick her out and she would be on her own. Between these moments of blossoming and withering, she took on the roles of devil and elf, troll and demon lover.

If she writes about Magnús, she fears she might miscarry. If she chooses to describe every encounter with a boy or girl in high school or the fishermen, or mere strangers, she will go mad. And the months in Klepp are impossible to write. When her mother immigrated with her to Canada, it was supposed to be a fresh start, yet the old evils haunted them. She knew what she was—her mother made that clear, calling her 'little whore' every day in Toronto, both before and after she closed the door, sending her out into the streets to . . . to be a whore.

She does not give excuses. She writes the facts and lets Eirík interpret them. What she left behind in *Ísland* was a broken body and a scarred soul, a thousand thoughts that turned to dust with a snap of her fingers. There was beauty in her childhood, she recalls, when father was father and mother was mother and they were a good family. She knew no harm and had no punishment. There were songs and dances, feasts and picnics, on wildflower hillsides above Eyjafjörður, the long blue neck of the sea that ran inland to the town of Akureyri. She remembers that, and writes it.

The birds sing and Íris awakens. She halted only a moment, yet fell asleep. She stretches on the floor beside her laptop. The sky is lavender as she gets up and looks outside, reminding herself that she is here in

Wichita, Kansas—not back in Akureyri.

She makes a cup of tea, then studies her letter. It is eighteen pages. She has arrived at the University of Toronto and met Professor Hirsch. She went one afternoon to fill in for Beth, her Wiccan sister, also a dancer at Club Venus. Such an amateur! She had stood naked in the center of the room, waiting for the class to begin.

"And you are . . . ?" asked the flamboyant old man.

She kept her face on guard. "I am Íris."

He repeated her name as though it were a strange, new color: "*Eeee*ris."

"*Já*," she said, and added a curt nod.

He walked around her, examining her nude figure, calling her perfect. Then he had asked about Beth and Íris gave a satisfactory answer.

"All right," he said with a laugh. "Let's give you a try."

Hirsch taught her about art and showed her a different kind of life. In her first semester, she worked at the club at night and went to classes by day. The two worlds pulled her apart, so she quit the club on her birthday, December 30. She had not planned to quit that night, she types. After two stage acts and a round of sitting among customers, dancing on their laps, she decided to leave—just got up off that lap and went to the dressing room, put on clothes, and left.

She wipes away some tears, realizing not so much has changed. Art is only a way to delay a future that does not exist, not the start of some wonderful new life. Even standing naked in the center of a room, surrounded by artists, or up on a stage in a strip club, or on her knees in the Back Room—she does not exist. Nobody sees her. A woman—a toy, *já*—yet never *her*, never this girl who was torn from the soil of *Ísland* and left for dead in an alley behind the CN Tower—

She falls back on the floor. The ceiling seems to descend and she feels a kick. It does not hurt yet it makes her rise up on her elbows so she can watch her belly. *My baby is calling to me. He tells me to write a letter, to explain what is wrong with me, so everyone will know.* She needs to make promises to everyone. A test follows: some blood, a microscope, some chemicals swished around a petri dish, and . . . *vá*, judgment!

The altar at the end of the room has gathered dust. She strips and kneels before it, hoping to rekindle some magic. She lights the tapers and bows her head, whispers an old incantation.

"O Goddess mine," she calls, focusing on the silver chalice on the table, "hear me in my time of sorrow, in my time of need. Hear this, my call for help, and come to me. I am unworthy yet she who is lost is most in need. Come into me and guide me. O Goddess mine, hear me now and come into me."

She waits and listens to the birds as dawn blossoms outside the window.

There is no change.

"Goddess, I need some fucking advice!"

Silence.

She repeats her charge yet she remains alone.

All Sunday she writes, pausing only to politely decline Sandra's offer to go to church, and when Monday morning arrives too soon, she awakens with strength renewed. The letter is finished. It is a Tarot reading of Íris, the daughter of Heiðr. It is a casting of Runes for Íris, the daughter of Magnús. It is truth in all its tarnished glory. It is her—twice as real as Cory's statue of her.

Linden Hall is busy when she arrives at mid-morning. Classes are letting out.

Like most art students, she usually dresses casually. Today, however, she wears her finest dress: the black one with gold lines and a white lace collar, the finest she can squeeze into. Her belly protrudes, making the dress tight. She slides her legs into dark hosiery and her feet into three-inch black pumps. The heels put her at eye level with him. She wants to look into his eyes. Because she expects her meeting with him will result in a kiss of reunion, she brushes her teeth thoroughly, rinses with mouthwash, flosses her teeth, and stares a while into the mirror.

The door to his office is open. She steps quietly to it, daring to enter.

He is at the desk, grading papers.

As soon as he sees her, his face seems to reflect a foul mood.

"What do you want?" he asks, neither happy to see her nor concerned about her feelings. She wants to run away.

"Is this a bad time?" What she means is inconvenient. She cannot, will not run away.

"Any time is bad." He sits back, takes a deep breath. "This is not a good time to talk. I have so many papers to go through this morning. I'd like to give them back this evening. I've got twenty more." He looks up. "Are you going to give me any?"

She steps forward, arm extended. Her hand holds a thick envelope, its flap glued shut.

"Here is the letter you wanted me to write," says Íris. "Everything is there. Everything bad I have done in my life."

He accepts it, eyeing its thickness. "Thanks."

"Now it is yours."

"I really did not expect so much," he says, and she detects an improvement in his mood. "A couple pages would do."

"My life is . . . complicated, *já*. You wanted me to write all of it."

She watches him lay it on the desk. Casually, to the side.

"Are you going to read it?" she asks.

"I will, but I have so much to do right now."

"I worked on it all weekend. Except for the fashion show." She frowns. "I did not see you there."

"I was there," he says, and she knows it is a lie to soothe her ego. "You were very lovely. Quite professional."

"*Já*, I was."

She cannot wait. Her composure is about to crack as he returns to his student papers.

"Please read the letter." Her throat tightens. "You refuse to talk to me, even when I beg for your time. I am not just a student of yours. What is in my belly is yours, too. That is what you want, *já*? You have to hear me, Eirík."

He turns in his chair and gives her his full attention.

"I thought I could explain everything to your satisfaction," she says.

"You said I should think about why I did it and how I came to be the way I am. You said to write a letter, so I did. There it is. Read it."

"Íris, I promise I'll read it as soon as possible. Tomorrow, okay?"

"You are not serious about our relationship, are you? You have got your freedom back these four weeks and you are ready to abandon me. And the baby. You are surprised I wrote it. That is what you wanted, *já*? Read it and you will know everything."

His face melts into a smirk and he tries not to shake his head.

"When you're finished, I will be waiting," says Íris, pointing out to the benches by the elevators. Her eyes are wet.

"You don't have to wait," he says.

She chokes back tears that always fall too easily, whether in joy or sorrow.

"Eirík, I cannot do anything else. I will wait for you to read it. Then we will talk."

"Talk . . . ?"

There has never been anyone who stood before her more a stranger than he does at this moment. She sniffles back her emotions.

"*Já* . . . talk."

She watches him examine the letter in its envelope, weighing it in his hand as though calculating how long it will take to read. As he considers it, she begins to suspect he still may set it on his desk and not read it right away. She must know today.

"I will wait out there . . . no matter how long it takes you to finish reading it."

He looks up and their eyes meet. A tear runs down her cheek.

Without thinking, the words fall out of her mouth: "After you read the letter you have to decide. You will come out and embrace me, tell me you forgive me, or if you cannot forgive me, and that is your decision, just close the door. Close the door and I will go away. And I will never bother you again."

Before he can respond, she turns and exits.

36

ERIC SHIFTED THE ENVELOPE IN HIS HANDS, deciding what to do. There were three stacks of student papers on his desk and he needed to go through one of them before the afternoon meeting of the *Journatalia* staff. Albright had made his selections and would reveal them at the meeting. This was certainly not the day to have to deal with Íris and her apologies.

He slid his thumbnail carefully under the flap, opening the envelope. *What is the problem? You've already decided to take her back, haven't you? So why not start acting like you are back together?* It was his way of punishing her for the transgression, he realized suddenly. Yes, he had suffered seeing her with the Spring Break boy, and he wanted her to suffer, too. At least for a while.

He glanced at the clock: now it was just an hour until the meeting. How many papers could he grade by then? The letter from Íris would have to wait. By this point in the semester, with a little more than two weeks until final exams, everything was coming to a climax. She had waited this long; she could wait a couple days more.

Setting the envelope and the letter on the bookcase next to his desk, he resumed grading papers.

After a half-hour which seemed much longer, Eric took a break. He slipped out to the restroom and saw that Íris was sitting on the bench near the elevators. She smiled, seeing him, stood awkwardly, and took a step toward him.

"You finished it?" she asked, cheerfully.

"What? The letter?" He veered for the restroom. "I told you, I have a lot to do. I'll get to it later, when I can give it a good, thorough reading. When I won't be distracted."

"You promised."

"And I will keep my promise, but the world is shouting at me to hurry up with seven different things at once."

"Is one of them our future?"

Eric stopped. He turned and regarded her—saw her eyes red from crying, almost matching her auburn eyebrows, bronze eyelashes, and the Mango Morning hair that framed her pale face. *Who is this woman?* Not the same woman he had met months ago at an art exhibit. Not the one he had picked up in the rain, nor rolled playfully with in the snow. Not his fantasy woman. He noticed her formal dress, in fact, her entire elegant, stately presence.

"All right," he said, exasperated. "As soon as I flush, I'll come back and read the letter, just to make you happy."

"Thank you," she said, sitting.

He did his business and returned, glancing at her as he went to his office. What was he supposed to do? Read what she had written about her past, her present, and the problems she had developed? Anything else? It was all a formality.

The envelope had his name handwritten on it. The dot over each 'i' in *Eirik* was a snowflake.

As he pulled out the bundle of tri-folded pages, a pendant fell onto his desk. He picked it up, examined it. The silver pentacle had Runes around its rim. The pendant was on a leather string that had obviously been worn before. By Íris. For many years, it had swung between her breasts, against them. *Is this some kind of peace offering?* He flipped it in his palm, decided it was nice, a wonderful token of her sincerity. He set it aside and unfolded the pages. With a sigh, he turned to the last one: number twenty-nine. They were all single-spaced, printed on a computer, with narrow margins—the kind of writing he did when he was hot with the muse and could not stop for any misspellings or the end of the page.

He stared at the first page without reading, just thinking. *I want you back in my life and I need you to be with me, not only for the sake of our son but for my sake, as well.* That's what he would say. For now, he must read the letter, just to verify that she had indeed spent the required time thinking about the problem and its solution. He grinned, glancing with awkward amusement at the stack of problem/solution essays he had been grading. Here was the motherload of problem/solution essays!

```
dear eirík-

here is the letter you asked me to write. i
think it is good to do because it made me
really think through my life and find the
origin of my troubles. it is painful to
return to the details yet in this journey
is my hope that everything will be answered
by the final page.
```

So far, so good, thought Eric. He continued, reading of facts such as her date of birth and the names of her kin. She had a certain style that was spare yet compelling, like the Icelandic sagas, and he was drawn into the letter. He drifted through her idyllic childhood and the boat trip with her father from Akureyri to Reykjavik, her words almost poetic. He could not stop reading even when it turned bad in her fourteenth year. He forced himself to read through the day of her rape and the pregnancy that became known to her only when it ended in a frightening miscarriage, and how her father became apologetic and affectionate after. She learned what power she had. For the next two years, she was his temptress, and Eric could not contemplate what it must have been like for her. Or for her father.

She wrote about her father's fishing partner, her uncles and cousins, and their friends who assaulted her on shore and aboard their boats. She could not tell anyone what happened because of her father's situation; she didn't want Magnús to be arrested. Weeks later, she was again taunted by those fishermen and she give in to them rather than let them become violent. When her father discovered it, he tried to intervene but could not halt the abuse. They threatened to expose the truth—which continued at home, either as her perverse duty or as her torturing of her father. Word got around her school and she became popular with several boys who took turns walking her home—stopping in an alley or in the park or behind a car. At that time, her mother was often away, researching the mating habits of the North Atlantic cod instead of being at home investigating what was happening to her daughter.

He could understand how a young girl could get into trouble that way, but he was not prepared to read how she paid off her father's debts, how she was teased by classmates, how her father continued forcing himself on her—until the day she arranged for her mother to catch them. Magnús ran out, went straight for his boat and sailed off, never to be seen again. The boat was found locked in ice, no body aboard. He was presumed drowned. Heiðr fell into shock and the wild child was taken to a psychiatric hospital. On page sixteen, she arrived in Toronto with her mother but was soon kicked out of the household.

Eric brushed his hair back, took a deep breath, and continued reading about her job at Club Venus. She waitressed, danced, stripped, but was clumsy at all of them. He read how she was taken to the back room and found work she could do, work she enjoyed. He hated reading it, but he could not stop. His eyes ran along the lines, his mind stabbed by the details. She wrote of parties and the 'dates' arranged for her, and about Big Joe, and Beth, Renée, and Fritz, and the roommates and lovers she had. Then Beth introduced her to the art professor, Hirsch, who was fascinated by her "modern primitive" drawings and believed she had talent.

That was the beginning of the present era. Art came first and last. Hirsch taught her everything he knew. He arranged for her to get the scholarship at Fairmont College by way of his former student, Ray

Ferguson. After Hirsch died, she took lesbian lovers before and after moving to Kansas. Then she met a professor who seemed at first glance to be far too conservative for what he did with her. She analyzed the situation perfectly: he desired someone to worship and she desired someone to worship her. He wanted to be wild but could not, did not know how; she did not know how to hold back and eventually reached her limit of self-control. They were opposites. They did not belong together yet here they were, struggling to be a couple, to be a family.

When the baby made its awkward appearance on page twenty-four, their fate was sealed. She did believe in fate, she wrote. For better or worse, they must get to know each other and live in a world of crazy distractions. She never wanted to go south for Spring Break. Her life lay in the north, and there were too many times she had told him that fact. Through all of that, he stayed focused on the baby, the family, the appearance of propriety before the judgment of his relations. He could not be outrageous. So she would be—

Eric wiped his eyes. Only then did he notice the time. The staff meeting had been on for an hour and would likely be done by the time he could clean himself up and put on a happy face. He sat back, conceded missing the meeting, and pondered his role: the man who would be father to their baby and perhaps someday the husband she deserved but never imagined finding. It was his responsibility to fight for her, to help her kill the demons and tear off the shackles that had imprisoned her. He must polish his armor, saddle that white horse, and ride to her rescue!

He needed to jot down some lines of poetry, so he stretched for the legal pad he used to collect random inspiration. As he reached for it, the phone rang. His chair was already rolling across the floor toward the side desk when he tried to halt its movement and simultaneously reach back to the phone. The chair teetered precariously at the second ring. He lost his balance and went tumbling onto the floor. The third ring. The accident startled him; it happened so fast. A fourth ring. He shook his head slowly and picked himself up, brushed off his pants. Fifth ring. His foot had hit the door just enough to swing it shut with a quiet *hummph*.

He picked up the phone as he righted his chair. "Hello?"

Whoever it had been had lost patience and hung up.

He grabbed the notepad and sat again at his desk. He scribbled several lines about forgiveness—or about forgetfulness. They were so close, he mused in verse. They were neighbors on the boulevard of synapses, he considered with a grin. Twenty-eight lines and several cross-outs later, his eyes drifted onto the door.

37

As she waits on the bench, Íris thinks of Georgia at Stork Fashions, wishing she had gotten the second outfit. She misunderstood. Instead, Georgia gave her a discount at her sister store, Li'l Darlings. She will be a customer soon. What will her baby want? What will this little boy need?

Li'l Darlings, she repeats in her head. *Darling*, she ponders. Megan used the word a lot when they talked a few days before. Yvonne had used *darling*. The conversation replays in her head. After her initiation into Megan's Wicca circle, Yvonne gave her a business card. A few weeks later, before Íris had ever used the number on the card to call Yvonne, she got an e-mail from Yvonne, asking how she was, wanting to know what she thought of the coven. Typical topics, *já*, but Íris now realizes that YVONNE666 could have been anyone. Then YVONNE666 joined her Excite.com community and posted a few messages. From time to time Íris had e-mailed her about what was happening in her life. Then Megan makes a strange return, a woman full of unrequested guidance and *darling* thrown out so casually that Íris did not notice.

They must be the same, Íris decides: Megan in flesh-and-blood and the online Yvonne. Íris was never communicating with the original Yvonne. All along it was Megan, the psychology student—who has taken six years to get to graduation! Megan, self-appointed Wiccan priestess—that bitch!

Íris curses so hard that tears come to her eyes. She has been betrayed, and she hates the feeling. That woman has played with her, teased her, and pulled her in so many different directions that she is about to go insane. And when she needed someone the most! She confided in that Yvonne yet she was actually revealing her secrets to Megan. She thinks of how Megan put a spell on the pendant she has been wearing all of her life.

Now it belongs to Eirík. If he opens the letter, he will find it inside. He promised to stop his work and read the letter, and she is waiting. Eirík will find the truth in her heart: that she fell in love with him, and not knowing what love should feel like, let it escape. He will come out of his office and rush to her, embrace her, and kiss her, not caring who sees them, and they will twirl around like the happy couples do in the cinema, and the lights will fade and the credits will roll and the image of two people deeply in love will be frozen on the screen like an ice sculpture, through the final notes of the soundtrack—

A small group of students sweep past Íris, knocking her back to reality. She watches them step onto the elevator and as the doors close, she glances down the hallway. The doors are closed, as they have been since she arrived. All of them. She counts the doors, finds the one that is Eirík's.

She stands and counts the doors again. She goes down the hallway a few steps.

Rubbing her eyes, she looks again.

The door is closed.

She collapses in the hallway. Her knees hit the tiles and a woman rushes to help her. She picks her up and asks what is wrong, yet Íris cannot say anything. An older woman arrives and the two of them help Íris to the bench where she was sitting. They offer tissues to wipe her face, want to know if they should call anyone, or if she needs medical assistance. They see she is pregnant. She cannot stop crying and when the elevator returns, she breaks through them and hurries onto it, letting the doors close, blocking her view of the door to his office.

He does not want me. He doesn't want his baby. And Megan has tricked me, maybe cursed him. Sandra pities me. Jean despises me. Cory thinks I am a fool. Ray takes me for a slut. My father is dead because of what I did, and my mother is trying to forget me. I am alone.

She hurries through the Plaza of Heroines, feeling like a traitor for letting this man ruin her life.

In the counseling center, where she is well-known, the receptionist tries to stop her. Íris brushes past the desk and heads down the hallway. She knocks hard on the usual door, waits, becomes impatient.

"It's Íris! I need to talk!"

Another woman comes out, willing to help her.

She needs *her* counselor, who already knows her secrets.

"I can't wait until next week!" She pounds on the door and they tell her that her counselor is off today. "*Vá!* I need to talk! This minute! It cannot wait!"

They try to console her yet she is hysterical as she struggles to break through their ring of concern. She rushes out, ripping her dress on the corner of the reception desk.

She cannot see where she is going through her tear-filled eyes, yet she finds her way to Dickerson and pulls Sandra out of her studio.

"Please take me home," she begs Sandra.

"Yes, of course," Sandra quickly agrees. "What in the world is wrong, Iris?"

"It's finished," she sobs. "Everything is finished!"

Sandra guides her out to the car and the drive is silent except for sobbing. Íris hates cars; she has been crying in them a lot. Sandra doesn't ask questions.

At the house, Sandra helps her walk to the veranda, arm around her waist, a hand holding her arm. Sandra sees her up to her room, eases her down on the bed.

Sandra can guess what is wrong, that her plan to bring Eric and Íris together has failed miserably. She is as shocked and disappointed as Íris—perhaps more. Sandra is not familiar with failure. Everything works out for her. God performs miracles on her behalf and for her friends. This time she has failed. God doesn't like this friend of hers.

"He can't really reject you, not just like that," Sandra says, referring, Íris thinks, to Eirík and not to God.

"He was very clear. Very clear!"

Sandra tries to calm her, rubbing her shoulders, letting Íris weep against her.

"My sister had a baby last month," Sandra offers, trying to distract her. "A girl. Did I tell you? She's such a cutie—"

"Everybody is having babies, *já*. It's a disease!"

"Since I've been here at school, I've missed all the excitement." Her arm tightens around Íris's shoulders. "I wanted so much to be with Brenda. But I can't see the baby until after graduation." Sandra releases her, regards her face to face, smiling. "Would you mind? Could I listen to your baby?"

Íris gets control of her sobbing and nods. Sandra scoots away and lowers her ear to the belly. They do not match, so they adjust their positions, Sandra sliding down the bed. Íris lies back as Sandra presses her ear to the abdomen once more.

"Usually it's after I eat a meal," she tells Sandra, rolling up the dress to expose her belly, "so it is not a good time to hear him."

Sandra shifts her ear, settles it against Íris's skin. "I know. He's in there . . . sleeping. Sweet little baby. Someday I hope to be a mother. But for now, I just want to imagine."

"You like babies, *já*?" Íris asks her, moving her hand down to Sandra's head, brushing her soft, brown hair. "I know you will be a wonderful mother."

Sandra listens and as she does, her breath tickles Íris's skin. Slowly Íris strokes Sandra's hair, fingers strumming like a guitar. She seems to relax and Íris thinks it is a sign. Her hand caresses Sandra's cheek—

"No, no, no," Sandra mutters, resisting. She pushes Íris's hand away and sits up.

Íris rises, too, anxious and aroused. They are face to face. She looks into Sandra's eyes. Heartbeats fill the gap between them. Suddenly, Íris presses her lips against Sandra's.

"No, Iris," says Sandra sternly, pushing away. "I don't want that."

"I love you." Íris begins to cry. "I love you!"

Sandra hesitates, not wanting to touch her now, so Íris reaches for her. Sandra slaps her hands away and jumps up.

"You don't love me, not like that, Iris. Not like a man and woman love each other in holy matrimony." She goes to the door.

"I need you, Sandra!"

"You need something. I wanted to help you, but I think I've done all I can. Now you're misdirecting all your emotions. They're scattering in all directions, Iris."

"I need you!"

"You need Jesus."

"You're all I have!"

"No, you have God."

"The Goddess has abandoned me."

"There is no Goddess, Iris."

Sandra shakes her head and steps into the hallway, pausing as if deciding whether to abandon her. Then she does.

The house is silent after the front door slams shut. Everyone is still on campus or gone to a job. Íris has no classes, no job, no friends, no peace. There is nothing for her.

Rather than sit in her room, thinking of a place she has forgotten, she tears off the elegant dress, rips it and smashes it into the floor with all of her fury. She kicks it, stamps on it, picks it up and hurls it at the altar at the end of the room.

On the altar table, the candles are dusty, the chalice tarnished. The silver pentacle hanging on the wall is askew. She picks up the athame, the dagger used in her rituals. She turns it over and over, catching the light, knowing that, though it is not sharp, with enough rage she could push it through flesh. She could kill with it. The point scores her arm as she wonders where her Goddess is.

A shadow sweeps over her.

She kisses the blade and places its point against her belly as tears flood her face.

Suddenly the life inside her kicks, or she thinks he does, and she touches her abdomen, gently, as though caressing him, remembering him. A bead of blood stains her fingers. She stares at her belly and she knows she is not her mother. Tears drop onto her belly and mix with the spot of blood. It is a work of art: *Glacier II* or *Arcadia III* or *Íris IV*—

She crashes to her knees and the blade falls out of her hands and rolls on the floor.

"*Fyrirgefðu, elskan,*" she whimpers, begging forgiveness from her baby. "*Fyrirgefðu, elskan. Mér þykir þetta leitt . . . .*"

She breathes deeply, feeling the blood drain out of her heart.

By the Four Winds, where is my Goddess? *Já,* she's dancing with Megan and Celia and Amber, Darcy, Vivienne and the others. And they are laughing at me! Look at that stupid Íris, so caught up by her own psyche, so clouded, so lost, so much in trouble—all through her own silly mistakes. She is ready to strangle herself. What a fool she's become!

Her eyes fall upon the dress, crumpled and dirty on the floor in front of her altar. This dress, the black one with gold trim and lace collar, is cursed. These black heels, picked out by Jean, are useless. The hosiery is also cursed. And the curse has rubbed off onto her. She must burn them to remove the curse. Gathering the dress, shoes, and hosiery in her arms, she steps from the room and makes her way downstairs.

"Iris? What're you doing?" asks Tracie, when she passes by her open door on the way out to the backyard. Tracie is curious because Íris is carrying her clothes, not wearing them. She follows.

In the backyard, Íris tosses them down on the stone grill at the edge of the patio. She takes out matches from the box that was on her altar and starts a flame on the hosiery.

"So what if they're outta fashion," calls Tracie from the doorway, "You don't hafta burn 'em. Give 'em ta Goodwill."

Íris ignores her and places the dress on the burning hosiery, then the shoes, and coaxes the flames higher, until the whole pile is ablaze. Watching the fire grow, she waves it up to the sky. The smoke settles around her, chokes her, and she sweeps it away. She steps back and it follows her. She runs to get the hose and turns on the water to put out the fire. The clothing is ruined—that was the idea. She has killed the curse in them.

She drops to her knees beside the smoldering grill and cries out: "O Frigga, wife of Óðinn and goddess of mothers, goddess who guides us safely through childbirth. I call out to you, after so much time apart, because I have returned to you, to you and your kin. I am yours, Frigga!"

She waits a moment to let the words circle the universe. She gazes up at the sky, sees the clouds gathering, blotting out the sun, and feels a sudden chill. There is something different in the yard now. The horizon is orange like her hair—and all the houses and trees are black, drawing a shadow across the yard as she regards the golden countenance of Frigga. With her skyclad back toward the house, Íris listens for a voice.

"O Frigga, my father called you long ago to watch over me."

If Frigga is with her, she thinks, she need not speak loudly. Perhaps she need not speak at all. Frigga hears her heart.

"I closed my eyes to you. I became blind and wandered the world giving hurt and pain and taking the same in return. There is so much I want to tell you, but there is not much time. I need to know now—today, or tomorrow at the latest—what I should do. I need to know. So I seek your guidance."

A breeze sails through the yard, shaking the branches, dropping a few petals upon her from the blossoming trees.

"*Já*, I must forgive in order to be forgiven," she says, suddenly feeling the spirit within her. It is so elementary. She shouts: "Heiðr, Magnús, I call you!"

We say we must 'forgive and forget,' but it is impossible, she repeats in her head. It must be forgive *or* forget. That is the way of virtue, the wisdom of Óðinn and the good heart of Frigga.

"Heiðr, I forgive you! Even as you bid me no peace, I thank you for my life and the acts of good you did that I never recognized. Magnús, I forgive you! Even as you tried in your way to show me love, I thank you for the lessons I could not learn. You do not know what you did, Heiðr! You do not know what you did, Magnus! You do not know what you did, Eirík! O Frigga, hear me, and direct my words to them. As I have now forgiven, please forgive me for all I have done."

She stops, out of breath, and the cool breeze washes over her.

"I have a child and his father left us. All I ask is a sign—anything—that shows me the way. Give me a sign what I should do, dear Frigga, wife of Óðinn, goddess of love and marriage and children and the home. I call on you to give me a sign." She sniffles back tears and clears her throat. "And I shall honor you until the day I die!"

She feels the chill consuming her. She must feel it—the beautiful chill that guides her, that shows her the way. That is the truth she seeks. With her cry for help, she sits back on her bare feet, holds her clasped hands in her lap, resting on the gray patio stones in front of the old grill. The world is black and orange, the clouds fleeing in Frigga's blustery arrival, the blue sky of dusk fading into a cool taupe-gray—

Suddenly, a fatal coldness strikes the back of her head, a deathblow that freezes her. Icy wetness slides down her neck. She reaches behind. When she retrieves her hand, she sees that it is snow. Cold, beautiful snow! It melts as she tastes it—fresh, pure, surreal. She looks around the yard. Another breeze blows past her and she rises to her feet, catching her balance on the grill.

She turns and sees Richie at the balcony.

"No clothes?" he calls down.

"They were cursed."

"What are you doing?"

"Praying."

"Sorry about the snowball," he says. "I was saving it for summer, but when I saw you trying to make a fire out of your clothes, I decided to use it today."

"You threw a snowball at me?"

"Sorry. Did it hurt? Was it hard? Was it cold?"

She shook her head, stretching to the sky, arms out and chin up, round belly projecting as she gazes at the wonderful spirit of Frigga.

"Thank you," Íris calls to the wind.

"Thank you?" Richie asks.

Já, he cannot know how he has been used. It is clear Frigga entered him, seized his snowball, probably saved since the last snowfall, and compelled him to climb onto the balcony and throw it at her. It was the sign she was looking for—snow! The guidance she needed. Her path is clear: *snjó—fylgja snjór.*

"I said: Thank you, Richie. Thank you, Frigga."

"What?" he calls.

Íris stays in the yard and welcomes the cold wind blowing in. It is a sign: north. Follow the snow.

There is only one place for a wayward woman and her unborn baby. She must go there, where she belongs: home—*heima.* To the place of her dreams—not of her memories. There is such a place, she knows. It is a springtime meadow of colorful wildflowers and golden sunshine, still dotted with snow, there on a gentle hill that overlooks Eyjafjörður's blue throat. There, she was a child who knew nothing of pain or sorrow or the evil that people can do. She ran barefoot through green fields, rolled in the wild grasses, swam in the sky. That is what she remembers: the endless day, the lush hillside overlooking the sea, the orange-haired mother adorning her child's orange hair with a garland of white flowers hand-woven with love. That is what she wants for her baby. That is what she wants for herself.

"*Já,* there is a dream . . . buried under the snow, waiting for me."

And she will call him *Vé*—a natural place of worship and sacrifice, a stone circle where *Ásatrúar* gather, where they meet their gods and goddesses, where she will praise Frigga for all time. And his name will be *Eiríksson.*

Já, because he is.

38

Eric dashed into the hallway. Olivia Jones and Dr. Liz were still talking about the agitated, pregnant woman. They gave Eric a glance. Maybe they suspected he was responsible. He was, after all, a man.

He stood in the foyer a moment, listening to them, pretending to be waiting for the elevator until they left. Then he gazed out the windows, searching the campus for an orange-haired woman. None.

The elevator arrived, and out spilled Lance Albright in a sport coat that did not quite meet across his Santa Claus gut. He shifted the sheaf of papers in his hand as he greeted Eric. He was coming from the *Journatalia* staff meeting, down in the conference room.

"What's the hurry?" he asked. "Thought you'd be in the meeting."

Eric went toward the open elevator but Albright stood in his way.

"Sorry to miss it, but something's come up."

"That's all right," Albright said, for perhaps the first time in his life. "Got the winners right here." He handed Eric the sheaf as the elevator doors closed.

"Excuse me, but I really have to go now."

"Oh! And Eric, my boy—don't be offended, but Megan's asked to do the intro at the reading Friday night. You don't mind, do you? Nothing to do with the bang-up job you did last time. It's just that, heck, with this crazy farewell party she's got planned . . . well, you see, it wouldn't be right to refuse her."

Eric, frantic, nodded his head, pushed the call button several times.

"Good. I'll tell the woman it's all hers." Albright sucked in his gut and gave Eric a wink. "Confidentially, I think the lady's got the hots for me."

Eric waved him off as the next elevator arrived. "Gotta go. Sorry."

The elevator stopped at the third floor, where three *Journatalia* staff members got on. They quizzed him on his absence and he put them off with his emergency situation. It *was* an emergency. Misunderstanding always is: the misspoken word, the misinterpreted gesture, the unintentional *faux pas*—they could not go without rebuttal!

The elevator reached the first floor and the others exited before Eric. He glanced around. She might be waiting for him there. Maybe she went for a snack or a drink. He checked the canteen, called into the women's restroom, then headed for the Student Center and by the time he reached the Plaza of Heroines he was jogging.

Inside the Student Center, an hour after the lunch rush, he saw no one in the dining hall with orange hair. He walked through the bookstore, past the credit union office, even checked the arcade. He called into two more restrooms. He caught his breath at the ice cream stand, wondering where she might go if she were upset.

The Art department, of course! Her private studio would be the place to go to dry her tears and mope about his misdirected love. He did love her. But he wanted her to be perfect, pure and clean. But this was not a time to decide what he wanted; he had to think what Íris would want. She was upset. She had gotten tired of waiting for him, he decided, and despite her vow to wait to the bitter end, she must have chosen to take a break, thinking he might not be reading the letter yet. Or at all. Giving him the letter was a futile effort, she would no doubt conclude. Maybe she was even now painting some new fantasy, a surreal landscape peopled with fallen women, something like *Roses*, only happier.

And a brave knight in shining armor, mounting a mighty steed, ready to slay the dragon, ready to save her!

Eric paused as he arrived at Everett Hall, out of breath. He gazed at the trees overhead, at the lampposts lining the drive. The same spot, he recognized, where he had picked up Íris that rainy night long ago. Now the afternoon sun was warm though a chilling breeze blew. This was not her season.

With a cramp in his calf, he dropped himself onto a bench in front of the building as a few students exited, carrying book bags, art supplies, portfolios under their arms.

If she were upset—and she had a right to be—she would need a couple of days to cool down. Then he could approach her, fully prepared to woo her again, as though nothing quite so dramatic had happened—not April, not Spring Break. Their halcyon February would return. The lingering winter would bring them back to life, he thought, in the twisted logic of his ice princess. They could travel north during the heat of summer.

He would give her time. Then, perhaps Wednesday evening, he would show up at her house with flowers and chocolates, and whisk her off to a fabulous dinner and a night of romantic lovemaking. That's how they would celebrate their reunion—the same way they had celebrated their union. Yes, by Wednesday, he could finish all his school work, clear his schedule, and fully devote his attention to Íris. She deserved that. In two days, she would be calm again and ready to accept him back—just as he had already decided to accept her.

Íris persuades Richie to drive her over to the campus, to the credit union office inside the Student Center. They arrive a few minutes before closing, enough time to close her account. She withdraws one thousand dollars and change, all she has in the world.

Returning to the house, she goes up to her room and packs her clothing, sweeps her altar items into a box for Celia. She leaves a note telling Cory he can have her bicycle to sell, to pay for the materials he used for his sculpture. Her clothing is for Jean. She has no use for her journal—silly counselors!—so she will leave it behind. She scribbles a note warning Eirík of the spell Megan put on the pendant. If he wears it, he will never fall in love again. She thinks about the note, then tears the paper into tiny pieces. It is better that he not suffer the same fate with the next woman.

From the shoebox under the bed she gathers important papers and two passports—Canada and Iceland—symbols of her dual life, before and after. When she opens the cover of the Icelandic passport, she sees a girl she no longer recognizes: the nearly seventeen-year-old slut with the short-cropped hair, a too-cool expression of annoyed boredom crossed with seething rebellion. She was a girl who thought she knew so much. There were many more lessons to learn. Now she is a woman, wiser in many ways yet still lost. It is neither of them she seeks. She is looking for that innocent girl who was forgotten among the wildflowers on a hilltop above the *fjörður*.

In front of the mirror, she takes the scissors to her hair until she sees that girl again.

Her bath is long and hot, using the only tub in the house, down on the ground floor near Tracie's room. The others have gone to bed and the house is silent. She soaks for two hours, until the water is cold and she is wrinkled.

This is how I will look as a crone, *já*. The image in the mirror is horrid. Tears come.

There are no dreams that inhabit her sleep and she awakens with the singing birds.

When Cory is leaving for campus at seven, she is ready. Dressed in the green jumper with blue butterflies over a white, long-sleeved blouse, she is the model of a pregnant bride. Her hair is sheered randomly.

"Can you give me a ride?" Íris asks him.

She sees the surprise on his face.

"What'd you do to your hair?"

"I need a ride," she says, and Cory agrees.

She hurries back to her room and tries to gather everything in her two arms. Going down the stairs, she drops her suitcase. It is too heavy. Cory says they have to hurry. He has an early class and today is a major exam. She leaves the suitcase on the landing and, with only the laptop, her portfolio, and the small bag she used at Spring Break, she joins him at the door.

They walk out to the car and she notices the gray sky streaked with high, feathery clouds—full of ice crystals, she recalls from a science class—and they point north. Frigga has planned this for her, and she nods.

A few blocks away from the house, Íris asks: "I know it is out of the way, yet can you take me to the bus station?"

"The bus station?" asks Cory. "You're not going to school?

"Will you take me or not?"

"Are you going somewhere?"

She repeats the question, and he realizes she doesn't want to talk about it. He glances at her, sees her tearful face, and agrees to take her.

"Thanks," she says.

She is shaking. The more he questions her, the more she questions herself. Yet the kick in her belly reminds her that Frigga has shown her the way. The final blocks are silent and when the car pulls to the curb, Cory announces the destination.

"Where are you going?" he asks, cautiously.

"Home," she says.

Cory is surprised. "Why're you going there? Was there a death in the family or something?"

"*Nei*, there is no death," says Íris, "only rebirth."

Eric stood before the Shakespeare class and asked the pregnant question: "Has anybody seen our classmate, Íris?"

"I got Graphic Design with her," said Ginger Grundy, "and she hasn't been coming to that class either. For about a month."

Eric thanked them and began the lesson, an introductory lecture on *Macbeth*, with a brief explanation of witchcraft in the Middle Ages thrown in for free.

After the class, he drove by her house, scanning the windows for the one he knew was hers. It was dark. He waited for almost an hour beside the curb, then drove on and eventually returned to his quiet apartment. It didn't matter, he thought, she was probably doing her rituals at the altar and the candle light would not be enough to illuminate her window.

He spent most of Wednesday in his office, finished the grading of final papers from his composition classes. The Shakespeare students had until next week to turn in their final reports. Then came the final exams for his composition classes.

In the evening, he went by Dickerson Hall, stopped in at Open Studio but did not find Íris there. A young man sat behind the desk, guarding the art supplies cabinet.

"Íris around?" Eric asked and the young man looked up.

"Iris? Haven't seen her for about a month."

Eric nodded, exited before he could analyze the situation. Íris hadn't been going to any of her classes. That disappointed him. How could she graduate?

She was around, he felt certain, just hiding from him. He went next to her private studio in the basement of Dickerson and found the door locked, of course, but he knocked on it several times anyway.

With no answer, he went to his car and drove to the mall. No one in the picture frame shop, or her friend at the boutique next door, had heard from her in over a month. Something was wrong, he decided, and, being worried, he drove past her house once more, circled the block six times, slowly, watching for the window to be lit—but it remained dark. There might be a medical emergency, he thought. A miscarriage? He went to the campus clinic, closed at that hour. He returned to his apartment and found the doctor's card, called the service and asked if Íris had gone to a hospital. No such message had been logged.

Eric awoke Thursday morning determined to find her and went straight to the house at seven o'clock, expecting to find her in her room. He no longer cared that he would seem like a fool, so pathetic and desperate, or that his reunion would be so abrupt that it might ruin the whole plan. He had to see her face to face.

He burst into the house, startling the four students sitting down to breakfast, and scaled the stairs two at a time. He pounded on her door until Cory, the kid across the hall, came out to ask what was going on.

"I'm looking for Íris," said Eric, panting.

"She's gone," said the kid, shifting his book bag on his shoulder. "But, hey, she left something for you." He retrieved a notebook from his room and handed it over. "Looks like some journal she was wri—"

"Gone?" Eric felt his chest tighten. "Where'd she go?"

"She just said she was going home."

Friday evening Eric put on his darkest suit and went to the campus, retracing his steps through the Dickerson Hall atrium, pausing at the refreshments table to sip a cup of red punch and stare forlornly at the gray-green statue named *Iris*, cast in life-sized nudity, clutching a real flower. The blank eyes seemed to look back at him as he leaned against the table. She had turned to stone.

He smiled, a slightly insane scowl, then crushed the empty cup in his hand, tossed it into the wastebasket, and trudged on to the gallery.

Lance Albright was more subdued at this reading than the one on Halloween, though he still had a good amount of humor to throw at the audience. He read a story titled "Noisy Whispers" which he explained had been written during his year at Fairmont College. It was a simple tale of an affair between a male student and his female Psychology professor. He quietly apologized for its rough spots, as any draft would have—but Eric did not notice any places in need of polishing. Even Dr. Liz sat quietly through the reading. The others sat in awe of Albright's craft and when he was finished, the tall, rotund man in white beard and bald head, decked out in a red-and-blue striped shirt and bolo tie, its clip an ivory goose in flight, bowed his head reverently—until Megan on the front row began the applause.

Eric remained on the back row, nursing a cup of coffee, swearing off the wine, as his sober colleagues slowly filed out, their chatter echoing against the gallery walls.

He stared ahead.

He gazed at the podium at the front of the room.

Behind the podium hung his painting, the one he had bought, the one he allowed them to display for everyone to enjoy: *Roses*. He studied it, smiling at the irony that piqued his eyes, wishing the flowers were irises, not roses. He marveled at the subtle expression of calm that had settled over the woman's pallid, thorn-scarred face.

Her pain was gone.

And his?

Her image was already branded into his brain. Like a tattoo, he decided, taking out his pocket pad and a pen, ready to write a poem. Like a tattoo that would never be finished.

Vé-Þórr Eiríksson was born 8 August 2000.

In Iceland.

Today Íris makes her home in Akureyri,
where her son is the light of her life.

She teaches art to children at the primary school.

Notes

For readers who may have questions about references or incidents in the novel, the author offers these notes.

The account of Christian priests overseeing the ritual burning of pregnant house maidens was taken from *Óðsmál*, written /compiled by Guðrún Kristín Magnúsdóttir, Ásatrú priestess, 1997 (no relation to the heroine of *A Beautiful Chill*).

Other information concerning the beliefs, rituals, and lifestyle of those practicing Ásatrú have also come, generally, from *Óðsmál*, as well as from *The Masks of Odin* by Elsa-Brita Titchenell (1985) and *Northern Mysteries and Magick* by Freya Aswynn (2nd ed., 1998).

Historical and cultural information on Iceland used in the novel has come from *The Anthropology of Iceland* (ed. by E. Paul Durrenberger and Gísli Pálsson, 1998), *Viking Age Iceland* by Jesse Byock (2001), and *Daughter of Fire: A Portrait of Iceland* by Katherine Scherman (1976).

Depictions of the effects of childhood incest on adult women have been based on information provided in *Promiscuities: The Secret Struggle for Womanhood* by Naomi Wolf (1997) and *Secret Survivors: Uncovering Incest and its Aftereffects in Women* by E. Sue Blume (1990).

Additional influences on the writing of the novel have come from the following:

Angels of the Universe (*Englar alheimsins*) by Einar Már Gudmundsson (1993; trans. by Bernard Scudder, 1995);

Pan by Knut Hamsun (1894);

Independent People (*Sjálfstætt fólk*, 1946) and *The Atom Station* (*Atomstadin*, 1948) by Halldor Laxness;

The White Goddess by Robert Graves (1948);

Icelandic texts known as *The Poetic Edda* (trans. by Carolyne Larrington, 1996) and *The Prose Edda* [of Snorri Sturluson] (trans. by Anthony Faulkes, 1987);

Music from the album *Miriam* by Miriam Stockley (Virgin Records, 1999), and the entire catalogs of Björk and Sigur Rós.

Acknowledgements

Special thanks to Heiðrún Bergsdóttir, a student of Icelandic folklore at the University of Iceland, Reykjavík, for her gracious and valuable assistance in carefully checking all Icelandic words and phrases used in the novel.

Thanks also to Maríana Matthiásdóttir at the MÁL OG MENNING bookstore in Reykjavík for her endless patience in answering the author's questions about Icelandic literature and customs.

Takk fyrir allt.

About the Author

Stephen Swartz grew up in Kansas City where he was an avid reader of science-fiction and quickly began emulating his favorite authors. Since then, Stephen studied music in college and, like many writers, worked at a wide range of jobs: from French fry guy to soldier, to IRS clerk to TV station writer, before heading to Japan for several years of teaching English.

Along the way, Swartz obtained a Master of Fine Arts degree in Creative Writing, requiring him to study not only the Classics and the English literary canon, but Old Norse literature. *A Beautiful Chill* was originally his MFA thesis, and was based on the faculty, peers, and campus he encountered during his studies; he maintains it is a work of fiction.

Swartz is now a Professor of English and teaches writing at a university in Oklahoma. He can always be found writing his newest novel, usually late at night.